# The Glacial Rogue

Book Three of the Roanfire Saga

C.K. Miller

Copyright © 2022 Author CK Miller
All rights reserved.

Edited by Melissa Frey

Cover art, layout, and interior graphics by C.K. Miller

www.ckmillerbooks.com
ISBN-13: 978-1-7324544-2-2

To the fans that keep me going!

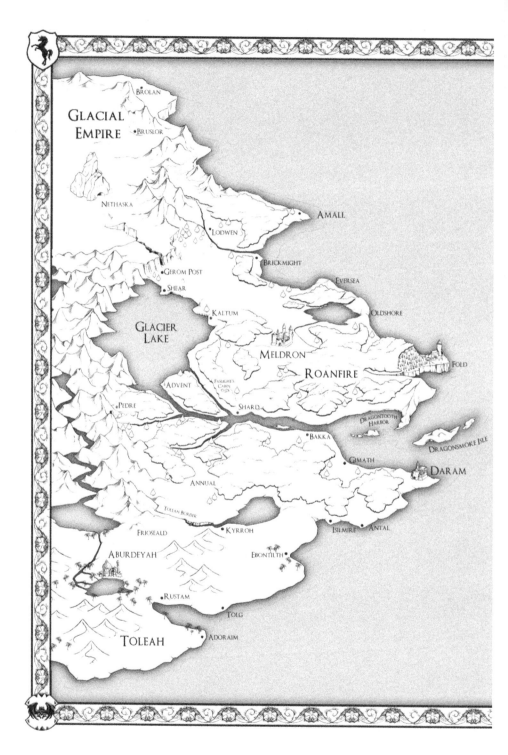

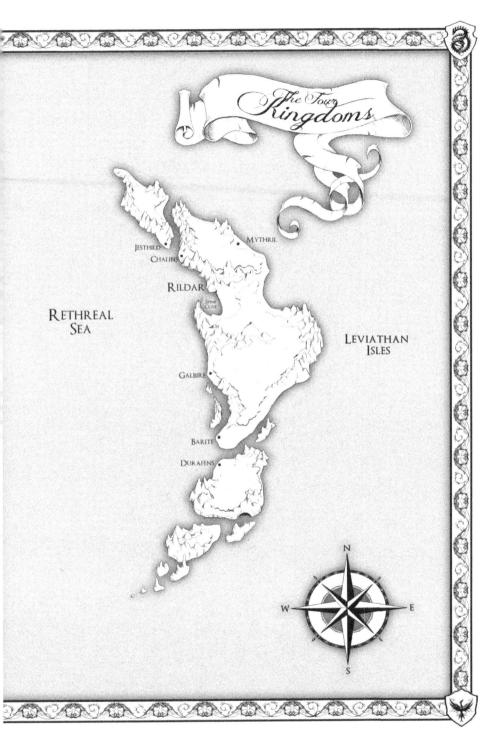

CK Miller

# CHAPTER 1

# "YOU *ARE* AWAKE"

His arms jerked strangely as he lifted his hands to cover his ears. Everything was too loud. He needed silence. The endless rush of screeches, the flapping of wings, and grinding claws that echoed through the black cavern—he needed to think. Every bone ached as if a hot rope coiled around them, twisting and stretching his body within an inch of breaking. The feeling wasn't foreign to him. It was the bane of being a lycanthrope. But the sensation should have ended by now. He was done transforming.

Grinding his teeth against the pain, he rolled to his knees.

He paused. By the scales of the Leviathans, what was wrong with his hands? Dark fur covered his humanlike limbs. These weren't his hands. They couldn't be. They were trapped between man and wolf, undecided about which form they should take.

He drew his hands back, the claws effortlessly grinding clean, silvery lines into the stone beneath him. This body—whatever it was—was built for destruction.

*His heart hammered against his ribs like the sea against cliffs. This . . . this was only a nightmare. When he woke, he would have Kea by his side. She would understand. With her hand in his, he would tell her about the dream. And she, in turn, with tears glistening in her stormy-blue eyes, would assure him that she would put an end to this.*

"You should thank me."

The deep voice dug into Ikane's chest with a warning. His head snapped up, searching for the source. But his movement was too quick. Spasms ignited along his newly developed spine, and white sparks flashed across his vision, blurring the shrouded figure standing beside him.

The hooded figure crouched, and a gust of sharp, foul air hit Ikane's nose as his black cloak settled against the stone.

"I've always wanted a son," the man said.

Ikane's blood curdled. He was the seventh son of Dagun Ormand, prince of a rich Leviathan bloodline. How dare this withered old carcass imply otherwise.

"I am not your son." Ikane paused. Scales, what was wrong with his voice? It was deeper, tinged with an animal-like growl as if it, too, couldn't decide what shape it should take.

He ran his tongue across his teeth, feeling sharp and jagged edges. "What have you done to me?"

"I have fulfilled your potential," the man said. "To be a lycanthrope is a rare gift; it should not be hidden. It should be embraced, revered, and respected. Rion would have savored your essence if I hadn't explained your glorious potential."

Ikane shook his head. This was not his lycanthrope form. This was an abomination. He'd rather be dead than imprisoned in a misshapen form of man and wolf.

"Change me back."

The cloak stiffened. "I saved your life."

Was the old carcass hard of hearing? "Change. Me. Back," Ikane repeated.

The old man's bone-thin shoulders dropped. "I expected gratitude." His tone was threatening. Slowly, he raised his hand, displaying a tiny sapphire stone glittering between his thumb and index finger.

Ikane's heart jumped behind his spine. He scrambled back, claws clicking against rock, joints aching. Scales, no. He . . . he had the stone.

"Do you feel her?" the old man asked in a low whisper. "The way she burns with life? Her energy? Her power? She was born to be a goddess, to save the world from its own destruction and hate."

This withered skeleton was as delusional as Rion. Her power wasn't life—it was feasting, gluttony, and greed. Her power had surged through Ikane like untamed fire, forcing his body to move, to kill.

And he hated it. Oh, how he hated it.

She'd forced his hands to tighten around Kea's neck. He could never forget the image of her face turning red, her eyes pleading for him to stop, her mouth open as if that alone could bring air back to her lungs. He'd tried everything in his power to refuse Rion's control, but even with his mind and heart screaming for him to stop, his hands continued to tighten.

His eyes rose to the hooded figure. "Rion is a monster."

The man snapped the Phoenix Stone into his fist. He stood, rising to his full height. His eyes burned beneath his hood, rage flowing from him as thick as smoke. "Never speak of her in that manner again." His booming voice sent the black walls of the cavern into a frenzy. "She is the mother of Roanfire, the future of the world. She has more power than you or I."

Ikane flinched as something black dropped from the ceiling, arching at a strange angle for his head. Ducking, he felt wind rush across his fur as it whipped by his ears. He scanned the cavern, finding jagged, toothlike rocks punching through the ceiling and floor like the fangs of a serpent. And clinging to every crack, fissure, and crevice, was a black-winged creature.

The Deathbiters' lair.

Ikane shut his eyes, remembering hundreds of bat-like creatures falling upon him like sharks to prey. Fire tore through his skin as their talons dug in. The air around him had burned with tear-welling stench as their wings flapped wildly, lifting him from the ground. They'd carried him away from Kea—and brought him here.

He shook his head again. This had to be one of the worst dreams yet. Was Kea experiencing it, too? She'd shared his dreams in the past. It was both a comfort and a curse to know she was in his mind, her soft white glow touching the edges of his blue . . . but right now he couldn't feel her.

"My poor, confused son. Your mind is troubled."

Ikane glowered at the black cloaked figure standing over him; at the white eyes shining beneath the shadowy cowl. The man held the Phoenix Stone between them like a trophy, its blue color belying its true nature.

"Once Rion returns to the Phoenix Stone, your mind will be free," the man said. "Open your mind to me, my son. I'll make it quick."

Ikane's fur bristled up his spine. The man had already deformed his body; his mind was the only thing he had left, even if it was tainted by Rion. He couldn't let this husk of a man invade it, too.

Slamming his eyes shut, Ikane turned away, pressing his fists against his temples. "Wake up. Wake up. Wake up."

The man's deep laugh vibrated against his back. "You *are* awake, my son."

Ikane stopped his chanting. He stared at the silvery streaks his claws had left in the stone as effortlessly as drawing a finger through sand. Perhaps this wasn't a dream. Perhaps he truly had been transformed into this monster. He ached for his swords. He had to fight. He had to get out of here, away from this delusional man. Flexing the powerful muscles in his fingers, he watched as his new claws flashed like black steel. He didn't need his swords. His entire being *was* a weapon.

And he would use it.

Whipping around, he aimed the black steel claws for the old man's torso. A rending noise filled the stale air as the man drew his cloak away. *For someone so withered, he was remarkably lithe and quick.*

"It seems you have yet to learn respect." *The man's jaw hardened dangerously as he stretched his gray bony hand toward Ikane. A strange energy crackled between his fingertips.* "You. Are. Mine."

Snap. *Lightning ripped through Ikane's skull, black rippling through his vision as something burrowed inside, deep and invading. Ikane clutched his head, claws digging into his flesh as he collapsed onto his side.*

*No. Not his mind. It was the last thing he had.*

"No, Ikane. No."

"Brendagger, wake up."

Hands gripped my shoulders, my body jerking as someone shook me awake. I couldn't leave the dream now. Ikane needed to know I was with him. He needed to know that I hadn't left him to face Rion and her ally on his own.

A hand brushed my forehead, coaxing my mind away from the nightmare. I didn't want to leave him, but he was already gone. The stench, the tacky thickness of the air, the never-ending flutter of wings, and the abrasive screeching had all been replaced by silence and the scent of fur and cold leather.

White light shone through my eyelids, the light too bright to open them and scold whomever had woken me. I shoved the hand away. "Leave me." The words came through a tongue dry and thick, and my lips stuck to my teeth.

"I was beginning to worry."

I knew the voice. Melodic and strong.

Broderick.

"You've been asleep for five days," he said.

What? I forced my eyes open, squinting at the unbearably bright whiteness of icy walls around us. Five days? That meant Ikane had been in the hands of that monster for nearly a week.

"Where . . . where are we?"

"We are in the Glacial Capital, Nethaska." Broderick's cool hand rested on my forehead. "Your fever is gone—that's a good sign. How are you feeling?"

What did it matter how I felt? Ikane was the one suffering. I needed to get to him.

I sat upright, pushing the weighted blankets of furs from my body. "We need to go back."

"Easy, now. Don't rush, Kea. You're still healing."

My aches couldn't compare to what Ikane was enduring. "Ikane needs us. Now."

"Is he still alive?"

How could he ask that? I glowered at him, hoping he could see the ridiculousness of his question in my eyes.

He stood, his dark leather clothes creaking as he stalked over to a circular table standing in the center of the room. Ice. Everything was made of it. The table, the nooks in the walls, even the platform making up my bed.

He crouched to the knee-high table, lifted a clay teapot, and poured its milky contents into a pair of mugs. Steam burst from the top like thick smoke from a chimney. "We need to talk about what happened in Glacier Pass."

Talk? Now wasn't the time for tea and talk. We needed to move. We needed to gather an army.

I threw the blankets aside, swinging my legs over the icy platform. "Where is my coat?"

"Kea." His tone was reprimanding and firm. He lifted the mugs, handing one to me. "You can't ignore it. It will happen again."

Warmth seeped into my fingers as a sweet honey-tinged smell wafted from the milky drink. I didn't deserve this, any of it. I'd failed at the one thing I'd promised to do: free Ikane of Rion.

I slipped from the bed, my feet sinking into a carpet of furs strewn around the circular table. "How far is it to Glacier Pass?" I asked as I set the mug beside the teapot.

"You won't make it if you don't get something nourishing into your stomach." Broderick lifted the mug once more, pushing it into my hands again. "Drink."

If that's what it took for him to give me the information I wanted, I'd drink.

I took a sip, then paused. What was this drink? It was creamy and smooth, with a sweet floral smokiness that danced on my tongue and tempted my mind away from the topic.

Broderick lowered his mug from his own lips. "The guard post to Glacier Pass is less than a day's ride from here. But it's too late in the day to leave now."

"Then we should make preparations," I said. "Do they have plated armor here? Shields? Anything strong enough to withstand the Deathbiters?"

"Kea, you're ignoring the issue."

"And you're ignoring the fact that Ikane needs our help." My voice rose. How could he not feel the urgency?

Broderick set his mug on the table, eyes growing hard beneath his brown curls. "How do you expect to help him? With brute strength? With shields and swords?" He narrowed his eyes and peered into my soul. "Or do you plan to use Thrall again?"

Thrall. The word felt sour against my ears like the grinding of steel, or the gut-wrenching tear of a knife drawn from flesh. My mind pushed against it.

His voice grew softer. "You came here for a reason: to find the letter written to Emperor Skarand so you could learn the answers. If you go after Ikane now, you will go down a path you cannot come back from."

My eyes fell to the brown-gray mottled furs under my feet. "It may be too late by then."

"Tell me this," Broderick said. "If we did go after Ikane, if we did find him, how would you help him?"

My hands began to tremble, the milky tea rippling in the mug. I had no answer . . . save for the power I didn't want to think about.

"What you did in Glacier Pass cannot happen again," he said. "You used Thrall. It nearly consumed you and everyone around you. Do you understand?"

Feathers, why wouldn't he stop talking? I didn't want to remember. It was wrong. It was filthy and terrifying. It was unlike anything I'd ever felt—and for some reason, I wanted more.

He set his mug on the table. "Look at me, Kea."

His voice was too powerful to ignore, and I looked up. His stormy-blue eyes reflected the ice around us. I'd always loved his youthful face and brown curls. There was an innocence to him that denied his dangerous training. But something was different. Was that a new scar running down the corner of his lips?

Heat surged through my blood. Those accursed Deathbiters. First my face, and now his. I had to put an end to them. To everything Rion created.

"I tell you this not to hurt you, but because I care." His lips pulled differently, the scarred corner moving with less vigor than the other. "I need you to understand the severity of your actions. You lost control, Kea. Given the circumstance, I understand why. We were overrun and overpowered. Fear took hold."

The horrific events at Glacier Pass flooded my mind: the white cliffs trapping us in the narrow pathway, the foul-smelling mist, the Deathbiters. My link to Ikane hung like a severed ribbon, tattered and waving in the smoke-filled air of a battlefield.

I shook my head; I didn't want to go there. Darkness waited to engulf me, draw me down, suffocate me, and threaten my sanity. I pushed the memory away.

He stepped closer, gently taking my hand in his. His grip was firm, and his fingerless leather gloves felt soft against my palm. "The power you released could have destroyed us," he whispered.

"It destroyed the Deathbiters, didn't it?" I said. "It saved us." Perhaps I was groping for some form of validation, that what I had done wasn't as terrible as he made it out to be. But something inside bit and gnawed at my chest.

His grip tightened. "It killed our horse, and it would have killed me, too. My skill as a Wind Wardent was the only reason I was able to deflect the magic."

The gnawing dug deeper, tearing into my heart. His words burrowed into the pain entombed there. And it all came flooding back. The power surging like a hurricane. The Deathbiters disintegrating into ash. Ice cracking, shards ripping through everything in their path.

For all the mess I caused, why was he being so kind? He should just say how it was. I had almost killed him. Not it. *I* did it.

My legs shook, too tired to support my weight. The scar on his lips was from me, not a Deathbiter.

"Broderick," I breathed. "I'm . . . I'm so sorry."

He wrapped his arms around me. How could he stand to touch me after what I'd done?

"You didn't intend to hurt me," he said. "Thrall has a mind of its own."

I crushed him, fearing that if I let go, I would lose his friendship forever. "I don't even know how I summoned it."

"Thrall feeds on raw emotions," he explained. "Our emotions were running hot with fear."

"I don't understand; I've felt fear before." Tears streaked down my cheeks, falling against his leather coat. "I've used magic to fight against Rion in my mind. But it's never . . . it's never . . ."

"Manifested physically?" he finished.

I drew back.

"I was wondering when it would happen. There is much for you to learn. More than I can tell you in a day, and more than I am capable of teaching." He reached up, running his thumb across my cheek. "But I will be by your side. I will help in any way I can. You are not alone."

A sob tore from my throat, tears rushing to the surface as I wrapped my arms around his solid torso, burying my face in his shoulder. I didn't deserve his help.

By the flaming feathers of the Phoenix, a part of me didn't want his help. I wanted *more*. I wanted this power to grow and thrive and tear everything Rion built to shreds. Maybe I could. Maybe that was the reason for it.

"What about Ikane?" I whispered.

"We'll go after him as soon as you've found control over Thrall."

I pushed away. "But that could take too long."

"Then we should get to work." He gave me a crooked smile that ripped into my chest. I would never hurt him like that again. "Erin has been infected. She needs healing."

Sniffing, I wiped the moisture from my cheeks. "What must I do?"

"Heal her."

## CHAPTER 2

# HONEY PUFFS

Slipping my arms into my leather coat, I followed Broderick down the three icy stairs to the leather curtain hanging over the arched doorway.

He held it open for me. "She's just down the hallway."

Ducking my head, I stepped through.

This wasn't a hallway; this was a tunnel. A massive passageway wide enough for five men to ride abreast was carved beneath a vaulted ceiling with intricate pillars lining the path. Blue light penetrated the walls, slanted beams of fluid water bearing through thin sections above. Arched doorways lined the tunnel walls, some carved to glistening perfection, others holding the natural lumpiness of frozen water, each one covered by a leather curtain door.

Citizens dressed in heavy furs and leathers came and went, greeting each other as the people did on the streets of Meldron. Dogs barked, glacial ponies whinnied, and children darted across the space.

A girl in a heavy coat skipped past me, and a brown-coated dog chased after the bone in her hand. Spinning on her toes, she giggled as the animal's teeth snapped the air where the bone had been.

I swallowed. The hound's face held similar features to a wolf. The pointed ears, the bushy tail, the thick fur around its neck . . . but it was so small compared to Ikane.

I tore my eyes away, following Broderick down the street. I had to focus. I had to learn quickly if I was going to have any chance at saving Ikane.

"You know your way around here pretty well," I said.

"I should," Broderick replied. "I was born here."

"What? I thought—"

"I know what you thought. Most people do. But I am a citizen of the Glacial Empire, apprenticed to Master Chanter years before Princess Lonacheska came to Roanfire. It was part of the contract. I was to be her eyes and ears in Roanfire," he said. "Master Chanter saw differently. It's been hard serving two masters. You gave me the courage to break free, to do what I was sent to do."

I stared down at my feet. "And now you're here with me . . ."

"It's what Queen Lonacheska wanted," he said.

"You really think I can do this?" I asked.

"I know you can. But it won't come easy."

I fell into step beside him. "If I fail to heal her, you need to do it."

He slowed. "You won't fail, Kea."

"But if I do. Erin's been suffering for five days." The faint memory of pain searing through my body with Deathbiter poison pushed to the forefront of my mind. The hallucinations. The sleeplessness. The raging fever. "You can't let her suffer."

"I'm confident you'll succeed." He stopped by a doorway, pulling the curtain aside. "After you."

The light dimmed as I stepped inside.

The smell hit me first. The crisp air was tinged with the sharp odor of Deathbiter poison, and I scrunched my nose against it as my feet climbed the three steps to the circular landing. A low round table sat in the center, just like in my room, and furs were also strewn across the floor. A figure lay on the matching icy platform.

Phoenix help me—that couldn't be Erin. Her skin held a sickly gray tinge that grew more pronounced when compared to the snow-white walls around her. Her ebony curls, oily and matted, splayed across her pillow, made wilder by the dazed rocking of her head. The whites of her eyes flashed between rapidly fluttering eyelids.

Broderick sank to the bed beside her, placing a hand on Erin's brow. Her rocking stilled, and a soft moan filled the circular chamber.

"The hallucinations have started," he said.

How could he let her suffer for so long? With every passing day, the Deathbiter venom burrowed deeper, yet he'd waited for me. This had been his plan all along.

Broderick slid Erin's arm from beneath the furs, pushing her sleeve to her elbow. Unwrapping the white bandaging on her forearm, he exposed three festering gashes. Black vines spread beneath her skin like rivers and streams on a map.

"I have everything ready," he said. "The ash pail is beside you. Believe me, it was not easy acquiring that. They don't burn fuel here the way they do in Roan—"

"How dare you?" A torrential voice flowed with a gust of air surging through the leather curtain. Icy needles stung my cheeks, blinding my eyes. I held my arm up, shielding my face as a buzzing noise grew louder.

Ali? Her tiny transparent form surged into the room.

Broderick lowered his arm against the dying wind. "Ali. Please—"

"I told you I didn't want her anywhere near Erin. Get out." Ali's voice roared with wind, pushing against me again as if a barbarian warrior had shunted me in the shoulder. Pain flared through my ribs as I staggered into the wall, knocking over a piece of pottery sitting in an icy nook.

Broderick leapt to his feet. "Ali, she needs to do this. She needs to try—"

"By the power of the White Wardent, don't you remember what she did?"

I held my side, my heart sinking lower than I thought possible. My stomach clenched; I didn't blame her. This was how Broderick should have reacted.

"I do remember," Broderick said. "She does, too. Let her try. Erin agreed to this. She knows what Kea needs to do."

"Erin was already delusional with fever and pain when you coerced her into it." The faint warble of air spun to me, white sparks glinting across her fluttering wings like light across a dagger. "Do you know how much damage you've caused? You didn't just taste Thrall; you consumed it. You gorged yourself on emotions too dark to forgive. You've been tainted."

"Ali," Broderick warned.

"Don't try to shelter her." The windsprite whirled back to me. "Those who use Thrall never come back. They live for the feast, for the idea of invincibility."

My mouth went dry. Why did her words sound so true?

"Don't listen to her, Kea," Broderick said. "You can come back. That is why I brought you here."

I hugged my ribs. No. Ali was telling the truth. I did long for it. I wanted to use it again.

"Kea. Every Wardent faces what you are facing now," Broderick said. "Thrall is in all of us. It takes training and discipline to keep it from devouring us."

"Did you . . . did you face it, too?" I didn't dare look at him. Broderick was perfect, his heart too good. How could he ever think to tamper with what I had wielded?

"I did," he said. "And I do still. Every day."

My eyes rose.

He watched me intently, Ali's warbled form beside him. They were so different. His face glowed with faith and hope, where Ali's white sparks danced with unforgiving sharpness.

"Ali," Broderick pleaded, his tone even and calm. "It isn't your job to take care of Erin anymore. I'm asking you to trust me. I won't let any harm come to her."

The buzzing moved across the room and back as she paced. I hugged myself tighter with every back-and-forth movement. Maybe she was right. Maybe I shouldn't do this. The risk of calling on Thrall was too great. I should just leave it alone and focus on battling Rion in my mind as I'd always done.

But what if Thrall infested that part of me, too? It was the same power Rion used. When I tried to use it against her, it only made her stronger.

Why did it have to be so complicated?

Ali stopped. "Alright. One try."

My heart sank. I'd been hoping for another answer.

"Thank you, Ali," Broderick said.

The windsprite whirled on me, fluttering so close her wind made my eyes water. "If you so much as brush a thought toward Thrall, I'll conjure a gale so strong it will blast you all the way back to Roanfire."

I didn't doubt her. I nodded once.

She fluttered to a shelf on the wall, her form shimmering with white edges as she sat beside the small oil lamp there.

"Ready?" Broderick asked, removing his gloves.

"Why are you helping me, Broderick?"

He tilted his head at my question.

"Ali is right. I should be banished, flogged, and marked for what I've done."

Broderick placed his hand on my shoulder. "Everyone makes mistakes. I would be a hypocrite if I judged you for this one misstep, however severe it may be."

Erin jerked upright, arms flailing at the air, trying to shield her face. "No! Help. Someone, help! They're everywhere."

Broderick grabbed her wrists. "Hush, Erin. It's alright. You're safe."

She tossed her head, black curls flying wild, eyes scrunched tight. "Get them off! Oh, Phoenix, help. My babies. They are taking my babies!"

Broderick wrestled against her. "Hurry, Kea."

Something about her words struck deep. She lost her children in an avalanche, not by Deathbiters. But the image of Ikane surrounded by black leathery wings as they pulled him into the sky surged behind my eyes.

That was what she saw now. But instead of Ikane, she saw her children. It was a hallucination, that's all. But why did it hurt so much?

"She needs you, Kea." Broderick pushed her onto the pillow, pinning his arm across her chest.

I sank to my knees, plunging my hands into the pail of black-gray soot from a fire burned long ago. This? This was all the protection I had against the Deathbiters' venom? The venom that burned like fire, poisoned the blood, and tortured victims with hallucinations for an entire fortnight before death claimed them?

I pushed the doubt away.

Broderick had done it; so could I.

Erin's thrashing stopped. Broderick leaned back slowly, his brow creasing as he positioned her infected arm at her side. The smell was revolting.

"This won't be easy," he said.

I had to do this for Ikane. I needed to change my path.

Twisting to face her, I turned my soot-covered palms down, hovering them over the three festering gashes.

"That's it." Broderick smiled. Would I ever get used to the crookedness? "You remembered. The closer you get, the easier it will be to reach the poison. But touching the skin directly won't give the poison a path to follow. Understand?"

I nodded.

"Now." He knelt beside me, his shoulder pressing against mine. "This is where you must find the right source to draw from. I find the easiest way is to think of why you want the person to live. Why are you sacrificing so much energy for them?"

I shut my eyes. That was easy—Erin was selfless. She might put up a hard front, but she'd risked everything to help us. She took us in after the first Deathbiter attack. She brought us to Gerom Post. She risked her life guiding us through Glacier Pass.

For what? Why? The only explanation was her heart, her goodness. She deserved to live. She deserved happiness again—happiness with Eamon.

"Did you find it?" Broderick asked.

"I think so."

"Alright. Now reach for the darkness inside her. See it writhing. See it trying to take what makes her so valuable." Broderick's voice was soft and distant, like he spoke across a summer prairie.

The darkness was thick, coursing through her veins like Leviathan ships surging into Roanfirien waters.

How could this have happened to her? She'd been through enough; she'd lost her children and husband. She'd lost everything, and now this? Her kindness had been rewarded by Deathbiter venom ready to take her life. Rion would pay for all the lives she destroyed.

"Brendagger!"

Something struck my forearms, slamming my wrists against the corner of the icy platform. My eyes flew wide.

Broderick sat back, curling his fingers. "Sorry. You turned to Thrall. I had to break it somehow."

Thrall? That easily? All I did was think of what Erin deserved. My heart dropped into my rolling stomach like a rag tossed into churning waves. Who was I fooling? I couldn't do this.

Ali was right. Thrall already had hold of me. Why didn't she strike already?

Biting my lip, I looked at the shelf where I'd last seen her. A tiny ball curled on the slab, the windsprite clutching her legs to her chest, wings trembling. Glittering tears spilled from her scrunched eyes as her sobs filled the circular room.

I pushed myself off the edge of the bed, my hands leaving black streaks on the snowy platform. "I can't do this."

Broderick rose. "You just need more time."

"Erin doesn't have any more time." My voice came harsh. "Look at her. Look at Ali. I can't do this."

"Just . . . just try again. You can do this."

I scrunched my eyes against the scene of the trembling windsprite. "No. You have to do it."

"Kea." Disappointment flowed with his tone. "You only lose if you give up. Please."

I couldn't take it anymore. I didn't want magic at all. Spinning, I sprinted down the three ice-carved stairs, pushing through the leather curtain. I wasn't like Broderick. I wasn't skilled with magic, patience, or calm.

I turned my face skyward. Ice. Everything was ice, bearing down on me like a tomb. I needed the sky, the openness, the fresh air, the wind. I needed to see the stars . . . with Ikane.

"Lady Brendagger!"

I glanced over at the people milling about. None of my companions called me by that title, and the voice was female, rich and strong.

"Lady Brendagger. Over here."

A mitten-covered hand waved above the sea of fur-lined hats. A woman pushed through, her thick, long white hair sitting in a loose braid over her left shoulder. Her skin held years of smiles, yet she was the most handsome woman I'd ever seen. There was something familiar about her, regal and poised. Something about her eyes . . .

"You look lost," she said.

How did she know me? I'd never seen her before. "I'm . . . I'm not sure where I'm headed."

"In life? Or in these tunnels?" There was a mischievous glint in her dark eyes. She chuckled. "Don't think too hard about it. Navigating through Nethaska can be a bit intimidating at first. But once you understand the layout, it's quite simple. See how this tunnel is lined with doors?"

I nodded.

"This is a housing passage. There are dozens of them throughout Nethaska. Most of its citizens live here. Each one is marked by a symbol on the curtains." She pointed to the nearest door with her mitten-covered hand. "See there. This one is marked with the arctic bear on the bottom right corner."

She waved to the far end of the tunnel where a deep shadow of blue opened to the right. "That is the entrance to the trade district. There are three of those in the city, and each one leads to the core tunnel. The core tunnel runs from the city's entrance to the main market, and from there to the palace."

The palace. That was where I needed to go. Queen Lonacheska's ring sat in my bag back in my room. Which one of these arched doorways was mine? My mind had been too occupied to keep track.

"Did I confuse you?" the woman asked.

"No, your directions were clear. I just can't remember which room is mine."

Her smile broadened. "Each family has decorated their doors to their liking over time. But yes, I can see how you could get lost. Look at the markings on the curtains." She waved her gloved hand at the bottom corner of the nearest leather curtain. A symbol had been burned into the hide: a bear with seven black stripes across its back.

"Your door is the fourth on the left."

"What?"

"Follow me." She turned, leading me past three curtained doors. "Notice anything?"

I squinted at a curtain as we passed. The one before it had six stripes sitting across the bear's back. This one had five. That meant . . . "The next one is mine."

"Clever girl." Pulling my curtain aside, she let herself in.

I paused. Who did she think she was? I wanted to be alone. I didn't have the energy to be civil.

Gathering a deep breath of chilled air, I pushed through the curtain, climbing the three stairs to the landing. I homed in on my bags, tossing the flap open, sinking my arm deep inside. The ring was here somewhere.

The woman stopped at the table, her white brows furrowing at the empty mugs and cold tea kettle sitting on the table. "No honey puffs?"

"Honey puffs?" I asked.

"I told them to bring you honey puffs as soon as you woke."

My fingers found the cold, round surface at the bottom of my sack. I clutched the ring, turning back to the door. "The tea was good," I offered. "I've never had anything like it."

"Ah, yes. Reindeer milk with vanilla, cardamom, cloves, and ginger. It accompanies honey puffs quite well."

Did she ever think of anything other than honey puffs, whatever they were?

"I don't mean to be rude, but I must be going," I said.

"Where to?"

I took the first step down the stairs. "I need to see the empress. It is urgent."

"Urgent, you say?" Her tone held a mocking edge. Small lines deepened near her deep brown eyes. Was she laughing at me?

"Did I say something amusing?" I asked.

"Oh, not at all," she said. "You'd best hurry. You don't want to keep the empress waiting."

I took the second step.

"How is my little reindeer, Lonacheska? I haven't heard from her in weeks."

My feet froze, chest tightening. Flaming feathers. This was the empress?

I turned slowly. She was nothing like I imagined. I expected her to be stoic and poised like her daughter, always proper. Always guarded in her words. And definitely not standing there with a childish grin on her face.

"Your Majesty." I bowed. "I . . . I'm sorry. I didn't know."

"Oh, honey puffs, it's too late for that now. Stand up, dear." She sighed, leaning back on the platform holding my unmade bed, stripping the mittens from her hands. "It was fun while it lasted. But in truth, I haven't heard from my daughter for some time. What news comes from Roanfire? How is she?"

"I . . . she . . ."

"Oh, come now. Don't be so tongue-tied. You had no problem speaking to me before you knew who I was. And call me Chrysla. I've never been fond of any other title." She knelt by the table, patting the furs beside her. "Tell me, how is Lona?"

Swallowing, I climbed the stairs, lowering myself to the floor. "She . . . she's worried. She sent me here."

Chrysla tilted her head, her silver-white braid moving softly over her shoulder. "What for?"

I set the ring on the table, sliding it to her. "I am here to find a letter written to Emperor Skarand."

Her smile faded. "That is a very unusual request." She picked up the ring, twisting it in the soft blue light radiating through the walls. Her eyes darkened. "It must be serious for her to send this with you. Is she in danger?"

I bit my lip. "Not yet."

Chrysla slipped the ring onto her finger, placed her hands on the table, and pushed herself up. "Then we must do as she asked. Come. I'll take you to the Cavern of Records." She moved to the steps, her smile returning. "And on the way back, I'll introduce you to the most amazing treat in all the four kingdoms."

She was talking about honey puffs again, wasn't she?

## CHAPTER 3

# SKARAND'S LETTER

*A* gentle moan flowed up the winding stairs leading into a mouth of darkness. The tunnel shimmered with frozen waterfalls, and icicles pointed from the arched ceiling like swords ready to fall.

"The hard part is coming back up," Empress Chrysla said as she removed a mitten and dug into her pocket.

"How deep does it go?" I asked.

"Deeper than Nethaska's rising spires. Don't be in a hurry. It'll take time." White light burst from her palm as she withdrew it from her pocket. A vial sat in her hand, smooth and cylindrical, glittering and glowing with white dust. I'd never seen so much at once. That vial alone would be worth twenty gold in Roanfire.

"Watch your step now. And don't rush. We have a long way to go." Chrysla took the first step into the gaping maw, her footfalls echoing deep into the endless darkness ahead. The glow flooded the stairway as the walls ignited into shimmering ripples of light and shadow moving as we descended.

"What do you hope to find in Skarand's letter?" she asked. "It was written over four hundred years ago."

"Clues."

"Clues to what? You need to be more specific, dear. Is this about the White Wardent?"

"You know about him?" I asked.

"I know of him. I haven't met him personally."

"But you believe he exists?"

She paused, looking back at me. "You don't?"

"I . . . I'm not sure what to believe," I said.

"Well, I can tell you for certain, he is as real as you or I." She resumed trekking down the stairs. "You can't expect a magical being like that to make his whereabouts known to just anybody."

Something pricked my chest, rolling down my spine. No, I couldn't. But by the burning feathers of the Phoenix, he was the cause of all this mess. If he hadn't forged the stone for Rion in the first place . . .

And now he left everything to me, but I didn't know what I was doing. He should at least make himself known to me.

"Finally," Chrysla breathed.

An arched doorway stood at the bottom of the stairs, and a leather curtain hung over it with an engraved image of the One-Horned Wonder in the center.

It looked so much like Gossamer—thick, powerful legs kicking the air, a strong neck, its mane full and lush. The horn sitting in the center of its forehead curved upward like a Tolean sword, identical to Queen Lonacheska's ring.

"Here." Chrysla pressed the glowing vial of windsprite dust into my hand, pulling the curtain aside. "After you."

When had the moisture fled my lips? I licked them, swallowing hard. My heart throbbed.

This was it. This was my last hope.

I ducked inside, the white glow of windsprite dust spreading across icy shelves carved into the circular cavern. The chamber was no bigger than my housing quarters above. As seemed standard for every chamber in Nethaska, a circular table—made of ice, of course—sat in the center. But the walls were entirely created of nooks and cubbies carved into the ice with creamy pages of books, scrolls, and tomes packed to bursting. Wicker baskets and crates held overflow.

How in the blazes was I going to find a single letter in all this? All my hope rested on the Glacial Empress.

"Put the vial there." Chrysla stepped beside me, removing her mittens and dropping them on the table. A small, circular dent sat in the center of the icy table, just big enough for the glass vial to slip into. Carefully, I dropped the vial into it with a soft *clink*. The room flared with unwavering light, penetrating the dark corners of the shelves.

Chrysla ran her fingers along the smooth edge of a shelf, inspecting the items. "Let's see here. Emperor Skarand..." she muttered to herself.

I bit my lip, praying, letting her focus.

Crouching, she tipped a book from the ledge, inspecting it. She slid it back into place. "Are you going to tell me the reason my daughter sent you on this errand, or do I need to pry it from you?" she asked.

I flexed my fingers inside my mittens, feeling the strands of fur glide between them. "It's a long story."

"I can take as long as you want to find the letter." Her look told me she meant it.

She was good. No wonder the other kingdoms didn't mess with the Glacial Empire. Even if she wasn't the empress, she deserved an explanation. It concerned her granddaughter, after all.

I removed my mittens. "Around four-hundred years ago, Fold was destroyed, and the last female heir to the throne of Roanfire perished with it."

"Queen Damita, I know. She had been recently crowned. Such a tragedy." Chrysla resumed searching the shelves.

"Since that time, there have been no female heirs born to the throne of Roanfire." My stomach clenched, bile rising in my throat. "It has recently come to light that there was a curse on the Noirfonika line long before Queen Damita was destroyed. A curse that claimed Roanfire's princesses while still in their youth."

Chrysla paused, leaning back on her heels. "Are you telling me . . . ?" Her dark eyes exploded with light, her face breaking into pure elation. She leapt to her feet. "Honey puffs, you are. My little reindeer is with child."

*That* was what she took from my story? Not that her granddaughter was in danger, but that her daughter was with child? Why hadn't Lonacheska shared the news with her mother? "You . . . didn't know?"

"I haven't heard from her in weeks. Her last letter was filled with sorrow so deep it bled from the ink. I've been worried. But with news like this?" She clasped her hands, clutching them to her chest. "Oh, she must be overjoyed." She leapt forward, taking my hands. "Tell me. How far along is she? When is the child due?"

"Late fall. Early winter, maybe."

"Oh, I must send her a gift." She dropped my hands. "A bow perhaps? Yes, a bow made from the cedar trees of Bruslor. And arrows with heads from the finest reindeer antler. No grandchild of mine should be without proper archery equipment."

This was all wrong. I should be celebrating with her. Lonacheska should be reveling in happiness. Yet here we were, terrified to the core of what would happen to the child if I did not find a way to stop Rion.

"Your Majesty, the letter?"

"Oh, yes." She whirled back to the shelves, her fingers dancing over spines of books like a butterfly. She plucked a weathered scroll from a shelf as if she'd known the exact location all along. "Here you are."

Every part of me trembled as she handed the parchment to me. It was here. In my hand. The broken red wax seal remained on the edge embedded with a symbol I couldn't make out.

My knees barely held as I knelt at the table and unraveled the scroll. Crisp black ink worked down the page as if it had been written yesterday.

My eyes burned, and a lump tightened my throat. For the first time, something was right. For the first time, the answers would be clear.

*My dear friend, Emperor Skarand Kovant of the Glacial Empire,*

*You were right.*

*You warned me, and I refused to listen.*

*I could blame it on Queen Rion's beauty and flattering words, but that would not be the truth. The truth is, I wanted to do it. I wanted to see if it could be done.*

*Now, Rion's greed has warped the magic, and Roanfire's daughters are paying the price. I have learned but an hour ago that the last Queen of Roanfire, Damita, has died.*

*I can't allow this to continue, but I am powerless to stop it. Everything I try has resulted in more death.*

*To protect Roanfire's daughters, I will administer a tonic to King Theon, his sons, and every son with ties to the Noirfonika line. Roanfire will henceforth be barren of female heirs. I hope that by doing this, I can suffocate Rion's source of power.*

*My method is but a bandage; the wound still festers. Eventually, a female heir will be born, and she will need help.*

*I ask you, my friend, to please keep these instructions safe. Watch for a daughter of Roanfire, and aid her in any way possible.*

*Your friend and faithful servant,*
*Yotherna Lonnir*

My hand moved down. I'd unrolled the entire scroll, hadn't I? My fingers held the edge; there was nothing more. The slamming of my heart increased. Feathers, please.

I flipped it over.

Blank.

"Where is the rest?" I asked.

"The rest?" Chrysla looked over my shoulder. "This is the only letter I know of."

"No, it can't be. Look." I pointed to the section where he'd explained there was another part to this letter. There was more. Specific instructions for me, for Lonacheska's daughter.

Chrysla tapped a finger against her lips as she turned back to the shelf. "If it is here, it should be on this shelf." She withdrew another scroll.

I unraveled it next to Yotherna's letter. A map? Something about the garrison sitting atop the seaside cliffs was familiar. Black ink displayed tunnels and paths winding beneath, leading to the sprawling city below.

Wait. This was Fold. And these paths—these were the caverns I'd discovered when I'd fallen from the cliffs. There was a tunnel leading to Fold City. It was right there. I could have made my way from the maze of tunnels in mere hours if I'd had this map.

"That should probably be returned to Roanfire." Chrysla leaned over my shoulder. "You take it."

I let go, the scroll snapping shut. I didn't come here for a map—I came for the letter. But I stuffed it into my pocket anyway. Then I stood. "Let's keep looking."

"Try those shelves over there." Chrysla returned to her shelf, checking scrolls and dropping them on the table.

Why did the letters get separated? This was supposed to be it. This was where my answers should be, the step-by-step instructions on how to destroy Rion. To free Ikane. To free myself. I had defied my king, lost Ikane, and faced death to come here. I had nowhere else to turn.

My fingers grew numb, skin cracking as I handled scroll after scroll, book after book, each one another fail. Another useless page. Something stabbed my chest like a betrayal. Had I come all this way for nothing?

"We should take a break," Chrysla said from her perch on the floor, scrolls and books scattered all around her. We'd torn the place apart.

Desperate, I pulled a tome from a shelf. *Hunting Courtship of the Glacial Empire.* I opened it anyway. The black letters blurred together.

I'd done everything I knew how, but there were no more clues. No directions. The White Wardent toyed with me time and time again, appearing in visions, coming to my aid, but never actually helping me.

Stuffing the book into its place, my head sank against the edge of the shelf. Cold seeped into my forehead, but it couldn't freeze the tears burning behind my eyelids. I'd come all this way for nothing.

"Chin up, dear." Chrysla came to my side. "We'll come back. Share a plate of honey puffs and golden milk with me."

I swallowed the lump in my throat.

Chrysla's sigh mingled with a compassionate whimper as she rested her hand on my shoulder. "Lonacheska is fortunate to have someone so passionate about the future of her child helping her."

If only she knew.

"Kea!" Broderick shot to his feet as I stepped through the curtain. "Where have you been? I've been searching everywhere for you."

Standing aside, I held the curtain for the empress. She ducked in with a tray of her obsession in hand, little round golden-brown pastries glistening with honey. The tea kettle and mugs rattled as she straightened.

"Empress Chryslacheska." Broderick bowed, touching his middle two fingers to his brow.

"Oh, honey puffs. Had I known you'd be here, I would've added another mug." Chrysla said. "Don't even think of eating all my honey puffs. You're worse than I am."

Was she this casual with all her subjects?

"That's debatable." He grinned.

My stomach clenched at the sight of his lopsided lips. Would I ever be able to look at him without the nightmare of Glacier Pass flooding into my mind?

"Don't just stand there—give me a hand." She held the tray up. "My knees can't take much more abuse."

He jumped into action, hurrying down the stairs and taking the tray from her. Why didn't she just let me carry it? I'd offered, but she'd insisted on doing it herself, saying something about me sneaking a taste of a honey puff behind her back.

"Where were you?" Broderick asked, holding his elbow out for her.

She slipped her arm through his as they climbed the steps. "The Cavern of Records."

Broderick glanced over his shoulder at me, a flicker of hope burning behind his eyes. "Did you find it?"

"Not the part I was looking for," I said.

The hope in his eyes evaporated.

"Don't you worry. We're going to look again." Chrysla patted his arm before releasing it and sank to the fur-covered ground. "Emperor Skarand wasn't exactly known for his organization. It's there somewhere."

I sank to the table. A part of me wanted to believe her, but something in my stomach knew it wasn't there. It should have been with the other letter, but it wasn't. It was lost. Possibly destroyed. And every day I spent searching was another day Ikane suffered at the hands of Rion and her ghastly, cowl-shrouded ally. There was nothing left for me to do.

I was done searching for clues.

Broderick knelt beside the empress as she poured creamy tea into the mugs. The smell of warming spices filled the chamber.

"Would the elders know where it could be?" Broderick asked, reaching for a honey puff.

"Perhaps." Chrysla slapped his hand. "Ladies first." She nodded to me expectantly.

I wanted nothing to do with her honey puffs and spiced milk. The sour taste in my mouth would spoil them anyway. But the anticipatory spark in her eyes had me reaching for one of the little round pastries. The golden glaze stuck to my fingers. Drool practically ran down the corner of her lips as she watched me bite into the soft, cloudlike pastry.

It was Mayama. It was home. It was a slice of soft wheat bread fresh from the oven slathered with warm honey-butter. It washed the bitterness from my tongue, flooding my eyes with tears. Oh, how I wanted to go home.

"Oh, dear." Chrysla's brows crowded. "Is it that bad?"

I sniffed, swallowing the little bite of heaven. "No. No, it's . . . it's wonderful."

She smiled, pushing a steaming mug in front of me. I grabbed the mug, pulling it to my lips, adding the creamy spices to the taste of home. It was wonderful. Too wonderful. How could I sit here and enjoy such a treat while Ikane suffered?

Broderick snatched a puff, the entire thing disappearing into his mouth in a flash.

Chrysla eyed him with a smile. "Well. You two, enjoy." She braced against her knees as she stood. "I'm going to ask the elders if they know where the other half of the letter went."

"No honey puffs?" Broderick mumbled through his mouthful, looking up at her like a chipmunk.

She ruffled his curly mop of hair. "I'll see myself out. You'll let me know if you decide to leave this time, won't you? You disappear for months on end without a trace."

"Don't worry. We're not going anywhere for a while. Not until we've gotten what we came for," Broderick said.

What did he mean by that? That we weren't going after Ikane until we found the letter? It wasn't here. We had nothing.

"I'll send word this evening with news from the elders." Chrysla descended the steps, slipping through the curtain.

Broderick pulled the second steaming mug to his lips.

"You promised, Broderick," I said.

He lowered the drink. "And I will keep my promise."

"The letter is gone."

"You don't know that."

My fist curled on the table, the sweet creaminess in my mouth evaporating to a bitter tang. The image of Deathbiters dissolving into black ash snapped into my mind.

I had magic.

I had power.

I didn't need him.

I didn't need anyone.

"I don't think I've ever seen you draw a bow," Broderick said.

A bow? Where did that topic come from?

He stuffed another honey puff into his mouth and stood. "We should practice. There is an archery range near the main stables."

"Now?" I asked.

He stepped down the first stair. "Why not? We could both use some exercise."

I tugged my bottom lip through my teeth, looking at the plate of honey puffs in the center of the table, half-empty mugs of cooling spiced milk sitting beside it. I hated archery. I wasn't any good at it.

"Can we spar instead?" I asked.

"When was the last time you lifted a sword?"

Everything in me deflated. It had been nearly a month.

"Archery is a good place to start to rebuild your strength," Broderick said.

I huffed. "What about my confidence?"

He chuckled, the corner of his scarred lips stiff. "Come on. It'll help pass the time."

## CHAPTER 4

## FOCUS, STEADY, RELEASE

Broderick's arrow sped across the courtyard and crashed into an icicle dangling from a slanted rooftop. Deep shadows pulled on the surrounding buildings as late afternoon sunlight filled the open space. The sky. If Broderick had told me I'd be able to see the sky at the range, I would have run here. The blue was like Ropert's eyes, bright and vibrant with life and freedom.

"Your turn." Broderick thrust a bow into my hand. "Take your stance." He pushed me into position, handing me an arrow.

"I don't want to do this, Broderick. I know how to use the sword, and that's good enough for me."

He gestured to the string of icicles along the wall. "Shoot."

He wasn't even listening. "Broderick."

"Focus, Kea."

"What's the point?"

"The point is you must learn to subdue Thrall, or it will overpower you again," he said.

"What does archery have to do with it?"

"Everything."

Fine. If he wanted me to hit an icicle, I would. The sooner I did, the sooner we could leave. I nocked the arrow, drawing the bow. My muscles strained. Newly healed scars across my back and arms pricked and throbbed. I exhaled, vapor fogging the row of glistening icicles ahead.

"You have excellent form," Broderick said. "Are you sure you've never done archery before?"

I was accustomed to gripping a sword, not pinching the narrow shaft of an arrow to a taut piece of string. My fingers ached. "Stop toying with me, Broderick." I lowered the bow. "Why aren't you listening to me? Don't you care what happens to Ikane?"

"Of course I do."

"Then what are we doing here?"

He rested his arm on the end of his bow. "I'll make you a deal. You hit your target, and I will tell you anything you want to know."

"Promise?"

"Promise."

I refocused my energy, muscles jerking and adjusting for better strength.

"Breathe," Broderick said.

White vapor puffed as I exhaled. I released. The arrow flew blindly, and I heard the harsh chink as it struck something. The noise was followed by clatter. Either I had hit my target and the icicle had come crashing down, or the arrow had missed and bounced off the icy wall behind it. As soon as my vision cleared, I realized it was the latter. Behind the dangling row of icicles lining the rim of the sloped glacial roof, sat a spider web of cracked ice in the wall. I had missed by two inches.

Broderick whistled. "Not bad."

I glowered at him. "I missed."

"Try again."

I selected another arrow from the quiver set beside me. Drawing the bow was easier this time. I held my breath, keeping the fumes from marring my vision, and released. The arrow zipped away and thunked the ice just above the icicles—not my target. The ice cracked, the entire row of dagger-like teeth crashing down.

"You didn't breathe," Broderick said.

He lifted his bow, chose an arrow, and strung it. Inhaling, he exaggerated the movement of his expanding ribs. "The first breath focuses." He pulled, his black leather coat straining against his shoulders, and inhaled again. "The second steadies." He took aim, setting his hand against the corner of his scarred lips, eyes fixated on his target. "The final breath releases the tension." He exhaled slowly, uncurling his fingers. The arrow whistled. A sharp click echoed through the courtyard as it hit one of the remaining icicles clinging to the corner of the slope. The ice snapped and crashed to the ground.

"Focus, steady, release." He lowered the bow. "Breathe every time."

I grabbed another arrow, trying not to scrunch the white fletching in my clamped fingers. He made it look so easy.

"Aim for the center of the dent you made in the wall. See if you can't get the arrow to burrow in."

Sunlight glinted against the ice, the small spider-web crack a black mark against whiteness.

"Breathe," Broderick whispered.

Bitter cold air bit my nostrils as I inhaled. I drew the bow, my muscles steadying as my chest expanded and drove my shoulders back. The soft fletching brushed against my cheek. Inhaling again, I focused on the center crack of the spider web.

"One more breath," Broderick reminded.

I inhaled. My lips parted, releasing air in a slow steady stream. My fingers uncurled. The string snapped, stinging my forearm, driving the arrow forward. A gentle thwit raced through the air, followed by a sharp crack. The web of fractured ice exploded, the shaft of the arrow embedding in the wall.

I missed. Only by an inch. But I missed.

"Well done." Broderick clapped my shoulder. "What do you want to know?"

I blinked at him. "I missed."

"That is still a kill. Besides, I was more interested in your breathing than aim."

My breathing? I didn't understand. More questions flooded my mind, more than he could answer—or *would* answer. I should've bargained harder, made him answer more than just one question. Knowing him, he would give me half-truth, or withhold just enough to keep me guessing. He was a trained assassin after all, a spy. He would only tell me what he wanted me to know.

"Why aren't we going after Ikane?"

He nocked an arrow, raising his bow. "We will. I promise, Kea." He released, his arrow flying true, embedding dead center in my original spider web of cracks. He lowered his bow. "But you are in a fragile state of mind right now. If you can't learn to control your emotions, or learn to subdue Thrall before it overpowers you, you won't help anyone."

"You have Thrall too? Why subdue it? Why not channel it, use it? Why else would this magic exist?"

Broderick withdrew another arrow. "What keeps an arrow flying straight?"

He was changing the subject again. "The fletching?"

He stroked the white feathers with his thumb. "The fletching certainly helps, but the fletching can't do its job if the arrow's balance point and physical midpoint are too close together. The key is harmony."

"I don't understand what that has to do with magic?"

"You asked why Thrall would exist if not to use it. Thrall is the symmetry to Etheria."

"Etheria?"

He chuckled, knocking the arrow. "Etheria is the magic of the elements. Some of us have parts of it. Like me." The arrow zipped away. "I am a Wind Wardent. I can ask the wind to push and pull. I can ask it to purify and clean. But I can't command it the way you can."

"Now you've lost me."

He faced me. "As far as I can tell, you have Etheria similar to the White Wardent's. You have the ability to command all four elements. If this is the case, it is even more imperative that you learn to balance Thrall with Etheria. Thrall is easy to summon. All it takes is a spark of anger, hatred, or loathing. It feeds on it, creating more emotions, twisting all rationality. If you're not careful, it will devour your mind."

"How do you know so much about it?"

He smiled, gesturing to the quiver. "Get another arrow."

I folded my arms across my chest. "No."

"You've got to work on your breathing."

"Why? I'm never going to shoot a bow. I am a swordsman."

"You have twenty-two arrows left. Hit my arrow and I'll tell you why we are doing this," he said.

"Everything is a wager with you, isn't it?"

He shrugged. "Not generally, but it ignites something in you. You like to prove yourself. So, prove to me you can shoot a bow."

Grudgingly, I nocked the arrow, studying his perfectly aimed shot down the shaft. The white fletching blurred with the ice behind it.

This was not my idea of fun.

I released the twenty-second arrow, my fingers blistered and raw, my back muscles spent, my forearm aching where the string repeatedly slapped against it. The thickness of my coat took away the initial sting, but it would be purple and blue by tomorrow. All twenty-two arrows struck within the vicinity of his, but none of them came close to the mark I intended. I hated archery.

"I think you're ready." Broderick unstrung his bow.

"Ready for what?"

"To heal Erin."

I froze. "You mean you haven't healed her yet? Broderick, she will die if she's not healed soon."

"I know. And I think you are ready now. At least try."

"No." I unstrung my bow. "No. I can't do it. I hurt Ali. She'd sooner blow me back to Roanfire than let me try again."

"She understands," he said. "She's agreed to not observe this time."

The image of the little sprite curled up on the shelf made my lungs tighten. The faith he had in me was beyond comprehension. He was either the most loyal friend in all of Roanfire, or the biggest fool.

I grabbed the empty quiver. "This is my last try," I said. "If I fail again, you must heal Erin today."

"Agreed."

Why was I looking for her? I knew she wouldn't be here. The room stood empty of her glimmer. No movement, no breeze. Just the darkening walls closing in on us like a tomb, the sour stench of Deathbiter poison thick enough to touch.

Unnatural blue veins spread under Erin's eyes, flowing down her cheeks. She lay still, her breathing shallow and weak, the only evidence of life coming from a faint throbbing vein in her neck.

My fingers trembled as I brushed her black curls from her forehead. She was dying.

Broderick uncovered her arm, the smell stimulating the gag reflex in my throat. The poison was spreading fast. Had my wounds looked like this? Had the smell been just as repulsive? How did my friends tolerate being in the same room with me? I suffered for ten long days, alive, but wishing I was dead.

"You can do this, Kea," Broderick said. "Focus, steady, release."

I dipped my hands in the ash, a gentle gray puff exploding from the pail. It was so light. How this frail barrier worked was beyond my understanding. But Broderick had done it. He had labored over me, drawing poison from the dozens of cuts and bites on my skin. I could do one, couldn't I? Just one wound.

Holding my breath, I knelt beside the platform, my hands hovering over the three gashes on her arm. Heat radiated from her swollen flesh.

"Remember to breathe," Broderick said.

I inhaled. Feathers, the smell. My chest clenched. How could I breathe with this acrid sourness burning my nose and making my eyes water?

"Is your mind ready?" Broderick sank to the floor beside me. "Think of Erin and why she deserves to live."

I shut my eyes, the sight of my soot-smudged hands vanishing. Erin's pale face. The black veins. All that remained was the smell and the heat radiating under my palms.

"Focus," Broderick whispered.

My mind stretched. This was for Erin. She'd given up everything to get me here. The least I could do was try.

Inhaling, a familiar warmth entered my chest, slowly trickling like water droplets down my arms to my hands. It wasn't exhilarating. It held little energy. But it was firm, like an armor-clad knight rooted to the pinnacle of a mountain. It was an old friend, something constant, always coming when Ikane needed protection from Rion's fiery assaults. How could I have forgotten the taste, the sweetness, the calm reassurance that I was safe? Why had I left it to collect dust and cobwebs?

Dark heat pulled at my hands, threatening to draw me into Erin's misery. I struggled to keep them elevated, shoulders trembling, holding onto the vibrant heat in my chest.

"Breathe." Broderick's voice was distant. "Breathe, Kea."

I forced an inhale, staggering my breath against the strain of my body.

"Draw it to you."

My mind struggled to comprehend his words, like I was surrounded in fog. The poison wanted to devour me. It wanted to infect me the same way it did Erin. Etheria flickered and spun, streaks of light like shooting stars whirling through my mind.

"Steady."

My arms shook, straining against the weight.

"Breathe." Broderick's reminders were becoming a lifeline, a guiding hand I could trust.

My lungs gathered breath.

"When you are ready, release." Broderick's voice was soft and strong.

I was ready.

White light expanded, silver fragments of power driving through my arms, hardening them like an iron sword. The treacherous darkness resisted, slimy weight settling against my palms and fingers, absorbing into the charcoal on my skin. I pulled. This was not going to take Erin. This would not be how she died.

The pull released with a snap. My body rocked back, my mind thrust into awareness of my surroundings. The white walls spun and twisted.

Broderick caught my shoulders. "You did it, Kea." The joy in his voice was as tangible as his crooked smile.

I was exhausted, my arms shaking. The smelly black ooze coating my hands dragged them down like stones. "Is... is it always this taxing?"

"You'll get stronger. Just like learning to wield a sword, ride a horse, or draw a bow, you will grow stronger every time you use that muscle." He held me close in a celebratory embrace.

All I wanted was to wash this horrid, foul-smelling slime from my hands.

A drawn-out sigh came from Erin. Blue veins no longer clung to her eyes and the harsh lines of pain on her brow softened. Her body sank deeper into the furs, rosiness returning to her lips and cheeks.

How I wished I could sink into sleep like that right now.

"Wait." Broderick leaned over, studying her arm.

My heart thumped. Had I missed something? Did I not do it? I peered over his shoulder, catching sight of three pale scars on her skin. Nothing seemed amiss. What was Broderick looking at?

"What is it?" I asked.

Broderick looked at me, his blue eyes wide with excitement. "You not only drew out the poison. You healed her completely. I couldn't do this. I drew out your poison, but the wounds still needed time." He tucked Erin's arm under her blankets. "And you did it without touching Thrall," he said. "I'm proud of you."

A strangled whimper escaped my throat. I hadn't realized his approval meant so much to me.

"Come." He gripped my elbows, helping me rise. "Let's get you cleaned up."

My legs moved sluggishly as he steered me to the washbasin. He lifted the wooden pitcher, poured a generous amount of water into the large bowl, and pulled a vial from his coat. A soft red glow radiated from the dust inside. Popping the cork, he tipped the mouth of the vial over the bowl. Glowing red flakes shimmered into the water like dust caught in a sunbeam. A soft hiss ignited as the granules struck, steam rising from the water.

He tucked the vial back into his coat. "It helps cut the poison from your skin. And it's warm." He winked.

I dropped my weighted hands into the water. Hiss. A heavy plume of sour smelling mist exploded, acrid steam flooding into my eyes. Arching back, I coughed fumes from my lungs.

Trying to keep my face away from the fumes, I washed. My legs shook, ready to give out under my weight. Wrists resting against the rim of the bowl, my hands hung in the water like limp rags, shoulders too tired to lift my arms. Black ooze pulled away from my skin in ugly threads, collecting in the bottom of the bowl like tiny misshapen rocks.

Broderick handed me a towel. "Did you feel Etheria? The way it shields you?"

The name suited it perfectly. It was bright and faultless, wispy, fragile, and light. It was like wielding a silk ribbon in place of a sword.

I dropped the towel beside the washbasin.

Broderick wrapped his arm around my shoulders. "You look like you could use some rest."

"Can we go help Ikane now?"

## CHAPTER 5

# ALONE AGAIN

*H*e clung to his memories like clutching the rigging on a ship in a storm. How much longer could he endure? Wave after wave of brutal power washed over him, pulling and twisting, determined to sever his connection.

He gasped as it receded, dragging against him, gathering strength for the next burst. He shifted his hold, bracing for the following swell.

A suffocating surge of fierce power rushed forward, slamming into him, jeopardizing everything he was, everything he could become.

He was born on the water, a prince of the sea. A warrior and brother. A friend and lover. Without his memories, he was nothing.

The power ebbed, dragging against him. A memory slipped from his grasp—the vision of himself as a young boy in wolf form and his older brother, Teilo, trying to soothe him. He scrambled after it, but it disappeared in the roaring power.

This was beyond him. He couldn't hold on forever. Rion no longer infested his mind, but this was worse. This threatened to destroy everything he was.

"You have no need for these memories." The old man's voice cracked above him like thunder. Another breaker washed over him. Another memory lost. Was it about a friend? A brother? It was someone he cared about, but the face was swallowed up. The emptiness left behind was like the dark abyss of the sea, growing wider with each severed memory.

"Stop. Please."

"I am freeing your mind. It is what you wanted."

Not like this. He wanted Rion gone, that was all. Not his mind changed.

Where was Kea? They could fight this together. He couldn't do it alone. Whatever silver-blue energy he had did not rise to the surface without the first spark of her white embers.

"Kea." Why did he call for her? He'd cried out her name so many times he'd lost count. She wasn't there. She couldn't hear him.

Her smile flooded to the front of his mind, the light smattering of freckles across her cheeks and nose, her stormy blue eyes. She moved like water on the battlefield, slipping past his defenses, her strikes rippling up his arms. She knew her skill and used it. Her ability to . . .

To what? What was he thinking about?

The hole in his chest grew wider as the wave receded, the emptiness deeper, the fear stronger.

"Stop," he croaked.

Power rolled over him, spinning him like an abandoned ship at sea.

He couldn't hold on anymore.

*Ikane. I'm here. I'm with you. I see you.*

My mind reached and stretched, but something held me back. Why couldn't I get to him?

My heart ached with each throb, like a knife drilling through my ribs. I sat upright, curling over my chest, trying to relieve the pain.

His mind was under attack, and there was nothing I could do, nothing but watch.

If only I'd gotten to him sooner. If only Broderick would have let me leave. The pain in my chest shifted to heat, roaring through my blood. We should have left as soon as I'd awakened.

Enough was enough. I couldn't wait anymore. It might already have been too late.

Throwing the furs from my legs, I pulled on my boots and grabbed my saddlebag. I didn't have much to pack. Two pairs of woolen stockings, fresh trousers, a cotton shirt, a comb, a bar of soap, flint, my vials of firedust and waterdust, and my small box of herbs. I added my sword, scabbard, and two small knives to the collection. All I needed now was armor or hides thick enough to resist the Deathbiters' talons.

"Kea?" Broderick called from the curtain. "Are you awake?"

*Feathers, not now.* I flipped the corner of the heavy fur blanket over the stash on my bed. "I'm up."

The curtain parted, and Broderick stepped inside, two quivers slung over his shoulder, two bows in his right hand. "I thought we could practice archery again."

How much archery did he think I needed? We were wasting time. "I did what you wanted—Erin is healed. It's time to go after Ikane."

Broderick's face contorted with pity. "You healed her, yes. But you have yet to master control."

"He's suffering, Broderick. I see it. I feel it." I clutched my chest, trying to keep the pain from overpowering my heart.

"Did you dream of him again?" he asked.

"Yes."

I saw his mind process, calculate, and measure. It was a good sign. If I pushed a little more, he might consent.

"Please."

He straightened, gathering breath. "Not yet, Kea. You're not ready."

He didn't understand. How could he? The emotions weren't there. "If we don't leave now, there will be nothing left of Ikane to save."

Broderick glanced away for a moment as if considering the idea. "Can you be certain?"

"I can feel him giving up, Broderick. We are running out of time."

His hand landed on my shoulder, drawing my eyes to his. "I know this is difficult, Kea, but please trust me when I say you are not ready. You still need practice. You will be no help to Ikane like this."

Closing my eyes, I gathered a breath. There was no fighting him on this. "I'm not up for archery today," I said. "My fingers are blistered, and my arm is bruised."

"I thought you might say that." He pulled something from his coat pocket. "I brought you these."

I stepped down the stairs before he could come up. His eyes were sharp. If he caught a glimpse of anything on my bed, he'd know what I was up to, and he would ruin my plans.

"Hold out your arm." He shook his head when I complied. "No, the other one. The one you hold the bow with." He slipped a leather armguard onto my forearm, twisting it so that the solid portion sat on the inside of my wrist, covering my bruises from the day before. "Most archers wear these," he said, lacing it up to my elbow.

"Then why in the flaming feathers didn't you give this to me yesterday?" I asked.

"You're spirited today." He gave me a crooked smile, drawing attention to his scar.

My stomach clenched.

"Give me your hand," he said.

He slipped a fingered leather glove onto my other hand. A small notch separated my middle and forefingers, right where I would hold the arrow. My raw skin ached as he secured its leather string around my wrist.

"There." He stepped back, scanning his work. "You're ready."

"I'd rather spar."

"We can. But later," he said. "It is good to learn a new skill. You could be a decent archer if you trained enough."

"I don't want to be an archer."

"Oh, you've made that clear," he said.

I sighed. Very well. I'd practice once more, just to satisfy him, and then I would go.

"Let me grab my coat," I said. Stepping back onto the landing, I noticed the tip of my leather scabbard peeking out from under the fur blanket on my bed. My heart rate quickened. He hadn't indicated he'd seen it, but he was good at hiding things from me.

I grabbed my coat then shrugged it on as I hurried down the steps.

"Erin is awake." Broderick held open the curtain. "She and Ali would like to share supper with us."

"Are they coming back to Roanfire with us?" I stepped into the barren passageway, struggling to fasten the wooden toggles down the front of my coat with Broderick's finger guard.

"I think so. She's ready to go home."

"When do we leave?" I asked.

"Patience, Kea. You may have succeeded in healing Erin, but that was with my coaching. You need to be able to do it on your own. The strength of will needed to resist Thrall isn't going to come easy."

My feet stopped. "How long before you feel I'm ready? Ikane has no more time."

"That depends on you," he said.

"Flaming feathers, Broderick." I tore my hand through my hair, tugging on the ends. "I thought you were Ikane's friend."

His face hardened. "Don't say that."

"Then prove it. Let's go. Now. He's... he's suffering, Broderick. His mind... his body. It's all wrong."

"You can't help him if you don't train, Kea."

"Forget this." I tossed the bow at his feet, stripping the armguard and finger glove. "You're just content to stay here where the Deathbiters don't bother us, stuffing your face with honey puffs and spiced milk while Roanfire suffers. While Ikane suffers. I came here to find a way to defeat Rion, and nothing has changed."

A few onlookers paused in the street.

"Kea, calm down." Broderick's voice was furiously relaxed. Every part of me bristled, heat running through my limbs, spreading up my neck. Did this man not have any passion? Perhaps that was why he made such a good assassin.

I pitched the leather equipment at his chest. "There are no answers here. We are wasting time."

He caught the armguard, his eyes finally holding some hint of emotion. "Kea. Breathe."

"Don't tell me to breathe. Ikane is suffocating." I was, too. My chest was too tight, too filled with heat and rage.

Broderick took a step back, throwing his arms wide, keeping the glacial natives from drawing any closer. "Get back," he told them. "Go."

The growing crowd stepped away, eyeing us from far walls and doorways.

Why was he so concerned about them? Ikane was the one suffering. I was the one whose heart was bleeding.

A hot wind floated through the air.

"Kea, please. Think of what you are doing." Broderick's eyes were wide, his brows crowding his face, his hands held up as if I held a sword to his throat. "Listen to your thoughts. Your mind. Tame the rage in your heart."

Something flashed inside, something under too much pressure to contain. This was the same power—

It released. Broderick threw his arms over his face, and his body sailed backward. The crowd screamed as he hit the icy road, tumbling.

What had I done?

Broderick's muscles trembled as he pushed himself from the street, red dripping from his nose.

"I . . . I'm sorry. I didn't . . . I didn't mean . . ." Oh, Phoenix help me, I couldn't breathe. I backed away, the crowd looking on, eyes wide, mouths agape. I clutched my chest, trying to ease the crushing weight from stopping my heart. This was not who I was. I was meant to be a warrior, a protector, a friend to those who had none.

My feet moved, carrying me down the street and through my curtain door, only stopping at the bottom steps in my chamber.

What was happening to me? My knees gave out, and my body sunk to the first step. I couldn't breathe. No matter how many times I inhaled, it wasn't enough. My fingers dug into my shoulders and squeezed, and my body rocked as cold tears trailed down my cheeks, dripping from my chin.

Broderick had already forgiven me once. He wouldn't do it again.

Ali was right.

Thrall had me.

My bag leaned against the base of my bed, ready to go. He would tell me to leave. It was only logical. I was out of control and a danger to everyone. Did I dare ask for provisions or armor? I wouldn't blame him for withholding those basic needs.

"Kea?"

Something squeezed around my heart at the sound of his voice. Why had he come? Didn't he understand? I was lost. There was no helping me.

The curtain drew aside, and Broderick entered slowly, his eyes falling immediately to my bag. His lips pressed tight as he climbed the stairs, sitting beside me on the bed. Inhaling through his nose, he leaned back, hands on his knees. "I never told you what kept me from meeting you at Midpoint."

I swallowed, keeping my eyes fixed on the plate of half-eaten honey puffs on the table. If I looked at him, the tears would come.

"The Phoenix soldiers regrouped and gave chase with much more skill than anticipated," he said. "I held them at the entrance for a time, much longer than intended. By the time I lost them, it was too late. I knew I wouldn't make it to Midpoint before nightfall."

Why was he telling me this? Why didn't he scold me? "You should have gone back," I whispered.

"That may have been the easier path, but not the right one," he said. "Ali found me just before nightfall. She spent the night watching for Deathbiters, blasting them away with powerful bursts of wind."

I glanced at my bag sitting at my feet. Where was he going with this? Why didn't he just tell me to be gone, that I was too much of a danger to be around anyone?

"By morning, she was spent. I put her in my pocket and rode hard, trying to catch up to you," he said. "By the time I reached Midpoint, strange clouds were building in the sky. I'd never seen anything like them. They were so thick the sun couldn't penetrate. I knew then something was wrong."

I remembered. I remembered the cold burrowing deeper as the sun vanished. "Why are you telling me this?" My voice was quiet and weak.

"Because I know where the Deathbiters' lair is."

Something in me stood at attention, eager for the information, but I still couldn't look at him. "Where is it?"

"It's roughly four furlongs west of Midpoint," he said.

I stiffened, daring to look at the bandoleer strapped across his chest. "We'd already passed it?"

"It's easy to miss," he said. "The strange gray mist seeping from the crevice drew my attention to it. And the stench. It will take some climbing to reach."

My lip quivered, the pain of losing his friendship tearing into my heart like a Deathbiter's talon. I understood why he was telling me this now. He had to protect himself. He had to protect everyone here in Nethaska. He was letting me go.

I swallowed against the painful lump tightening in my throat, my eyes falling to my boots. "I'll leave at first light."

"Kea, you're not going alone."

I took a good look at him, at the new pink-and-blue bruise on his cheek, at the scar on his lips, at the brown curls hanging over his brow, at the sincerity in his eyes. "You would . . . do that? After what I just did?"

"Believe it or not, I was where you are now." He straightened, his eyes turning to the smooth dome ceiling. "I almost let Thrall take me."

"How did you stop it?"

"With time, patience, and practice," he said. "With holding on to the belief that I could change. And by refusing to use Thrall, no matter how tempting it was."

I looked at my palms, at the empty flecks of gray burned into my skin like an inverted starlit sky. "But Ikane doesn't have time."

He sighed. "I know. And I see that keeping you away from him is only making Thrall dig deeper and want more. But I still don't think you are ready."

Hope surged through my body, my fingers aching to grab my bag, my legs ready to run. But something held me back, like chains dragging against my arms and legs. What if he was right? If I hurt him again, I would never forgive myself.

Feathers, what if I hurt Ikane?

What was wrong with me? I'd been fighting him all this time, wanting nothing more than to go after Ikane. But now . . . "Broderick, I . . . I'm not sure—"

The curtain parted.

Chrysla stepped into the room, her smile igniting the walls in sun and warmth. "Someone is here to see you." She held open the curtain.

A woman with dark curls tumbling down her shoulders in waves of black silk entered, a heavy skin of white-and-gray fur wrapped around her shoulders.

I stood. "Erin."

She looked good. Pink touched her cheeks, and her lips held color again.

"I hear I have you to thank for saving my life," she said.

The words curdled in my stomach. I did nothing. It was all Broderick.

"Is it time for supper already?" Broderick asked.

Chrysla's grin widened. "It is. And I've had a feast prepared of Nethaska's finest delicacies." She waved to the door, and three glacial natives entered carrying trays laden with bowls, plates, saucers, and cups. They spread the meal across the table, the warm aroma of roasted meat filling the room. The servers each bowed to the empress, touching their hands to their foreheads before they left.

"Go on, sit," Chrysla urged us, taking a place at the table. There was no mistaking why she chose that spot. It was nearest to the plate of honey puffs. She waved a hand across the meal. "There's sea lion meat, smoked fish, bear, cabbage, salt wafers, aged reindeer cheese, and—of course—my favorite, honey puffs."

Broderick and Erin sank to the carpet of furs surrounding the table. My legs moved slowly, a part of me unsure if it was safe for me to be with them. What if Thrall arose again? What if I lost control?

Chrysla spooned roasted cabbage and a slice of beautifully browned meat onto her plate. "I've spoken with the elders about the letter. I'm sorry to report that they have no insight on the whereabouts. I have seven scribes combing through the Cavern of Records as we speak. If the missing half of the letter is there, they will find it."

"So you haven't found what you came for." Erin eyed me.

"Not yet," Broderick said. "But we can't wait any longer. We're leaving for Roanfire tomorrow."

"So soon?" Chrysla's smile faded into a pout. "I haven't gotten to show you the snow bison herds or the coal mines of Levgough."

Broderick chuckled. "We're not here as tourists, Your Majesty."

She jabbed her fork in his direction. "How many times have I told you to call me Chrysla?"

I glanced across the table at Erin, who was taking polite bites of her meal, chewing slowly. She gave me a forced smile.

Feathers, it hurt. "How is your arm?" I asked.

"Like it never happened," she said.

I took a bite of my meal, barely tasting it, barely hearing the lighthearted banter between the empress and Broderick. What was Erin thinking? How much did she remember? Did she see the destruction I caused in Glacier Pass? Did she understand it was me? Did she realize I was the one who gave Broderick the new scar on his lips?

"Kea?" Broderick nudged my shoulder, pulling me from my thoughts. "What do you think?"

"About what?"

"There's been a long-standing debate whether snow bison hides are stronger than the steel armor of Roanfirien soldiers," Broderick said. "I, personally, think steel armor better."

"It's heavier," Chrysla said. "You must take that into consideration."

"That's not the point. We're talking about protective qualities, not lightness or ease of wear."

"Are you saying we have a choice of either wearing steel or snow bison hides as protection from the Deathbiters?" Erin asked.

"No." Chrysla chuckled. "We don't have steel here."

"Then why are we debating it?" Erin tilted her head at them. "We need protection from the Deathbiters. Snow bison is the only option."

Leave it to Erin to dull the mood.

Chrysla leaned back. "I suppose you're right. I'll have three coats brought to you this evening."

"Three?" An airy voice broke into the conversation like a whirlwind, a loud buzzing tearing through the room. "Erin. You're not considering returning with them, are you? Not with her." The sprite hovered above the table, her form warping as steam rose from the various dishes.

Erin's eyes darkened. "Ali." There was a warning in her tone.

"No. Don't look at me like that. You were almost killed once. I will not see you intentionally put your life in danger again." White sparks leapt from Ali's form as she spoke.

I lowered my fork, the knot in my stomach making it impossible to eat.

"Don't point fingers," Erin warned. "We all make mistakes. Even you."

"It's not the same thing," Ali said. "She used it again when she tried to heal you, and a third time just hours ago. Just look at Broderick's face. How you can sit here eating with such darkness spewing from her countenance—it makes me sick."

Erin looked away, tugging at her bracelets. "Do you really want to discuss this here?"

Ali's silver-edged image dulled, the buzz of her wings losing vigor. Her bleached eyes narrowed at me, and something stabbed at my chest with her glare. "I suppose not. But we will speak more of this tonight." Wind tore through the chamber, ruffling my hair, blasting against the curtain as Ali disappeared.

"Well, I must say, I've never seen a sprite with so much passion for the wellbeing of a human." Chrysla turned to Erin. "There must be an intriguing story there."

"It's not one I like to share." Erin lifted her fork.

Broderick reached over, his hand resting on my knee. "Are you alright?" he whispered.

The dark roast blurred on my plate, and a thousand icy shards burrowed into my eyes. Ali was the only one treating me the way I deserved to be treated. I was going to use Thrall again. I could feel it. It churned and bubbled, waiting for another moment my emotions became too overwhelming.

It was happening all over again. The isolation. The inability to feel at ease around others I cared for. But this time, it wasn't because Rion threatened to devour them. This time, it was me.

"She's right," I whispered. "You're not safe with me. No one is."

"Kea—"

I held up a hand. "I'm sorry. I... I can't..." I stood, wiping my cheeks furiously as I ducked out of the room.

My feet stopped outside the door. I didn't want to be alone, but I couldn't let them be around me, either.

It was like reaching for an outstretched hand only to catch air. The emptiness. The hollow nothing centered in my chest had become a place for Thrall to reside like an unwelcome parasite.

"Kea?"

Scrunching my eyes at her voice, I turned away, tears burning down my cheeks.

Erin stepped beside me, hugging the heavy fur draped around her shoulders. "Ali would never admit it, but she understands what is eating you up inside. I think that's why she's being so hard on you."

How could Ali know anything about this? Ali despised Thrall. She wouldn't brush it with the edge of her wind.

"It was Ali's use of magic that killed my children." Erin's voice was tight. "She lives with that guilt every day. And so, she stays. There are days I wish she'd leave me in peace, days I wish I could squash her like a bug. But the strange thing is, I love her."

"But you sent her away. You don't want her near you." Knives tore through my throat.

"That doesn't mean I don't care about her."

I didn't understand. Did she want me to leave or not?

"The point is, we all make mistakes." She shrugged. "Feathers, I made the mistake of helping you."

I blinked at her. Did she just make a joke? The Erin I knew didn't have a lighthearted bone in her body.

Her eyes grew serious. "Don't let guilt eat at you, Kea. I may not know much about magic, but I know guilt will devour you from the inside out."

I brushed the tears from my cheeks. "I'm so sorry, Erin. I didn't mean for any of this to happen."

"I know." She opened her palm, white light bursting across the tunnel as if she held the sun in her hand. The teardrop-shaped vial rolled to her fingers. "And deep down, Ali knows it, too."

Windsprite dust?

"From Ali." Erin pushed it at me.

What was she saying? That Ali was giving this dust to me? It was too much. It was rare to find windsprite dust at all. Something this pure was unheard of.

"Oh, for the love of the Phoenix, take it already." Erin grabbed my hand, pressing the vial into it.

A soothing energy pulsed through my fingers, rushing up my skin like a tempered breeze—almost, almost like an embrace. My body shook, a fresh wave of tears rushing from my eyes. "I don't deserve this."

"Who really gets what they deserve?" she asked with a shrug. "Now, come back. Don't make me eat with those two 'the world is perfect' people by myself." She ducked back into my room.

I glanced at the glowing vial in my hand, the radiance stinging my tear-blurred eyes. Why did speaking with Erin always leave me confused? Did she care for me or not? Her lack of emotion was more frustrating than Ali's overpowering anger.

Gathering a deep breath, I pulled the curtain aside. The least I could do was respect Empress Chryslacheska's hospitality.

## CHAPTER 6

# ROGUE

*His* silvery-white hair rippled like silken ribbons, caressing his flawless skin, whispering across his broad shoulders as he drifted closer. He was too perfect, too immaculate to be real.

Why were his eyes never the same? His irises had been red once, then blue. There was a time they'd been as white as his unblemished hair. Now, they shone like a newborn forest, greens flickering like fresh leaves spinning in the wind.

How dare he show his face. How dare he come to me again, mocking me, flaunting every answer I needed, holding it like a crust of bread before a starving child's face. The last time I'd seen his vision I was plagued with Deathbiter venom, fighting for my life. He said help was coming. He said he was sending it.

But it was Broderick who saved my life.

This man was nothing to me. Nothing but a horrible vision of beauty and promise that was always out of reach.

"What are you doing here?" My voice trembled, edged with blackness I couldn't hide.

He stopped, silvery brows knotting. "What... what happened to you?" His voice flowed like warm cream, soft and rich, sinking deep into my chest like an unwanted embrace.

"Don't pretend you care."

His green eyes searched around me, and his perfect face morphed into confusion. "I can't see. Where are you?"

"The Glacial Empire. And the letter isn't here. There is nothing here. I've lost everything." A black thread snaked around my chest, curling around my heart. "I've lost Ikane."

He took a step forward. "What have you done? I warned you not to go to the Glacial Empire. I told you the letter wasn't needed."

"Then help me!" Shadow pushed from my heart, leaking like smoke through the gaps in a door. "Tell me what I need to do to defeat her. Stop giving me riddles and telling me what I don't need. I can't do this on my own. I can't . . ." Every part of me trembled, sorrow welling in my chest. If only I could cry, let the pain bleed through my tears. "I'm failing."

His beautiful brows knotted, his head tilted, and his forest-green eyes burned with something bordering on fear and empathy. "Oh, my dear child. How have you become so dark? You must let it go."

Who was he to tell me what I should do? He never answered my questions. He was the one who created this curse, and the princesses of Roanfire had suffered for it. The thread around my heart thickened, growing tighter, and shadow spilled from me like a dense fog. Curse his pale beauty and perfection. Curse everything about him.

"You are the reason for this plague. You. No one else. Rion wouldn't be who she is if you had left it alone—let her be taken by old age like any other normal human," I said. "But you tampered with magic. You admitted it yourself. And you blame me for turning dark?"

He flinched as if I'd punched him, his white vision flickering. "I know."

"Then help me."

"I am trying," he said.

"Rubbish. If that were the truth, you would be here with me, guiding me, teaching me, helping me." The darkness crept in, gnawing on my pain. "Yet you hide in my dreams. Coward. Where are you? Are you even real?"

"I am as real as you are."

"Then by the burning feathers of the Phoenix, why aren't you here?" The shadow expanded with my words, pushing against him, stinging his arms as he shielded his body.

His eyes slammed shut, teeth clenching. "You are going down a path I cannot follow."

Strange how Broderick had said the same thing. But what else was I to do? Trying to follow the White Wardent's trail was like hunting for mouse tracks in the woods. It was impossible.

I steeled everything inside me. "Then perhaps this new path will get me somewhere."

He pried his eyes open, glistening beads of perspiration forming on his brow. "You will fail if you do."

"I'm failing now!"

"Please... don't do this," he said through gritted teeth. "Don't push me away. Think about what you are doing."

I didn't need to think. He should be the one to suffer, not me. Shadow thickened, eating at the raw parts of my pain. If only it would surround him, snuff out his pastel glory, erase him from history. He had to know the heartache I felt, the loss, the fear, the uncertainty.

He stumbled back, his white form growing darker like the sun blotted out by clouds. "Don't... don't do this. Don't push me away."

"You've already done that," I hissed.

His green eyes bored into the deepest parts of my energy, flickering with a sadness so deep, my resolve almost wavered. Almost.

"I'm not giving up on you," he said. His white form vanished, and my shadow was left hanging like vapor in his void.

My eyes flew open, and tears already clung to my lashes as cold droplets slid to my pillow. Phoenix, how could the pain be so deep and raw? The cry tearing from my throat couldn't release it. The sobs didn't relieve it. I clutched my chest, hoping the motion would somehow ease the throbbing ache inside.

I was done waiting for help. I was done trying to do it the right way—whatever way that was. Thrall was given to me for a reason. If it meant I could get Ikane back, I'd use it. Forget Broderick's balance.

Fists tight, I pushed the tears from my cheeks.

I was going to get him back.

I laced my fur-lined boots, slipped into the coat from Queen Lonacheska, secured my knives and sword, and hefted my pack. Orange light shimmered across the outline of the curtain hanging over the door as I stepped into the quiet tunnel, empty in the night. My feet carried me quickly down the passageway. The stables weren't far from the archery range.

A soft light radiated from the arched doorway of the stable, unwavering, white. Pressing my back against the wall, I peered around the corner. The glow came from a vial of windsprite dust hanging from a leather cord in the center of the quiet stable, illuminating rows of ice-carved pens lining the circular room with gates constructed of leather and bone. A dozen long-haired glacial ponies hung their heads in sleep. Despite the cold, the sweet smell of hay and honey-coated oats tinged by horse manure was thick.

Slipping inside, I hurried to the nearest pen, clicking my tongue softly. The glacial pony, its rump to me, lifted its head.

I reached over the gate. "Come on," I whispered.

Its ears twitched, and recognition hit. It was the horse Erin had ridden through Glacier Pass. The image of her standing on the road, clutching his reins, staring at me like I'd sprouted Deathbiter wings flooded my mind. Did he remember?

My breath stopped as he turned around. Warm, moist air pushed from his flaring nostrils against my outstretched hand.

He jerked back, a panicked whinny tearing through the silence. Whirling in the stall, he tossed his head, eyes wide in terror.

He did remember.

I was a monster.

The entire stall came alive with movement, horses straightening, heads pushing over gates, ears twitching.

"What's going on in there?"

The feminine voice came from outside. White light shifted across the tunnel walls as someone drew near.

Leaping into an empty stall, I sank to my heels, pressing my back against the icy wall, heart pounding against my ribs like a battle drum.

The white light in the room grew brighter as footfalls echoed through the stall. "What's gotten into you, Sprint? Come here, boy. Everything is alright."

Her gentle voice almost soothed me.

"There. It's alright," she said.

I closed my eyes, imagining her stroking the poor animal's neck.

"You've been through a lot, I know. But there are no Deathbiters here. See?"

Her light traveled down the row of pens, drawing closer. "Now, go back to sleep. All of you."

The light faded as the woman left.

I exhaled slowly, muscles sighing. I'd have to find a horse that didn't recognize me. Tucking my feet under myself, I rose slowly, my nose brushing the edge of the pen. The stables stood quiet once more.

Something warm and moist blasted against my ear. I jerked away, finding a shaggy glacial pony staring back at me, her dark eyes curious. Stretching out my hand, I stroked her forehead.

"You should be afraid of me," I whispered.

Her gray ears turned forward at the sound of my voice. The poor little horse had no idea what she'd gotten herself into.

I saddled her, wrapped her hooves in torn scraps from my extra shirt, and led her from the pen, her steps giving off a muffled clop against the ice. Stroking her neck, I glanced at Sprint, barely seeing his back over the edge of his stall. I'd ruined him. He might never be able to set foot in Glacier Pass again.

"Come on," I whispered, tugging the unsuspecting glacial pony from the stables, guiding her to the main tunnel. It was expansive, wide enough for five wagons to ride abreast. Fewer arched doorways lined the street, replaced by smaller tunnels leading into darkness. It turned a soft bend, opening to the deep blue sky speckled with winking stars, beckoning me from this icy prison.

I stopped. This was too easy. Where were the guards? Where were the gates? Did the Glacial Empress have that much faith in her city?

The pony nudged my shoulder.

There was no turning back now.

After removing the cloth wrappings from her hooves, I mounted then gathered a deep breath of chilled air. I was doing what I should have done days ago.

My heels dug into her sides. Her muscles bunched beneath me, hooves clapping like ringing hammers through the tunnel. Rising in my seat, I urged her into a gallop, icy wind rushing against my cheeks. We exploded from the shaft.

Thousands of stars filled the obsidian sky, free and endless. Vast plains stretched on, reflecting starlight like a sea of ice. Far ahead, the long, faint silhouette of Glacier Pass blocked out the stars on the horizon.

*I'm coming, Ikane.*

Morning light struck the solid wall of ice, igniting the edges in a fiery glow. Glacier Pass sat in the cliffs like an irreparable cut in a piece of armor, edges torn, narrowing as the walls plummeted to the pathway swallowed in shadow. The pathway leading back to Roanfire. The pathway hiding the Deathbiters' lair.

A faint wail whispered through the Pass, crawling up my spine as I slipped from the saddle, my muscles groaning. I should rest. I should close my eyes for a moment, sleep, wake with a clear head for the task ahead of me. But I couldn't stop now. I was so close.

And Broderick was bound to come after me. If I fell asleep now, I wasn't sure I'd wake before he caught up to me. And I couldn't let him witness what I was going to do.

But why didn't my feet move? I stood at the opening, fist clutching my stolen horse's reins as though my life depended on it, staring at the gaping fissure in the ice. Sunlight touched my cheeks, teasing them with the promise of warmth and safety. Deathbiters didn't fly in daylight, but that hadn't kept them from attacking us in Glacier Pass before. What if they attacked me now?

I swallowed.

If I couldn't get Ikane back, what did any of this matter? The Deathbiters wouldn't be searching for me. They'd gotten what they came for.

And I was going to get him back, no matter the cost.

The cliffs consumed me in shadow as I stepped between them, and the temperature plummeted as the horse's clopping hooves echoed forever. Sunlight danced on the ledge high above, like the snow was rimmed in fire. Two slick ruts were carved into the road from years of trade between our two kingdoms. Trade that had now halted because of the Deathbiters.

I'd find their lair today. I'd find their source and put an end to it.

Something lay ahead, a small black mass crumpled against the base of the cliff. My heart thundered as I moved closer. Black veins stretching through leathery wings became more defined, and the upturned snout, the large ears, the fangs, and the talons were all frozen in place. Its eyes stared at the sky, hazy and frosted.

Dropping the horse's reins, I slid my sword from its sheath.

Another one lay a few yards away with a wing missing. Beyond that stood—

*Phoenix help me.*

Something crushed my chest, and my heart struggled to beat beneath the squeezing vise. My stomach rolled, bile searing up my throat. I did this?

The walls bent outward into a jagged sphere larger than the Hall of Records, and fragments of shattered ice were scattered around the rim. In the heart, the road curved upward like a dish, black streaks exploding from the center as if charred by fire. Broken bits of Deathbiter lay among the icy rubble, touched with white frost. And on the edge lay a glacial horse, shaggy fur unmoving in the wind rushing through the Pass, neck twisted strangely, eyes glazed with white.

My knees buckled as I pushed a trembling hand over my mouth. Bile curled over my tongue. Ali was right. What I had done was unforgivable. How in the name of the Phoenix did Broderick look at me? How had he survived this?

My stomach convulsed, and foamy yellow liquid hit the icy road. What was happening to me? When had I become such a monster? I hadn't thought it would feel like this, so dark, so deep, so petrifying. This power consumed and grew; it knew no bounds.

Why didn't I listen to Broderick? If this was what I could do without meaning to, what would I do if I intended it?

I had to get away from this place. I shouldn't have come here on my own, but it was too late to turn back now. The Deathbiters would be upon me by the time I reached the entrance.

My legs shook as I stood. Midpoint. I'd go to Midpoint and wait for Broderick there.

Grabbing the horse's reins, I kept my eyes on the path ahead. I would not look. The deformed section of the Pass was like a scar, forever reminding the world of my mistake.

Climbing into the saddle, I urged the horse away.

Frozen cascades jutted down the walls, rippling with shadow and light as the sun reached its highest point. I was almost there.

Something foul touched the air, the stench of rot and acid wafting through the Pass. I stiffened, scanning the crevices above. By the burning feathers of the Phoenix, there it was, standing like an open wound against the gray-white cliffs. Black streaks ran down the ice like oil stains on castle walls after a siege.

Their lair.

*Ikane? Are you there? Can you hear me?* The words hung in my mind, unable to move through the walls of ice.

I swung from the horse's back, boots landing hard on the road, my eyes fixed on the blackness towering above.

What was I thinking? After seeing what I'd done in Glacier Pass, why did Thrall tempt me now?

Because he was within reach.

And I'd promised.

## CHAPTER 7

# BLACK SPARKS

My knife pressed against my leg, wedged tightly in my boot, and my sword hung against my hip, solid and heavy. The snow bison coat was buttoned securely up to my neck. This was the best I could do.

Taking the glacial pony by the halter, I positioned her beside the cliff, calculating the distance to the lair's entrance. I climbed onto her back, standing in the saddle, and the sharp sting of Deathbiter stench hit my nose like a punch as I came eye level to the black gaping tunnel. I blinked against tears.

Was I making the right choice? Was it wise to go after Ikane now, with my magic so new and confused? But what would happen to Ikane if I waited? Was it already too late?

I shook my head. I couldn't think that way. I wouldn't believe it.

Holding my breath, I set my arms on the ledge, hoisting myself up, Deathbiter filth clinging to the beautiful pale coat. I braced against the wall, struggling to breathe without coughing. Pulling the collar of my shirt over my nose did little, but Ikane had been stuck here for nearly a week. I could endure it a moment.

Pushing off the wall, I ducked under the low ceiling and stepped into the darkness. The walls shifted from pale icy formations to solid rock slick with moisture, and Mina's firedust gift ignited the jagged formations in an orange-red glow. Tears burned down my cheeks, lungs tightening with every breath. Muggy heat pushed into my fur-lined coat.

*Kea, don't. Go back while you still can.*

I stopped. "Ikane?" The rancid air cut my throat. It was his voice—I was sure of it. I'd know his beautiful Leviathan accent anywhere.

His voice was as clear as if he was standing right beside me. He was here. I felt him, the gentle brush of his mind against mine, frantic and pained, hanging on by a thread.

I squinted into the black void ahead. *I'm here, Ikane. I promised.*

*Go back,* he said. *Leave.* Even in his mind, his voice took on an animal-like edge.

*I'm not going to leave you.* My feet picked up the pace.

Something black slammed into my shoulder, the impact driving me against the ragged wall. Leathery wings whipped my face as the bat clung to my coat with poison-infested talons. Its jaw opened; its fangs bared. I groped at its flailing wings, the slick leather slipping through my gloved fingers. My heart stopped as it bit the collar of my coat. No sting.

Catching its wing, I jerked the creature from my neck, a rending noise echoing through the tunnel as its claws pulled through the thick snow bison leather. Every muscle in my core fired as I whipped the creature against the stone wall, a solid crack echoing through the tunnel. It screamed and thrashed, arching its back, twisting its head to bite. I flogged it against the wall again and again, each time the body growing limper until it became dead weight in my hand.

Dropping it, I staggered back, coughing as I gulped putrid air. My legs shook.

How had Ikane survived this long?

"Ikane." My voice trembled. "Ikane, where are you?" My mind opened, reaching for his silver-blue energy. *Please, don't send me away. I've given up too much to come here.*

Sorrow filled his blue energy, the pieces of his mind rippling like broken banners in the wind. *I'm not . . . I'm not what you remember.*

*Neither am I,* I said.

*Kea.* His mind took on a strangled edge, darkness pushing against him, the blue fading. *I . . . I love you.*

I was losing him. *Ikane, no.* My boots hit the uneven ground as fast as I dared, following the tunnel's curve. A massive cavern opened.

My stomach lurched into my throat as the ground dropped, and my boots slipped down a slope of loose dirt and slick rock. Arms flying wide, I groped at a giant black pillar punching to the cavern ceiling, my fingers catching stone. Sharp edges dug into my gloves, and my body jerked to a halt, cheek smashing against the hot surface. I hugged the pillar, gasping the thick, foul air.

*How convenient for me.* Rion's voices slithered through my skull, every hair on my body standing on end. *You've come to sacrifice yourself after all.*

I braced against the slope, my boots slipping on the grimy stone. Pebbles tumbled down the incline, rolling into a sea of black Deathbiter filth. *I'm here for Ikane.*

Her voices laughed. *He's beyond help. He's forgotten you already. He is an empty vessel, ripe for molding. He will serve me.*

*Haven't you taken enough from me already?*

*I have nothing until I have Roanfire,* she said.

Something dropped from the ceiling.

My heart stood still, muscles turning to stone. The cavern rippled like a thick lake of tar, thousands upon thousands of Deathbiters clinging to stone. Three more dropped from their perch, arching toward me.

I ducked against the hot pillar, the air from their bodies blasting against the back of my head. Something jerked my elbow, the frantic beating of wings slapping against my shoulder. Pressure from the Deathbiter's jaw clamped down on the thick leather.

A black spark struck my chest like flint against steel, hot and smoldering. It was powerful, like Ikane's strikes rippling up my arms. No. Like a catapult. Like thunder.

Thrall caught a memory, bringing it to the front of my mind: the day the Deathbiters had left me with pain, scars, and a voice forever altered. The flames burned hot, quick, and violent, consuming the memory, exploding from my core.

Deathbiters disintegrated into wisps of ash and dust, twisting in a strange, foul-smelling wind.

The power sputtered out. It had burned too hot and fast.

Hundreds of Deathbiters dropped from the ceiling, arcing toward me.

Phoenix curse and burn these demons. I would not abandon Ikane. Not to them. Not to Rion. Not to the decrepit old skeleton helping her.

I shut my eyes, searching for the source of the power. It fed on sorrow, pain, and anger. I had more than enough—

Fire exploded through my shoulder, trailing down the back of my triceps like hot oil. Spinning, I slammed the flailing black creature into the pillar, and a ripple of crunching bones vibrated up my arm.

Another beast raced for my face. I ducked, losing hold of the pillar. Loose rocks slid down the slope with me. Leathery wings slapped my face, following my descent, sharp talons catching and jerking the thick leather of my coat.

Images flooded my mind: my sweaty palm clutching Ikane's waist, hoofbeats thundering beneath me, a black cloud of Deathbiters gaining on us. Of my flesh burning as the demon creatures pulled me from the horse, tearing into me like ants devouring a crumb of bread.

It would never happen again.

The black spark took hold of the memory, feeding on the pain and fear, growing with my own anger.

My body came to a stop, boots sliding on mounds of bat droppings scattered on the ledge. Arms covering my head, I curled into a ball.

Thrall needed more—more pain, more heartache. Black sparks leapt away, searching for more.

It devoured the image of Deathbiters swarming Ikane, carrying him away. It snatched the tightness in my chest as Ikane told me to leave. I'd risked everything to find him. I had defied Broderick, abandoned my quest for Queen Lonacheska, and still he pushed me away.

I couldn't contain it anymore. It surged through my chest, wanting to be released like a scream. My body opened, Thrall smashing into the Deathbiters like a hail of arrows, ripping through flesh, crushing bone, shattering stone. Horrid screeches filled the cavern, fragments of leather and bone dropping to the sea of toxic waste.

My breath came hard, choking on the thick stench inside my lungs. The ceiling rippled with Deathbiters as hundreds dropped from their perch, darting across the cavern like midnight arrows.

"Where is he?" My voice tore through the cavern, rising above their deafening screeches. "Give him back!"

Stray black embers floated through my mind like sparks from an unattended fire, catching any memory it touched. Wait. That one was a pleasant memory. Yes, it was tinged with heartache, but it was a memory of love and kindness, of Broderick reaching beyond himself, urging me to become something more. Thrall twisted it, wringing it out like a waterlogged garment for every drop of pain.

Broderick didn't want me to find Ikane. He didn't want to help me find the White Wardent. He manipulated me, first into archery and then into using Etheria.

A second spark flared across another memory. The Glacial Empress's easy smile morphed into a devious grin. She hid

Skarand's letter from me. She knew where it was. She knew where to find the White Wardent. She didn't want to help me. She wanted to see me fail.

Thrall screamed from my core. Some Deathbiters burst into dust, others rent in two, bodies plummeting around me.

I fell onto my hands, fingers sinking into shadowy mounds of filth and rubble, arms trembling. When would it stop? When would it be enough?

More Deathbiters dropped from the cave. They were as endless as the stars.

Phoenix help me. What was I thinking? Thrall couldn't destroy them all, not without tearing my mind apart—

Ali was a selfish windsprite, blaming me for magic I couldn't control. She had no right to judge me for using it. She'd killed Erin's children to save herself.

Ropert was—

No. Wait.

I shook my head, scrunching my eyes against the falling ash and Deathbiter fragments. A black flame licked across a bittersweet memory of when Ropert had come to the training arena to comfort me in his own soldierly way.

"No," I breathed. "Stop. Don't take—"

Ropert's smile twisted. It was wrong. He wanted nothing more than to see me enslaved to the Tolean Prince.

Hot tears burned down my cheeks. This was what I wanted, wasn't it? The Deathbiters were disintegrating, turning to ruins. But my mind . . . my mind was falling apart, cut through by daggers, pierced with arrows, bleeding from every pore.

Why hadn't I listened to Broderick? He'd warned me this would happen.

Oh, Phoenix help me. I'd rather the Deathbiters destroy me than have my mind torn apart this way.

"Stay your magic." The voice was unfamiliar and deep, and it resonated through my ears like a command.

I searched for the source through frantically beating wings, bubbling heat, and tear-warped vision.

"I can't!" I cried. Thrall pushed through another memory, twisting it. "Help me."

Magic burst again. Bats puffed into clouds of smoke.

An ember fell across a memory of Eamon.

"Breathe."

The deep voice boomed through the cavern, vibrating against my chest like a beacon, turning my attention to my lungs. I couldn't. It was like a boulder sat on my chest. I blinked through the frenzy of agitated bats at the dark figure standing on the ledge above, a black cloak shrouding his features. Broderick?

"Breathe," he said, moving around a jagged black rock. "Just breathe. I'm coming."

I closed my eyes, pulling myself back to archery lessons. Inhale. Just inhale. Putrid air seared down my throat.

Embers sputtered, starved of fuel, winking out one by one.

"Breathe." The man's black boots skidded down the slope, rocks and pebbles breaking free. He was too tall to be Broderick.

I took another breath, focusing only on the spasms in my chest, the sting of sour air in my nose, the taste of ash on my tongue, the way my ribs pressed against my coat.

Another ember flickered out.

The blurry figure skipped off the slope and onto the landing.

Could it be?

"Ikane?" I asked.

No, not Ikane. He was young—not much older than myself—and tall and lanky, like a willow tree. His leather trousers and boots creaked as he sank to his knees, placing a reassuring hand on my shoulder. "Breathe," he said, his rich voice soft and soothing against my chest, easing the boulder away.

I blinked the tears from my eyes, breathing deep, the last ember flickering out.

"Good." He squeezed. "Good."

"My memories..." My voice was raspy as if I had been screaming. I crushed my fists to my head. "They are wrong. All wrong. They've been—"

"—changed. I know," he said. "It's alright. They will repair over time."

I scrunched my eyes shut, shaking my head, wanting these strange, altered memories out of my brain. "It's not right."

Something dark flickered awake.

He gripped both of my shoulders, thumbs pinching. "Stay with me. Breathe. Just breathe."

Foul air filled my lungs, driving Thrall back. I was exhausted, my arms and legs feeling as though they were weighed down by armor or tar. Sweat clung to my back and beads ran down my neck and chest.

"That's it." The man leaned back on his heels, resting his pale hands on his knees. His skin seemed to glow against the deep color of his trousers and cloak, creamy and smooth.

It couldn't be.

My eyes shot up to his face, hoping against hope that he'd finally come to help. His black cowl hid his eyes, revealing only his sculpted jawline and perfect lips. "Yotherna?"

"Beg pardon?"

He looked so much like the pale, willowy man in my visions. "You're not Yotherna?"

"No." He stood, holding out a perfect hand. "My name is Alder Grayhorn."

Numb and trembling, I took it. He was cold.

Ash dusted his black hood and shoulders like gray snow. The Deathbiters. Why weren't they attacking? I looked up to find the creatures clinging to rock, darting from one section of the cave to another. Didn't they see us? Didn't they see the destruction scattered on the cavern floor? Didn't they see the ash swirling through the cave? Instead, they climbed over each other, grooming and pawing like ordinary bats.

"It's alright. They won't bother us," Alder said.

I didn't dare raise my voice above a whisper. "How can you be so sure?"

"Because I am shielding us from them." He turned back to the slope. "But I can't hold the barrier forever. Thrall does have limits."

What did he just say? "You're . . . you're using Thrall?" I asked. "Right now?"

"I am." He took a first step onto loose rock at the base of the slope, his long legs agile and strong. "I'll explain once we're out of here. Come."

I followed clumsily, rocks breaking free under my weight. Every sound of flapping wings sent me ducking.

"What are you doing here?" Alder climbed onto the narrow ledge, drawing his floor-length cloak up after him. He extended his ghostly pale hand out to me. "This isn't an easy place to find nor a place anyone should visit."

"I am looking for someone," I said, "a man named Ikane. Have you seen him?"

He pulled me over the edge with one strong tug, drawing our clasped hands clear to his chest. I thought he was tall before. Standing so close, I realized just how tall he was. My head barely reached his shoulders.

He smiled down at me. "I haven't seen anyone here but you."

I couldn't see his eyes, but something in the way his lips moved made my heart race.

"I admit, I was stunned to see anyone else in these tunnels," he continued.

Deathbiters screeched. I flinched, but he held me firm.

"Let's get out of here." He dropped my hand, keeping close to the narrow ledge.

I surveyed the cave once more, the pillars reaching from floor to ceiling, the bats scurrying across the rock. *Ikane, where are you?* How could I be so close and yet so far? I was a fool to give up now. But I'd be an even bigger fool if I tried to keep going.

Thrall had nearly destroyed me. Broderick was right—I wasn't ready.

"Are you coming?" Alder glanced over his shoulder.

I followed, watching his tall frame maneuver around bulging rock formations. He ducked under a low-hanging shelf, proceeding like someone who could roam these tunnels blindfolded.

"Hold on." I caught up to him. "Why are *you* here?"

"I study bats," he said. "Did you know they hibernate in the winter months? Especially here near the Glacial Empire. I've been to this cave many times. Imagine my surprise when I heard of bat sightings in the area. Large ones. When they said the bats were coming from Glacier Pass, I needed to investigate. It's astounding how much they've changed in such a short time." He stepped over the lifeless body of the Deathbiter I had smashed earlier like it was nothing but a rock in his path. "You see, bats are not normally poisonous."

That was obvious.

"And even more peculiar is that they not only have poison in their mouths but in the claws on their feet and the thumb on their wings. It's like the poison courses through their entire body. It's odd, really. Most venomous creatures have a special sac or gland holding the poison." He glanced back at me. "We should probably tend to your injuries as soon as possible."

I barely felt my wounds, as the adrenaline still numbed the pain. "How do you do it?"

"Do what? Study bats?"

"Use Thrall like this."

"Like what?"

"With . . . with control."

He chuckled. "It isn't easy to master."

Master? Broderick said the exact opposite. "It can't be mastered. It *becomes* the master. That's why it's called Thrall."

He looked over his shoulder. "Is that what you've been told?"

My brows furrowed. Broderick, Ali, and the empress agreed on that. I couldn't trust them. They were manipulative and greedy, looking out for their own—

I shook my head. Something about that thought was off.

"Thrall can be broken just like a wild horse," Alder said. "I can show you how. You have the gift."

Light grew in the blackened tunnel as we neared the cave entrance. The soft whistle of the wind rushing through the Pass echoed faintly. Fresh air. Light.

Black rock shifted to filthy snow as we drew nearer. My pace quickened.

But Alder's pace slowed, his body blocking my path as he braced himself against the wall. "You know what else is odd about these bats?" he asked, his question disjointed as he breathed around the words. "They simply attack to infect. They don't eat their prey. It goes against the natural behavior of the entire animal kingdom."

"Are you alright?" I asked.

"Like I said, I can't shield us much longer."

I squeezed into the space beside him. "Lean on me."

"What do they call you?" he asked as I pulled his arm around my shoulders.

"My friends call me Kea."

"I appreciate your help, Kea."

My muscles trembled, almost buckling under his weight.

We staggered to the opening, cool air and warm sunlight touching our black-smudged cheeks. I inhaled the fresh wind, clean and sweet, letting it brush the cobwebs from my mind.

Alder's body grew heavier, and he sunk to the edge. He clung to my arm, pulling me down with him. His head fell against the wall, his teeth clenching as if something pained him.

"Alder?"

"It's . . . it's nothing. I'm alright. Just help me out. Once we're in the sunlight, I won't have to use so much energy."

"Kea!"

My body tensed.

Below, on the icy path, stood Broderick, tending to my horse and his own. He hurried to the entrance, his face a mix of worry and rage. Why was I so confused? I couldn't trust him. He was manipulative and a liar.

My head ached. Why was I thinking this way? He was a friend, wasn't he?

His eyes widened as Alder's legs slipped over the ledge.

"You found him?" Broderick asked.

"Get the horse," I said.

Broderick positioned one of the horses below the entrance, holding the animal steady as Alder lowered himself to its back with my help. His grip was crushing.

A flash of white shocked my eyes as Alder's boots hit the saddle.

The surrounding cliffs moved and warped. I braced against the tunnel entrance.

Alder's powerful grip released as he slid from the horse's back, his cloak dragging after him.

Broderick eyed him. "You're not Ikane."

Alder drew his shoulders back, stretching to his full height, his chest expanding as he inhaled. "That's twice I've been called that."

I was going to pass out. I swung my legs over the ledge, the movement sending the cliffs whirling again, so I fell forward, stomach lurching. I dropped onto the horse, clutching her mane as my body slid.

"Kea." Broderick's hands shot out, catching my waist. I couldn't stand; my muscles shook under my weight. Broderick's arms were the only thing keeping me upright.

"Careful," Alder said. "She's used a lot of magic."

"Magic?" Broderick's eyes flew wide as he gaped at me. "Kea. Please, tell me you didn't use Thrall."

"I . . ." The white flashes of light softened behind my eyes, but the cliffs curled and distorted. My head rolled against his shoulder, and everything caved in to darkness.

## CHAPTER 6

# TRUST

A soft red glow fell across my eyelids, and warmth radiated against the right side of my body. Thick furs cradled my limbs as my lungs expanded with deep breaths of cool air. When was the last time I'd opened my eyes without drowsiness or the sticky crust of sleep?

Smooth ice reflected the soft orange light of a fire overhead. A deep, dark crack ran through the ceiling. Midpoint. We'd made it to Midpoint, tucked away in the center of Glacier Pass.

I rolled onto my side. I hurt everywhere, especially my left arm behind my elbow. Pushing myself from the furs and blankets, I faced the brightly burning fire in the center of the cavern, the warmth penetrating my thin cotton shirt and trousers. A black kettle, steaming and bubbling, sat near the edge of the fire.

"You're awake," Broderick said, his voice echoing from the stable side of the cavern. He patted a horse gently then slipped from the pen, closing the gate. His eyes remained lowered, hidden beneath his mop of brown curls as if too enraged to look me in the eye. "Are you feeling alright?"

Why did he care? He tricked me, twisted my arm into practicing archery when he knew I despised it. He kept me from going after Ikane. If we'd left sooner, Ikane would . . . he wouldn't be . . . he . . .

I shook my head. Why didn't anything make sense?

Hugging my shoulders, a sting flared through my arm.

"My power isn't as strong as yours." Broderick crouched by the fire, lifting the kettle with a mitten-covered hand. "I managed to draw out the poison, but your body will have to do the healing."

The sound of water sloshing into mugs filled the strained silence between us.

I scanned the manmade cave. All but two stalls stood empty. The table and benches sat near the door, where Ikane had left them before . . .

Where was Alder? He *had* come to my aid, hadn't he? I didn't think I'd imagined it. "Where is Alder?" I asked.

"I think the better question is: *Who* is Alder?" Broderick came to my side, handing me a steaming mug before sitting on the blankets beside me like a familiar friend. My mind bristled, but my body remained strangely comfortable in his presence, like my heart somehow knew he was genuine.

"What does it matter?" My voice was strangely calculated and tight.

Broderick glanced up, the firelight flickering across his furrowed brows. He considered me for the space of five unnerving breaths, minty steam silently curling from the mugs in our hands. The scar stretching across his lips ignited something in me. Guilt? Why was there guilt when this was a man I didn't trust?

"Oh no," he breathed.

What was wrong with him?

"How deep did Thrall go?" he demanded. "How many memories have been altered?"

"What?"

Broderick rubbed his face, pushing his brown curls from his forehead. "It's me, isn't it? Your memories of me have been altered."

"I . . . I don't know." Setting down the mug, I struggled to my feet. "Where is Alder? I want to talk to him."

"Do you trust him?" Broderick asked.

"More than you."

He winced.

Why did my chest tighten at his expression?

Broderick sipped his tea. "Alder doesn't have a mount," he said.

What did that have to do with anything? This was just like archery. "Don't try to change the subject. Where is Alder?"

Broderick shrugged, lifting his mug to his lips again. "I suppose it's not impossible to travel through Glacier Pass without a horse. But without food and water? Without a bedroll? And with a threadbare cloak?"

Now that he mentioned it, Alder's cloak had been rather thin and worn. In fact, I'd noticed a tear on the right corner.

I shook my head. No. Broderick was trying to sway me, to turn me away from the only person looking out for my wellbeing, from the only person willing to teach me how to use this power. I wasn't going to lose focus.

"Where is he?" I asked.

"Outside." Broderick lowered his mug, staring at the flames. "He's studying a Deathbiter carcass. You'll want your coat."

I reached for the fur-lined coat lying beside the fire, my hand freezing. Black smudges covered the pale color, and tears and holes gaped from the armor-like leather. A thick stain of brown-red crust saturated the left sleeve. The smell wafting from it overpowered the mint from Broderick's tea.

The last thing I wanted was to put it back on.

Broderick stood, lifting my mug, holding it out to me. "It's warm," he offered. "And it'll help with the pain."

I cupped it in my hands, staring at the endless gray-green herbs swirling around the bottom like a constellation of stars.

He did this often. That part of my memory was sound. Broderick found comfort in warm herbal beverages and always offered me a mug. I took a sip, and soothing heat ran down my throat, spreading to my limbs in a rush of wind.

"I hope you don't mind," he said. "I used some dust from Ali."

He smiled, the scar on his lips whipping guilt against my conscience like a rawhide strap.

"Erin and Ali didn't come with you?" I asked.

"They plan to catch up later. I left in a rush to find you."

Why?

Why would he do that for me if he didn't care?

Alder leaned back with a satisfied groan rumbling from his chest, licking his perfect lips. "Thank you for sharing your provisions," he said. "I am a man of little means."

"Or any," Broderick muttered into his mug.

It was the first time anyone had spoken during the meal. Trust hung between us by fragile threads, ready to snap at any moment.

Alder still hadn't removed his hood, and Broderick kept a wary eye on him. I couldn't decide what to make of it. Broderick was the manipulative one, always changing the subject, always pushing his own agenda. Alder, on the other hand, had helped me calm Thrall. He'd saved me.

Alder rubbed his abdomen. "I would like to return your kindness."

Broderick lifted his mug. "By cleaning the dishes?"

Alder smiled, his teeth bright and linear. "By teaching you both how to use Thrall."

Tea sprayed from Broderick's lips. "What? Are you mad?"

Alder shrugged. "Some seem to think so."

Broderick shook his head, his brown curls flying wild. "No. We don't accept. Don't you see the damage it's already done?"

"All the more reason to learn." Alder leaned forward, lacing his long fingers together on the table. "I can teach you how to direct Thrall's hunger to memories of your choosing. I can teach you to create your own so Thrall will not damage ones you hold dear. I can teach you to channel it through your body."

"Is that how you manage to keep control?" I asked.

"It is. You see, with the right leverage, Thrall cannot overpower—"

"Stop." Broderick set his mug on the table.

Alder tipped his head at him, his smile melting. "I see," he said slowly. "You've lost the knowledge. And what we don't know, we fear. What we fear, we hate. It's not as black and white as you think. Tell me this, Master Broderick, why would wardents be endowed with this magic if they were not permitted to use it?"

Broderick's brows furrowed. "I can't believe you are asking that. Thrall is the balance to Etheria, but it does not mean we should use it. Its name is Thrall for a reason. It traps the mind, destroys what we know. It cannot be tamed. If you were any sort of wardent, you would know this."

"Oh, I am a wardent." Alder reached across the table, slid his pale fingers around Broderick's wooden mug, and drew it to him. His breath plumed in a slow, soft cloud in front of his hooded face.

I stiffened as pressure bore down on my ears.

Broderick's eyes widened as a faint hiss escaped his mug. Thick steam rose, blending with Alder's foggy breath. The pressure vanished as Alder removed his hand, gesturing to the freshly heated tea. "Thrall. Controlled and tamed."

I swallowed. How? His control was beyond comprehension.

Broderick's eyes narrowed. "Who are you?"

Alder leaned back, folding his arms. "A man of science and magic."

Broderick slammed his fists on the tabletop, and the table shuddered. "Stop deflecting!" He leapt to his feet. "Who are you? Why do you keep your face hidden under that cowl? What are you? A criminal? A wanted man?"

I'd never seen him lose his temper like this. "Broderick," I snapped.

"It's alright." Alder touched my hand, and a shiver raced up my arm.

His skin was arctic.

"He asks valid questions." Alder paused for a moment as if considering his next move, then he reached up, pulling the hood from his head. His hair hung across his face like black steel curtains, falling past his shoulders in silky strands.

Then he dragged his gaze up to meet mine.

My heart leapt into my throat. It couldn't be.

Alder held the same chiseled features of the White Wardent—the same slender jawline, the same high cheekbones, the same straight-edged nose.

But his eyes.

Faded pink scar tissue stretched over his left eye, deforming his brow and pulling his eyelid into a narrow slit, and the iris was glazed over and white. The other was stunning, its silver iris glinting like the polished blade of a knife. Even with his scarred face, he was beautiful.

"Are . . . are you sure you don't know Yotherna?" I asked.

He laughed, pulling his hood over his head, hiding his stunning features. "Of course, I don't know him. If he were alive, he'd be what? Six hundred and eighty-nine years old?" He paused, tilting his head at me. "Why do you ask? Have you seen someone like me?"

"Only in my . . ." I stopped. How crazy would I sound if I told him I'd spoken to someone like him in my dreams? "It's nothing. You just look like the image of the White Wardent on the stained glass window of the Meldron library." I stood, gathering the dishes. "I'll wash tonight."

Alder grabbed my wrist, his hand so cold it burned. "You need to rest. Broderick and I can manage."

As if on cue, the cavern walls spun. I sank back to the bench. Had using Thrall really taken that much of a toll on me? How did Alder do it? He didn't seem phased at all by the use of his power.

Broderick slid my plate and mug away, glancing suspiciously at the hooded man. "Help me prop the table over the entrance, will you? The last thing we need are the Deathbiters finding us here tonight."

"As long as I'm with you, you're safe," Alder assured.

I hadn't known Broderick's eyes could get any harder. "I'm not willing to risk that."

He didn't trust Alder.

I didn't trust Broderick.

And who knew what Alder was thinking under that black hood.

Broderick's fingers danced across the lute strings, firelight reflecting on the polished surface of his new instrument. I leaned back in my bedroll, the sweet, warm melody desperately trying to coax the nightmare of the day before from my mind.

It couldn't.

Even with Broderick's rich tenor voice adding to the song, my heart ached. Ikane told me to go. He was only trying to save me, but there had been something in his voice, something saying goodbye forever, like he was letting go.

"You're deep in thought," Alder whispered, leaning closer.

I dug at my fingernails, pulling crusts of dirt from beneath them. Thrall had overpowered me. But though I couldn't control it, I knew Alder could. "Will you go back into the lair with me?"

Broderick's hand slipped, an ugly tune ringing through the cavern.

Alder straightened. "Why do you want to go back?"

"For Ikane."

Alder glanced at Broderick.

"Ikane means everything to her," Broderick explained. "But the Deathbiters took him."

Alder's hood rippled as he looked back at me. "My darling girl, from what I've learned of the beasts, your friend is no more."

"You don't understand." I sat upright. "They didn't infect him, not the way they did me. They don't want him dead. There is an old man with him, an old, decrepit man who changed Ikane into something . . . something monstrous."

"How do you know this?" Alder asked.

"What does it matter how I know or not? Ikane needs our help, and you are the only one who can do it." I pushed to my knees, facing Alder. "Please."

Broderick set his lute aside. "Kea, if what you say is true, what can we do for him?"

"We have to try."

"You already did."

"But not with Alder."

Broderick's face darkened.

"I'm sorry, darling." Alder's head dropped. "I agree with Broderick. We can't go back, not now. There is too much we don't know. We could be walking into a trap."

"We can't just leave him." My voice rose. "I promised."

Broderick rested a hand on his lute's neck. "And I will help you keep that promise."

"When? You know what will happen once I set foot in Roanfire. I'll be arrested and carted back to Meldron." I tore a hand through my hair. "This opportunity will never come again."

"Not if I can help it," Alder said. "You have potential and power. All you need is guidance."

"Don't give her false hope," Broderick said.

"She doesn't need hope." Alder looked at me. "All she needs is a tutor."

"And you think you're the one to coach her?" Broderick folded his arms across his chest.

"I'm only saying she has more potential than I've seen in a long while." Alder turned to me. "I would be honored to be your tutor, but the choice is yours."

Broderick watched me, his eyes pleading with me not to accept, to remember what he had already taught me. And something in my mind began to mend, to understand Broderick's friendship and loyalty again. How could I have allowed Thrall to twist such fidelity into doubts and lies?

But if it could save Ikane . . .

I bit my lip. Why was this so hard?

"No need to decide right now." Alder curled onto the ground, pulling his threadbare cloak over his legs. "Either way, it is unwise to go after your friend right now. Think about it, darling. You have talent and strength. Don't let it go to waste."

Broderick reclaimed his lute, strumming a bittersweet melody, his eyes growing distant with frustration and worry. His lips parted, and his beautiful voice was touched with pain as he began to sing a well-known lullaby of Roanfire.

*You wander roads lost in tale and time*
*A path unknown to the stars*
*Silver flow'rs crown your steps with truth*
*Guiding your way toward the heart*

*Clouds reach up to the moonlight*
*A silver crown in the sky*
*Dreams cast shadows across your way*
*Hiding the pain within your eyes*

How much truth could a song hold? The words I'd heard time and time again suddenly spoke to my heart as if he had written the lyrics just for me.

My eyes began to burn.

Alder was right. I had to let Ikane go. But feathers, it hurt.

*Come away, to land I have conquered*
*Leave the day and the shadow behind*

*You have all the answers*
*Every breath a gift divine*
*A twist of hope and freedom*
*Will seal your heart to mine*

My heart crumbled into a thousand shards. I thought I would have Ikane by my side forever. I thought I could keep him safe. I should have listened to Eamon months ago, when Ikane first came to Daram. I should have stayed away.

# CHAPTER 7

# THE AXEMAN INN

Broderick led the way, and Alder followed, his thin black cloak hugging his tall, lean frame in the wind. With every step, the storm intensified, pressing against our backs as we descended the ever-sloping pass. Through the narrow gap looming above, the sky changed from pale blue to violet. The sun was setting, and the end of Glacier Pass was nowhere in sight.

Broderick needed to pick up the pace, or we would be caught in the dark—with the Deathbiters.

"You look worried." Alder slowed his pace, taking position beside me. He followed my gaze to the sky, unveiling his perfectly chiseled jaw and well-formed nose as he looked up. "If you're worried about the Deathbiters, don't be. I can shield us from them."

I rubbed the back of my neck. "Will you teach me?"

He glanced down. "I am honored. But you must learn the fundamentals before I can teach you something as intricate as repelling Deathbiters."

"When do we start?"

His smile was easy. "Eager, aren't we?"

"I'm tired of waiting for things to change. I need to take action, and this is the only way I know how."

"Very well," he said. "But first, tell me about your scars. They look like the marks of Deathbiters. Ones sustained not too long ago."

My chest tightened, and I glowered at the icy road.

"Ah, not a pleasant memory, I see."

"I was attacked by Deathbiters."

"Did you use Thrall?" he asked.

"I didn't even know I had Thrall until last week."

"Then how did you survive?"

My hands tightened around my horse's reins. Beneath the warm leather mittens, my palms were riddled with gray specks where firedust once glowed. I still didn't understand how it had worked. "Firedust," I said.

"Firedust?" His voice held a genuine question.

"I don't know how to explain it. All I know is that firedust spared my life."

He stared ahead. "Interesting."

"Since we're talking about scars, how did you get yours?" I asked.

"You're not one to beat around the bush, are you?"

I gave him a look. I'd told him about mine; it was only fair he returned the favor.

He sighed. "I was dabbling with a unique combination of elemental dusts. Something went wrong."

"That's it? You're not going to give me any more details?"

He chuckled. "It's as vague an answer as you gave me."

"Fair enough."

"Alder, Kea," Broderick called over his shoulder. "Prepare yourselves. The wind is going to get stronger in the next few minutes. And you might want to pick up the pace, or we'll be stuck out here after nightfall."

My feet moved faster, the wind pushing me forward.

"How long have you known Broderick?" Alder asked.

I gazed at Broderick's back, his lean frame moving with strength and purpose. He had so much confidence. Confidence I wish I had.

"Awhile," I said.

"But he didn't tell you about Thrall?"

My teeth ground against my cheek. "Not until recently."

"For someone as powerful as you, he should have. Letting your power manifest like this was irresponsible. His stubbornness against using Thrall is blinding him."

The wind intensified, blasting Broderick's hood against the back of his head. Alder's cloak whipped around his long legs.

They were so different and yet so similar.

But who knew the truth? Was Thrall really as dangerous as Broderick said? The twisted memories in my mind were evidence of that. And yet Alder used it with control and conviction.

Could they both be right?

I pushed my back against the wind, my hood's fur lining whipping around my face, blurring my vision. I hadn't anticipated the pressure change to be this brutal. My boots slipped on the slick road toward a field of snow beyond the sheer walls of the Pass, the glacial pony becoming my support. She kept her head lowered, and her steps were deliberate like she'd passed this way a hundred times before.

As we broke from the narrow gorge, the wind dispersed. My ears rang, and I fought to find my balance in the absence of pressure at my back.

A red blur flashed in the corner of my vision. Hands pinched my arms, drawing them behind my back. The cut from the Deathbiter flared with pain. A solid kick to the back of my knee sent me to the ground and cold hardness bit against my wrists, the rattling of chains indicating shackles.

There was no need for this. "I'm not going to resist," I said.

The soldiers ripped the hood from my head.

"Orders are orders," the female soldier said. The way her dark hair was pulled back into a tight braid made her face hard. "You can settle the matter with Sir Ropert."

I flinched. Ropert, the liar who wanted to betray me to the Tolean Prince. That sly, manipulative, mewling, boar-pig of a—

Wait. What was wrong with me? He was my friend. His bright blue eyes laughed with me. His easy smile eased away tension. The way he wrapped his arm around my shoulders was nothing but supportive.

How long would it take until my mind sorted through the mess Thrall had made?

I caught a quick glimpse of Broderick and Alder on their knees as two soldiers steered me across the open space toward the village of Gerom Post. Gray clouds billowed from smokestacks, curling to the darker gray clouds overhead as the sunlight faded in the evening.

"Hurry now," the taller soldier said. "There isn't much daylight left."

The hard-faced female released my arm as we stepped between the first two buildings, sprinting around thigh-deep snowdrifts in the street and disappearing around a corner. I was left with the taller soldier holding my arm like a vise.

"The shackles aren't necessary," I said. "I am turning myself in."

He said nothing as he jerked me around a corner. Rows of timber-framed buildings lined the snow-covered street, and warm light glowed between gaps in boarded windows. Deep gouges from Deathbiter talons splintered the wood, and unnerving marks sank into the creamy plaster of houses. The Deathbiters had overrun Gerom Post.

A door flew wide, light spilling onto the snow as a broad-shouldered man bolted into the middle of the street wearing only his cotton shirt, trousers, and boots.

His blue eyes fell on me, and my feet froze to the snow. Ropert. His strawberry-blond hair had grown, reaching his shoulders in supple waves. Had I been gone that long?

The female soldier emerged behind him. "She didn't give us any trouble," she said.

Ropert swallowed hard, his breath pluming in the darkening sky. Where was his smile? His expression was filled with too many emotions to count—betrayal, relief, anger, wonder, frustration—each one strained under a forced composure.

"There were two others with her," the hard-faced female said. "We are bringing them in for questioning."

"Good." Ropert's voice was tight. He stepped forward, taking my elbow. "I'll take her from here. Hurry and bring the others indoors before the Deathbiters emerge."

"Yes, sir." The soldiers saluted and turned back toward Glacier Pass.

Ropert's grip grew tighter and tighter as he watched the soldiers disappear around the corner, a vein standing out on his neck.

I worried this would happen. I knew he would be angry with me. But Ikane convinced me Ropert would understand. How foolish could I be? I'd betrayed Ropert too many times to deserve his forgiveness.

He jerked my arm. "What were you thinking?" The words spat through his clenched jaw. "Why?"

I kept my gaze on my boots, the way they sank into the snow, the way the leather darkened with moisture. Queen Lonacheska had ordered me to go alone. She ordered me not to share anything with him. "I didn't want to," I whispered.

"Dagger." Ropert pulled me against his hard chest, his solid arms encircling me as his cheek rested on the crown of my head. He was warm and smelled of iron, leather, a hint of herbs from the inn's tavern, and undying friendship. He was trembling.

My body locked. What was happening? Wasn't he angry with me?

He held me at arm's length, his nose wrinkling. "Feathers, Dagger, what is that disgusting smell? It's worse than . . ." His eyes widened as they trailed the length of the three scars running from my brow to my cheek. He took in the filthy tattered coat with new horror. "Deathbiters?"

"They nearly killed me," I said.

He shook his head, blinking in disbelief. Then he produced a key from his pocket, stuck it in the iron cuffs, and the lock on my wrists clicked. "Let's get you a hot bath and some new clothes. Then we can talk."

I rubbed the cold out of my wrists.

"What the—" Ropert grabbed my wrist, turning my hand over. His fingers pressed against mine, feeling the resistance. "When . . . how did . . . when did you regain mobility? The last time I saw you, your arm was as limp as a deboned fish."

"It's a long story."

He pulled me into a sidelong embrace, steering me toward the inn. The wooden sign hanging on iron hinges above the door was layered with a thin dusting of snow. The Axeman Inn. The same inn Erin had brought me to after I'd been attacked by the Deathbiters.

This was where I had lain dying of fever and hallucinations, listening to Deathbiters scratch and screech through the night. This was where Broderick had healed me of more than Deathbiter venom.

Ropert opened the door, warm air and rich smells wafting from the building. "Is Ikane with you?"

The question stung, burrowing deep, cutting down to the core of Thrall. The magic flickered, trying to catch hold of the pain.

Alder's voice rushed through my mind.

*Breathe.*

My lungs opened, my mind turning to the expansion of my ribcage, and Thrall sputtered out like a candle in the wind.

"Dagger?"

"Ikane . . . is gone." My voice broke at a whisper.

"What?"

Scrunching my eyes shut, tears slid down my cheeks like fire. "Don't make me repeat it."

He pulled me to him. "We should let Eamon know."

I buried my face in his shoulder, letting grief run its course. It was better to let the pain flow through tears than be consumed by Thrall. It was better to just let go.

The wooden stairs creaked as I followed Ropert to the upper rooms of the inn. It was strange hearing my boots thump against wood instead of ice. The sound was hollow like the void left in my heart.

The doors lining the hallway stood open. Why were the windows open, too? Wasn't it cold enough? Small fires burned in each hearth. Parents and children, travelers and soldiers lounged in beds, played card games, cleaned weapons, or mended clothes.

A young soldier stood guard at the last door on the right, the only door along the hallway that was closed.

"Sir Ropert." He saluted.

My brows rose.

"At ease," Ropert said. "Is he awake?"

"I think so, sir."

The young soldier produced a key, the lock clicked, and the door swung open. I followed Ropert inside, eyeing the soldier as I passed. I'd never heard anyone address Ropert so respectfully.

"Kea?" Eamon leapt from his chair, nearly knocking it over. He dropped the feathered quill onto the small desk, heedless of the ink blotting the paper. His brown eyes filled with moisture as he took five giant steps toward me, wrapping me in arms built to wield a sword. I hugged him back. He was warm and solid like a father should be.

"My little Brendagger." His voice was filled with relief. "Thank the Phoenix you are safe. Did you find it? Did you get the letter?"

I didn't want to talk about the letter. Eamon rarely showed his affection for me, and I needed his embrace now more than ever. He tried to pull away, but I hugged him tighter.

He held me close, stroking my hair. "What's wrong, Kea?"

"It's Ikane," Ropert said.

Eamon's hand froze on my head. "What about Ikane?"

I swallowed once. "He's gone."

Silence.

Eamon pried me away, holding me at arm's length. "Tell me it isn't true." His brown eyes shone wild.

"Deathbiters," I said. "They took him."

"They took him, or he's dead? Which one is it?"

"I . . . it's more complicated than that."

Eamon shook me, pinching me tighter than I'm sure he intended. "Tell me what happened. Where is he?"

"We were attacked in Glacier Pass." I tried to keep my voice even as if I were reporting an incident to a superior officer. But inside, my chest ached. "Deathbiters overwhelmed us. They carried Ikane away. He's been transformed."

"Transformed?" Ropert asked.

I freed myself from Eamon's grip. "It doesn't matter anymore. I tried. I tried to save him and failed. He's gone." What was I saying? Was I really giving up on him? I'd heard him in the Deathbiters' lair. But he was weak, his mind struggling to remember what was truth and what wasn't. Just like Thrall did to me.

"He's alive then?" Ropert asked.

I hugged my shoulders. "I don't know."

Eamon slumped onto the edge of his bed, running a hand over his salt-and-pepper beard. "Feathers, Kea. Don't scare me like that."

"You don't understand. He's not Ikane anymore."

"Sir Ropert," Eamon said. "With your permission, I would like to stay in Gerom Post and find Ikane."

Ropert scratched the red stubble on his chin. "I don't think—"

"Please." Eamon stood. "He's like a son to me."

I glanced between the two of them. "What is going on here? Why are you asking Ropert for permission?"

The younger man shifted uneasily.

Eamon shrugged. "I made the choice to help you escape to the Glacial Empire, and I do not regret it," he said. "I knew my reputation wouldn't spare me King Sander's wrath. I have been stripped of all rank within Roanfire's militia. Ropert, on the other hand, is now Captain Ropert Saded, head of a small squadron of men sent to bring us back to Meldron."

"Captain?" I scanned Ropert, taking in his open hair and untucked shirt.

Ropert folded his arms across his chest. "Don't judge. You caught me just as I was about to take a nap. I didn't have time to put on my uniform."

"Napping on the job?" I asked, fighting a smirk.

Ropert rolled his eyes, turning to Eamon. "Yes, Eamon. I will let you stay. I'll assign a few men to help you."

"I'd appreciate it."

Ropert moved to the door. "Come on, Dagger. Let's get you some food and a bath. I think the innkeeper's daughter might have something you could wear."

## CHAPTER 8

# PHEASANTS AND CIDER

Red uniforms crowded the tavern. The smell of mead, body odor, roasting meat, overcooked stew, and burnt wood melded together, bringing me back to my days as a soldier in Daram.

My previous stay at the Axeman Inn was a blur, as I had been too sick to notice anything. Now, everything seemed new and bright, with rustic lanterns hanging from the wooden beams above. A massive stone fireplace sat in the center of scattered tables, a support for the upper floor that spread warmth throughout the entire building. But it was too warm—my freshly washed skin was already tacky with perspiration.

Ropert waved to me from a table already occupied by Alder, Eamon, and Broderick. The eyes of all but Eamon strayed to my feminine curves as I claimed a seat between Ropert and my surrogate father. I almost wished I was wearing the shredded coat again.

A serving girl with soft brown curls appeared. "Good evening, Sir Ropert. Eamon. I see you have new company tonight." She smiled at me. "That dress suits you."

"Thank you for lending it to me." I hated it. It cinched my waist too snugly, and the neckline sat uncomfortably low. The girl was nearly a head shorter than I was, causing the hem to hit me mid-calf. The sooner my trousers and shirt could be washed and mended, the better.

Ropert gestured around the table. "Melody, this is Keatep Brendagger, Alder Grayhorn, and Broderick Ironshade."

Broderick glanced up as he was introduced, and his mouth opened to say something, but nothing came out. His eyes froze on her.

Was he blushing? I'd never seen him so flustered. My lips ached to grin when her cheeks went a shade brighter.

Ropert cleared his throat.

Melody straightened. "I have a roast pheasant with your name on it, Sir Ropert."

He grinned. "I could kiss you."

Broderick's eyes filled with alarm.

"And for you?" She turned to me.

"I'll have what Sir Ropert is having. And some bread, cheese, and butter to share. And some spiced cider if you have it."

Ropert whistled. "Your appetite hasn't changed."

"She didn't eat much in the Glacial Empire," Broderick said. "Save for honey puffs."

I hated to admit it, but honey puffs weren't my favorite. They might have been the most decadent food I'd ever tasted, but the events leading up to the treat soured the experience.

"You're from the Glacial Empire?" Melody turned to Broderick. "I've always wanted to visit, but I've never had the opportunity to venture through Glacier Pass. Now, it seems I never will." She sighed. "Oh, forgive me. I didn't mean to burden you with my dreams. What can I get you?"

"The phea . . ." Broderick cleared his throat. "The pheasant sounds good. And you don't bore me."

Her cheeks flushed.

Eamon grunted. "I'll have the pheasant, too."

"Of course, Master Eamon. And for you?" she asked Alder.

"A sampling of your spiced cider would be splendid." His voice was smooth and rich. "And the pheasant sounds lovely. Could you perhaps add an apple?"

Melody tucked a strand of hair behind her ear. "Apples are not in season. We have a few, but they are better suited for pies and cider."

"I'll take one anyway," he said.

"Very well." She bit her lip, looking over her shoulder at Broderick as she turned away.

Ropert nudged Broderick in the ribs. "Love at first sight, eh, Thundercrack?"

I'd almost forgotten the nickname Ropert had given the assassin.

"Lay off." Broderick's face went bright red.

"She's a sweet thing," Ropert said. "You could do worse."

Eamon leaned in, his hand tapping the table. "Hush."

Just as the word left his mouth, my skin crawled. A stillness swept through the tavern. Spoons paused in midair. Patrons glanced nervously at the walls. Melody stopped by the counter, her large brown eyes following the length of the chimney to the roof.

A high-pitched shriek penetrated the walls, boring into my ears. Every scar on my body prickled, my hair standing on end.

Something hit the shuttered window. My muscles reacted, reaching for my sword and driving me from my seat. My chair rocked back, hitting the floor with a solid bang.

Three more screeches responded to the noise, the shutters rattling.

Ropert grabbed my hand, preventing me from pulling my sword from its sheath. His touch was warm and strong. "It's alright. They can't get in."

I swallowed hard, the scar on my neck tightening, clamping down on my throat.

Eamon stood my chair upright, coaxing me into it. "We're safe here."

Quiet conversations arose, ignoring the scrapes and screeches outside. The soft clattering of spoons scraping against bowls resumed. Melody hurried to the fireplace, tossing extra logs onto the already roaring flames. Sparks flew and wood snapped, but she stoked it hotter, glancing up the chimney as she worked.

"The Deathbiters try to come down the flue," Ropert said. "The fire prevents that."

"Are they here every night?" Alder asked.

"Since before I arrived." Ropert took a sip of his drink. "It's a feat making sure there is enough firewood to last the night. This area is so barren of trees."

I scanned the woodpile sitting beside the hearth. That was it? Their supply would barely last a few hours. My chest tightened.

Ropert squeezed my hand. "There's more by the back door."

Phoenix bless him. He always knew what to say.

Melody returned with our drinks, her hands shaking as she distributed them.

"So, Alder. What is your story?" Ropert asked. "Kea tells me you're from Lodwen?"

"From a village nearby, yes."

"And what is your trade?"

"Well." Alder tapped a pale finger on the side of his mug. "I've dabbled in many things. Perhaps that is the reason I am such a pauper." He chuckled. "As you can see, I'm not a man of means. Bat study isn't exactly a lucrative profession."

"If you can call it a profession," Broderick mumbled into his mug.

"You study bats?" Ropert leaned forward, releasing my hand. "Have you learned anything about the Deathbiters?"

Alder shrugged. "They dislike sunlight, their bite is lethal, and they attack for the mere sport of it. I can't determine an agenda." Alder lifted his mug, paused to inhale the aroma, and sipped.

"Alder can repel the bats," I said. "I've seen him do it."

"Really?" Ropert asked. "That would be most helpful as we travel to Shear tomorrow, especially if we get caught in a storm. Apparently, they are very common around here."

Alder's perfect lips pulled into an easy smile, flashing linear white teeth. "And my offer still stands to teach Kea."

Broderick slammed his mug on the table. "Leave her alone."

"Hush." Melody appeared with a tray laden with plates. "Do you want the Deathbiters clawing at your bedroom window all night? Keep it down."

She distributed the dishes around the table, placing Alder's requested apple beside his plate. The red skin was soft and wrinkled like that of an old man. Her hand lingered on the fruit, her gaze repentant. "It's the best one I could find."

He covered her hand with his. "Thank you."

Her eyes flew wide at his touch, and the blush drained from her cheeks. She jerked her hand away. "Ex . . . excuse me." She hurried away without looking at Broderick.

"What was that?" Broderick leaned over the table, teeth bared at Alder.

The other man lifted the shriveled apple to his nose, inhaling deeply, savoring the smell as he had with his cider. "A woman's touch can change the bitterness of any season." He bit down, a rough tearing noise bursting from the old skin.

Broderick banged his palms on the table, chair rocking back as he stood. "That's enough."

"Broderick, ease off. He didn't mean anything by it," I said.

"You should talk," Broderick said. "You don't see the way he makes moves on you? Touches your hand, brushes against your shoulder? Feathers, Kea. How can you be so oblivious? He's trying to get to you."

Is that what Alder did? I thought back on my encounters with him. He just wanted to help, didn't he?

"I think I've caused enough trouble for one night." Alder pushed his chair back, stood, and picked up his plate. "I'll take my meal to my room." He slipped between the chairs, weaving through tables as he headed out of the room.

Broderick tore through his curls, leaving them wild. "I'm sorry, but something isn't right about that man. I can't put my finger on it."

"You're just upset that he wants to teach me what you refuse to." I stood. "Can you repel the Deathbiters?"

Broderick's mouth clamped shut.

"No, you can't. But Alder can. We need him. I need him."

"Kea." Broderick sighed.

"I'm going to bed."

"You've hardly touched your food," Ropert said.

I grabbed a wedge of bread and tried to tuck it in my pocket. Feathers, this dress had no pockets. "Goodnight Ropert, Eamon. I'll see you in the morning."

The nightshirt clung to my skin as heat radiated from the stone chimney rising through the center of the inn. Melody wasn't taking any chances—she kept the fire roaring hot. Any rustling through the flue quickly turned to a death cry as the invading Deathbiter caught fire.

Beyond the bulky shutters, Deathbiter screeches pierced the night. Claws scraped against the walls. The chaos was occasionally interrupted by a roof tile shattering on the street.

It was a war zone, and I was helpless to do anything about it. My sword lay lonely and abandoned atop the single table in my room. When was the last time I'd used it? Not for sparring, but actually wielding it in defense?

I growled, rolling onto my side, and the bed creaked. Why couldn't life be simple again? I wanted to be back in Daram with Mayama and Eamon. I wanted to feel the sun on my shoulders as I sparred in the training arena, see the dust swirling around my boots. I wanted to smell the sea, taste the sticky air. I wanted to drill, laugh, and fight. I wanted to walk along the beach with the moonlight glowing on the white foam at night.

But most of all, I wanted Ikane back.

My stomach clenched.

How could I do it without magic? It had become my choice of protection, seemingly the only defense against the Deathbiters.

I closed my eyes, tears sneaking onto my pillow.

*Curse you, Rion. Curse you. This is what you've turned Roanfire into, a poisoned battlefield of black death and fear.*

If she could hear me, she didn't reply.

"Don't let them leave, you hear me? This is as far as they get." The deep voice was ragged, matching the bony figure it belonged to.

"Yes, Master."

*Was that Ikane? He'd changed. His voice was different, rumbling with a growl, submissive, unquestioning.*

"She is vulnerable. Now is the time to strike."

"Yes, Master."

*Master? Oh, Ikane, what has he done to you?*

"Are you ready?" Master asked.

"I am always ready," Ikane said.

A cry tore me from sleep, sharp and violent.

I gasped, getting a lungful of heavy, suffocating air. The room was too hot. Perspiration dripped down my back and chest, and my hair clung to my neck. If only I could open the window or toss some snow against my face. Or better yet, jump into one of the snowdrifts outside. But I couldn't.

Fanning my shirt, I opened the door to the hallway. A wave of heat wafted against my face mixed with the unpleasant smells of the tavern below.

No good. We were all trapped here until daybreak.

Shutting the door, I leaned against it, sliding to the ground. I closed my eyes, resting my head against the door, Ikane's voice burning through my brain.

He couldn't be working for that monster. It wasn't in his nature. He was kind and pure, always searching for the goodness in others, even his brothers.

But this was different. *He* was different. Something was very wrong.

I hugged my knees.

*Ikane? If you can hear me, please remember that I love you. I always will. No matter what.*

A Deathbiter screeched in return.

## CHAPTER 9

## MUSCLE AND FUR

*B**ang, bang, bang.*
　　　The door rattled against the back of my head. I jerked awake. My neck ached.

"Dagger?" Ropert's muffled voice sounded through the door. "Are you up? It's time to go."

Now? When it was finally quiet enough to sleep?

I rubbed my face, dragging my hands through my damp hair. Pale blue light radiated through the gaps in the shutters.

"I'll be down in a minute." I pushed myself from the floor, staggering to the window. I threw the shutters wide, and cold air flowed into the room, caressing my damp skin like a summer rain. I glanced at the bed, the pillow askew from my restless sleep last night, the blankets shoved against the footboard in a heap.

Five minutes. That's all I needed.

With a good steady pace, we could reach Shear before nightfall.

The bed creaked as my body sagged onto the mattress. My head sank into the pillow as the cool breath of fresh air wafted into my room like a whisper . . .

I pried myself from the bed, blinking at golden sunlight stretching across the floorboards.

Flaming feathers!

I tossed the blanket aside, jumped into my freshly washed clothing, and strapped my sword to my waist. Why didn't Ropert wake me?

Ripping the door open, I hurried down the stairs, taking them two at a time.

Ropert and Broderick sat at the far end, bowls of half-eaten porridge steaming in the cool air coming from the open windows and door.

"Ah, there she is." Ropert grinned at me.

"I am so sorry." I sank to the chair beside him. "I didn't mean to fall asleep again."

Melody approached with a ready smile. "Good morning, Lady Brendagger. I hope you slept well. How would you like a warm bowl of porridge this morning?"

"Do I have time to eat?" I looked at Ropert. "I can be ready to go in two minutes."

Ropert laughed. "Eat. We're not leaving today."

"We're not?" Broderick blinked at Ropert over his half-empty bowl. He pushed it away. "In that case, I'm going back to bed. Those Deathbiters kept me up all night."

"That is the new norm around here," Melody said. "Most of us sleep during the day now."

"When do *you* rest?" Broderick asked. "Haven't you been up all night stoking the fire?"

"I catch a few hours between shifts." She turned to me. "I'll fetch you that porridge."

Broderick stood. "And I'm going back to bed." He excused himself, sluggishly climbing the stairs to the rooms.

"Have you seen Alder?" Ropert whispered to me.

"I just woke up. I thought he'd be here with you."

Ropert shook his head. "You left in a hurry last night. I wanted to talk to you about him. Did you notice the way Melody flinched yesterday?"

"When he touched her hand?"

He nodded. "Is what Thundercrack said true? Has Alder been pressing unwanted attention on you?"

"Did Broderick put you up to this?"

"What? No. He didn't say—"

The front door slammed against the wall. Two shadows stood in the threshold, blocking the light filtering into the room. The figure on the left hung limp, something dark and sticky running down her arm.

Ropert sprang from his chair as the newly arrived soldiers shuffled to a table. The woman's face contorted in pain, her skin pale, her teeth clenched tight as she sank into a chair. The tight braid holding her dark hair back had come undone.

I stood. She was the same soldier who'd marched me back to Gerom Post yesterday.

Melody pushed through the crowd, assessing the woman's injury. "She's going to need sutures. Get her upstairs. I'll send for Malcom."

Chairs and boots scraped against the floor as soldiers and patrons worked together to carry the woman to a room.

Ropert cornered the soldier who'd carried her in. "What happened?"

The man licked his lips, breathing hard, his eyes locked on some distant horror.

"Soldier," Ropert snapped.

The man's glazed eyes drifted to Ropert.

"What happened?" he repeated. "That is not a Deathbiter injury."

"It . . . it was . . . oh, Phoenix help us." The soldier's hands began to shake uncontrollably. "First, the Deathbiters, and now this. We won't survive."

"Tell me what happened," Ropert growled, gathering a fistful of the man's uniform.

"It was a monster. A terrible monster. Larger than a man. It was too fast. We didn't see it until it was upon us."

Ropert's brows crowded his forehead. "Where is it now?"

"When I left, it was at the entrance to Gerom Post," he said, his eyes flying across the room. "We tried to hold it off. Phoenix help us. We need to flee. We can't stay here."

Ropert shoved the man against the wall. "You are a soldier of Roanfire," he hissed. "Keep it together. The last thing we need is for everyone to panic."

The soldier swallowed hard. "You don't understand. It has the head of a wolf—"

I heard nothing more.

Ikane.

My boots thundered from the tavern, digging into the snow. Sunlight flickered between the stone and timber-framed buildings as my legs pumped through the main street of Gerom Post. A gentle curve kept the North Gate from full view, but cries of battle carried through the street. Cold burned my lungs as I turned the corner.

A dozen soldiers stood in a line between the two main buildings at the entrance. Something towered behind them, moving with the speed of a snake. Soldiers screamed. Three of them fell back, swords glinting.

By the burning feathers of the Phoenix, what had Rion done to him?

The dreams didn't do this bare-chested creature justice. He was built for destruction, a creature of solid muscle, power, and rage. He slipped beneath glinting swords, striking out with claws as long as Broderick's throwing knives.

A soldier screamed as his hand hooked a soldier's boot, ripping it from under him. Ikane leapt back, jerking the soldier with him. The man twisted, grabbing at loose snow.

"Ikane!" I shoved between the line of soldiers.

"Stop." A soldier with a bleeding forehead jerked me back. "Stay in formation."

My heart beat against my chest in massive bursts as Ikane's jaw opened, exposing jagged, gleaming white teeth, his powerful form towering over the terrified soldier.

*Ikane, don't.*

He bit down. The soldier's cry gurgled in his throat as teeth punctured flesh. The wolf twisted, a spray of red coating the snow.

I fell back. This wasn't my Ikane.

He would never do something like this.

The massive creature stood on his hind legs covered in tattered remains of trousers, tail whipping as he threw his head back and howled. The sound sank deep into my chest, fracturing the fragile hope in my heart. How could I have let this happen? I had been so close. I'd felt him in the Deathbiters' lair, within reach, and I'd turned away, saving my own skin.

A black spark ignited, catching the fragmented pieces in my chest. No breath could tame it now, not even if I wanted it to.

His massive form blurred behind fiery tears. I was too late.

*I'm sorry, Ikane. I'm so sorry.*

His howl drew to an end, and his wolflike head swiveled to me, his black eyes hollow pools of nothing. He sank to the snow, shoulders shifting in a great ripple of muscle and fur as he stalked forward.

"Ikane. This isn't . . ." My voice broke, pain flaring through the scar tissue in my throat. "This isn't you."

His ears twisted forward at the sound of my voice.

I stepped from the line of soldiers, one careful movement at a time, my hands raised. Ikane followed, fur bristling.

"Please, Ikane," I said.

"Watch out!" A soldier screamed as the monster sprang forward, clawed hand ready to tear through flesh and bone. *My* flesh and bone.

My sword flew from my hip, feet sliding aside. It would have been easy to slice his arm. All I needed to do was let my sword fall. But I turned my blade, the flat of it slamming against his outstretched wrist.

The impact surged up my arms like I'd struck stone.

The wolf coiled, tumbling into the snow. Before the explosion of white dust settled, he rolled back to his feet, rich brown fur bristling up his back. His lips retracted, exposing white teeth and pink gums, and his black eyes centered on the polished steel in my hand.

"Ikane." I said his name with as much emotion as I dared, willing him to come back. "Please, remember who you are."

His teeth snapped together, cracking like a hammer on steel. The darkness in his eyes deepened.

He was gone.

Teeth and claws bared, he lunged.

I dropped my sword. Tears flooded my vision. That old man had destroyed Ikane. He'd turned my Leviathan prince into a heartless monster. My Ikane. My loving friend whose heart was bigger than the Rethreal Sea was destroyed.

The black fire already dancing through my pain flared, consuming every shred of my broken heart, bursting with hot energy. I couldn't call him Ikane anymore. He was gone. He was—

Power rushed from my chest, flattening the snow like a boulder crashing from a catapult. All sound caved in as the twisted creature reversed direction, muscle and fur spinning through the air. Snow burst around him as he tumbled into the open landscape outside the village.

A hollow emptiness gaped wide in my chest. The black flames curled up the sides of my mind, reaching for more.

The creature pushed from the ground, shaking off snow, his black eyes staring at me. He snorted. "This isn't over."

A hailstorm of arrows burrowed into my heart. His accent. He still held his Leviathan accent even in this hideous form.

He turned and bolted, kicking up snow behind him as he raced on all fours toward the gaping fissure of Glacier Pass.

"Dagger."

Soldiers stepped aside as I turned, finding Ropert standing in the road, jaw slack, bright blue eyes wide with a look I'd seen before. The same look on Erin's face when . . .

I glanced down and saw my feet standing in a crater of flattened snow.

What had I done?

Where was Alder when I needed him?

Ropert's eyes flicked to the shadowy figure growing smaller as it raced across the open field then back to me, his expression unchanging. When had I become as dangerous as that deformed creature?

"What is happening to you?" Ropert asked.

I fell back, suddenly wishing I was running alongside Ikane. "Where is Alder?"

Ropert's eyes hardened. "Was that Ikane? Is he the monster who attacked my soldiers?"

Black energy surged through my brain, reaching for memories to twist, bend, wring for every scrap of pain no matter how insignificant.

"Alder. Where is Alder?"

"Answer me, Dagger. Was that Ikane?"

My fingers dug into my scalp. If I didn't stop it, Thrall was going to emerge again. And this time, it would be against my friends.

"Ikane is dead!" Tears burned down my cheeks. "He's gone."

Ropert swallowed hard, his eyes softening.

Didn't he feel the energy growing inside me? It was like a black cloud, consuming, growing, reaching. I ducked my head, legs pumping as fast as they could carry me.

"Dagger, wait." Ropert's footfalls thumped loudly on the stairs behind me.

My fists clenched, nails digging into my palms. I couldn't look at him. I saw the way he gaped at me, like I was just as deformed as Ikane.

The sparks in my mind continued to smolder, searching for sustenance. The ache in my chest deepened, threatening to fold in on itself, pulsing with a relentless desire to consume. If I didn't tame it, I knew it would turn to memories I cherished.

I needed Alder. I glanced down the hall—his room was the fifth door on the right, the only door still closed.

The rest of the inn stood open, doors and windows allowing cool air to flow. What good did it do? We'd be cowering inside by nightfall, suffocating in heat. If Alder taught me how to use this power, we could do something about the Deathbiters. We could do something about Ikane.

The door beside Alder's opened wider.

"Kea?" Broderick said.

The last thing I needed was his interference. I pushed by.

He grabbed my arm, pulling me to a stop. "Kea."

I jerked away. "Leave me alone."

"Dagger," Ropert said. "We're only trying to help."

I whirled. "Right now, Alder is the only one who can help me."

Ropert stiffened, brows raised.

What was Thrall doing to me? They were only trying to help ... or were they trying to hold me back? A spark latched on to the thought, growing.

"Get her inside." Broderick gripped my elbow, jerking me into his room. Ropert followed, pushing the door shut.

I didn't have time to make them understand. The magic grew hot and fierce, ready to burst. I had to get out of here or I would hurt them—or worse.

I reached for my sword but gripped air. A stone dropped to my stomach. It still lay in the snow, surrounded by blood and fallen soldiers.

Broderick raised his hands. "Breathe, Kea. Breathe."

I gulped the air, my lungs choking on hatred. How dare he. Did he think he could use the same words as Alder to tame Thrall? He knew nothing about it; he'd said so himself. He refused to learn or teach—unlike Alder, who offered freely.

Pressure built behind my eyes, bearing down on my ears, muffling his words. I scrunched my eyes shut. I was going to burst; the energy was ready. My fists clenched at my temples, trying to keep it inside. I was going to hurt them. Didn't they see that? I was dangerous.

"Get away." The words pushed through clenched teeth.

"Remember the bow, Kea." Broderick's voice was calm and reassuring. "Focus, steady, release."

Thrall snapped. Energy crashed into him. His body lifted from the ground, collided into Ropert, spun, and slammed against the door with an audible thud. Ropert crashed into the small table beside the bed, a variety of glass bottles and herbs spilling to the floor like a hundred delicate bells.

Phoenix help me. Thrall roared, feasting, growing, building into an unstoppable force. It latched onto my fear like the hook of an axe, pulling my feet from under me. My legs buckled. I braced myself on my hands and knees, eyes on Broderick's crumpled body.

He was no enemy; he was my friend. He helped me escape Meldron when I was framed for murder. He vouched for my innocence. He defended me against assassins. He healed Ikane. He healed me. He was a shadow, always there, unnoticed but vital. The darkness to the light.

These thoughts snatched the anger from Thrall like severing a limb. The flames grew weaker but flickered with rage, sparking. Embers scattered, flying through my thoughts.

*Focus.*

I found my breath.

*Steady.*

I inhaled.

*Release.*

Exhaling, I released the anger, the vengeance, the desire to destroy. All I wanted was to feel alive again, to see Broderick smile that crooked smile, to know he was there, watching my back.

"Broderick?" Ropert pushed the overturned table away, wincing as he scrambled to Broderick's side. He rolled the assassin onto his back. Blood trickled from a wound beneath Broderick's mop of brown curls.

The embers latched onto the guilt rising in my chest, sputtering like fire on damp wood.

"Is he . . . ?" I couldn't say the word.

"He's breathing." Ropert's voice was tight and calculated. He looked at me, his brows furrowed. "What is happening to you?"

No one was safe with me, not even my friends. I couldn't stay. I couldn't go back to Meldron with Ropert, not until I learned control. What if Thrall did this again? I'd hurt Broderick twice with this magic and nearly destroyed myself.

I needed Alder. I didn't care if Broderick disapproved, as long as he was safe.

My legs trembled as I staggered to my feet. "I . . . I need to go."

Ropert leapt to his feet, blocking my path. "You're not well, Kea."

Didn't he see what I just did? I could do the same again without warning. It was a miracle he didn't burst into ash the way the Deathbiters did. I had to get out.

Broderick groaned, pushing himself from the floor, holding his head.

Ropert crouched, resting a hand on Broderick's shoulder. "Easy, now."

Broderick looked at me, blood trickling down the side of his face, curving as it hit his cheekbone. "Kea?"

I hugged myself, new tears burning my eyes. How could he bear to look at me? "I didn't mean . . . I'm sorry. I'm sorry . . ."

Magic was not supposed to be a part of my life. It wasn't supposed to be a part of my world at all. I was a soldier, a warrior, a fighter. My strength was in my hands, not my mind.

Ropert helped Broderick to his feet.

The assassin swayed, holding Ropert's arm for balance. "It's alright, Kea. You did it."

How hard did he hit his head? The fool was smiling at me. A light shone in his eyes, a joy, a triumph I didn't understand. He needed a surgeon.

"Don't you see? Once Thrall has a hold on you, it is nearly impossible to break free. But you did it. You drove Thrall back on your own. You released it not by force, but by forgiveness," he said.

"Thrall?" Ropert asked.

I swallowed, feeling lightheaded. "I want to be rid of it, Broderick. Tell me how to get rid of it."

He released Ropert's arm. "You can't. You would end up destroying Etheria as well. You can't have one without the other."

"I don't want either! I don't want magic at all." My knees were ready to fail.

"Then you won't be able to help Ikane," he said. "And the Phoenix Witch will win."

My legs folded, hands bracing against the floor. "Ikane is already gone."

Ropert knelt beside me, but his hand stopped before touching my shoulder. I'd scared him. I saw it in his eyes, even though he forced a smile to hide it. "It's going to be alright." He braved a touch, squeezing my shoulder gently. Then he glanced at Broderick. "Isn't there anything you can do?"

He picked up a vial from the floor. Brownish liquid sloshed inside the cylindrical tube as he held it up. His eyes churned, and I could see the idea burning behind them. "Perhaps . . . perhaps I can make a tonic . . ."

Hope burned in me. "Please. Do whatever you can."

Broderick erected the table. "Some herbs numb senses. Thrall's energy comes from strong emotions of anger and fear. Perhaps a bit of baneberry . . . or aconite? Maybe belladonna." He was speaking to himself now, his voice growing quieter. "Nightshade? No. That one's too strong." He set the bottles on the table and leaned on the edge, his eyes distant. "Perhaps a bit of Tolean Rose . . . it's milder. But where am I going to get that?"

"First things first, Thundercrack." Ropert pinched the back of Broderick's neck. "You need to see a healer."

Broderick touched his forehead, a little smile curling on his lips when he saw the blood. "I suppose I do."

Ropert winked. "Any excuse to see Melody, right?"

Broderick slugged Ropert's shoulder.

How could they banter so easily after what I'd done?

"As for you." Broderick turned to me. "I want you to practice archery. It'll keep you focused until I can make the tonic."

I didn't care about how much I hated archery. I would do whatever he asked if it meant keeping Thrall at bay.

## CHAPTER 10

# BRODERICK'S TONIC

My arms trembled, new blisters burning my fingers as I drew a chair from the table. My back and shoulders would feel the ache tomorrow; the familiar throb of hard physical labor, of training my body, of getting stronger. There was something tranquil about archery, but I wasn't about to admit that to Broderick.

A strange silence spread across the busy tavern. Whispers rose around tables, eyes turned to me over the rims of mugs.

"Is it true?"

I whirled to Melody standing beside my table, her large brown eyes watching me with a strange curiosity. She leaned closer, keeping her voice hushed. "They say you did it again. That you single-handedly frightened off the beast twenty soldiers couldn't fell. It was like the battle for Meldron all over again. Leviathans, Deathbiters, unnatural creatures. You can destroy them all."

Is that what all the gossip was about? My power? My stomach rolled. "It's a bit more complicated than that. How is the soldier upstairs? Is she going to be alright?"

"She may never regain full use of her arm, but she'll live."

My heart ached for her. I knew exactly how she felt.

Melody slipped into the chair beside me. "They say you found the lair of the Deathbiters." She leaned in so close I could smell the rosewater on her skin. "That you tried to destroy them." Her brown eyes scanned my face. "That's why you have so many scars."

"Who told you that?"

"Is it true?" she asked again.

I didn't care if it was true or not. No one knew about the Deathbiters' lair save Broderick and Alder. Broderick wouldn't boast about something like that—he was ashamed of Thrall. Alder, on the other hand, just might.

But why? Why would he share that about me? That was private, not something I was proud of.

"They are already calling you Brendagger, the Biters' Bane," Melody said. "Is it true? Can you destroy them?"

I stared at her. "What do you think?"

She stood, a smile spreading across her face. "I think you are a hero, and a hero deserves a good meal. I'll have my father make a fresh batch of honey herb fritters just for you." She winked.

The last thing I wanted was anything related to honey.

"What, no fritters for me?" Ropert pulled out the chair beside me. Eamon joined us as well.

"Good evening, Sir Ropert. Master Eamon. Roast pheasants for both of you?"

They nodded.

She wiped her hands on her apron. "I'll be back in a moment."

I turned to the men. "Did you know about the rumors?"

Eamon inched his chair under the table. "I just heard them myself. The tales have gone quite elaborate."

"I don't know what to say." I leaned back in my chair.

"Don't say anything."

"But they're not true."

"Not everyone who wants to know the truth can handle it," Eamon said. "The rumors will fade over time. Trust me."

I rubbed my forehead. He was right. Eamon was a legend among the soldiers. I'd heard the stories. They'd spread like wildfire across Roanfire. For the first time, I wondered if all of them were true.

"Suppertime already?" Alder's deep voice rumbled through my chest. He took a seat across the table, his hood still hiding his face. "I must say, Lady Brendagger, you are looking worse for wear. Didn't you sleep well last night?"

My throat tightened. "Where have you been all day?"

"I've been studying the aftermath of the Deathbiters. They entered three homes last night through splintered cellar doors. It appears that they've been working at it over the last week, not just one night. That alone is telling."

"What do you mean?" Ropert asked.

"It means they are determined little creatures. If there's a way in, they'll find it, even if they have to work at it night after night."

Eamon's eyebrows furrowed. "We should probably suggest the mayor have everyone reinforce their cellar doors. And check the shutters."

"Agreed," Ropert said.

Melody returned, spreading our dishes across the table like a banquet for a king. Not only did she bring soup and pheasant, but bread, butter, cheese, pickled beets, and a large tankard of cider. "The fritters will be out in a moment. Can I get you anything else?"

Alder's tongue ran across his lips. "What is the occasion?"

"Haven't you heard?" Melody asked. "Lady Brendagger is a hero here in Gerom Post."

"Is that right?"

Why was he playing dumb? He knew exactly what was going on. He was the one who'd spread the rumors.

"As long as it brings us meals like this, let the rumors fly." Ropert tore into his pheasant.

Melody turned away with a satisfied smile but paused. "Broderick, what are you doing out of bed? I told you I would bring you your supper."

Broderick approached our table, a layer of white bandaging peeking from beneath his mop of brown curls. He gave her a crooked smile. "I'll be back in bed before you know it," he said.

Then his eyes fell on Alder, and his smile crumbled away. "What are you doing here?" I could tell there was something deeper behind his question.

Alder spread his hands across the table. "Sharing a meal with my friends."

Broderick's lips tightened, jaw muscles throbbing so deep I feared he would dislocate it.

"Did you do it?" Ropert asked.

Broderick placed a cylindrical vial on the table before me. Red glittering flecks like smoldering embers swirled inside the amber liquid. "Two drops in the morning and two in the evening," he said. "Any more, and you could end up poisoning yourself."

Alder leaned forward as I lifted the bottle from the table, holding it up to the candlelight.

"Is that firedust?" Alder asked.

"It is a very good numbing agent," Broderick said.

"Are you trying to numb her emotions?"

"Traveling back to Meldron will be trying enough with the Deathbiters on our tail." Broderick took a slice of bread from the table. "It will be one less thing to worry about."

"'One less thing'?" Alder's voice shot an octave higher. "Her emotions and magic could be the one thing that gets us safely to Meldron."

Broderick lifted an eyebrow. "Us?"

Alder threw his hands up. "I'm coming with you. Who will protect you from the Deathbiters if you won't let Kea use her magic?"

I slammed my palm on the table, dishes rattling with the impact, the conversation quieting. "*Let* me?" I whirled to Alder. "Broderick isn't keeping me from using the magic. He's protecting me from it. You have no right to accuse him of this. You didn't see what happened today. Thrall is too much for me."

Alder leaned back. "I see. You are jealous. Both of you are, even after I've offered to share my knowledge with you, to train you, to make you as skilled with this magic as I am. I saved you from the Deathbiters. Do you remember? I did it using Thrall. And still you push me away."

"I'm not like you!"

He stood. "That much is clear." He turned for the door.

I hadn't meant to be so harsh. "Alder, wait."

He glanced over his shoulder. "I can't believe you'd let him numb your emotions like that. I'm worried for you. Broderick is wrong about Thrall. You have the potential to be legendary."

"I just want to be a soldier."

"Therein lies the fault." He slipped out of the tavern.

I sank to the chair and let my head fall into my hand, the warm vial of swirling red dust still clutched in the other.

Was Alder right? Or was Broderick? Did I have the strength to wield Thrall the way Alder did? Or was it better to leave it untouched?

The way I'd tamed it in Broderick's room proved I could, but the bandage around Broderick's head and the stiffness in Ropert's ribcage convinced me of its danger and unpredictability. How many friends would I injure trying to control it?

*Leathery wings blotted out the stars, those beautiful glittering stars that shone down on him night after night, calling to him, reaching deep into a part of him he didn't understand. He knew each constellation by heart, something drilled into him from a time when . . .*

*The memory ran black, blotted out, sinking into the blackest part of the depths. He couldn't escape his blurry past. His mind was an open sea, stretching endlessly in every direction.*

*But the stars. Something about them felt like purpose and direction, a map to his past and future. Each one glittered with a shape, brightness, and size of its own. Twelve stars to the east formed the great Leviathan, the sea serpent in the sky, the three stars near the tail pointing his way home.*

*Wherever that was.*

*Salt water stung his skin, and his legs tensed as if balancing on the deck of a ship. The sea rolled and crashed, powerful and unyielding. He belonged there, and yet he'd never seen it.*

*Pressure bore down on his skull, blurring the memory. He shook his head, trying to ease the sensation.*

"I am disappointed in you, Marrok." Master's voice thrummed through his mind, deep and seething. "You did not kill her. You didn't even fight."

He saw the young woman in his mind's eye, her face scarred, worried, and somehow pained as she gazed at him. "She startled me, Master. It will not happen again. I will hunt her down and tear—"

"Never mind the girl," Master said. "Leave her to me. I have a different target for you. A man clothed in black, shrouded in daggers and poison tonics. He is dangerous."

"I know of whom you speak."

"Wait for my signal. It won't be long."

Marrok? Was that Ikane's new name?

I sat up. As predicted, my back ached from hours of archery practice and swordplay. My head felt heavy, like it was filled with rocks ready to drag me into the deepest part of the sea. Opening the window didn't ease the thick sensation, neither did washing my face.

Water dripped from my chin as I eyed Broderick's vial sitting on the table. Red specks glittered inside. I had taken a dose before bed.

The taste had been unpleasant, but warmth had bloomed from my chest and spread to the tips of my fingers and toes, numbing every ache and throb in my body. The relief was incredible. And when it finally circulated to my mind, the night became as still as moonlight on a pond. The heat from the tavern's roaring fireplace dissolved, and the Deathbiters' cries dulled to a gentle hum. I hadn't slept so soundly in weeks. Even the dream didn't bother me as much as I thought it should.

I opened the cork, dipped my finger inside, and allowed two more drops to fall onto my tongue. It leached all moisture from my tongue, coating it in bitter dryness. I smacked my lips, waiting for the heat to spread to my limbs.

It wouldn't be long now, and everything would be fine.

Three knocks sounded on the door. "Kea? Are you up?"

Eamon.

"I'm coming." I buckled my sword around my waist, hefted my bag, and opened the door. "I'm not late, am I?"

"No. I thought I would escort you to the stables. It'll be some time before we see each other again." He handed me a large woolen bundle. "Ropert asked me to give this to you."

I traded the bundle for my saddlebag. The brown fabric unraveled into a thick woolen cloak lined with a layer of tan fur. Anything was better than my old Deathbiter-filth-stained coat. But this? This was the most beautiful, practical cloak I'd ever seen.

Swinging it over my shoulders, I fastened the three wooden toggles across my chest. It felt like an embrace, a warm reminder of how much I meant to Ropert. I ran my hands down the front, discovering narrow openings on either side.

My eyes shot to Eamon's. "It has pockets!"

He chuckled. "He thought you'd like it."

"I love it."

"Come on." Eamon tossed my bag over his shoulder. "Let's not keep them waiting."

We descended the stairs into the main tavern. The early morning was quiet, with tables cleared and chairs still turned upside down. I vaguely remembered seeing Melody and Broderick quietly conversing by the hearth when I'd gone to bed.

Now, a boy lay curled up by the dying embers of the fire, ash and soot smudging his face, marking him as the one who'd kept the Deathbiters from coming down the chimney. Our hero for the night.

"I found tracks this morning," Eamon said as we moved between the tables. "Hybrid-wolf tracks, in the alley."

A wave of heat soared through my body followed by sudden weightless tingling. Not now. Eamon was telling me something important, something I needed to know.

The darkened room became more vibrant, and every grain of wood stood out in variegated hues of beautiful brown ripples. I shook my head. The herbs were beginning to work.

Feathery lightness pushed through my body, dispelling the spark of concern I'd felt seconds ago.

"Kea? Are you alright?"

I glanced at Eamon, his brown eyes, his salt-and-pepper hair, his strong jaw and broad shoulders. This man was incredible. Through the years, I had seen him flourish, be beaten down, and rise again. He held a reputation as the champion warrior of our time, but his heart was soft. He was everything I wanted to be.

"Why are you smiling like that?" he asked.

"Like what?"

Eamon raised an eyebrow. "It's Broderick's tonic, isn't it?"

I opened the door, swinging it wide to the cool morning. Clay shingles lay shattered in the gray-blue snow. The Deathbiters must have knocked them loose in the night.

I glanced up between the timber-framed buildings, the clear sky faintly glowing with the rising sun. My breath plumed, mixing with the smoke curling from the chimneys. "It's such a beautiful day."

"Flaming feathers. What has Broderick done to you?" Eamon grabbed my arm, steering me down the street. "I think we need to talk to Ropert."

We turned a corner, coming to the main square. It was quite impressive for Gerom Post's size, a relaxing stop for merchants traveling between Roanfire and the Glacial Empire. The community stable bustled with red uniforms, causing the lone merchant wagon to stand out.

"There you are." Ropert stepped around a chestnut warhorse. "How do you like it?"

"It?" I asked.

"The cloak. How do you like the cloak?"

"Oh." I stroked the inner fur lining with the back of my knuckles. "It has pockets."

He laughed, handing me the reins to the horse. "This is Stalwart. He'll be your horse for the trek."

Eamon released my arm. "Ropert, may I have a word?" Eamon hefted my saddlebag over Stalwart's back. "You might want to keep a close eye on Kea. The tonic Broderick gave her seems to . . ."

My attention was drawn to the large-bellied merchant who was addressing a soldier. He tugged a graphite stick from behind his right ear and opened a thick leather-bound book. "How much? Surely you'll consider escorting us for a price."

The soldier crossed his arms. "Bribery won't work. No wagons. We ride hard."

"But it is our livelihood." The merchant gestured to the wagon. "Our livelihood," he repeated, waving his arm as if the soldier couldn't see it.

"It won't do you any good if you're dead."

"He's right, Papa." A young girl appeared from behind the wagon, two golden braids hanging from the fur-lined cap on her head. She led two horses, saddled and packed. "The goods won't spoil. Let us go home; that's all that matters. We can come back when the Deathbiter situation is under control."

"That is the wisest thing I've heard all day," the soldier said.

"Very well. Very well." The merchant tucked the graphite stick behind his ear and closed his book.

"Kea." Ropert's voice was harsh, snapping me from the scene. "Did you hear me?"

"Sorry. What?"

"I said I think Broderick should ride with you."

"Broderick is good company. Do you think he'll play his lute?" I stroked Stalwart's thick neck, admiring the way the morning light made his red coat shimmer. It reminded me of the silken fabrics Queen Lonacheska wore.

Ropert arched an eyebrow.

"The soldiers are ready," Eamon said.

Ropert clasped hands with Eamon. "Will you help Kea get situated? I'll send Broderick over."

"Ride on the wings of the Phoenix," Eamon said. "I pray you make it before dark."

"And I hope you find Ikane."

Something sparked inside me hearing his name, but a fluttering sensation pushed the thought from my mind. I didn't need to worry. Everything was going to be alright.

Ropert took position at the head of the platoon, climbing onto the back of an impressive warhorse. He gave a quick order to a nearby soldier.

Eamon secured my bag, checking the straps. "I don't think you should take any more of Broderick's tonic."

"Why?"

Eamon paused. "Look at you. You're grinning like a fool. The Kea I know wouldn't leave so readily. You've lost all fight."

I pondered that for a moment. "I haven't lost all fight. I've simply chosen a different battle."

Eamon shook his head, tugging another strap tight. "You've taken the easy way out."

Eamon grabbed Stalwart's bridle as all ten horses moved at once, following Ropert through the main street of Gerom Post. A black horse bearing a familiar figure veered toward us.

"What's going on?" Broderick asked, pushing his hood from his head, his brown curls flying wild. His bandage was missing, revealing a mottle of purple on his brow. "I was told Kea needs assistance."

He was such a dashing young man, dangerous and sly. I was fortunate to call him a friend. His blue eyes watched me, deep and churning like a stormy sky over the Rethreal Sea.

One of his brows rose. "Oh."

"Your tonic has made her . . . flippant," Eamon said.

I didn't understand the fuss. It was a beautiful day with clear skies, mild wind, and a temperature growing more bearable as the sun rose. We would easily make it to Shear by nightfall.

Broderick bit his lip. "I think I need to adjust a few herbs."

"It's a little late for that now," Eamon said. "Come on, Kea. Climb on. You've got to catch up."

I placed my boot in the stirrup and swung my body skyward, my head soaring with lightness as I sat high above the ground. If I spread my arms, I would fly.

"I'll watch her," Broderick said.

"I'd expect nothing less. Off now." Eamon slapped Stalwart's rump. The horse moved forward, hoofs jarring against the snowy cobblestones. I waved to Eamon over my shoulder. I was going to miss him.

Windows stood wide in the buildings flanking the road, and sunlight flashed on the glass panes. Gerom Post was a simple collection of buildings with no wall or watchtower of any kind. There had never been a need; it was a simple trading post. No gate marked our exit. We simply stepped out of the shadow of two buildings into an endless landscape of snow and blue sky.

Ahead, the small party of horses cast miniature shadows on the ground. Ropert didn't need to push so hard. The day was young and the sky beautiful, the wind at our backs a gentle nudge.

I kicked Stalwart's sides. The towering cliffs in the distance floated by, my horse flying as if he'd sprouted wings. Wind rushed through my hair, filling my ears, crisp and fresh.

"Kea." Broderick shouted from behind. "Don't push too hard. We have a—"

I slowed, waiting for him to finish.

His horse whinnied behind me, the sound shattering the weightless sensation through my bones. Why was he so silent?

I turned in my seat to see Broderick's riderless horse gallop back to Gerom Post, saddlebags flailing.

My heart slammed against my chest like a battering ram, crushing my lungs.

A hulking mass of deep chestnut fur crouched over Broderick's prostrate form lying in the snow. The assassin's arm flew up, shielding his neck from the wolf's powerful jaws. The sound of cracking bone split the sky.

Broderick roared.

Phoenix, no.

Adrenaline soared, grounding my mind.

I pulled Stalwart around, the horse stomping and tossing his head. His powerful body bunched beneath me as I spurred him toward the beast.

The wolf thrashed his head, jerking Broderick's body back and forth like a scrap of old cloth. With a powerful twist, the beast pitched Broderick into the air. His body tumbled across the snow, a trail of red streaking across white.

Broderick scrambled to his feet, stumbling for me, his legs pumping hard. His left arm hung twisted and limp at his side.

The wolf gave chase.

I slipped from Stalwart's back, racing for Broderick. The soft hiss of my sword flying from its scabbard was dulled by a familiar whistle.

The creature's shoulder jerked as an arrow embedded into its flesh. It didn't miss a step.

I wouldn't make it to Broderick in time. Ikane was too close.

The beast lunged. Another whistle. A second arrow sank into Ikane's arm. He barely flinched as his claws raked down Broderick's back, sinking deep into his leg. Broderick landed facedown in the snow.

I swung at the wolf, my boots sinking deep as I skidded to a halt over Broderick's body. "Get away from him!"

Ikane arched back, the silver glint of my blade whistling past his shoulder and catching a small tuft of dark fur. I swung again, driving him back until I stood between him and Broderick.

This was not Ikane. This was an empty shell. He deserved the new name "Master" had given him. Marrok the Monster.

Hackles standing on end, Marrok lowered himself to the snow.

"Go on, do it." It would give me a reason to run him through. I braced for his lunge, ready to plunge my sword into his belly, ready to feel his claws digging into my skin, ready for the bite of his teeth. If I died freeing Ikane from Rion's control, then I would be satisfied.

A sharp *thwit* raced past my ear. A chunk of fur ripped from Marrok's neck, drawing a gruff snarl from the wolf. The arrow struck the ground behind him. He staggered back, clutching the side of his neck. Another arrow hit his shoulder, plunging deep beside the first.

He turned away.

Two more arrows chased him, landing harmlessly in the knobby tufts of grass at his heels.

Ropert's entire platoon rushed toward us, the archer keeping her bow strung. The merchant girl.

Stomach clenching, I whirled to Broderick, seeing his rent coat and thick blood pooling by his leg. He lay so still. Falling to my knees, I rolled Broderick onto my lap.

"Broderick?" I squeaked.

His eyes fluttered dangerously, his face as white as the snow around him.

"Don't you dare die on me, you hear? Broderick."

His lashes closed.

I shook him. "Broderick!"

## CHAPTER 11

# BLOOD OF KINGS

The door slammed against the wall. Boots scuffed across the floor as soldiers carried Broderick's limp body into the tavern. Ropert swung his arms over the nearest table, pitching every mug, bowl, knife, and scrap of food onto the floor with a loud clatter.

"Hurry. Lay him here."

I couldn't tell who said it. Patrons scrambled to their feet, and Melody froze by the bar with two bowls of steaming porridge in her hands.

"Tighten the belt on his leg." This time I could tell it was Ropert giving the orders. "We need to stop the bleeding. Where is that blasted healer?"

"I'm here." A middle-aged man burst through the open door with the young merchant girl on his heels. I recognized the healer instantly. He was the one who had first treated my injuries after my initial Deathbiter attack. Malcom.

His apprentice followed, a young girl carrying a large satchel and basket filled with the tools of a healer's trade.

"Give him room." Ropert pushed the crowd back with outstretched arms.

Healer Malcom's graying hair slipped over his shoulders as he leaned over Broderick. "I need towels, rags, scraps of clean cloth. Whatever you can find."

Melody dropped her bowls onto the bar. She sprinted to the back.

Malcom grabbed the leather belt around Broderick's thigh, fumbled with the buckle, and drew it tighter. The blood dripping from Broderick's calf eased. "I need a knife. Get his clothes off. I need to see what we're dealing with."

Three soldiers and his apprentice stepped forward, stripping, tearing, and cutting away at Broderick's black attire.

Ropert blocked my view. "Come."

I shook my head, craning my neck to see the healer pull at the sticky sleeve of Broderick's shirt. I needed to stay. I needed to know if he would survive.

"Dagger." Ropert's hands squeezed my shoulders, steering me toward the door. "There is nothing we can do."

"No." I wriggled from his hands, catching a glimpse of Broderick's unnaturally bent arm between the bustling bodies around him. I choked. If he lived, he would never be able to play his lute the same way again.

Ropert pulled me out the door, the cold air burning the tears on my cheeks. I couldn't do this again. I couldn't lose another friend and ally.

I struck the wooden doorframe three times, and pain shuddered through the side of my fist. I cried out, my voice rough and hoarse, not caring who heard.

It was my fault. I'd been warned. I'd heard Master give the order. Because of Broderick's tonic, I couldn't comprehend it.

No, I comprehended it. I just didn't care.

I struck the doorframe again. This was all my fault.

Ropert pulled me to him, crushing me against his solid frame. Fingers clawing at his back, I screamed into his chest, his tunic crumpling against my lips. I wished, for the first time, that Thrall could devour this ache in my heart.

Eyes stinging from the tears and throat raw from screaming, my legs numbly carried me to the stables. I stepped inside, my eyes adjusting from light to dark.

What was I doing here? Our horses had been returned to their stalls, unsaddled, groomed, and fed. We wouldn't be traveling to Shear today.

Broderick's horse stood in one of the stalls, a brown blanket draped across its back, hiding the scratches from Ikane's claws. My chest tightened as a new wave of tears threatened to pour from my eyes. Ikane was no more. He was Marrok. A monster.

The horse's ears twitched as I drew near. It hung its head over the gate, nostrils flaring as I held my hand to its nose. I scratched its forehead. How could it be so calm? I was still screaming inside.

"I heard what happened." Alder's voice carried through the stable.

Broderick's horse jerked back, retreating into the stall.

I turned to Alder, his dark hood hiding any emotion.

"I am so sorry," he said.

"Say it. You warned me, and I didn't listen," I said. "I shouldn't have taken the tonic."

"You said it, not I."

I swallowed hard, staring at the stray pieces of golden hay on the floor. "Can you heal him?"

"Thrall doesn't work that way. It can draw out the poison from the Deathbiters, but it cannot heal."

I blinked at the wooden beams supporting the stable roof. Etheria could. I'd done it before. But I couldn't do it now. I was too broken, too bitter, too numb.

"Dagger? Are you in here?" Ropert called, his form a black silhouette in the doorframe. He stepped inside, blinking as his eyes adjusted to the darkness. His pace slowed as he noticed Alder. "You heard?"

Alder nodded soberly. "I came to offer my condolences."

Ropert took my hand. "Melody needs help cleaning up the tavern. I thought it would be good to keep busy."

Squeezing his hand, I moved for the door.

"Will you reconsider my offer?" Alder asked.

I stopped, glancing over my shoulder at him. Even if I did take him up on the offer, my heart ached too much. Thrall would overpower me in an instant.

"Not now. I need . . . I need time."

"Fair enough," he said. "I am ready whenever you are."

Healer Malcom descended the stairs one heavy footfall at a time, wiping his hands on a severely bloodied apron. Crusted redness streaked his arms, and a smudge ran along his cheekbone, clotting a strand of his graying hair and groomed beard. His apprentice followed, blood coating the front of her apron and skirt.

Eamon, Ropert, and I leapt from our chairs, our meal untouched on the table.

"How is he?" Ropert asked.

Healer Malcom was tall and lean with shoulders any man would envy. But they slumped as he eyed my mug of cider. "Are you going to drink that?"

I handed it to him.

He drank deeply, clearly not caring that it dribbled down the sides of his lips. It was painful to watch. I wanted news, and the longer he took to relay it, the more I feared.

He tipped his head back, finishing off the cider. After wiping his lips with the back of his hand—the only part of him that wasn't bloody—he set the mug on the table.

"Well?" Eamon pressed.

By now, even the soldiers were looking on, eager to hear the news.

"He's in poor condition," Malcom said.

Something coiled around my throat. "Can I see him?"

Malcom sank into my vacant chair, dropping his forehead into his hand. "I don't know what more I can do. He's lost a lot of blood. Too much. He won't be awake for quite some time . . . if he wakes at all."

I looked at Ropert.

"Go on," he urged.

I took the stairs two at a time. The third door on the left stood ajar, the light of a candle flickering shadows onto the floorboards. My breath caught as I stepped inside.

The room smelled of a thousand herbs mixed with the sharpness of iron and burnt flesh. Swallowing hard, I stepped around the first bed. The movement of my body sent the single candle standing between the two beds into a frenzy. Deathly shadows danced across Broderick's pale skin, and white strips of fabric peeked out from under the heavy quilt draped over his body.

"Broderick?" I brushed his unruly mop of brown curls from his forehead, his closed eyes sunken in his slumber. His chest barely rose and fell with breath.

Ropert entered the room, coming to my side. "He's going to pull through. He's strong."

His words were a plea to the Phoenix, a prayer, a wish, a hope.

I twisted the vial between my hands. I didn't need his herbs now. I'd shed all the tears I could until I felt dry and empty inside.

My mind, clear of his numbing tonic, focused on the blue tinge of the flame burning closest to the wick of the candle sitting on the bedside table. The flame flickered and trembled, layers upon layers of pale wax clinging to the side like frozen tears.

I felt like the candle—burning but empty, each drop of wax weakening my resolve. When would my flame go out? When would I have nothing left to give?

A knock pulled my attention to the open door.

Eamon stood in the doorway, empathy creasing his handsome features. "May I come in?" His voice was hushed, but there was no need. Broderick hadn't stirred since I'd come in, and that had been over six hours ago.

The bed creaked as Eamon sat down beside me. "This isn't your fault."

"Yes, it is." My fist tightened around the vial, wishing it would shatter. "I had a vision. I knew Broderick was in danger. I heard Master give Ikane the order. But I was too caught up trying to rid myself of magic that I ignored it."

"Master?" Eamon asked.

I pinched the bridge of my nose, seeing the hooded old man in my mind's eye, his pale knobby fingers twisting the ruby. "He's the one who took Ikane. Ikane calls him Master. He turned him into . . ." My throat tightened painfully. He was the one who "killed" Ikane. "He is working with Rion."

Eamon placed a hand on my back, his warm touch radiating through my tunic with life and love. My body absorbed it, and the tears I thought dry burned my eyes again.

"It's not your fault. Even if you had warned him, he wouldn't have stayed behind to save his skin." Eamon pried the vial from my fist, setting it on the table beside the weeping candle. "You and I both know that he would have risked his life for you anyway."

"But he would have been better prepared. We could have defended him, stayed in a group, surrounded him with soldiers." I rubbed my thighs, watching Broderick's slow breathing. I kept my voice at a whisper. "I probably would have taken Alder up on his offer to learn Thrall. I could have protected him."

"Kea." Eamon squeezed my hand with his calloused one. "You're holding a knife to your own throat. You won't be able to move forward holding on to guilt. What happened, happened. It is a terrible thing. But you need to get up. Move on. Press on. Fight. You are Keatep Brendagger, a warrior. And not all warriors wield a sword." He reached up, tucking my hair behind my ear, something that I could only remember him doing twice in my life. "You are my daughter. The blood of kings flows through you. I couldn't be prouder of the woman you've become."

I scanned his brown eyes, finding nothing but sincerity in them. "You think I can do this?"

"I know you can."

Wrapping my arms around him, I buried my face in his shoulder. What more could I say? His confidence in me was overwhelming to the point of empowering. All I could do was draw on it.

After a few long breaths, he pulled back, holding me at arm's length. "You had best get some sleep, young lady. Dawn will come before you know it."

"You'll look after Broderick for me?"

"You know I will." He leaned over and pinched the wick of the candle with his thumb and forefinger, plunging the room into darkness. The only light came from the muted red glow of the vial sitting on the table. I curled onto the bed, not bothering to strip my boots.

Eamon slipped into the hallway, but I called to him before he could walk away. "Eamon?"

He turned to regard me, a silhouette in the doorway.

"If you do find Ikane, kill him." It didn't hurt as much as I thought to say the words. Ikane was dead. Marrok was a nefarious replacement, a nightmare, a tortured reminder of what he once was. He was a monster and a danger to Roanfire. If I could stay and hunt him, I would.

"Goodnight," he whispered.

"Goodnight, Eamon."

Three gentle knocks pulled me from sleep.

I rolled onto my back. Was it morning already? Crust scratched my eyes as I rubbed them, and I sat up.

Wait. Why hadn't I dreamed? I'd expected a vision, a hint of what fiendish plan Master had in store. But there was nothing. A blank night.

I hadn't heard the Deathbiters, either. My shirt clung to my skin, damp with sweat in the heat of the stuffy inn. How in the blazes did I manage to sleep so soundly without Broderick's tonic?

Light from the hallway spilled into the room as Healer Malcom stepped inside. "You're awake." He looked like a different man, changed, washed, and groomed. The top portion of his graying hair was bound away from his face, giving him an air of brightness and energy.

Melody entered behind him, carrying a wide wicker basket filled with white linen strips. Her smile didn't quite reach her eyes as she gazed on Broderick's unmoving form.

"How is he?" she asked.

I swung my legs over the edge of the bed, eyeing Broderick. "I don't know."

Healer Malcom bent over the unconscious man, pressing his fingers against the side of his throat. "His heart still beats, but he is weak and cold." He pulled the blankets up to Broderick's shoulders.

Melody set the basket on the foot of my bed. "This room smells of death." She moved to the window, opening it, allowing fresh air and pale morning light into the room. Smoke floated lazily from chimneys into the hazy morning sky. Today, gray clouds covered the blue.

"He didn't deserve this," Malcom whispered, glancing down on Broderick, a crease forming between his brows. He tipped his head at me. "I remember you. I was unable to heal you after the Deathbiter attack." His eyes turned back to Broderick, looking on him as a father would a son. "Broderick was the one who saved your life."

"I remember."

"He didn't just save you. He saved many." He laughed bitterly. "If only I could heal the way he did. The boy is selfless." Malcom pulled a vial from his pocket. It glowed white and blue, swirling like wind and water. "Since that time, I've experimented with the sprite dusts. Mind you, it wasn't easy. My supply of dust is dwindling rapidly. But I've found a way to draw out Deathbiter poison without the use of magic."

Without magic? "How?"

Malcom uncorked the bottle, pulled Broderick's cracked bottom lip down, and tapped. A sprinkle of blue-white powder rained into his mouth.

"Water, wind, and earthdust mixed with a paste of ash," Malcom said. "It takes time and a lot of applications." He stoppered the vial, his face going grave. "But it doesn't look like another Dust Hunter will come this way soon. This is the last of my winddust."

Melody stepped up beside me, rubbing her arm. "What are his chances?"

"The problem is that he no longer has the proper amount of blood flowing to his organs. Windsprite dust can compensate for that, and watersprite dust aids the replenishing of blood." Malcom sighed, tucking the vial back into his pocket. "I don't have enough windsprite dust for him to fully recover. He needs this blend for five weeks minimum. I only have enough for two."

He turned to me. "I need you to make a choice, Lady Brendagger. Is it fair for me to use what precious dust I have on a man who is already dying? Or should I use the dust to draw out the poison from those I know I can save?"

Broderick couldn't die like this. He had been through so much. He was wise beyond his years. He knew where to place a knife to kill and where would cause minimal damage. He knew which herbs would poison a man, render a man unconscious, or heal. He knew history and cartography, alchemy, magic, and music. He lived through my outburst of magic three times. He survived a night out in the open with the Deathbiters.

This could not be how his life ended. If only Ali was . . .

I suddenly knew what to do.

Diving for my saddlebag, my knees hit the floorboards hard. It was here somewhere. I moved my spare shirt, and a white shine burst from the pack like sunlight glistening on freshly fallen snow.

I presented it to Malcom.

The whites of his eyes glowed. "Flaming feathers of the Phoenix. How . . . ? Where . . . where did you come by so much pure dust?"

"Is it enough?" I asked.

He lifted the vial, scrutinizing it. "This will outlast my supply of water and earthdust." He engulfed the light in his fist. "Do you have those?"

I glanced at Broderick's saddlebags. He had every tonic and herb known to man in there. Surely, he'd have some sprite dusts, too.

Kneeling by his pack, I opened the flap, digging into the assassin's world. Leather rolls lay neatly inside, each one holding endless vials of things I knew nothing about. A faint glow radiated near the bottom. I removed the leather roll, unbinding the cord. Three vials glowed inside—red, green, and blue—but they were all half-spent.

I gave them to Malcom.

"I'll find more dust in Shear and send them your way," I said.

"I've already asked them to send more. They have nothing," Malcom said. "You'll need to send it from Kaltum."

"I'll bring them back myself if I must."

"Dagger, there you are." Ropert stepped into the room, his cloak draped tightly around his shoulders. "How is he?"

Melody sat on the edge of Broderick's bed, gently brushing his curls from his eyes. "No change."

Ropert hesitated. "We can't wait any longer. The weather is changing fast."

I swung my cloak around my shoulders and hefted my saddlebag, glancing once more at Broderick's gear. Two familiar weapons peeked out from under the bag—the recognizable curve of the pommel creating the head of a sea serpent, the three sharp spines on its head, the coiling body around the hilt. No one could wield them the way Ikane did.

I pulled one out, my reflection warping on the black steel. This was a part of him I could hold on to, something strong and tangible. Something Rion could not change.

Would it be a sin to separate them? They were meant to be together, a balance, a dance.

But that didn't matter now. Ikane didn't need them anymore.

Tucking one of Ikane's black steel swords into my belt, I left the other with Broderick.

## CHAPTER 12
## BURNING CANVAS

My eyes and neck ached. How long did I need to keep looking? The buildings of Gerom Post had long faded into the distance. The Gyroh Mountains dominated the east, massive formations of gray and white. Marrok, no matter how skilled, couldn't blend with the wide snowy plains given his dark coat.

Three hazy white trees, tiny specks in the distance, sat to our left. I squinted at the base for a shadow or movement. Nothing. It was tempting to pull my hood over my head against the bitter cold breeze and ride. But that's what he wanted. That's when he would strike.

Ropert slowed his horse, taking position beside me. "Anything?"

"No."

His blue eyes looked as tired as mine felt, bloodshot and droopy. "We can't stop."

"I know."

"Have you noticed the clouds?" he asked.

I dared to take my eyes off the horizon. Gray clouds hung low in the sky, pressing down like thick smoke, and a familiar crisp smell burned my nose. Snow.

"We need to pick up the pace," he said. "Keep watching for Ikane."

"Don't call him that. The creature is Marrok."

"What?"

"Ikane is dead."

Ropert's lips pressed into a tight line. "How . . . how do you know?"

"Trust me."

I scanned our surroundings again. I'd rather face Marrok than be caught in the dark with the Deathbiters. Marrok, I could fight. Feathers, I *wanted* to fight him. I'd take Ikane's sword and run him through.

"Let's pick up the pace," Ropert hollered over his shoulder to the rest of our party.

The terrain changed from a blanket of soft whiteness to windblown grassland. Scattered evergreens, too thin to be called trees, stood like torn banners in a battlefield.

Tiny specks of ice hit my cheeks as the horizon became hazy with white crystals. The storm was coming fast, faster than I'd ever encountered one. From the first smell of snow, I could usually count the hours before it fell.

We pressed on, hoods pulled up, trying to keep the multiplying flakes from our eyes. The horses slowed, heads lowered as they pressed against the wind.

Ropert pulled his horse to a halt. "We're not going to make it." His voice was muffled by the turned-up collar of his coat, his blue eyes framed by snow-dusted lashes.

Shear was too far, and night was pressing in.

He pulled his collar down, turning to the rest of the party behind us. "We're stopping here. Set up the tent."

I slipped from Stalwart's back. My hips ached. And charred rachis, needles of ice stabbed my toes. Grabbing my saddlebag, I slapped Stalwart's rump, urging him to join the other horses as they huddled together on the open prairie.

Four soldiers stretched the tent fabric against the wind. Three more set the poles, staking the guylines into the frozen ground. As soon as the tent stood firm, canvas bracing against the storm, all thirteen members of our party ducked inside.

My ears rang as I removed my hood. The tent wasn't built for so many.

I pushed to a corner where the merchant and his daughter had taken refuge. Dropping my saddlebag, I sank to the snow-packed ground, trying to find a comfortable position for my rump between thick tufts of grass.

Ropert entered last, a heavy layer of snow clinging to his shoulders and head. His red-rimmed eyes scanned the dark tent, counting the individual shadows huddled together.

Satisfied, he stepped around the soldiers, sinking down beside me. "How long do you think this storm will last?"

"It won't be long," the merchant girl said. A bright-red glow came from her hand, illuminating the tent. Firesprite dust. "Sorry, I didn't mean to eavesdrop. My father and I have made this trek for many years. These storms are brutal and hit hard and fast, but they also move on just as quickly." She turned to her father. "What do you think, Papa? It should taper off in about an hour or two?"

The merchant looked up from his ledger. "What? Oh, yes. Not long. Not long at all." He squinted back down at the book, scribbling something on the page.

I eyed Ropert. That didn't bode well for us. By the time the storm lifted, it would be full dark and prime prowling time for the Deathbiters.

"What is your name, young lady?" Ropert asked.

"I'm Tanja, and this is my father, Master Cornell Brickwater."

"Tanja," I said. "Thank you for your help earlier. You have good aim."

Her smiled faded. "I'm sorry I couldn't do more. I hit that creature three times, didn't I? What was that thing? I've never seen anything like it."

I shrugged, pretending to be as clueless as she was. "How long have you been shooting?"

"Since I was three," Tanja said. The red light in her hand dimmed as she tried to find a more comfortable position. "That would make it ten . . . no, eleven years."

"You're only fourteen?"

She looked insulted. "I am a grown woman and will take over my father's business in less than two years."

I held up my hands. "That's not what I meant. I've been around warriors all my life, and I've known dozens of exceptional archers. I am impressed with your skill, especially for how young you are."

A smile stole across her lips. "You know, I like you. I've heard some crazy things about you, but you're just as normal as the rest of us."

Ropert chuckled, stretching his legs between two soldiers in the cramped tent. "You have no idea." He lay back on his saddlebag, tucking an arm under his head.

I slapped his shoulder, but feathers, he was right. Nothing was normal about me.

Tanja followed Ropert's example, lying down as best she could. She tucked the vial of firesprite dust into her coat, resulting in several outbursts from the soldiers as well as her father as the tent plunged into darkness.

"Alright, alright." She pulled it out again, letting it rest against her chest. "Serves you right for not bringing any yourself."

She and Ropert closed their eyes, and a few soldiers did the same.

How could they sleep? This storm wouldn't protect us forever.

I watched Master Cornell's graphite stick make a jot here and there, listening to the howling wind, the shaking of the tent, and the occasional whinny of a horse.

There must be something I could do to prepare for the impending attack.

I slumped back against my saddlebag, hugging my torso, eyes heavy. What had we gotten ourselves into? I should have taken Alder up on his offer.

I was returning empty-handed to Meldron. Queen Lonacheska expected me to find answers, yet I had nothing. Nothing except for Thrall. Even my dreams of the White Wardent had been nonexistent since I'd ... since I'd pushed him away. Since I'd gone into the Deathbiters' lair in search of Ikane.

I'd crossed a line. What did he expect? I was alone in this, stumbling through magic since the first nightmare made my nose bleed.

Eyes burning, I closed them, just for a moment. I would not be asleep when the Deathbiters attacked. I knew their sting too well.

*His eyes were blue this time.*

*Clear and radiant like a summer sky, shifting from the lightest hues to the deepest azure.*

*He looked so much like Alder save the tension in his jaw, as if he was expending tremendous effort to be here.*

*Here. In my mind. Reaching for me again even though I'd pushed him away.*

*Didn't he understand? It was torture to see him, to know what he'd done, to be the one who'd lost everything because of his mistake. And now he expected me to fix it? It wasn't fair.*

"Keatep." He said my name like an anxious father, his silver-white brows knotted with struggle and worry.

*I couldn't see him, not the way I had in the past. The white curtains that typically accompanied his vision were obscure shadows in the back, and his white robe faded into gray. The usual sweet scent of lilies smelled weak and tainted.*

"What ... what is this darkness?" He strained to say the words. "This isn't your doing. Something ... something is keeping you from me."

I bristled. "Now you want to help?"

*His jaw clenched with effort as a shadow pressed in on his vision. He drove it back.*

*Were those beads of perspiration on his brow?*

*"I would come to you if I could." His eyes scrunched tight.*

*"Then tell me where you are. I'll come to you."*

*He shook his head, white hair falling over his face, his image darkening. I'd never seen him so distressed, so overwhelmed, so disheveled. "Can't . . . can't hold . . ."*

*"Where are you? Tell me what to do."*

*"Leander." The name pushed through his clenched teeth, his voice dulled by the growing darkness.*

*"What?"*

*"Prince . . . Leander."*

*Shadow swallowed him, his vision bursting into a cloud of ash on the wind.*

I jolted from the dream to a darkened tent, the soft red glow of firedust illuminating the cramped sleeping forms.

I'd fallen asleep.

I ground the heels of my palms into my eyes.

The Tolean Prince? What did he have to do with Yotherna? Did he know where I could find him? And what was the darkness pressing in on him? It wasn't me.

At least, I thought it wasn't. I didn't want to touch magic ever again, Thrall *or* Etheria.

Tanja stirred, her vial of firedust slipping from her chest, darkening the tent. Master Cornell slumped against one of the tent poles, his mouth open, drool glistening on his chin.

It was quiet. Too quiet. The tent didn't sway and tremble. The wind didn't howl.

The storm had passed.

I held my breath.

A screech tore through the canvas.

They were here.

I shook Ropert's shoulder, and his eyes flew open. I held a finger to my lips. Our best defense right now was silence. Maybe the Deathbiters would never know we were here.

Mouth pressed tight, he sat up.

Screams from our horses ripped through the tent. Tanja's eyes flew wide.

My hand flew to her mouth, clamping down hard. If she screamed, it would be the end of us.

Panic burned in her eyes as I motioned for silence.

She blinked once, nodding against the pressure of my hand. I released her.

She sat upright, her hand suffocating the red glow of firedust at her side. She clutched it to her chest.

Ropert silently moved among the soldiers, waking them. Wide-eyed and momentarily disoriented, they sat up and drew weapons, every hiss and clank of metal setting my nerves on edge.

I gestured for Tanja to wake her father, freezing mid-wave. A Deathbiter was above us, the air of flapping wings warbling the tent's fabric.

My mouth went dry. Would licking my lips be too loud? Would breathing?

Ropert crouched amid his soldiers, white knuckles gripping his sword. No fear showed on his face, only determination. He was ready. We hadn't come this far to be destroyed by oversized bats.

Horses screamed outside. Master Cornell stirred, the tent pole swaying under his weight. His graphite stick fell from his ear, a soft tick sounding as it struck the leather binding of the book in his lap.

It might as well have been a thunderclap.

A terrible screech drilled through my ears like stone on steel. The tent flew into a frenzy, tears and gashes splitting the canvas as talons pierced the beige canvas.

Ropert leapt up with a growl, his sword plunging through the canvas, hitting a shadow behind. Soldiers followed suit, a dozen cries exploding from the creatures as sword tips cut into their skin.

I drew my sword. "Tanja. Open the firedust."

She curled over the vial, and flashes of red light burst through her fingers.

I jabbed at a shadow above us, and the canvas tore open to the night sky. Blurs of bat wings and talons flashed, blinking out the stars.

Flaming feathers, there were thousands.

"Now what?" Tanja shouted over the turmoil.

A terrible face appeared in the gaping hole above me, hissing. Its mouth opened wide, teeth dripping with venom. My sword shot up, the tip sliding into the leathery skin on its neck.

Tanja froze as the creature dropped at her feet.

"Don't just stand there," I spat. "Set the tent on fire."

The girl ducked away, soldiers and swords filling the space she had occupied.

Shredded scraps of tent dangled above us, holes exposing us to the unbelievable swarm of black-winged creatures twisting to the sky like a tornado. I stabbed again and again. We couldn't hold out much longer. What was taking Tanja so long?

Red-orange light flickered to life, spreading up the torn fabric. Deathbiters scattered as firelight spread across their black leathery skin.

Ropert sliced through the canvas behind him, making a door. "Go!" He stepped out into the night, soldiers following.

"Keep your backs to the fire!" he ordered.

I looked at Tanja and her father. "Stay with me."

Cold night air struck my face, followed by the sour stench of demon bats. Lazy snowflakes, caught in our battle, swirled wildly as hundreds of black leather wings circled the sky.

Phoenix help us. Half the lair was here.

I pressed my shoulder against Ropert's.

"Any more ideas?" he asked, his eyes fixed on the angry blur of wings and talons darting around us. "The tent won't—look out!"

His arm swung over my neck, pulling me down with him as an oversized bat sliced the air where our heads had been. The thick smoke roiling to the sky couldn't mask the sour stench burning my nostrils. My eyes watered.

Ropert whirled, sword slicing up and hitting a Deathbiter square in the chest.

There were too many. Whatever Master and Rion were planning, it was working. We wouldn't survive this. Not without . . .

No. I gripped my sword tighter. I would not use Thrall again.

A bat dropped, sinking into the snow at my feet. Was that an arrow protruding from its chest? The animal twitched as I looked closer. The fletching looked familiar.

I blinked at Tanja.

She raised her bow, arm drawn back with perfect posture, taking aim. Her arrow flew, ripping through a Deathbiter's wing and into another's face. The former panic in her eyes had been replaced by a solid resolve. She was a fighter.

And yet, her father cowered beside her, holding his ledger over her head like a shield.

What were we thinking? They weren't warriors. We should have never allowed them to come with us. They should have stayed in Gerom Post.

A soldier cried out.

I whirled, seeing the long leathery wings of a Deathbiter slice by him. He clutched his arm, red blossoming on his sleeve, sword dropping from his hand. I knew the sting. I knew the burn that seared into his flesh like the hot brand of iron, curling into the blood. But he did not have the luxury of nursing the injury now.

"Pick up your sword," I cried. "Fight!"

Firelight deepened the pain on his face, but he gritted his teeth, grabbed his sword, and swung at another Deathbiter.

"Look out!" someone shouted.

Hot air blasted against my face as the tent collapsed, sending smoldering sparks and ash exploding into the air, the blessed raging flames diminishing into useless glowing embers. Weak fire licked up the tattered canvas clinging to a lone standing corner post.

Now things would get intense.

Ropert slipped to my back as Deathbiters plunged at us in the absence of light. Tanja screamed, curling into a ball beside me. Her father became a blur as wings and teeth swarmed around us.

I swung, my sword jerking as it hit a body, then another. The second creature wrapped its talons around my blade, clinging to the weapon like heavy rust. It hissed at me, baring daggerlike teeth dripping with poisonous saliva. Whirling, I slammed my sword against the smoldering heap behind me. Red embers exploded on impact.

The Deathbiter screamed, releasing my sword as its skin ignited in a flash of blinding hot fire.

Light didn't just repel them—it burned them.

"Use the fire! Toss them into the fire!" I roared.

Bright bursts of flame hissed and flared as soldiers followed my advice. With each flash of light, Deathbiters dispersed, giving us precious moments of reprieve.

Ropert grunted, whirling to the fire.

Sparks hit my face as he smashed his forearm into the embers. The bat attached to him screamed, but it didn't let go as its body burst into flame. Fire licked up Ropert's sleeve, and he banged his arm down again. The smell of burning human flesh mixed with the overwhelming stench of Deathbiter and smoke.

"Ropert!"

I clawed at the burning mass, heat biting my palm as I tore it from his arm. It writhed on the muddied ground.

"Kea!" Tanja screamed.

I whirled.

Three demon bats pecked at the girl lying in a fetal position and screaming into her knees.

The air whistled around my sword as the blade sliced into the first and second Deathbiters. The third escaped to the sky.

I scanned the battlefield. There was nowhere to run, nowhere to hide. No place to seek shelter. Soldiers cried out, buckling under the pain. Two lay lifeless, Deathbiters ripping into their skin like savage animals.

There was no escape.

Not unless I did something. Not unless I reached for the untamed magic waiting to consume me.

I didn't want to.

Something barreled into my shoulder, knocking me forward. My boot hit the cowering girl's leg, and my body pitched over her, landing hard on the compacted snow, pinning my sword beneath me. I rolled to my back as two black-taloned beasts plunged from the sky, throwing my arms up.

I fought the urge to cry out as fire raced through my forearm, a burning sensation leaking into my blood. It was happening all over again. They would overpower me. They would tear me apart.

I'd barely survived last time. If it hadn't been for Broderick . . . oh, feathers, Broderick.

Shutting my eyes, I reached for the black spark always ready to consume. It seemed . . . confused. The spark flickered like I was trying to start a fire with rain-soaked wood.

How could I not have enough rage, fear, or hatred? We were in the middle of a massacre.

A blast of ash and cinder blew into my eyes. The Deathbiters clinging to my clothing lifted. The battlefield grew silent.

Slowly, I lowered my arms, daring a look at the sky.

A swarm of black circled above like a thick cloud, blotting out the stars and silver moonlight, almost... almost spellbinding. They weren't attacking.

I... I hadn't used Thrall, had I?

"Dagger." Ropert staggered to me, blood and ash coating his clothing and skin, but he wasn't looking at me or the sky. He was looking across the open field, back the way we had come.

I rolled to my knees.

A tall, hooded figure sat on a horse beyond the smoldering rubble that was once the tent.

Alder.

## CHAPTER 13
# INSIDE OUT

Tanja's cry was so deep, so real, so raw, it pulled tears from my eyes. The girl held her father's head in her lap, rocking back and forth as glistening streams ran down her cheeks like an endless waterfall.

I was no stranger to death. It was part of a soldier's life. But seeing it never made it easier.

Three soldiers lay in puddles of sleet unmoving, their crimson tunics dusted with a layer of ash and snow. It was easier to not think of them as people, to not remember their faces, their smiles, their laughter, or the life in their eyes. And it was easier to not remember that they had families, friends, and loved ones.

But seeing Tanja like this . . . my heart couldn't take it.

Alder stepped beside me. "Are you ready to learn now?"

I tasted ash. If he'd asked me an hour ago, I would've taken him up on his offer. But it was my use of Thrall that severed my connection from the one who could help me the most. I couldn't touch it. Ever. I was ashamed for even reaching for it earlier.

I brushed tears from my cheeks. "No."

"No?" Alder gestured to the crying girl and the lifeless soldiers. "You could've prevented this. All of it. I watched. I waited. I hoped you would find the strength to use it."

What did he just say? That he stood by and watched? As we were fighting for our lives? As our horses were driven off, infected, and torn to shreds? As the soldiers bled?

He folded his arms across his chest. "You could have done it."

Was he trying to blame me? He was the one with power. He had the knowledge and skill. I didn't. This was not my fault.

"Don't you dare turn this on me," I said. "You know I have no control. Feathers, Alder. You could have spared them."

"I spared the rest of you, didn't I? Once I realized you wouldn't."

"I tried! I reached for it, but it didn't come."

He tilted his head, and I imagined his brows rising in question beneath his hood.

"It didn't?" he asked.

"No. Feathers, Alder. I wanted to protect them. I wanted to save them all."

He groaned. "And that is why it didn't work. Thrall feeds on fear and anger, not the urge to protect."

Was he saying I had reached for the wrong power? That since I wanted to protect, I had reached for Thrall when I should have been reaching for Etheria?

That didn't matter. What mattered was how he stood by and watched innocent men and women die when he could have prevented everything. When he could have saved Tanja's father.

He was irritating. No, not just irritating. He was completely wrong in the head. How could he justify saving me but not the others? He might have control over Thrall's unbridled power, but at what cost?

"You're injured." He took my arm, his hands cold and firm.

I shook him off, staring at the tattered, bloodstained sleeve of my forearm. My wound was nothing compared to what others had suffered. That this was the only venomous injury I'd sustained was a miracle.

"Don't try to change the subject," I said. "Four good men died because of you."

"The way I see it, they died because of you."

I tore my hands through my hair, turning away with a growl. He couldn't see it. His mind was too damaged by Thrall. I couldn't look at him.

"What? Is that it?" he called after me. "I'm beginning to think you would've rather I let you die. Let the Deathbiters tear you asunder. Is that it? Is that what you want? I can still oblige."

I stopped, scrunching my eyes shut. Crazy or not, he was still keeping the Deathbiters aloft.

"I didn't mean to sound ungrateful," I muttered.

"You could have fooled me."

"Kea." Ropert's voice was tight as he approached, and a deep crease of pain etched between his brows. His skin glistened with perspiration—with fever. The venom was working quickly.

"We have two soldiers with severe lacerations. Four infected with minor bites. All our horses are either lost or dead. I don't know how it happened, but Tanja has managed to come out unscathed." He looked at the girl still weeping over her father. "Well, not entirely."

"You don't look so good yourself." Alder scrutinized the mottle of red blisters covering Ropert's forearm. "That doesn't look like poison."

"A Deathbiter caught fire while attached to my arm," Ropert said. He sucked air through his teeth. "The burning hasn't let up yet."

Alder's mouth pulled into a frown. "May I?"

Ropert kept his face stoic, but a muscle twitched in his jaw as Alder's slender fingers cradled his arm.

"The Deathbiters have a very flammable oil on their skin," Alder said. "It's why they smell so bad. Do you see this?" He drew attention to the thickest part of Ropert's arm where the blistering was worst. "These six marks are where the talons dug into your skin." He leaned closer. "Fascinating."

Ropert's brows rose. "What?"

Alder straightened. "It looks like more than venom has found a way into your bloodstream. The oil found its way inside as well."

"I don't think 'fascinating' is the word I'd use," Ropert snapped.

Into his blood? The oil? "What do you mean?" I asked.

The edges of Alder's hood swayed as he looked at me. "He's burning from the inside out."

Ropert and I exchanged looks.

"I can draw out the poison, but I don't think my magic will have any effect on the burning," Alder said.

Ropert swallowed hard. "Please, do what you can. But help the others first. I can wait."

Leaning back on his heels, Alder growled, his breathing heavy. His fingers flexed repeatedly.

"What's wrong?" Ropert asked.

"Nothing is wrong." Alder's voice was tight. "I'm tired. What do you expect after drawing the poison out of all your soldiers?"

I crouched beside Ropert, squeezing his shoulder. "Maybe you should take a break."

"I don't need a break," Alder snapped. "Give me your arm. I can do this."

Ropert extended his blistered forearm again, and Alder's pale fingers, long and slender, hovered over the injury. His jaw set as he bowed his head in concentration.

I wished I could see his face. He'd drawn the poison from the other soldiers with ease, transferring the sour-smelling blackness into tufts of grass, making them wither and die. It was a different method than Broderick used, but effective.

But now Alder's fingers shook, muscles standing out on the backs of his hands. His teeth clenched.

Then he sighed, dropping his hands. "It's no use. I can't do it."

My heart thundered. He couldn't give up. This was Ropert. "Maybe if you rested for—"

"I don't need rest." Alder stood abruptly. "Something is blocking me. I can't get through. I'm sorry, Ropert."

Ropert scooped another handful of snow over the blisters. "I understand."

"I don't." I stood. "Please, try again, Alder. I know you can do it."

"You do it," he snapped. "By the power of the elements, Keatep, embrace your gift."

If he couldn't do it, what made him think I could?

"It's alright." Ropert got to his feet. "We'll find a healer in Shear. Sprite dust should do it, right?"

Alder shook his head and turned away.

Ropert looked at me, his gaze questioning.

"I don't think sprite dust is going to help if magic can't," I said.

Ropert swallowed hard, his brows tightening. "What about you? You won't let him draw the poison from you?"

I hugged my arm. I would be fighting a fever within the hour. "I'm going to use Healer Malcom's recipe once we reach Shear. Besides, if you are going to suffer, then I will, too."

"Dagger, please, don't do it on my behalf."

I wasn't. If Thrall was keeping the White Wardent from me, then I needed to do everything in my power to stay away from it.

I stared at Alder's black cloak as he moved among the soldiers.

That included him.

Alder's tattered charcoal cloak billowed behind him. His horse—the only mount alive—carried a severely wounded soldier while the rest of us stumbled after him.

How had it come to this? Alder, a mysterious man with a past I knew nothing about, was leading Ropert's platoon.

Ropert staggered beside me, his face pale, lips and cheeks chapped from the cold, his jaw clenched so tight veins popped from his neck. His forehead glistened with the heat soaring through his body while my teeth knocked together.

Every smash of my jaw intensified the throbbing ache in my head. Despite the sun beating down on my shoulders and how tightly I pulled my cloak around my body, the air still bit and prickled across my skin.

More and more trees dotted the landscape. We were getting closer. Just a few more hours, and we would be safe within the walls of a warm inn with a fire, a bed, a hot meal, and a healer tending to our injuries.

I glanced over my shoulder, making sure Tanja was still there. Silent tears glinted on her chapped cheeks, glittering diamonds slipping to the small of her chin.

I looked away.

Her father, along with three good soldiers, lay in unmarked, shallow graves at the site of the attack. If only I could say something to comfort her, something to bring the fight back into her eyes. But every time I looked at her, my throat closed up.

How would I cope if I'd lost Eamon?

Ropert stopped, sucking air through his teeth, and curled over his arm, his hand locked in a pained claw. His eyes scrunched shut as I placed a hand on his trembling shoulder.

"Just a little farther," I said.

His head shook hard, his strawberry locks falling across his face. "It's . . . it's in my bones. Phoenix, it burns."

A sharp copper taste filled my mouth, and my stomach clenched. Ropert never showed signs of weakness. Twice, he'd taken a knife to the wrist. Twice, I'd stitched him up without so much as a flinch. Yet now he trembled, tears shimmering in his eyes, his voice shaking.

I coaxed his arm from his body. "Let me see."

Flaming feathers. The blisters were spreading, angry and red, moving down to his fingers and past his elbow.

"Dagger," he said.

I'd never heard his voice so tight.

"It . . . it needs to come off."

I blinked, and Tanja's eyes widened.

I must have been hallucinating. He couldn't mean that. Losing his arm would mean losing his career. No. We could do this. Just a few more hours. He could make it.

"Come on, Ropert. Don't stop. We'll find a healer as soon as we get to Shear." I pushed against his broad back, urging him forward, but he stood like a rock.

"Feathers, Dagger. It's burning up to my shoulder." He panted. "I hate . . . I hate to think what will happen if it reaches my throat—or my heart. It must come off."

I stepped back. "You don't mean that."

He drew his broadsword from the scabbard at his back, the blade glinting under the noonday sun. "Use my sword. The edge is sharper than yours."

"No."

"Dagger, please," he hissed, pain overpowering his muscular frame. "I need you . . . I need you to do this."

I choked on my own bile. I wasn't qualified for this. It took a trained healer to amputate a limb, and even then, the chances of survival were not promising. He could bleed out, get an infection, go into shock.

"We don't have a tourniquet. We don't have a fire to cauterize the wound. We don't have herbs to manage the pain, no alcohol or clean water. You won't be able to walk."

Ropert grabbed my hand, his grip crushing and hot. He was truly on fire inside. His glazed eyes searched mine. "I'm scared, too."

His sword was heavy, as heavy as knowing he was right. He couldn't keep going like this.

"So much for a hero," Tanja scoffed. "They say you destroyed the Leviathan Army, fought Deathbiters, overpowered a wolf-hybrid beast." Her swollen eyes hardened. "I don't believe any of it. You're nothing but a fraud. Alder healed everyone. Alder saved us from the Deathbiters. Not you."

Her words cut deeper than she knew.

"She's right," Ropert said.

What? My fever must be getting worse. How could he side with her? He knew the truth. He knew what I was struggling with.

"There are two sides to magic, right?" he asked.

I blinked at him.

"Alder has chosen one side, but Broderick taught you another."

Etheria.

Ropert's grip tightened. "You can do this."

Could he be right? Could Etheria succeed where Thrall failed?

What if I hurt him? What if I slipped into Thrall, lost control, hurt everyone?

"Try, Dagger," Ropert said. "For Broderick. For me."

My mouth went dry as I glanced at Tanja. My heart rate rose to that of a horse's gallop, the pounding in my head rushing red with every bang. Her safety and the safety of the party came first.

"Go ahead, Tanja. We'll catch up," I said.

Her chin rose. "I want to see this."

"I can't guarantee you'll be safe," I warned her.

Her eyes hardened. "By the burning feathers of the Phoenix, I will stay and witness this. I won't let the world be fooled by your lies."

I didn't have the energy to argue. If she wanted to risk it, so be it.

"Very well. But stand over there." I pointed at a spot ten paces away beside a little spruce barely tall enough to reach her knees.

Stabbing the tip of his sword into the hard ground, I turned to Ropert. "I don't know what I'm doing," I said.

"I trust you." He gave me his hand, blisters bulging from inflamed skin. I couldn't imagine his pain. Did it feel like his arm was emerged in smoldering coals? Or was it more like it was stuck in a blacksmith's furnace?

I'd felt fire in my bones before, so intense I couldn't breathe, and endured it time and time again as Rion assaulted me with her burning magic. But it did not leave physical scars the way these would.

We knelt in the snow, biting cold sinking into my trousers as our knees touched. I ran my tongue along my chapped lips, tasting copper. This was better than chopping off his arm. I could do this. I could try.

He held out his arm between us. "You can do it."

Closing my eyes, I inhaled.

*Archery,* I told myself. *Focus, steady, release.*

Heat radiated from his skin as I held my frozen hands over his blistering flesh. The frigid air swept across my mind like an oilcloth to a blade, wiping away distractions and thoughts blurring my vision.

A clear path opened into my mind like stone stairs spiraling into a tower.

The place was foreign, forgotten, cobwebs of past battles scattered between thoughts. Not that long ago, Rion had been here, tormenting me with her fire. Even Ikane's memories had filled my mind, heightening my senses. It was strange and empty without them.

But Ropert was here now, and he needed me. I couldn't abandon him again. I'd done that enough. It was time I stood my ground, defended what I cared for, what I believed was right. And right now, Ropert deserved healing.

Something warm flickered in my chest, a white star winking in the lonely space in my mind. It thawed the hard edges in me, as if I had stepped out of the rain and into a homely tavern filled with warm firelight and aromatic food, and spread, reaching for the tips of my fingers. It was pure and rich.

Another star sparkled to life, then another, until my mind spun with a sea of endless stars waiting for direction.

Oh, how I missed Ikane's touch of blue, the way his energy encircled mine, doubling its power. But now—

I shook my head. *Focus.*

Heat pushed into my fingertips. This was the fire burning Ropert. This was the pain slowly boiling through his body, killing him.

I reached for it.

Fire seared up my arms, flooding my chest, tearing through my lungs. Red heat filled my vision. It was just like Rion's magic. Everything about this pain was hers. The Deathbiters were hers. Ikane's deformed body was her doing. Master was working for her.

A black flicker warbled between the stars, ready to consume the rage building in my chest.

*Breathe.* It was almost as if Broderick said it, coaching me, keeping my mind on track. My lungs expanded. *Focus. Turn my mind.*

Ropert. Everything about this moment was him. Blue eyes, sly grin, strong jaw, strawberry hair. A soldier, my friend, my brother.

Thick black ooze glowing with red embers like molten floods of lava clung to his bone, muscle, and skin. It shrank from the white lights, burrowing deeper.

Ropert's muted groan struck my mind.

This fire would not take him.

I pushed like cavalry stampeding through the enemy line, thundering into the darkness. Streaks of white light reeled, wove, pulled, and coiled around the blackness, spinning threads like a spider around prey, every ounce of red-rimmed darkness cocooned in etheric light.

I drew it to me. Away from Ropert. It would never harm him again.

I opened my eyes.

Feathers, I was cold. Where had all the heat gone? I thought I was cold before, but this was something else. My body didn't have the energy to shiver, but still it jerked and trembled.

Ropert caught me in his arms, and my teeth chattered against his shoulder.

"Dagger? Are you alright?" He stroked my hair. "You stopped breathing."

"S-s-s-so c-c-cold."

He touched my forehead. "You're burning." He rubbed my shoulders and back, but the friction irritated my skin like a sunburn.

I squirmed. The cold was deep, and my bones felt brittle like ice.

"I don't believe it." Tanja stepped closer. "Sir Ropert. Look at your arm."

He lifted his arm, and I craned to look.

I'd hoped to see his flesh as perfectly healed as Erin's, but my heart sank into the pit of my stomach. His skin, from the tips of his fingers to the tattered sleeve of his burnt shirt, was mottled as badly as Alder's face, covered with raised veins of pink flesh and craters of white scar tissue.

Ropert flexed his marked fingers, testing his wrist.

I sagged against his chest, closing my eyes to the sight. "I'm s . . . s . . . sorry."

His arms wrapped around me once again. "Dagger, I was about to have you chop off my arm. I'd say this is a far better alternative. I knew you could do it."

"Ropert! Kea! What are you doing?" Alder's voice carried across the landscape. His cloak billowed, his hood hiding his features.

"We're coming!" Ropert hollered back. "Come on, Dagger." He hauled me to my feet. My knees knocked together. The white landscape spun.

"Ropert." I gripped his arms, waiting for the world to settle.

He slipped his newly healed arm under my legs, lifting me from the snow.

"Now it's my turn to take care of you," he said.

## CHAPTER 14

## DOUBLE-STITCHED LEATHER

My eyes fluttered open.

Wooden beams? A ceiling? When had we made it to Shear? I blinked at the dark timbers framing the small room, at the firelight dancing across the walls.

The last thing I remembered was freezing cold gnawing on my bones. Now, sweat drenched my cotton shirt, and my hair stuck to the back of my neck. The scent of dust and dry wood would have been pleasant if it weren't for the stifling heat.

The shuttered window and screeching beyond told me all I needed to know.

The bed creaked as I sat up, a dull pinch drawing my attention to my arm. White bandaging hugged my skin—the work of a healer. And a good one. The pain was almost nonexistent.

Another bed stood in the opposite corner of the room. Tanja lay there, her hands laced behind her head, her nightdress hiked up to her knees in the heat. Firelight flickered against her eyes as she stared at the ceiling, a single tear streaking down her cheek.

"You could have saved him," she whispered. Her voice was dark and thick with cynicism. "You have magic."

I looked away. I could never make it right in her eyes. I healed Ropert, but I had let her father die. She would never understand the wrestle in my mind, and feathers, I would never understand it, either. If I'd used Thrall to fight off the Deathbiters, I could have killed them, too.

"I did what I could," I said.

She sat up, her unbraided hair falling across her shoulders like brown waterfalls as her hands curled into fists at her side.

Her eyes. How they burned with hatred.

"You destroyed the Leviathan Pirates. You fought off Deathbiters and a beast and lived. Why couldn't you do it again, for me? For my father?" Tears streaked down her cheeks. "Why? Tell me why you refused to save us."

"It's not . . ." I rubbed the back of my neck. "It's not that simple."

"Why not?" She pushed to her knees.

No answer I gave her would suffice. Because I didn't trust magic? That was true, but that wasn't a reason not to try. Because I didn't know how? That was partially true, but she witnessed me using magic to heal Ropert. She would think I was lying.

"Because . . . because I fear it." That was truth. I feared magic. "I am sorry for your loss, Tanja. I truly am."

She blinked at me. "You didn't use it because you were afraid?" Her voice rose in pitch. "Did you think any of us weren't afraid? He's dead, Kea. My father is *dead*. And you didn't save him because you were afraid. You're a coward."

Maybe I was. "I'm sorry, Tanja."

"Sorry won't bring him back." A fresh wave of tears surged from her eyes, dark droplets staining the white cotton stretched over her thighs. She hugged her shoulders, rocking. "I'm not ready to take over the family business. I have more to learn. I need him."

The lump in my throat grew tighter. I looked away.

There was nothing I could do for her save making sure she was taken care of. I could arrange that with Ropert. I would see that her family would have money and food for the rest of their lives. It was a small gesture but the only gesture I knew to make.

I slipped from the bed, my bare feet pattering on the wooden floorboards. "I'll be back," I whispered.

Opening the door, I slipped into the hallway. The door clicked shut, and I leaned against it, hard. The muffled conversations flowing down the hallway couldn't hide her sobs that penetrated the wood.

This had to stop. All this death and destruction had to end. Rion hadn't even completed her goal, and Roanfire suffered.

*Prince Leander.* His name rushed through my mind. Why had the White Wardent said his name? Was there more to the Tolean Prince than I thought? Perhaps it was for the best that we were heading back to Meldron.

I dragged a hand through my hair. When I'd left Meldron, King Sander had had no choice but to imprison the young Tolean Prince in an attempt to stave off war. What if there was too much bad blood to repair the damage done between us all?

Pushing from the door, I ventured down the hallway. After walking past three closed doors, I came to a small room crowded with four long tables and sleepless patrons conversing over mugs of cider. All were dressed the same as I: barefoot, unbuttoned, and untucked, trying to endure the insane heat radiating from the roaring hearth. The stench of body odor was thick.

Ropert leaned against a beam, one leg propped beside him on the bench where he was sitting. His blue eyes were focused on something distant, his lips were pressed into a tight line, and his brows were knit in a look I rarely witnessed.

He traced the rim of the mug sitting on the table in front of him, and I noticed the sleeves of his new shirt were rolled up to his elbows. Feathers, his arm looked terrible. Scarred, mottled, pink and white, deformed. No wonder he looked so sour.

He glanced up as I slipped onto the bench beside him.

"Dagger." His scowl melted into a smile as he moved his leg to make room for me. "You look well. How is your arm?"

Why was he pretending with me? He knew he could tell me anything. "What's wrong, Ropert?"

"What do you mean?"

I stole his mug to take a sip of his lukewarm cider, but the sweet and warm spices did little to combat the heat. I set the mug back on the table. I didn't dare look at him.

"I know you hate it," I said.

His brows furrowed. "Hate what?"

"Your arm. The scars. I saw you scowling."

His face darkened. "That's not what I was scowling about." He tugged the mug from my hand, tipped his head back, and drank deeply.

"Then what is it?" I asked.

He set the mug on the table, wiping his lips with the back of his hand. "It's Alder. I don't trust him, but I'm not sure what to do without him. He's proven to be invaluable on our journey."

I knew exactly what he meant. "What should we do?"

"Will you keep an eye on him for me?"

"Me?"

"I would do it if I could, but I can't. Not with all the responsibilities I have as captain." He straightened in his seat. "I need to secure passage to Kaltum, gather supplies, and send a report to King Sander. I also need to visit with Lady Ferra and ask her to replace my injured men with fresh troops from Shear. Not to mention briefing them of the new developments with the Deathbiters and Ika—I mean Marrok, all before noon tomorrow."

I hadn't realized how much weight Ropert carried. But the thought of spending my time with Alder? My skin crawled, and a shiver raced up my spine. I rubbed my arms to stave it off. "He makes me uncomfortable, Ropert."

"Just tomorrow morning until I return," he qualified.

I stole his mug again, taking a deep drink. "What do you want me to do with him?"

"Horseback riding? Archery?" Ropert shrugged, then inspiration flickered in his eyes. "I need a new shirt. Why not take him shopping? He needs warmer clothing anyway."

I couldn't agree more. It was a wonder Alder's fingers weren't black with frostbite already. Perhaps Thrall had something to do with his tolerance of cold.

"Alright," I sighed. "On two conditions."

Ropert arched an eyebrow.

"I need extra spending money. Healer Malcom needs more sprite dusts for Broderick."

"Naturally," Ropert said. "And second?"

"Will you speak to Lady Ferra about Tanja? She lost her father under our care. Her family deserves compensation with the rest of the soldiers."

"I'll see what I can do," he said.

I tipped my head back, finished the spicy drink, and slid the empty mug back to Ropert.

He gave me a crooked grin and waved to the innkeeper. "Two mugs of cider, please."

Alder's breath fogged the windowpanes of the shop, obscuring the thick black cloak on display. He wanted it. I could feel it.

The clothes hanging on his lean, tall frame were nothing more than threadbare rags. He should be shivering. He should be sick with hypothermia or worse.

Even my head ached from the bitter air hitting my temples.

"Does the cold not bother you?" I asked.

He tilted his head at me, his breath pluming under his hood. "This cold would bother anyone."

"Come on." My boots thumped against the wooden steps to the long porch stretching from shop to shop. "Try it on."

He stood in the street, unmoving. "I make do with what I have. A man who studies bats for a living can't afford quality like that."

"Courtesy of Roanfire's militia," I said. "It's the least we can do after you saved us." The words tasted like rotten apples in my mouth. *I'm doing this for Ropert.*

The smile spreading across Alder's perfect lips seemed genuine. "If you insist." He followed me up the stairs.

The delicate chime of a bell rang as I opened the door. Smells of leather and fur filled the building, mingled with a spice I couldn't identify. How long had it been since I'd stood here with Eamon and Ikane? A month? It felt like a lifetime ago.

The same woman who'd greeted us then greeted us now with her gap-toothed smile, stepping out from behind the polished wooden counter. "Good afternoon." She paused. "I remember you." Her eyes scanned me up and down, lingering on the new scars across my face. She politely refrained from commenting on them.

Alder moved to the window display, scrutinizing the thick black cloak he'd seen through the glass.

For some reason she cornered me. I wasn't the one with the ragged shroud.

"That cloak." She fingered a patched gash in the shoulder. "I don't remember selling that to you. It's seen better days."

I pushed her hand away. This cloak was a gift from Ropert. I would wear it until it was as ragged and thin as Alder's.

"We're not here for me," I said.

She turned her attention to Alder, who had pulled the black cloak from the display. His long fingers glided over the seams.

She hurried over. "You have exceptional taste, young man. Here, let me help you." She reached for the frayed knot at his throat.

Alder's hand shot up, catching her wrist. She froze, color draining from her face. "I can dress myself." His voice was low and menacing. He released her, and she stumbled back, bumping into a rack of coats.

"A-alright. I . . . I'll be over here if you need me." She rubbed her wrist and hurried past me, head down as she scurried behind her wooden counter.

Why did he do that? Melody had reacted the same way.

I grabbed his elbow, jerking him to face me. "What was that?"

"I don't like being touched," he said.

Was he threatening me or still referring to the shopkeeper? I didn't care. "What did you do to her? She's white as a sheet."

"I didn't do—"

"Don't give me that rachis. You did the same thing to Melody."

"Who?"

"The innkeeper's daughter back in Gerom Post. The apple. She went white as a sheet then avoided you until we left."

"You're overthinking this." He turned his back to me and removed his hood, his long, silver-black hair falling down his back. Dragging his old cloak from his shoulders, he handed it to me without looking.

Why was it so cold? Shouldn't some residual body heat radiate from it?

His muscles rippled beneath his thin cotton shirt as he flung the new cloak over his shoulders. Had he been wearing that the whole time? It was thinner than his cloak—his skin showed through.

Something wasn't right with this man. I wasn't overthinking anything.

He flipped his hair over his back, adjusted the padded shoulders, and pulled the hood over his face. He turned slowly. "What do you think?"

The new hood didn't hang quite as low as his old one had, revealing more of his impossibly perfect features while still shrouding his scarred eye in shadow.

I pushed his cold, shabby old cloak at him. "You look warmer."

"I was going for majestic," he said.

"More like mysterious." I grabbed a shirt from a rack for Ropert, paused, and then grabbed another. Alder needed one, too. I dropped the items on the shopkeeper's counter.

She forced another gap-toothed smile at us. "The cloak and two shirts? That'll be three silver."

A stab of annoyance struck my chest. Her prices hadn't improved. For three silver, I should be able to get two cloaks as nice as the one Alder wore plus a pair of leather trousers.

"How much are those?" I gestured to a pair of fingerless gloves sitting on a shelf behind her.

"These?" She pulled them from the shelf, hands still shaking. "Five copper. They're meant for the sailors, to help keep the rope from burning their hands. Sturdy, double-stitched leather with extra padding in the palm. They're not suitable for warmth. These here are better." She reached for another pair.

"No, I want the fingerless ones. For three silver, I'll take those, both shirts, and the cloak." I slid three coins across the tabletop.

Her eyes dashed between Alder and me as she pulled the coins to her. "Thank you for your business."

The bell rang, triggering a new pounding in my head as we stepped into the little market square.

"Here. This one is for you." I shoved one of the shirts at Alder and tucked the other into my satchel. The gloves I pushed into my cloak pockets.

"You shouldn't have," Alder said, holding up the shirt.

"Should I return it?"

He folded it across his arm. "Thank you, darling. It's nice to be appreciated."

Something cold and slithering stole up my spine. Why did he call me that? He wasn't that much older than I was. But he spoke to me like I was a child.

"Call me Kea or Lady Brendagger," I said, "but please, don't call me 'darling' again."

He gave me a respectful nod. "As you wish, Kea."

We walked down the street side by side, checking the shops lining the small market square in the center of Shear. A cobbler's sign caught my attention, then my eyes fell to Alder's soft leather boots dusted with snow. They were thin and scuffed on the toes with a hole worn in the side.

"How did you heal Ropert?" Alder asked.

I looked up, catching a glint of his silver eye beneath his new hood.

"You know what I did," I said.

"I have my suspicions. Where did you channel the heat?"

"Nowhere," I said. "Come. Let's get you some new boots."

Alder grabbed my wrist, his touch leeching warmth from my skin like ice. "Are you telling me the fire is inside you? That you didn't release it? Kea, that is dangerous. No, that is downright idiotic. You must channel it elsewhere."

I jerked my arm free, the market square spinning with the movement. What was wrong with my head?

"You see. It's affecting you already," Alder said.

"That's not it." I shut my eyes, waiting for my vision to clear. But something in me wondered if he could be right. I slipped deeper, checking the cluster of stars cocooning the fiery Deathbiter magic. It stood strong.

"Whoa." Alder caught my shoulders, holding me upright.

The buildings spun faster, and my head rolled, my legs stumbling as the sky tipped.

Alder's arms slipped under mine, holding me close to his ice-cold solid chest. What was wrong with me? Was it lingering Deathbiter venom? Ropert had changed the poultice this morning—it was healing fine.

"Are you alright?" Alder's low voice rumbled against my cheek.

Bruising pain filled my eyes. This wasn't right. This was more than Deathbiter venom. I'd felt this way before, when we'd climbed from the Deathbiters' lair. Was it Thrall? Was it Rion?

I sank into my mind.

*Yellow eyes glowered at me beneath the shade of his black hood, deep lines etching his features. The ruby hung around his neck, and red light struck under his chin, nose, and brows like the flames of a campfire. He smiled, eyeteeth white and gleaming.*

*"You cannot win." His voice cut into my mind, sharp and stinging, searching for something. Like a knife cutting across skin, it darted from one memory to another. Spinning, it arched toward the solid sphere of Etheria.*

*He was trying to break it.*

*A resounding crack echoed through my skull as his power struck the outer surface. A dark line zigzagged on the shell, and black-red heat shot from it like raven sunbeams. Another blow, and it would shatter.*

*Focus. I pulled memories of Broderick to me, his gentle coaching flickering Etheria to life. But it was taking too long.*

*"Kea? What's wrong?" Alder's voice was distant and garbled.*

*"Yes, what's wrong, little warrior? Is the pain too much?" Master echoed. Another dagger of power spun from him, launching directly at the sphere.*

*No, no, no. My focus shattered. What meager lights I'd gathered dispersed like a startled flock of birds.*

*His power hit. The sphere burst into a thousand shards of glass. Dark fire expanded. Red sparks leapt like the flares of a blacksmith's hammer. Heat burned down my throat, searing* through my chest, racing to every limb, burrowing into bone. A scream stuck in my throat.

"You are beyond help." Master laughed. "Let's end this now. Give yourself to me, and I will make the pain stop."

I wanted to run. I wanted to fight. I wanted to surrender. Anything to quench the flames. "Rion!" It was strange hearing my voice through my head again. It had become second nature with Ikane, but now, it was foreign. "Are you too much of a coward to face me? You send your old lapdog to fight your battles?"

"You dare speak to her that way?" Master growled.

Yes, I dared. I would speak to her how I pleased. Nothing she did now could be worse than the fire already burning inside me.

It didn't matter anyway. I didn't need to fight for myself—it was for my friends that I resisted. For Ikane and Broderick. For Ropert and Eamon. For Melody, Erin, Tanja, and her father. For King Sander, Queen Lonacheska, and their unborn child. I fought for every innocent life she would devour if given the chance. If I died now, I would make sure my death wasn't in vain.

Etheria winked to life like stars emerging over the black water of the sea. Each light repelled the black fire like drops of water, sizzling and steaming. They grew in size and number, knitting together like a shield. My mind steadied as the heat recoiled, folding in on itself, surrounded.

Alder was right. This fire needed to be channeled somewhere.

Master's image wavered, the red glow of the Phoenix Stone flickering like a target on his chest.

Let them deal with it.

I pulled my mental bowstring taut.

Release.

Etheria drove the writhing mass of black fire at the ruby. A thousand voices mingled with his scream. He reeled back, disappearing.

Alder stumbled against the wall of a stone building, pulling my waking body with him. He groaned as I untangled myself from his arms.

My body ached deep unlike anything I'd ever felt. This wasn't like the soreness of hours of training nor the bruising from a battle—no, this was bone-deep and dull.

I blinked. Where were we? Where was Alder taking me? We sat in an alley, surrounded by abandoned crates and barrels.

Alder sagged against the wall with gritted teeth, hugging his chest.

"Are you . . . ?" My voice sounded strange. I cleared my throat. "Are you alright?"

He rolled to his back and rested his head against the wall, revealing blue veins through the pale skin of his neck. His nostrils flared with each breath. "I felt that."

Felt what? What was he talking about?

"I felt your use of Etheria." He bowed his head, curling over his chest. "By the burning feathers of the Phoenix, you are strong. What were you doing? What happened?"

I wasn't sure I wanted to tell him. There was too much to explain, too much personal information I wasn't ready to share. But he'd be happy to know I'd listened to his advice, so I said simply, "I channeled the fire."

He looked at me, arching his head so that his good eye glinted from beneath his hood. "I won't pressure you anymore. Thrall is not for you. Your magic is Etheria." He pushed himself from the wall.

I bit my lip, unsure if I was alright with him giving up on teaching me. Thrall terrified me. It was so powerful, so violent, so overpowering. I didn't know why I hadn't used it just now. I'd summoned Etheria instead.

It was fragile and scattered, but when it surged, nothing held it back. It was reliable. I trusted it. It didn't torment me or destroy memories. In fact, I felt a sense of humble strength as strong as the temporary euphoria from Thrall.

"Let's get you back to the inn." I pulled his arm over my shoulders.

The new cloak must have been doing wonders. He felt warm.

"What happened?" Ropert watched Alder stagger past the tables and down the hallway to the back of the inn. "I told you to take care of him, not pummel him."

I pulled Ropert to a bench as my heart fluttered. For the first time in weeks, hope made my limbs feel light. I had a chance. "I used Etheria," I whispered, keeping my voice low.

His brows rose. "On him?"

"No, not on Alder. On Master . . . on Marrok's puppeteer or whatever you want to call him. I struck at Rion, too."

"How?"

I looked at his hands, taking his scarred one in mine. It was soft with new flesh, dented with scars. "The fire."

"I don't understand."

"I took your fire. I wrapped it in Etheria to keep it from burning me. Master tried to break the containment . . . well, he *did* break it, actually."

His brows furrowed, and his fingers slipped between mine, squeezing my hand. "I'm not sure I follow."

"That's alright." I smiled. "Ropert, it was Broderick's training that helped me. I wouldn't have been able to do this without him."

Ropert's smile was tinged with sorrow. "Did you get the dust for him?"

"Not yet. Will you come with me?"

He stood, releasing my hand. "I hear earthsprite dust helps with seasickness, too."

Feathers, that's right. I'd nearly forgotten how sick he got on ships.

"Oh." I pulled the fingerless gloves from my pockets. "I thought these would help protect your hand."

His face lit up. "Thank you, Dagger." He slipped his scarred hand into one, testing the movement of his fingers as he secured it to his wrist. "This is perfect."

## CHAPTER 15

# BLACK INK

"I have a new assignment for you."

Marrok lifted his head, ears shifting. Why was the voice so tight, so frail? Master typically spoke with power and authority. Something was wrong.

"Are you well, Master?" he asked.

"She is stronger than I anticipated."

"Who?" Marrok demanded. Who would do such a thing? He would tear them apart, piece by piece.

"The girl. The one you failed to kill. Twice."

Marrok's jaw tightened. How could he have let a beautiful face get to him? Twice she'd startled him, and now this? She needed to die. "I will destroy her."

"No," Master said.

What was he saying? The girl had harmed him. She deserved death.

"Not yet. I have something else in mind. Something that will deal a blow so deep, she will never recover. A new target."

Marrok listened eagerly. What could be worse than her feeling his claws sink into her skin, his teeth crushing her throat?

"He is with the man in black."

*"The healer?"*

*"No. A warrior. You know him by the name of Eamon Brendagger."*

Eamon... the name struck something deep inside, flickering a memory to life. *A bearded man sat at a table, head in his hand, holding an amber bottle. The sharp smell of stale wine struck his nose. The girl stood there, tall and slender, her long auburn hair pulled back in a soft braid down her back. She cared for this drunkard.*

Marrok shook his head, jostling the memory from his mind. He knew the target. *"What shall I do with him?"*

*"Kill him."*

My eyes flew wide to dark, stuffy heat. Prickling surged through my chest, my heart drumming wild.

Eamon.

Marrok was hunting Eamon.

I sat up, running my hands through my damp hair, glancing at Tanja who was asleep with tearstained cheeks. Even in the darkness, her swollen red eyes exposed her shattered heart. This couldn't happen to me. It wouldn't.

Climbing from the bed, I slipped from the room and down the hallway to the tavern. Just as the night before, patrons and soldiers conversed quietly around the four long tables.

Thank the Phoenix, the innkeeper was awake. She stood behind the small wooden bar, methodically wiping down bottles on a shelf.

I slipped onto one of the stools, shaking so badly I placed my hands flat on the bar to stop the trembling. "Excuse me."

She sighed, dropping her rag on the bar, unenthusiastic. "What'll it be? Ale or cider?"

"Neither. Do you have paper and a quill I could borrow?"

Her thin brows rose. "Well, now. That's not a request I get every night. I suppose I have some in the back... but you'll have to pay."

I didn't care. I just wanted her to hurry. "You can charge it to Captain Ropert Saded's tab."

She shrugged and disappeared to the back room.

My legs danced beneath the bar. What if Marrok got to Eamon before I could warn him? I rubbed my fingers, flexing them, anticipating the feel of the quill in them. They could not shake. I needed this letter to be legible. It wouldn't do Eamon any good if he couldn't read it.

The woman reappeared, sliding a cream-colored sheet of paper at me. She set a bottle of black ink and a brown feathered quill beside it. "Just so you know, the pigeon master has lost over half his birds to the Deathbiters. He's not willing to risk sending them out anymore."

Charred rachis. That was a problem. Maybe I could catch the messenger I'd hired to bring the sprite dust to Healer Malcom? If not, I would go myself, even if it meant defying the soldiers again. Feathers, Ropert would hate me.

My fingers steadied as I opened the ink, lifted the quill, and dipped it inside. Inhaling deeply, I set the tip to paper.

*Eamon,*
*The beast has been ordered to kill you.*

I cringed at the words, unable to write *his* name. His real name. Ikane.

I couldn't stop loving him, even after his betrayal. Even after leaving my heart in a thousand scattered pieces. It wasn't his fault. He'd been altered. He'd been stolen from me.

I'd connected with him in a way others would never understand. I saw his soul. He was in me and I in him, our minds linked stronger than the blood in my own veins. We shared breath and sight and smell. We shared thoughts and memories. We shared love.

I blinked at the tears blurring my vision and dipped the quill into the ink again.

*He will try to kill you, just as he tried to kill Broderick.*

*Please, be careful. You are more than a caretaker or guardian to me. You were there when no one else believed in me. You've stood by me despite everything. Watching this young merchant girl lose her father has made me realize how much you mean to me. I wish I could be there with you, protecting you.*

*I am sending windsprite dust to Healer Malcom for Broderick. Please, see that he gets it.*

*How is Broderick? Please, send word. I am eager to hear. We will be boarding a ship bound for Kaltum in the morning.*

*All my love,*
*Keatep Brendagger*

I watched the ink turn from glossy black to matte as it dried. It was all I could do until dawn.

The innkeeper gathered her quill, wiping the excess ink on her rag. "Anything to drink?"

I pushed my hair back. I might as well. "Some water, please."

She tucked her scribe supplies under the counter and ladled a cup of sage water from a bucket.

"Can't sleep?" Alder slipped onto the stool beside me, his face hidden beneath his new hood. How could he bear to wear his cloak in this stifling heat? Most of the patrons had stripped down to their cotton shirts and shifts. Even I only wore my trousers and cotton shirt, leaving my feet bare. Still, my skin was damp with perspiration.

The innkeeper slid the mug to me.

"Anything for you?" she asked Alder.

"Cider, please."

She set a mug in front of him then turned to another patron.

I sipped at my water, the subtle taste of herbs leaving a cooling sensation on my tongue. "Are you feeling any better?"

"Nothing a little rest couldn't fix. What are you writing there?" He stretched his neck to look at my paper.

I snatched it, flipping it around. This was not something I wanted to discuss with him. "Sorry. It's private."

"Aren't we friends? Don't you trust me?"

"I . . . well, yes, we are, but it's . . ."

He lifted his drink. "You think I don't see the doubt behind your eyes?"

That wasn't fair. How could he expect me to open up when he always kept his eyes hidden? I was like an open book to him, but he was a mystery. If Alder wanted me to open up, then I would expect more than a conversation with a masked face. I wasn't going to try to decipher the meaning behind each twitch of his lips or tension in his jaw. Not this time of night. "If it's trust you want, take your hood off."

He stiffened.

"Look, I get it. You may be ashamed of your scarring. I am, too, but you don't see me hiding behind a cowl."

He stared at his beverage. "Your scars are beautiful," he whispered into the mug. "They look like rose-gold sunbeams across your skin, like you've been touched by a master jeweler. The one on your neck reminds me of a rose blooming in summer."

Heat climbed to my cheeks, adding to my temperature discomfort. I had expected him to defend himself, not compliment me.

I rubbed the back of my neck. This didn't mean I was going to show him the letter. Flattery wasn't going to build trust.

He set his mug down with a sigh. "Alright." He reached up, grabbing the sides of his hood with both hands. "I thought I was doing you a favor by keeping it on, but I can see it is upsetting you."

He pulled the hood from his head, releasing his shimmering black-steel hair. His angular features boasted impossible perfection while his knit brows gave the appearance of youth and innocence. He smiled with a touch of shyness.

He was beautiful. Just like the White Wardent from my dreams. How could they not be the same person?

His eyes locked on mine—one silver and sharp like the edge of a knife, the scarred one clouded over and pale. "I won't hide anymore."

This wasn't what I'd expected. His features were too distracting, too perfect, too familiar. He was right. He had been doing me a favor by keeping his hood on. All those times I wished I could see his eyes, read his face. Now I wanted none of it and all of it at the same time.

I swallowed hard, saliva catching in my throat. "I . . ." My heart fluttered into my gut. What was wrong with me? The last time I'd felt this dangerously attracted to a man was the day I first met Ikane.

His dark hair, olive skin, and easy smile flooded into the forefront of my mind. His mismatched eyes of sapphire and emerald were like the summer sky touching lush spring fields of grass. The memory stung, biting into my heart like an animal gnawing on a fresh wound.

Any attraction I'd felt toward Alder dissolved like sand blowing away in the Tolean desert. I was not ready for this.

Pursing my lips, I looked away, tracing the long, irregular wood grains of the tavern bar until his face no longer burned behind my eyelids.

"I don't understand," Alder said. "I expose my face, and still you won't look at me."

I grabbed the letter and slipped from the stool. "I'm sorry, Alder. I shouldn't have encouraged you."

"Are you leaving?"

"Goodnight, Alder."

"Kea, wait." Alder grabbed my wrist, his grip not quite as cold as I remembered. He struggled to replace the hood with his other hand. "I don't mean to upset you. I am trying to do what's right here. Please, give me a chance."

"Don't take it personally, Alder. I have a lot on my mind."

He released me, gesturing to the bar. "I'm here as a friend. My ears are open."

How could I refuse? All he wanted was friendship. Was it reasonable to deny him that?

I sighed, returning to the bar. "Why are you trying so hard?"

He turned back to his drink. "Wouldn't you?"

Now I felt guilty again. How did he always manage to do that? I had been so consumed by my own problems to notice his loneliness.

He was odd. His hood made him strange and intimidating. His unusual beauty didn't do him any favors, either—not to mention the hood he wore in the middle of this stifling heat. And he always carried a notebook filled with sketches and notes about the Deathbiters. I had thought the whispering patrons glancing sideways at us were gossiping about me. Perhaps they were talking about Alder instead.

I set the letter on the bar, keeping it facedown. I'd offer him friendship, but that didn't mean I was ready to open up about Rion and my lineage.

"Have you discovered anything new about the Deathbiters?" I asked.

He smiled, and even with his hood on, I knew it reached his eyes. It was a smile of gratitude and relief. "Well, the damage here isn't as severe as Gerom Post. I am curious how far into Roanfire they've gone. Have they reached Kaltum? Do they hunt on the open water of Glacier Lake, or do they stick to land? If they *do* hunt on water, would they go as far as the Leviathan Isles? But most importantly, what is their agenda?"

"Will you come with us to Kaltum then?"

"If you'll have me."

As much as I didn't want to be tempted by his Thrall, I couldn't say no. "You'll have to pay your own way."

He smiled again. "I can manage."

I finished my sage water, setting the mug on the counter. "I'm going to try to get some sleep."

"Sleep well, Lady Brendagger. And thank you. You cannot imagine what your friendship means to me."

Grabbing the letter, I returned to my room. Why did I still feel so torn? I blamed Alder for keeping the White Wardent from me. His Thrall was so strong, I felt it urging my own to emerge. I needed the White Wardent now more than ever.

Was I jeopardizing my chances of speaking with him again by keeping Alder in my life?

If things went poorly, we could part ways in Kaltum. I could live with that. What harm could three days aboard a ship do?

## CHAPTER 16

# GREEN STARS

A chill bit into my cheeks as the wind snapped the sails tight. Waning sunlight sparked across the water. I clutched the railing, my legs straining for balance as the ship rocked over a swell. To the north, the Gyhro Mountains stood as sentinels, plunging their thick base into Glacier Lake. Seagulls called overhead, a sweet sound compared to the screeches of Deathbiters.

The last time I'd been on a ship, I stood beside Ikane. His dark hair blew in the wind, his stance was solid, his eyes were distant and serene as he looked to the horizon.

But the place beside me was empty.

I scrunched my eyes against the scene. He was gone. I needed to accept that.

"That won't keep you from getting seasick."

I didn't recognize the rich, feminine voice. A short, stocky woman stepped beside me, her dark, braided hair windblown and unwashed. I'd seen her embark the ship earlier. It was hard to forget the large bump on the bridge of her nose, as if she'd broken it multiple times. Even through the strong wind, the pungent spicy aroma of ginger root wafted from her. Her right cheek bulged with the spice.

"Here." She pulled a knife from her belt, slicing a portion of the knobby root in her hand. "It'll help."

"I'm not seasick."

She paused, her thick, untamed brows rising. Although her edges were rough, she had a beauty about her.

"Well, then." She spat a chewed wad of root into the water and stuffed the fresh portion into her mouth. "More for me." She tucked the remaining root into a small pouch at her waist, leaned over the railing, and spun the knife around her thumb. Sunlight flashed on the silver blade. She had skill.

"You travelin' with the Phoenix soldiers?" she asked.

I nodded.

"Including the tall man with hulking muscles?" She straightened, halting the spinning of her dagger. "You know, the one with eyes like sapphire jewels and hair like a pot of gold?"

"Ropert?"

"Is that his name?" She brushed a stray strand behind her ear. "What I wouldn't give to touch those biceps."

I chuckled. "Perhaps I can introduce you."

"Would you?" Her face brightened.

"Not this moment. He's not quite himself on ships."

"Maybe he'd like some ginger?"

"It doesn't help," I said.

The woman shrugged. "Thought I'd offer." She tucked the knife into her belt. "Tell me, are you Lady Brendagger? Destroyer of Leviathans? Hunter of Deathbiters?"

My brows rose. Those were new titles.

She smiled, showing teeth spaced a little too far apart. "It is you. I can't tell you how pleased I am to meet you. The stories are fascinating."

"They're just stories," I said.

"You deny them?"

I struggled for the right words. "They're . . . subjective."

"Well, it's an honor. Where are you headed?"

"Meldron. You?"

She shrugged. "Wherever work takes me."

"Ho, there. You two." The captain approached, his lips set in a stern line. "All passengers below. No exceptions, even if you are sick. Grab a bucket, and heave up your entrails there."

Sailors shouted to each other, scurrying up the rigging, securing sails to the mast. Orange light hung in the sky like a dying fire, the water blackening.

"We stopping?" the woman asked.

"Aye." The captain crossed his arms. "Those demon bats have claimed three of my crew already. We weigh anchor for the night, barricade in the hull, and continue our voyage in the morning."

My stomach clenched at the thought of spending another night stuck in a hot, stuffy box sour with the stench of human waste. Was it too much to ask for one night of sleep with cool, fresh air in silence and security?

"Better do as he says." The woman headed for the hatch.

I followed, the wooden stairs creaking as we made our way into the belly of the ship. Body odor and other foul smells struck before warmth tingled my face. My stomach rolled up to my throat.

"You sure you don't want any ginger?" the woman asked. "Trust me. It bites back. The smells won't be so bad."

"Perhaps a little."

She cut me a wedge. "I'm Gale, by the way. Gale Harwood. I'll be over here if you need more." She pointed to a bunk near the far wall. "Or if your friend is up for making a new acquaintance." She winked.

I stuck the fibrous root into my mouth, its earthy heat growing more intense as I chewed. She was right. The smells became secondary to the burn in my mouth.

Flickering lantern light rippled across the groaning beams as I walked to the back, finding the group of crimson tunics dispersed between our two allotted bunks. Alder sat on the floor, leaning against the curved timbers, while Ropert hunched on the edge of a bottom bunk, pale and perspiring. He forced a smile as I approached.

"You look terrible," I said.

"Thank you. You do, too," he grumbled, pushing his hair back.

I sank to the bunk beside him. "Did you take the earthsprite dust yet?"

He nodded, dragging a hand down his face.

"One third of the bottle," Alder said. "This is by far one of the worst cases of seasickness I've ever seen."

Ropert hugged his abdomen. "Two days. I can handle two days."

He didn't have a choice.

Marrok crouched to the snow-covered earth, muscles tense. Orange light radiated through the cracks of the shuttered window on the second floor. His ears turned, listening beyond the walls, and he detected the steady thump of a strong heartbeat. He knew this pulse—the heavy thud, the rhythm.

A softer pound echoed in the background. Another heart so weak it was puttering. It shouldn't be beating at all.

A black demon bat slammed into the wooden shutters, clawing at the light beaming through the cracks. Pathetic, useless creature. How would he ever complete Master's errand if they kept making such a racket?

He lowered to his haunches, tensing his muscles. Exploding upward, he swiped at the leather wings, dislodging the demon from its perch.

Scales, it got away.

The bat regained its composure in flight, screeching at him. Flattening his ears didn't help dull the sound.

"Ikane?"

His head snapped up, eyes scanning up and down the deserted street. Who had said that? He hadn't heard it with his ears. The voice had been in his head, but it wasn't Master nor the Phoenix Goddess, should he ever find favor to have her speak to him.

He sank to the snow.

"Ikane? Can you hear me?"

Her voice was too sweet, too concerned, too hopeful.

He clawed at his ears. He wanted her out. He wanted everyone out of his head. Was it so hard to give him the privacy of his own thoughts?

And why did she keep calling him Ikane? He was Marrok. He was bred for destruction and violence, created by Master to serve him.

Wait. By the horns of the Leviathan, he knew that voice. The girl. The one who'd assaulted Master. The one who stabbed him in the stomach when he was . . . when he was . . . He shook his head, and released a growl, feeling it rumble through his chest and throat. Why couldn't he remember?

His claws dug into the snow, finding the cobblestone beneath. What did it matter? She was the enemy.

"You will suffer," his mind shot to her.

"Don't do it, Ikane. This isn't who you are."

Who was she to say who he was? "Get out of my head!"

Silence. Was that it? Was she gone?

"Look at the stars, Ikane," she whispered.

Unwilling, his eyes turned upward to the black night, and glittering stars winked at him between the frantic, leathery fluttering of bats.

How could she know . . . ?

"Get away from him!" Master bellowed.

The dream dissolved, my mind waking to the stuffy confines of the ship. I was wedged in the bottom bunk, sleeping in the rancid hull with two dozen other passengers.

A Deathbiter screamed outside, the sound enhanced by the open water.

I'd reached him. He'd heard me.

My heart raced—not with adrenaline, but hope. Perhaps Ikane wasn't lost? Our connection wasn't as strong as it had been, but our minds shared a bond.

*And he'd heard me.*

Now if only I could figure out how I did it.

Sailors pushed the hatch open, and morning light spilled down the wooden stairs, beckoning us from the stuffy hull. A soft touch of blessed fresh air teased my nose.

Ropert stirred as crew and passengers funneled through the hatch. I rolled from the bunk, ready to feel the wind on my face.

Hope burned through my chest. If I dreamed of Ikane tonight, what would I say?

The bunk creaked as Ropert rolled his head over the edge, looking at me from a comical upside-down position. His cropped hair stood wild, and his fire-red stubble brightened his face. His eyes shone.

I smiled. "Looks like you slept well."

"Looks like you did, too. You haven't slept like this since . . . I can't remember when." He grabbed the underside of the bunk, slipped his body over the edge, and flipped. His feet landed on the floor with a thud. Tossing his hair back, he grinned. "It's been forever since I've done that."

I rolled from the bottom bunk. How I missed this. It was just like Daram—sleeping in the barracks, waking for the morning drills. He'd always emerged from his bunk like that.

"I think the earthdust is working." He stretched, his hands pressing against the beam above his head. "I feel well enough to spar this morning." He dropped his hands, rolling his shoulders. "What do you say? Shall we try out the new gloves?"

I grabbed my belt and sword from the foot of the bed. I wouldn't say no to a sparring session.

"I have some good news, too," I said.

Ropert reached for his broadsword, but his hand froze before gripping the hilt. "Oh, no." He dropped his forehead against the bunk's thin mattress. The warm pink color in his cheeks vanished, leaving sickly blue crescents under his eyes. He clutched his stomach. "Not again."

I rummaged through his bag at the foot of the bunk, finding the small green vial in a side pocket. Flaming feathers, Alder wasn't kidding. It was half-gone.

The cork was pushed tight, making the vial difficult to open.

"Hurry, Dagger," Ropert groaned.

It popped, the cork flying from my fingers, and precious green dust spilled onto my hand. I paused. A soft caress like a blanket of sun-warmed soil in a garden bed ran up my arm. I gazed at my hand.

The webbing between my thumb and forefinger shimmered green, flickering with emerald stars like Ikane's glowing eye. I brushed my hand against my trousers, but the dust didn't budge. The scars had soaked it up.

Ropert bolted up the stairs, and passengers grumbled in his wake. His heavy footfalls thumped across the deck, stopping at the railing before I heard the faint noise of heaving.

"You've been touched by a sprite." Alder stepped up beside me.

I wished I could read his eyes, but the last thing I wanted was for him to unveil his face. The unnerving set of his jaw and the pull on the corner of his lips was enough for now. He wasn't happy about this.

I rubbed my hand against my trousers again, but the dust remained embedded in my skin.

"Why didn't you tell me?" His voice held a tinge of hurt.

"I thought they were just scars."

"What more must I do to earn your trust?"

"This has nothing to do with trust," I said.

"It has everything to do with it. I've done nothing but help you," he said. "You owe me."

My fist curled around the vial of green dust. Owed him? "We didn't ask for your help."

"Should I have let you destroy yourself in Glacier Pass? Let Thrall tear you apart from the inside out? Should I have let the Deathbiters devour your cowering cluster of Phoenix soldiers? You think buying me a cloak is enough?" His voice grew louder, and pressure bore down on my ears as a feeling of blackness pushed against my mind. Thrall.

"That's not . . . ugh! Flaming feathers, Alder. What more do you want?" My voice rose to match his. My own Thrall expanded, eager and starved. It grabbed hold of my frustration, egging it on like it wasn't quite ripe for consuming.

This wasn't good. I couldn't afford to lose control. But more words left my lips before I could stop them.

"If it's friendship and trust you want, constantly using the Deathbiters against me is not going to help."

"Let the lady be." A nasally voice cut into our fight.

The Thrall inside me panicked as my mind shifted to the stocky woman from the night before currently standing behind Alder. Light flashed against her silver blade, her fingers nimble and precise as she worked delicate skin off the ginger root in her hand. There was no mistaking the warning in her posture.

Alder tipped his head, making little effort to look at the woman. "This is none of your concern."

"I make it my concern when a lady looks as terrified as she does," she said.

I swallowed hard, trying to compose myself. The last thing I wanted was to appear fragile and scared.

The pressure from Alder dissipated. I gathered breath, focusing on the way it filled my lungs, pushing my own Thrall back into the corners of my mind. The woman couldn't know how grateful I was. Not because she stood up to Alder—I could handle him—but for reminding me that I was not alone, for helping me push the magic back.

Alder straightened. "We'll talk later." He turned on his heel and marched up the stairs.

I didn't understand. He pushed his way into helping us, making it seem like it was out of the goodness of his heart. But now he wanted compensation? Did he really just want my friendship, or did he want more?

"Flaming feathers." Gale pressed her shoulder against mine, eyeing Alder. "He may be a bold ruffian, but Phoenix feathers, he's a stunning specimen. What is your secret?"

I swallowed hard.

"Hey, now." She took my arm like we had been friends for months instead of hours. "Are you alright?"

"I'll be fine. I . . . I'm sorry you had to see that." I glanced at the vial of sprite dust in my hand, trying not to focus on the green stars embedded in my skin. "I need to get this to my friend."

"You mean the blue-eyed god? By all means." She moved aside. "Talk later?"

I nodded, turned, and climbed the stairs, all tension melting as crisp clean air caressed my face and sunlight warmed my skin.

Alder stood to my right, gaze fixed on the water, his black cloak snapping in the wind. Ropert hung over the railing on my left, clutching the banister with white knuckles as the ship rocked.

He looked up as I approached, his brows furrowed in miserable discomfort. Wet stains of bile and last night's supper coursed down the front of his new shirt, and a smattering of vomit lay on the deck beside him. He took the vial of sprite dust, put it to his mouth, and poured a glittering heap onto his tongue.

He swallowed. "So help me, I'm never setting foot on a ship again."

Ropert and I had an audience for the same pleasant distraction I had once shared with Ikane.

My muscles burned. Beads of sweat slipped down the length of my spine. My sword striking, grinding, and whipping across my body roused forgotten energy.

Ropert's muscles rippled with each stroke of his sword, and his bare chest glistened in the noonday sunlight. The mottled pink scars running up his arm stood out like dents in polished armor. If only I'd healed him sooner, braved the magic, maybe it wouldn't have traveled so far to his shoulder.

He wore one fingerless glove, protecting the fragile skin on his hand, but it didn't hinder his strokes one bit. They surged up my shoulders, jarring my teeth. My arms needed a reprieve.

A thick rope swayed in the wind, sparking an idea.

Deflecting Ropert's blow, I leapt onto the banister, grabbing hold of the rope. I coiled it around my arm, tightened my grip, and pushed off.

*Feathers.*

My body dropped. The solid thump of my buttocks hitting the deck jarred my spine. A triangular sail shot up one of the forestays as the heavy rope rolled down in a long line, falling on my head and shoulders.

A wave of laughter erupted from our audience, the loudest coming from Ropert. Why did I have to try something that idiotic? I knew nothing about ships.

Ropert untangled the rope from my shoulders, still laughing. "What was that?"

My face burned, probably going three shades of red. "I saw Ikane do it once."

Ropert extended a hand. "Did he land on his rump, too?"

I chuckled as he pulled me to my feet. "No. I did."

He laughed again, throwing his head back. "You never told me about that."

"Why would I? It was as embarrassing as this." I rubbed the sore spot on my posterior.

"Again?" Ropert asked.

"I think I'm done for the day." I slid my sword into the sheath at my hip. Ropert followed suit as the crowd silently dispersed.

Our boots thumped across the deck as we walked to the water barrel sitting near the captain's cabin.

Ropert grabbed the ladle, dunking it into the clear water. "What's going on with you, Dagger?" he asked. "Something is different about you. Did you take some of Broderick's tonic again?"

"What do you mean?"

"You're smiling a lot today."

My smile grew bigger. "I had a dream last night."

Ropert arched an eyebrow. "And that's good news?"

That statement touched me in a way he couldn't imagine. He knew how terrifying my dreams were. But this time was different. "I spoke with Ikane."

Ropert's brows furrowed. "But I thought you said—"

"I know what I said. I was wrong. At least, I hope I am."

"I'm not following." Ropert lifted the spoon, drinking deeply, water trickling down his chin and onto his bare chest.

"In my dream, I could speak with Ikane . . . or Marrok. It didn't seem like a dream at all, though. It was like . . . like it used to be, when we were linked in our minds. When he was a wolf. I heard his thoughts. At first, I thought he was too far gone. But when I told him to look at the stars, something in him shifted. He remembers, Ropert. I think I can bring him back."

Ropert lowered the ladle, but his eyes didn't light up as I'd expected. Had he heard me?

"Ropert?"

He rubbed the back of his neck.

"What is it?" I asked.

"I don't know what to say, Dagger. The last thing I saw was a wolf-hybrid creature tearing into Broderick. You just sent a warning to Eamon that Marrok was hunting him. He's being controlled by Rion and a hooded old man, but we don't know where they are. I just . . . I think we need to let go."

I felt my smile melt from my face, my sword suddenly three times as heavy against my hip. I thought he'd be happy.

"What do you want me to do, Dagger? Go back?" Ropert cringed. "We can't. I've been ordered to bring you back to Meldron. Don't make me chose between helping you and doing what I've been ordered to do again. I can't keep doing this."

I hugged my shoulders. "I understand." Feathers, he was right. And if Yotherna's clue about the Tolean Prince was anything, I had to stay the course.

"Eamon will be fine," Ropert said as he replaced the ladle on the rain barrel.

My throat tightened, and my heart suddenly felt heavy like it was beating through mud. "It's not Eamon I'm worried about. What if . . . what if Eamon kills Ikane before I get the chance to try?"

Ropert took my hand, his skin damp and warm. "Dagger." His blue eyes claimed my full attention, deep pools of summer sky. "You reached him in your dream last night, right? Do you think you can reach him again?"

"I . . . I'm not sure. It's never happened before."

He squeezed my hand with his scarred one, drawing my attention to it. "I believe in you."

I searched his eyes and saw a burning resolve staring back at me, sharp and pure. The pressure in my chest eased, and the sluggish feeling of mud around my heart shriveled, cracked, and flaked away. His confidence was infectious.

"That was quite a performance." Gale interrupted our conversation.

Ropert dropped my hand.

"Grabbing that rope was unfortunate but oh so entertaining." She winked at me.

"I won't be making that mistake again," I said. "Gale, I'd like you to meet Captain Ropert Saded."

Gale extended her hand to Ropert. His hand engulfed hers.

"You must be feeling better," she said, her eyes falling to his bare chest. "It was a pleasure to watch you in action."

Ropert dropped her hand, suddenly looking uneasy. His bright blue eyes flashed to me, pleading for help. I chuckled. My poor Ropert. When wouldn't he become tongue-tied around women?

"Gale gets seasick, too," I offered.

"Hence my perfume of ginger," she added.

"You know each other?" Ropert asked.

"We met last night." Gale slipped her arm though mine. "But we may as well have known each other for years. Where will you be staying in Kaltum? Perhaps we can share a room."

"There's an inn near the docks called the Drowsy Dreamer," I said. "Don't let the outside fool you. The interior is quite homely."

"Excellent." Gale released me. "Then we can chat about the transaction between Lady Brendagger and the devastatingly beautiful cloaked man this morning. Didn't take you for someone to stand for bullying."

"Bullying?" Ropert's brows narrowed. "What are you talking about?"

"The hooded man had Lady Brendagger cornered," Gale said.

Ropert rounded on me. "He *what*?"

"It was nothing I couldn't handle."

Gale turned to Ropert. "He only let her go after I stepped in."

Ropert's fists clenched as the rippling muscles throughout his body became more defined, and his eyes turned to storms as he scanned the deck. "Where is he?"

"Excuse us," I said to Gale, grabbing Ropert's arm and steering him away. "I have it under control."

"Alder is always pushing your boundaries, Dagger. Broderick saw it. I see it, too. He needs to be put in his place. I'm more than happy to pummel him for you."

"I can do my own pummeling," I said.

I glanced over my shoulder, making certain we were alone. Gale stepped to the railing, spat her old piece of ginger into the water, and slipped a new wedge into her mouth.

"This was what Alder was upset about." I pinched my leather glove, pulling it from my hand. Glowing green specks of sprite dust winked at him.

His eyes widened. "What in the . . . ?"

I tugged the glove back on. "I'll tell you everything, but not here."

"Let me grab my shirt," he said. "I'll meet you at the stern."

I rolled onto my side. The wooden bunk alone would've been more comfortable than the lumpy straw mattress. I bunched up my cloak, trying to find a comfortable position for my head. It was hopeless.

The ship groaned and creaked, sitting dead in the water. Passengers coughed, snored, and whimpered. The retching sound of someone emptying their bowels was just another addition to the horrendous screeches piercing the hull. Perhaps it was my imagination, but the Deathbiters didn't sound as numerous as the night before.

"Can't sleep?" Alder's deep voice rushed through my chest.

I opened my eyes. Nearby lantern light swayed across Alder's form as he lay in the bottom bunk across the way. He stared at the bunk above him, the profile of his face beautiful and unblemished. His hands were laced over his abdomen.

"I can't, either," he said. He rolled to face me, his stunning silver eyes glinting. Somehow, his scarred eye didn't seem so disfiguring. "I apologize for this morning. I realize I may have come across as judgmental."

That was an understatement, but I nodded, accepting his apology.

His fingers toyed with the edge of his pillow. "I need you to understand why I reacted the way I did. Elemental dusts can be dangerous."

"I'm listening," I said.

"Will you please tell me about your hands? Why is the dust embedding itself?"

"I don't know," I said. "A firesprite gave me a gift awhile back. She burned firedust into my hands. She said it would come to my aid when I most needed it. And it did." I stared at my hand, rubbing the glowing green flecks on the webbing between my fingers. It reminded me so much of Ikane's eye. "When the Deathbiters first attacked, the firedust expanded. It spared my life. Since then, I've had nothing but dull gray flecks there."

"And you haven't touched sprite dust since?" he asked.

I bit my lip. "Once. I washed my hands in water infused with firesprite dust. Nothing happened then."

He propped himself up on one elbow, his rippling black hair falling across his shoulder. "Would you be willing to try an experiment?"

I made a fist, suffocating the green glow, glowering at the gorgeous man across the way. "You have yet to tell me why you were so angry."

"Fair enough." He lay back on his side. "Did you know that blending all four elemental dusts can cause explosions?"

I nodded. It was Broderick's hobby.

"Well, it was an explosion that did this to me." He lowered his eyes, brushing a fingertip across the scarred space where his brow should have been. "I am worried for you, Kea. You must be careful handling sprite dusts. If you get all four on your hands . . ."

I opened my palm, staring at the green stars. "But why didn't the firedust sink into my skin before?" I asked.

"I have a theory," Alder said. "I believe it must be pure dust. You said the water was infused with firedust. Therefore, it didn't embed itself into your skin. Or it could be since you've already used it that firedust doesn't have an effect."

"And you want to test that theory?" I asked.

"It's the only way to be sure."

"But if it does embed itself?"

"That is a risk," he said.

That would mean I'd have two of the four dusts embedded in my skin. There had to be a way to release the dust already there. The firedust came out—the earthdust should, too.

I tucked my hand under my chin. "Perhaps another time." I didn't want to risk it, not until I understood what was happening.

Alder rolled onto his back. "As you wish. Just take caution, Lady Brendagger. I'd hate to see you lose your hands over something that could have been avoided."

I swallowed. I'd have to wear my gloves more often.

## CHAPTER 17

# HE CHANGED MY LIFE

His thighs ached. Crouching in the shadow of a few crates for the past three hours with his muscles locked was not the way he'd planned to spend his evening. He'd listened to conversations inside the building, watching men and women come and go, picking up scents he wished he hadn't.

The sky shifted from pale light to violet. The Deathbiters would be out soon, and their noises would fill the sky, making his task impossible.

Why was it so hard to get anything done? Master deserved revenge.

A dull crunch made his ears perk, the sound of someone walking through the snow. A bearded man, bundled to his ears in furs and leathers, hurried toward the inn. He opened the door, and warmth and light spilled onto the snow, voices greeting him as he stepped inside.

"I have an urgent message for Eamon Brendagger. Is he here?" The door creaked shut.

A message? From whom?

Marrok slinked closer, muscles prickling. This was important; Master would want to know. He strained to pick out *the voice among dozens of conversations inside, the sounds muted through the thick timbers, stone, and plaster.*

*"I've got three candles at home. I can bring them . . ."*

*Wrong conversation. He moved to the next.*

*"Darling, you should try to get some . . ."*

*He snorted.*

*"Don't think I haven't forgotten. You said you'd pay . . ."*

*Wrong discussion again. Where was he? Where was the messenger?*

*"They said you have a message for me?"*

*Marrok settled against the wall. This was it.*

*A crisp rustle paused the conversation, paper unfolding followed by glass chinks. Scales, he couldn't read through walls. Come on, say something. Read it aloud.*

*Other conversations buzzed in his ears as he strained to stay connected.*

*"What is it?" a gentle, melodic voice asked. It was Melody. The voices in the tavern changed from day to day, but hers was a constant.*

*"It's from Kea," Eamon said.*

*The name struck him hard. The girl. The one who'd assaulted Master. His fingers tingled, itching to cleave into her flesh. Why did he think of her so much? He saw her face, brows narrowed, stormy blue eyes daring him to fight. His wrist still smarted where her sword struck him. She was in his head. She told him to look at the stars.*

*Marrok's eyes turned skyward, but the heavens were still too bright to reveal the winking lights.*

*"What does she say?" Melody asked.*

*"It's not good. Ikane is hunting me now," Eamon sighed.*

*There was that name again. Ikane. Why did they call him that?*

*"I'll take the sprite dust to Healer Malcom," Melody said, her soft footfalls fading to the other end of the inn.*

*Black water and scales, she'd warned him. Now he'd lost the element of surprise.*

*No matter. He had strength and speed on his side. He was a creature born of magic and power. He was a being parallel to the guardians of Roanfire. Even if Eamon called every soldier in this pitiful city to protect him, Marrok would rend every one of them to shreds to avenge Master.*

Water lapped against the hull as our ship slid into Kaltum's marina, lurching as it bumped against the dock. I staggered into the railing.

Ikane wouldn't have stumbled. He would have stood as firm as a mountain, his hair flowing in the breeze, his face serene and full of wild energy from the water.

I closed my eyes, savoring the touch of sunlight on my skin, trying to ignore the ache in my chest. At least my warning had reached Eamon in time. But I still wished I could have told him more. That Ikane was still there somewhere, trapped in that horrendous creature's body.

Ropert's boot tapped anxiously on deck as the gangplank dropped against the nearest pier, his face growing paler by the second. He'd run out of earthsprite dust hours ago.

"I need to make an appearance at Kaltum keep after we get settled at the inn," he said. "Lord Everguard needs to sign off on supplying us with horses for the next leg of our journey."

"May I come with you?" I asked.

Ropert didn't miss my wary glance at Alder who stood at the bow, his hood hiding his face again.

"Wouldn't have it any other way," he said. "Now, if only these people would move."

Merchants and other travelers filed off the ship, boots thumping hollowly on wood as they merged with the crowds on the docks. Seagulls soared overhead, and sunlight lanced off their black-tipped wings like polished swords.

I pulled my bag over my shoulder. "Come on. Let's get you off this ship before you lose your breakfast."

"Freya?" A man's voice rose from the crowd below.

"Freya! Over here!"

A hand waved above the masses, one attached to a young man with a blue bandanna tied over his dark hair.

Was he looking at me?

I glanced over my shoulder to find Alder and three of Ropert's soldiers. Who was Freya?

The young sailor elbowed his way through a cluster of people.

"Do you know that man?" Ropert whispered.

Something was familiar about his long, dark hair, the stubble on his chin, and his worn shirt and trousers, but I couldn't place it.

I shook my head.

The young man stopped short of embracing me, grinning as if we were lifelong friends. "It is so good to see you. Is Eamon with you?" He craned his neck, searching over my head.

"Who are you?" I asked.

"Come, now. You really don't remember me?" He set his hands on his hips, tilting his head, his bottom lip protruding in a pout. "We shared a meal together at the Drowsy Dreamer. I sported a few new bruises that night from your old man."

The Drowsy Dreamer? The inn? Recognition flickered. How could I have forgotten? Eamon had taken on three rowdy young dockworkers here, besting all of them with his bare hands, and then invited them to eat supper. Eamon had given me the alias of Freya. But for the life of me, I couldn't remember Bandanna Boy's name.

"You do remember." I didn't think his grin could get any wider. "Please, tell me Eamon is with you. Wouldn't you know it? I was promoted to mate. I'm working as an apprentice to the Sailing Master now. All because Eamon saw something in me. He changed my life."

I gave him a sad smile. He couldn't know how much I wanted Eamon here myself. "I'm afraid not."

His smile faded a little. "You'll tell him for me, then? Let him know what he did for me? At this rate, I'll have my own ship and crew in three years."

"I will."

He scanned my face. "I don't mean to be rude, but you've changed."

I pursed my lips, trying not to look away. The scars.

"I like it. Makes you look intimidating. Wouldn't have tried harassing you with my dock mates if you'd had those scars then."

Great. That made me feel better.

Bandanna Boy perked up, looking to the ship on our right. "Work calls. It was good to see you again, Freya." He jogged down the pier.

"Wait. Remind me of your name again," I called after him.

"Rowan," he called back.

I watched him go.

Eamon had done it again, changed the life of a young man much like Ikane.

I needed to get through to Marrok tonight. I needed to convince him we were not the enemy.

"Freya?" Ropert asked, raising an eyebrow.

"It's a long story."

Ropert pushed his goldenberry hair from his face. "I guess you'll have to tell me. *After* we get settled at the inn. I need to sleep off the rolling in my stomach before we meet with Lord Everguard."

"Do I have time for a bath first?" I asked.

Ropert chuckled. "I'm sure that can be arranged."

There was nothing better than a hot bath and a nap after a gruesome two nights aboard a stuffy ship.

## CHAPTER 18

# KALTUM KEEP

The sun sat high, deep shadows concealing his black fur in the alleyway. He peered around the corner, watching unsuspecting people bustle in and out of the tavern, tantalizing smells and laughter spilling into the snowy street every time the door opened. Too many heartbeats throbbed inside, muddling his focus.

This was the second night he'd cowered in the alley, waiting for the man to leave the tavern and expose himself. Adrenaline sparked again when a broad-shouldered figure stepped from the building, laughing and stumbling down the three small steps. His smell was wrong, too full of mead, and his heartbeat was off.

Marrok slouched against the wall, sinking to his haunches. He dragged one of his massive hands down his face, his fur bristling as he stroked against its natural direction.

What if he launched through the door and tore through the bodies inside? What if he took them all out? What if he destroyed every one of those annoying throbbing heartbeats? Surely Master would approve.

He heard the door creak open again, but he didn't bother to look. It would be just another patron, just another annoying heartbeat hiding his true target.

*What was Master thinking? Why was this man a danger? Even the black-clad man he'd attacked had done no harm.*

*It was the girl that posed the threat.*

*He shook his head. It wasn't his responsibility to wonder. It was his job to do Master's bidding.*

*The warm smell of steel struck his nose. His head jerked up, recognizing the leather-like undertone.* He scrambled on all fours, peering around the corner of the building, spotting the broad shoulders covered by a warm cloak and a graying warrior's tail hanging down the man's back.

Eamon Brendagger.

The smile creeping across his wolf-lips felt unnatural.

The tavern door closed, and Eamon shrugged his cloak higher, scanning the sparsely populated street.

*Just one powerful lunge. That's all he needed. Then his teeth could clamp down and pierce the throbbing veins in Eamon's throat. His heart threatened to burst from his chest if he didn't move.*

Eamon turned his back to Marrok, walking the wrong way. A low growl escaped Marrok's throat. *He was so close.*

He darted back into the alley, sprinting behind the tavern, peering down the next lane. On the other end, Eamon walked past.

Marrok sprinted behind the neighboring building, leaping silently over discarded crates and barrels. This next alleyway was narrower, but it didn't keep him from dashing to the end. He stopped, sinking into the shadows.

Eamon's boots crunched in the snow, drawing nearer.

*Any moment now.*

Marrok crouched, his toes tight, his calves coiled, his thighs trembling in anticipation. He could already smell iron.

The distinct sound of metal hinges grinding echoed through the street.

*No, no, no.*

"Eamon," an unfamiliar voice said. "I'm glad you came. I have what you ordered."

*Marrok peered around the corner, catching the last of Eamon's cloak slipping into the building. The door clicked shut.*

*Growling, he threw his head back, striking the wall hard. Plaster broke and crumbled down his spine.*

*He'd failed Master again.*

My heart thundered in my chest, threatening to burst.

Marrok could have killed Eamon ... and I was helpless to do anything but watch.

Why couldn't I get through to him? How could I control these dreams? *Were* they even dreams? It was like I slipped into Ikane's mind, feeling everything he did, hearing his thoughts, moving as if I were him. It was terrifying and exhilarating. His power and strength were beyond anything I'd ever felt. He could scale the tallest of castle walls if he wanted to without working up a sweat.

I licked my lips, finding my mouth dry and sticky, blinking at the thick beams across the ceiling and cracked patches of white plaster in the walls. And I'd left Eamon to face him alone?

Sitting up, I ran my fingers through my hair. It was still damp from my bath. I couldn't have been asleep for more than half an hour. And it would have taken Marrok seconds to tear Eamon apart.

I needed to get back to Gerom Post.

Snatching my boots from the floor, I stuffed my foot into one. The other followed more slowly.

I couldn't. I couldn't do that to Ropert, not again. And the White Wardent. He said ... he said something about the Tolean Prince. If I went back now, I'd lose this opportunity. I'd lose any hope of finding the answer to defeating Rion.

I buried my face in my hands. What was I to do?

*Knock, knock.* "Dagger?"

I straightened. "Come in."

Ropert stuck his head in the door. He looked well—color had returned to his cheeks. A golden lock near his brow stuck up at an odd angle from sleep. "Are you ready?" he asked.

I stood, grabbing my sword belt, swinging it around my waist. "Ready."

"Uh . . . shouldn't you change into a dress or something?"

My fingers stopped mid-buckle. "What?"

"We are meeting with Lord Everguard, a highly respected man and an aristocrat. You are Lady Brendagger. Is it proper for you to dress like . . . ?" He gestured to my cream cotton shirt and brown trousers.

I grabbed my cloak from the foot of the bed. "It's not a noble gathering, Ropert. We are petitioning him for horses and supplies. Besides, I didn't pack a dress. Did you?"

He gave me his best crooked smile. "What if I did?"

"I wouldn't hold that against you." I shrugged my cloak over my shoulders. "Come on. You don't want to be late."

Kaltum keep dominated an entire stretch of the market square's border. Two soldiers wearing Kaltum's earthy-green uniform flanked the wrought iron gates set into the crenelated stone wall. Sunlight danced on the corbeled corner turrets hugging nearly every bend and angle of the inner keep. A single tower soared behind them, acting both as a lookout post and a lighthouse for the ships on the lake. A timber-framed building sat beside it, an air of warmth and homeliness radiating from its softer edges.

The soldiers on duty straightened as Ropert and I approached.

"What business have you at Kaltum keep?" one of them asked.

"Don't you recognize Captain Saded from Meldron? And the famed Lady Brendagger?" A middle-aged woman with a long mane of thick black curls appeared. Her tailored green uniform suited her feminine yet aggressive features. My brows rose at the impressive number of medals and emblems decorating her shoulders and chest.

She stood stiff, her dark eyes calculating, her thin lips pressed into a tight line. "They have urgent military business to discuss with Lord Everguard," she said. "He's expecting them."

"Of course." The guard quickly opened the gate.

The woman tipped her head to us in greeting. "I am Commander Durianna. Please, follow me."

We stepped into the inner courtyard. My heart raced seeing the soldiers training in the square, dozens locked in swordplay. How I missed my simple life as a soldier.

Artillery dominated the far wall. An archery range stood to the right, a large weapons hut on the left.

Durianna led us to the timber-framed building beside the tower, urged us through a heavy wooden door, and guided us up two flights of stairs and down a corridor lined with tapestries and iron sconces flickering with firelight. She knocked on a door with light glowing beneath the wooden frame. The welcoming crackle of a fire echoed beyond.

"Enter." The voice sounded distracted.

Durianna opened the door, warmth spilling into the hallway. The smell of warm dust flowed with it. She urged us inside.

A blazing hearth roared beside a heavy wooden desk sitting in the center of the room. Papers, scrolls, candles, and feathered quills cluttered the surface, but not without organization.

"Durianna. Is this document correct?" The young nobleman sitting behind the desk didn't look up. His soft brown curls hung over his brow as he tipped a document with a black seal to the candlelight. "Were there seven more infected last night? What about the others who . . . ?" His eyes lifted from the paper, widening as they took us in.

"Lady Brendagger. Sir Ropert." Dietrich dropped the report and pushed his chair back. "I have been looking forward to your visit. Please, come in." He waved to two cushioned chairs sitting on the other side of his desk.

"We are not here for pleasure," Ropert said.

"Yes, yes. You need horses and supplies for your journey back to Meldron," Dietrich said. "Commander Durianna. Will you please see to that? And send someone to fetch refreshments." He turned back to us. "I'm sure you can spare some time for a brief visit." He stepped around the desk, taking my hand, pressing his lips against my gloved knuckles. "It is such a pleasure to see you again, Lady Brendagger."

"And you," I replied. This man wasn't easily forgotten. He had been the only young, eligible nobleman not attempting to win my affections with flattery at King Sander's wedding. He was energetic and passionate, speaking only of Kaltum and its rustic beauty. He earnestly wanted me to see it. "I'll never forget your enthusiasm for the thunderstorms over Glacier Lake."

His face brightened. "You should return in the summer when they are most intense. The air grows rich with energy, crisp and bright."

"I'd like that," I said. But would I ever have that chance? If I did wed the Tolean Prince, I might never see Roanfire again.

His brown eyes openly scanned my face, and my smile faded. He was looking at my scars, wonder and confusion growing behind his eyes. He shook his head.

"Forgive me, but are those Deathbiter injuries?" he asked.

"They are."

"But . . . how? There is no cure. Fifty-eight of my people are infected with raging fevers as we speak. Seven more as of last night. They are dying by the dozens."

"There are—"

"We know someone who can help." Ropert cut me off. "His name is Alder Grayhorn. He's staying at the Drowsy Dreamer with us. He drew the poison from my soldiers. With the proper incentive, I'm sure he can be persuaded to help."

"I must meet with him," Dietrich said. "I will pay whatever he asks."

I eyed Ropert. Alder? Alder may be powerful, but he couldn't draw the poison from so many on his own. Why didn't he just give the remedy of sprite dusts Malcom had invented? "There is another—"

Ropert cleared his throat, his blue eyes growing sharp with warning.

What was wrong with him? People were dying, suffering. Whatever he was trying to do, I was not going to see innocent people die because of it. "A healer in Gerom Post discovered another remedy. His name is Malcom. He's shared this remedy with a healer in Shear as well. You could contact him for more information."

Ropert's jaw tightened.

But Dietrich's smile grew. "Phoenix bless you both. The hope you bring is invaluable. What more have you learned from the Deathbiters? I could use some insight on how to fend them off in our city."

"Alder may help with that as well," Ropert said. "He studies bats for a living. And he's taken a special interest in the Deathbiters."

"This Alder sounds like the answer to our problems."

Three harsh knocks sounded on the door like they came from a boot rather than knuckles.

"Come in," Dietrich called.

"Young man." An elderly woman's muffled voice came from behind the thick wood. "My hands are full, and I'm nearly as blind as a bat. Unless you want your refreshments to grace the floor of this cold hallway, I suggest you get your attractive little backside out of your seat and open the door for me."

Ropert and I exchanged looks.

"Alright, alright." Dietrich laughed and pushed himself from the desk. "Pardon my new cook. She can be a bit headstrong, but her cuisine is so magnificent, I would let her ream me for hours just to lick her ladle."

He pulled the door open, allowing a short, plump woman to enter. She squinted at the desk. "This is what you get for giving all my aides the day—"

"Mayama!" Ropert and I shouted simultaneously.

My arms flew around her. She smelled of onion, garlic, and sage. Her skin was soft, her plump figure warm and familiar.

"Heavens," Mayama said.

Dietrich took the tray from her startled hands as Ropert wrapped us both in his arms.

"What in the name of the Phoenix is going on?" She grunted under the pressure.

Ropert released us, but I wasn't ready to let go. Not yet. She smelled of home, of love, of freedom. She had been the mother to the soldiers, the backbone of our militia, the heart of Daram.

I clung to her, burying my face against her soft shoulder. "Mayama." My voice felt fragile, like it would crack and give way permanently. How long had it been? Months? Years? When had I seen her last—was it hiding in the woods with her sister, Faslight?

"Kea?" Her arms slowly wrapped around me. "Is that you, sweet pea?"

"Yes, Mayama." I sobbed. "It's me. It's me."

She stroked my hair. "And is that tall, hulking beast my Ropert?"

He chuckled. "We've missed you, Maya."

I sniffed, managing to pry my arms off her.

She cupped my face in her hands, her thumbs gently wiping the tears from my cheeks. Her eyes, once dark and piercing, looked clouded and pale. She squinted, her round cheeks making her eyes little slits. "Oh, how beautiful you are."

I almost began weeping anew. She was safe and healthy and in good hands with Lord Everguard. I couldn't have asked for anything better for her.

"I take it you know each other," Dietrich said.

Mayama took my hands, steering me to the cushioned chairs. "Tell me what happened, sweet pea. The truth. I've heard so many rumors after the war with the Leviathan Pirates, I don't know what to believe."

"Where do I start?" I sighed.

Dietrich folded his arms across his chest, a little smile tugging on his lips. "I think my visit with Lady Brendagger has been snatched."

Ropert chuckled, stepping to the desk, eyeing the tray of refreshments. He plucked a round sugary wafer from a plate. "I think we are going to be here longer than anticipated," he said.

Mayama patted my hand. "Start from the time you left my sister's cabin. Where did you go? Did the herbs help with your headache? Were you able to"—she lowered her voice—"were you able to destroy the stone?"

Had it really been that long since I'd seen her? Besides Ropert, Mayama was the only other person I could share everything with—my deepest wishes, my secrets, my desires, good or bad.

The door opened, and Commander Durianna entered. "The horses and supplies are being gathered as we speak," she said. "Everything will be ready by first light tomorrow."

"Thank you, Durianna," Dietrich said. "One more thing. Send for a man named Alder Grayhorn. He's staying at the Drowsy Dreamer near the docks. Tell him I will make it worth his while."

I twisted the mug on the table, watching the moist ring at the bottom leave streaks against the wood grain. Alder had been gone for hours, and the innkeeper was already locking doors and windows for the night. I wasn't worried. Alder could take care of himself when it came to the Deathbiters. But what would he do once he returned, once he learned that Ropert had tried to sever him from our party? Something about Alder told me he wasn't going to take this well.

"Why did you tell Dietrich about Alder?" I asked.

Ropert tore a chunk of rye bread from the large loaf in the center of the table, dipping it into his soup. "Oh, it's Dietrich, is it? Not Lord Everguard?" He winked.

"Ropert." I glowered at him. This was not a subject to make light of.

His mischievous glint snuffed out. "Alder has latched onto our party like a flea you can't itch. I don't like the way he treats you. He's always criticizing you, pushing you to do things you don't like. Alder's abilities would be better used here in Kaltum, defending the people," he said.

"Don't you think we should have asked him first?"

The front door opened, cold air spilling into the room, the sky outside growing deep violet behind the tall figure. Alder's footfalls were heavy and deliberate as he walked to our table. Tight-lipped, he drew out the chair across from Ropert, sitting. He didn't say a word—he didn't need to. Thrall radiated from him like the heat from the fireplace.

I swallowed, trying to ease the pressure building in my ears. He was livid.

"Well?" Ropert asked. "What did Lord Everguard have to say?"

"You know what he wanted." The words shot through Alder's teeth like daggers.

"I thought you'd be happy. You're always saying how a man of your profession can't afford simple necessities like warm clothing, bedding, and supplies. Now, you will have everything provided. You'll have—"

Alder's palm hit the table. "What makes you think you know what I want?"

His energy rushed to the surface, slamming into me like a battering ram. Red sparked behind my eyes, tugging on my own energy, threatening to draw it out. My lungs locked in place, sensing the darkness rolling through his body. Was he losing his control?

The black spark inside me felt it, coaxed by his heated rage. My hands clutched the edge of the table, digging into the wood. *Breathe.*

"I don't understand your anger, my friend," Ropert said.

"You dare to call me 'friend' after this . . . this *betrayal*?" Spittle shot from Alder's teeth. He tore his hood from his face, his silver eyes turning into swords. His beautiful features contorted with rage. "All I have ever done is help you."

"And now you have the opportunity to help others," Ropert said.

Why wouldn't he keep his mouth shut? Didn't he feel the pressure, the rising heat, the threat of blackened power ready to tear him apart? He was egging Alder on.

"Ropert, stop." I barely pushed the words from my lips.

Ropert leaned back in his chair. "I don't see why you are so upset, Alder. You can refuse his offer. It's not like we are forcing you to do this."

Alder's rage boiled, pushing against my mind like a collapsing mountain. He was losing himself. He was going to unleash Thrall here, in the tavern, with all these people.

"Alder. Breathe."

He leapt to his feet, the chair rocking back, hitting the floor with a bang. "Don't tell me what to do." His deep voice barreled against my chest, silver eyes growing sharper. "You.

You just let him send me away. After all I've done. After all I promised. I thought you were my friend."

"I am, Alder." I stood, bracing against the table. "Please. Just breathe."

His skin took on the shade of thunderclouds, his hair rising as if caught in a wind, energy rushing around him.

Phoenix help me, I had to protect Ropert. I had to shield everyone here. Thrall would tear them apart.

I slammed my eyes shut.

White stars flickered inside, dancing around the black flame trying to reach for Alder's power. I knew which one to catch. I knew which power would flourish under the growing desire in my heart. Protection.

Pale lights swirled and blossomed around every memory I shared with Ropert. His smile, his humor, his laugh. The way he cared for me. The way he cared for others.

Etheria pushed against Thrall like a wall of soldiers driving the enemy back.

"Breathe, Alder." My voice rang strong and firm. "Just one breath. You helped me. Let me help you."

His eyes whipped to me, flashing like arrowheads, ready to burrow into my chest. He stood as if in a whirlwind, his cloak billowing.

"Breathe."

The edge in his eyes flickered. The power rushing around him recoiled, compacting somewhere inside his mind. His black-steel hair fell across his shoulders, his cloak losing wind.

He staggered back, shaking his head. "I . . . I'm sorry."

Broderick was right. Thrall could not be tamed.

Ropert's chair scraped against the floor as he stood. The room was silent. Patrons gaped at Alder from their seats, spoons, mugs, and knives held silently in the air.

"You need to go," Ropert said.

Alder lifted his eyes, looking at me through shimmering black strands falling across his handsome face. "You would send me away for doing the same thing you did?"

His words hit hard and true. I had used this same power against Broderick three times, and still he remained with me. Being on the receiving end was terrifying. I was being a hypocrite by condemning Alder for his one mistake.

But I couldn't let him influence me anymore. I needed to break free, to find my own path.

I hugged my shoulders, my gaze falling to my boots.

"I see," Alder said. He pulled his hood over his head, hiding his face deep in the black folds. His legs carried him to the door in six long strides.

"Alder, wait," I said.

He reached for the lever.

"What do you think you are doing?" the innkeeper barked from behind the counter. "The door stays locked. The Deathbiters are—"

Alder ripped the door open, his cloak billowing, people crying out as black streaks darted between the buildings, screeching. They arched away from Alder as he stepped into the street.

"Get back in here, you fool," the innkeeper shouted.

Alder's head tipped, as if his silver eyes could see through the thick fabric of his hood, glaring over his shoulder at me. "You've just lost the greatest protection you had, Lady Brendagger. I will not come to your aid again."

He pulled the door closed.

I sank to my chair, my legs losing all strength.

"Are you alright?" Ropert asked.

My hands trembled like the first day I faced Ikane on the training field. I pressed them against my legs. Why wasn't Ropert as unsettled as I was? Hadn't he felt Alder's rage? Hadn't he sensed the danger he was in?

"Dagger." Ropert sank to his chair beside me, his scarred hand slipping over mine. "Don't blame yourself for this. We should have parted ways a long time ago."

I released a shaky breath. "You're not . . . you're not afraid of him?"

"That man is shrouded in black, Dagger. I'd be concerned if someone wasn't wary of him."

"Didn't you feel his power?"

He just stared at me.

"Pressure? Heat? A tightness in your chest? Anything?"

Ropert leaned back, fingers tapping the table beside his plate. "I saw a strange wind rise in him. But no, I felt nothing."

How? How could he not feel so much rage and pain?

"He's gone now, Dagger. You needn't worry about him anymore."

I shook my head, closing my eyes. "How can I justify sending him away when I made the same mistake? I used Thrall against you and Broderick. I struck you. At least Alder calmed his power before he unleashed it."

"It is one thing for you to unleash power you have not mastered. It is another for a man who claims he commands it," Ropert said. "I have no regrets. You shouldn't, either."

Despite his words, my eyes fell on the door. Had I really just pushed an ally away?

## CHAPTER 19

# BETRAYAL

"You have failed me again." Master's voice barreled through Marrok's mind like a wave hitting the deck of a ship.

Marrok lowered his ears. "He knows I am hunting him."

"And why does that stop you?" Master roared.

Black power drilled into Marrok's mind like an arrow, shadow roiling from the site like flames up the main mast of a ship. But his sails were empty. Master had cleared his mind of anything he deemed of no worth, and the power hovered in nothingness, sputtering.

"I have given you a form equal to the gods, and still, you cannot kill a lowly human," Master growled. "The goddess will not be pleased. I need you to take care of another problem, one that is immune to my powers, but until you accomplish this task, I cannot send for you."

Marrok ran his claws through the snow, five penetrating lines digging up the brown earth beneath. His place was at his master's side. He needed to finish this. But how?

The man named Eamon had taken precautions, only leaving the building for short periods or surrounding himself with heavily armed soldiers.

"What would you have me do?" Marrok asked.

*"You expect me to organize your every move? I don't care how you do it. Just finish the task."*

*Marrok glanced at the buildings in the distance—the crumbling plaster on timber-framed walls, the stone chimneys leaching smoke to the gray clouds, the snow-covered rooftops, the heavy doors, the fragile glass windows standing wide to the daytime air. He could invade easily. He could silence every beating heart cowering inside the buildings. His claws ached to dig into flesh; his tongue longed for the taste of blood.*

*"Yes, my pet," Master purred. "Now you are thinking like the creature you were created to be."*

*Marrok blinked. Was that what Master wanted? For him to tear the village apart brick by brick until Eamon was dead? Why . . . why did the thought hurt his core, like his body wanted one thing and his heart another?*

*There were so many people . . .*

*He sat his hand on his chest, fingers curling, claws piercing his thick skin over his heart. If only he could tear out the horrible sensation festering in his chest.*

*"You have until week's end," Master said, "or you shall suffer by the hand of the goddess herself."*

*Marrok's hands flexed, eager to feel wood and stone splintering beneath his palms. "Yes, Master."*

I pushed the thick porridge around the side of my bowl, watching the little black raisins peek through the pale substance like the earth stirred up under Marrok's claws.

It hadn't worked. I couldn't reach him. I'd tried everything I knew, but I couldn't penetrate the dream.

Knowing Eamon had been warned was a small comfort. But I needed to do more. The dreams were torture, a constant reminder of what I'd left behind.

My heart felt stretched, torn between duty and love. I pushed my breakfast away, my stomach too full of worry to eat anything.

"Done already?" Ropert came down the stairs, his bags slung over his shoulder. His eyes fell on my untouched breakfast. "Is Alder still getting to you? Don't worry about him. We'll be off in a few hours."

Hours? What was I supposed to do for hours? My bags were already packed and waiting by the door.

"Would you like to spar this morning?" I asked.

He dropped his bags by the table, a regrettable expression filling his eyes. He couldn't. He was too busy with preparations. Too busy organizing, briefing, and delegating. His new station of captain was like a wedge between us, every day another blow widening the gap.

I shouldn't be upset. It was what he wanted. What we both wanted. He was rising in station and rank within Roanfire's militia, just like we'd imagined. He was finally attaining that dream.

But I wasn't. Everything pulled me away from what I'd wished for, what I'd worked for, what I'd fought for. Now, I wasn't even considered a soldier of Roanfire anymore. My future was no longer mine to forge.

If only King Sander hadn't made me a Lady of Meldron.

I pushed my chair back. Who was I fooling? It wasn't King Sander's fault. My fate was sealed the day I was conceived. All because one foolish man had cursed the princesses of Roanfire to fight a monster he created.

"It's alright. I understand." I pulled my cloak from the back of the chair and slipped it over my shoulders. "Do you need anything from the market? I need to have my sword sharpened and send another shipment of dust to Healer Malcom."

The sorrow in Ropert's eyes didn't lift. "I'm sorry, Dagger. I miss our time together, too."

"Don't apologize. You've earned this." I forced a smile.

He slipped into my vacant chair, pulling my bowl of uneaten porridge under his nose. "Since you're offering, I've had a hankering for shortbread knots."

Ah, my Ropert, always thinking with his stomach. It was a shame he hadn't accompanied me to the Glacial Empire. He would have appreciated Chrysla's honey puffs.

"I'll see what I can do."

Orange sparks leapt from my sword like shooting stars as the blacksmith slid my blade across the grindstone. A skinny young man stood behind her, throwing his weight into the task of pumping the billows. The coals in the forge flared white-hot with every whoosh.

There was a time I had the same task. I remembered the sweat, the blisters on my hands, the burn in my forearms and shoulders, the smell of iron, coal, and body odor. But most of all, I remembered the rage in the blacksmith's eyes as I'd made the fire too hot and cracked his forge.

How things had changed.

"Lady Brendagger. I thought that was you."

I looked across the bustling street, finding Gale pushing through a crowd. She hurried to my side, tossing her freshly braided hair behind her shoulder.

"Shopping for a new weapon?" she asked.

"Just having mine sharpened," I said.

"A dull knife is as bad as not having one."

I smiled. A true warrior.

The grinding halted, and the blacksmith ran an oil cloth over my blade, the metal glinting in the forge fire behind her. She handed the weapon to me. "That'll be two copper."

"Thank you." I placed the coins in her calloused, scarred hand then slid my newly sharpened weapon into the scabbard at my hip. I turned to Gale. "I haven't seen you at the Drowsy Dreamer. Were you unable to find a room?"

"Sadly, all the rooms were booked," Gale said. "But I did find room at an inn close by." Her eyes scanned the surrounding area. "Where is that gorgeous blue-eyed hulk of yours?"

"He's busy making preparations for our journey." I moved down the street, eyeing the signs hanging over shop doors, searching for the apothecary.

"Pity." Gale fell into step beside me. "I could watch him all day. Tell me, does he have a lady friend? Oh." She stopped, her hand flying to her lips. "I'm sorry. Are you two—"

"No, we're not." I chuckled. "He's just a friend, but a dear one. He's not attached at the moment." When *was* the last time I'd seen him with a girl? Was it in Daram? He'd gone through a horrible heartbreak then. I hadn't seen him show any interest in another since. He threw himself into his training, pretending it never happened.

"Do you think a girl like me has a chance?" Gale asked.

"You'll have to ask him." I winked.

She smiled. "Where are you headed?"

"I need sprite dust," I said.

"What kind?"

"All of them."

"I know just the place. This way." She jerked her head, urging me to follow. "You've never been to Kaltum before, have you?"

"Not long enough to become familiar with it. It's a beautiful city, even if it does smell like day-old fish."

She laughed.

Gale turned a corner, leading me down a road less crowded than the main street. Snow lay in shallow drifts across the smoothly worn cobblestones.

"Charlotte's apothecary isn't the most well-known, but she sells the most pungent ginger root I've ever sampled. Imported from Toleah. It settles my stomach better than any other."

"Are you on ships a lot?"

"Sometimes work calls for it." She turned down a narrow lane, dark and shadowed, the lack of sunlight dropping the temperature between the stone buildings. I skirted around a rain barrel, the smell of old water permeating the space.

A tingling raced up my spine. Something didn't feel right. I glanced over my shoulder, seeing nothing.

"We're almost there," Gale said.

Licking my lips, I rested my hand on my sword, following. I scanned the alley window frames and the underside of roof overhangs.

What was I missing? Deathbiters? Flaming feathers, was Alder here?

I looked over my shoulder again.

"Kea," Gale said.

I turned to her.

*Poof.* A cloud of white powder struck my face.

I staggered back, hitting the wall, my eyes going dry like a blast of wind had sucked away all moisture. Tears blurred my vision, streaking down my cheeks. What was this? I rubbed my eyes, but it didn't help.

"Gale?"

"Don't fight it," Gale said. Her grip on my wrists was like iron as she wrung my arms behind my back, pushing me against the wall. Stone scraped my cheek. A cord began winding around my wrists.

She was trying to bind me. But why?

Something cold and hard brushed against my fingertips by her belt—an object I knew well.

Instinct took over. My fingers curled around the hard object, my leg shooting back into her shin. She buckled, losing hold of my arms. I whirled, elbow slamming into the side of her jaw with a crack. My vision flared with light as I groped at her collar, driving her against the opposite wall. She grunted at the impact.

"What is the meaning of this?" I pressed the edge of her dagger against her throat.

What was wrong with my eyes? What had she done to me? Everything shone like it was basked in noonday sun, even the alley.

Gale's brows furrowed as she scanned my face. Her jaw twitched where I'd struck it. "H . . . how? How are you able to see?"

I hardened my face. I couldn't let her see that I was asking myself the same thing. I slammed her against the wall again. "I asked you a question."

"You shouldn't be able to see," she said. "I've used winddust on all my bounties. It always works."

"Bounties? Are you a bounty hunter? Who put a bounty on me?"

"It blinds my target for a few hours. Nothing permanent. Just makes it easier to—"

"Focus." I smashed her against the wall a third time. "Who put a bounty on me?"

Her surprised expression shifted to determined resistance, her thick, untamed brows narrowing over her eyes. Her mouth flattened into a tight line.

Perhaps the press of the knife would loosen her tongue. She inhaled sharply through her nose as the blade dug into her skin.

"Who put a bounty on me?" I asked slowly.

"You won't kill me."

"Won't I?" The knife pressed deeper, and a line of red appeared on her skin. A crimson drop slid to her collar.

She sucked air through her teeth, eyes slamming shut. "Leviathans."

I eased the pressure. "What?"

"The Leviathan pirates put a bounty on you. Twelve thousand gold for your capture. Alive."

The Leviathan pirates? Here in Roanfire? I thought they were still at sea, testing our waters. "Where did you get that information? Did you meet with them?"

"They were right. You're not an easy target," she said.

The knife sank into her skin again. She arched back, inhaling.

"Tell me where they are!" Phoenix help us. With King Sander's attention turned to Toleah, the Leviathans could stab us in the back if they were already in Roanfire.

"I . . . I don't know," she croaked. "I saw the bounty on a bulletin in Capin."

Capin? That meant the Leviathans were deeper into Roanfire than I thought. How had they slipped past Eversea and Oldshore? Those prominent fortresses along the coast were the first defense against the pirates.

"It was just business," Gale said. "A bounty like yours would set me up for life."

How could she say that? This was beyond her and me. This meant Roanfire and all its people were at risk.

I jerked her from the wall by the front of her shirt. "I'm turning you in."

"I've done nothing against the law. As a bounty hunter, the laws apply to me differently."

It didn't matter if she had immunity or not. Fulfilling a bounty set by the pirates was treason.

Everything was too clear, too crisp, too detailed. Every cobblestone, crack, and pebble wedged in crevices stood out like looking through polished glass. Snowdrifts glistened like blinding diamonds in King Sander's coffers, forcing me to squint.

Winddust.

Gale used it to blind her bounties, but I already had firedust in my eyes. A bruised feeling built behind them. I wanted to shut everything out, bury my face in a pillow, and let my eyes rest. But I couldn't. One moment of careless attention, and Gale would bolt.

I pressed the knife into her back, and onlookers watching with curious and worried expressions slowed their errands as I marched the bound woman to Kaltum keep.

The guards standing by the gate stiffened as we neared.

"Lady Brendagger?" a guard asked, recognizing me from the day before. "What's this?"

I shunted Gale in the back. "This bounty hunter just tried to abduct me."

Gale stumbled forward. "I already told her I have immunity to—"

"She was fulfilling a bounty set by Leviathan pirates," I said.

The guards spun into action, one grabbing Gale by the arm, the other bolting into the keep.

With Gale held secure, I rubbed my eyes, closing them against every blinding detail bruising my sockets. How long would the ache last? It was like Mina had burned dust into my eyes all over again.

I pulled my hand away.

Something white flashed in my palm.

I blinked, staring at white specks glowing where the gray scars had been, glistening like stars in a skin-colored sky. Flaming feathers, the winddust. It must have happened when I threw my hands up to shield my eyes.

The sprinkle of earthdust glistening between my thumb and forefinger intensified in color and warmth, enhanced by the winddust's energy. I rubbed my hands against my sides. But why? I knew it wouldn't come off. Alder warned me about this. I should have been wearing my gloves.

The gate creaked open, and Dietrich stepped into the street, followed by two more guards wearing Kaltum's green uniform. Despite his cloak being crooked and unclasped and his hair tousled, he looked as regal as King Sander.

"Finally," Gale sighed. "Lord Everguard, I am Gale Harwood, a local bounty hunter. Credentials are in my pocket."

Dietrich eyed the stout woman, his face hard. "What is this about the Leviathan pirates?"

Gale's confidence wavered. "A bounty is a bounty. What does it matter who it comes from?"

"Have you met with the Leviathan pirates?"

"I . . ." Her face paled.

Dietrich's eyes narrowed. "You knew Leviathan pirates were on Roanfirien soil, and you said nothing? *That* is treason."

"I didn't . . . I wasn't thinking. I just wanted the bounty."

Dietrich held up a hand, and her mouth clamped shut. "Take her to the dungeons. I'll deal with her later."

The guards steered her away.

"Do you believe her?" I asked, pulling my gloves from my belt and slipping my hands into them. "That she wasn't thinking?"

"It is possible," Dietrich said. "A good sum of money can blind anyone to the real threat."

"She said the Leviathans put a bounty on me. I want to know why."

"Most bounty hunters don't care for a reason. In your case, I think it would be obvious. You destroyed their army. They want revenge."

"It would make more sense if they wanted me dead."

His brows furrowed. "They want you alive?"

"That's what Gale said."

"How much did Gale say the Leviathans would pay?"

How had I missed this? I'd been so focused on the threat of Leviathans in Roanfire that I completely disregarded the fact that they were willing to pay six times the amount King Sander did when I was framed for the murder of King Myron. "Twelve thousand gold," I whispered.

Dietrich's eyes bulged. "This does not bode well for you. Bounty hunters will come in droves for a price like that." He waved a soldier over. "You should not be alone. I'll assign another eight soldiers to accompany you to Meldron."

"Really, Dietrich. You've provided us with enough."

"You cannot comprehend that amount, can you? Believe me, I wish I could send a small army."

I rubbed my hands together, a strange airiness tugging on my skin beneath the gloves. "I should be getting back. Ropert will be wondering where I am."

"I'll walk with you." He waved to the soldier to follow us. "After news like this, it is imperative you make haste for Meldron. The less time spent on the road, the better."

"I'll be sure to inform Sir Ropert," I said.

"Now." He fell into step beside me, straightening his cloak. "We didn't get the chance to speak much about things not pertaining to Deathbiters after my cook stole your attention." He winked, offering me his arm.

I smiled, slipping my arm through his. "I'm grateful to you for taking her in. It's a relief to know she's safe."

"You see, she's not even here, and she's already snatched the conversation." He chuckled. "Enough about her. How are the wedding negotiations coming along with Toleah?"

I'd rather talk about Deathbiters.

## CHAPTER 20

# A BEAUTIFUL LIE

*T*he soothing rush of water lapped beside me. My stomach fluttered as the solid planks under my back moved up and down with the waves. A mast soared to the starless, ink-black sky.

Was I on a ship?

"Little Brendagger?"

"Ikane?" I turned my head.

Was this real? Was he really next to me? My Ikane?

He lay beside me the same way he had on the Otaridae the night we'd slept under the stars: his hands laced behind his head, his eyes fixed on... nothing. There were no stars to admire.

"Do you remember this night?" he asked in his beautiful Leviathan accent.

I'd never forget. This was the moment with him I cherished the most. The moment I clung to, hoping we could share more. "Is this... is this a dream?"

He looked at me, his beautiful, mismatched eyes gleaming like I remembered. His olive skin, his deep-brown hair almost the shade of midnight falling over his eyes, the scars crossing on his left cheek forming an uneven x.

*He moved a hand from the back of his head and reached for me.*

*My heart slammed against my chest as his fingers slid through mine. He was warm and strong, his skin calloused and solid. Almost as if he were real.*

*Oh, if this was a dream, let me never wake. Let tomorrow never come. I would live this beautiful lie for eternity if it meant I could have him again.*

*He rolled onto his side, propping himself on an elbow, his hand caressing my cheek. "I've missed you."*

*Tears flooded my vision.* "Oh, Ikane. I've missed you, too."

"Why have you abandoned me?"

My heart froze in my chest, threatening to crack. "I tried, Ikane. I did everything I knew to get you back."

"But you let Alder go."

Alder? Was he . . . feathers, had I made a mistake in sending him away?

"I couldn't follow his path, Ikane. It was dark. Consuming. Angry."

"So you will let me suffer?"

I sat up. "No, I won't. I will do whatever it takes to get you back. You are everything to me, Ikane. I can't tell you how much I hurt . . . how much my heart aches. I am searching for the White Wardent. I'm close."

He sat upright, resting his arms on his knees, turning his gaze to the starless world above us. "It may be too late for me by then."

Something flickered in the sky.

A single star.

"What can I do, Ikane?"

"Listen to Alder," he said. "Learn from him. He has so much to offer."

Another star flickered to life, brighter than the first. But something wasn't right. It was red. Both stars were. Another and another blinked awake, the sky bursting into a million embers of angry lights reflecting on the glassy black water below.

Ikane stared at me, his green eye burning beneath his dark lashes. "Help me, Little Brendagger. You promised."

The dream faded away, the vision and touch of my handsome Leviathan prince slipping through my grasp. It was like I'd lost him all over again. The tearing sensation in my chest was almost too much to bear.

Oh, how I missed him. How I missed his hand in mine.

I lifted my arm, turning my palm to see the glowing white stars embedded in my skin. Everything about the dream had been real and wonderful, a place I could have stayed forever.

Save the strange stars. They'd burned with so much rage and hatred, so much pain. That wasn't him. That felt more like . . . like Rion.

But feathers, it had been a beautiful, heartbreaking dream.

I sat upright, pushing my hair back, the light from my hands flashing across the dark room. Hazy morning brilliance pushed through the window shutters.

This had been my last night of freedom. My last night to breathe before King Sander locked me in a tower . . . or the dungeon . . . or the pillory.

I deserved all of them.

I'd betrayed his trust.

And for what? I hadn't found the letter. I'd lost Ikane and Broderick. All I had to show for my defiance were scars, heartache, and a growing magic that tried to destroy me.

A growing magic Alder had offered to teach me to control. But I couldn't go back for him now. Not when we were so close to Meldron.

Something about reaching out to Alder didn't feel right. It was like the previous dream I had of Ikane . . . of Marrok. Like my head and heart couldn't agree on what was right. I wanted to believe that Alder could help me, but my heart drummed with a warning.

Why?

A cool breeze brushed against my skin, blowing strands of growing hair across my face, obscuring the damaged great city of Meldron. From my position on the hillside, black scars smeared the white stone of the castle, a reminder of what had happened a few short months ago. Two towers braced by thick beams dithered on damaged foundations, leaning like wounded soldiers on canes.

Ropert stopped his horse beside mine. "Are you ready?"

Was anyone ever ready to give up their freedom?

My life was bound from the beginning, my fate tied to Rion by the White Wardent. Now my future was in the hands of my king who didn't understand my true purpose.

I squared my shoulders, kicked my horse's sides, and cantered down the hillside.

The soft thump of her hoofbeats shifted to sharp clops as the ground transitioned from dirt to cobblestone. Stepping through the arched gateway was like stepping into another world.

A woman watched me from her doorstep, her face gaunt, a tear-streaked child clinging to her skirt. A man with hunched shoulders stopped in the road, his eyes hollow and greedy as we passed.

Was it really that bad? Were the people so starved, so beaten, that they had murder in their eyes?

A ghostly emptiness filled the market square in front of the Meldron castle. No stalls or booths lined the street. Flurries whirled in the breeze, gathering in drifts on the gray stone, a haunting echo of the usual shouts of merchants bartering or soft clinks of exchanged money. Something foul carried in the wind, burning my nose.

We passed the library. The stained glass images of great scholars of the past looked down on the square as if in mourning. I now recognized the one as the White Wardent, Yotherna. Feathers, he looked so much like Alder, even in a stained glass depiction.

Another window portrayed a beautiful woman with blazing red hair. My stomach clenched at the sight of the Phoenix Stone around her neck, glowing like the mocking embers of a fire on a bitter night. The kingdom of Roanfire was built on her lies.

Four soldiers flanked the main gate, straightening as we approached. My heart raced, every beat hitting my chest like a punch as a soldier slipped through a small door set in the massive gates. He was going to inform King Sander I was here.

Ropert pulled his horse to a stop and swung his legs over the saddle, his soft leather boots hitting the cobbled street with a strange echo. His bright blue eyes found mine, uncertainty shining through. "Stay strong, Dagger," he whispered.

I swallowed and slipped from my saddle. What example would King Sander make of me?

The sound of heavy locks echoed through the vacant courtyard, and the thick wooden doors groaned open. A dozen fresh crimson tunics filed out. Two flanked me, pinching my arms, pulling them back. The rattle of iron cuffs rang as they clamped the cold metal around my wrists.

Ropert's brows furrowed. "There's no need for that."

"King Sander's orders," the soldier replied, his voice cold as he steered me through the gates, across the courtyard, and up the steps to the main entrance.

King Sander was not fooling around. Entering through the main doors was a statement.

Both doors swung open, heavy ironwork moaning. The Great Hall stretched on, hazy light shining in patches of blue squares on the floor from the wall of arched windows to the right. It was a dismal sight compared to the roaring festivities of King Sander's wedding.

King Sander shakily rose from his throne like he was pushing beyond his physical abilities. His skin was pale, and his eyes were sunken. He took three steps down the dais, his long cloak dragging on the floor like it was made of chain mail. His hands clenched and unclenched at his sides. Feathers, he was angry.

I glanced behind him. Queen Lonacheska sat on her throne, hands clasped in her lap, a perfect younger version of her mother. But she held an air of worry the Glacial Empress had not. Did King Sander notice? Would he suspect her treachery?

I averted my eyes as the soldiers drove me to my knees.

King Sander stepped forward but paused with one foot lingering on the bottom step of the dais like he didn't trust himself to stay composed once he reached me. Silence stretched through the Great Hall, the only sound coming from the roaring braziers beside the dais.

I focused on the seams in the stone floor. Why didn't he say anything? The sooner he passed his sentence, the sooner we could move past this.

"Why?" His voice was tight and measured, filled with too many emotions to count.

I shut my eyes.

"For the love of the Phoenix, stand up," he snapped, the rage surfacing.

I felt it, tugging on the black ember curled in the forgotten corner of my mind. But how? I thought only someone with Thrall could influence my power, like Alder. Did King Sander have magic, too?

My eyes shot to his.

I saw no magic in them. What I was feeling, what Thrall was sensing, was just the power of his anger. It was potent.

If I allowed it, Thrall could devour it. It would grow and flourish without feasting on any emotion of my own. I could . . . I could use this. I could use his rage, use the rage of anyone around me to fuel my power and spare my mind.

The soldiers grabbed my arms and hauled me to my feet, chains rattling.

King Sander moved from the step and stopped before me. "Do you have any idea what you've done?"

Oh, I did. Feathers, I did. I glanced away.

"Look at me!"

My eyes met his again.

New lines creased them, the dark circles making him appear older than his years.

"Tell me why! What was so important that you would leave and risk the safety of Roanfire?" His face burned red, and a small vein protruded from under the crown on his temple. "The people are starving. I needed you here."

What could I say? I was fighting an enemy he could not see or feel. An enemy who would do far worse to Roanfire than the Tolean army.

"Say something!" He cut the air across his body, the bejeweled livery collar around his shoulders ringing with the movement.

I couldn't look at him. "I'm sorry," I whispered. "That is all I can say. I am sorry."

"An apology will not save us. Feathers, I can't even look at you right now." He turned away.

I flinched. I'd never heard him use language like that before.

Queen Lonacheska rose from her throne, stepped down, and slid a hand onto King Sander's shoulder. Despite the rage rolling off him, there was something beautiful about the scene. They were together, the hurt between them somehow mended.

"Now is not the time, my love," she whispered. There was something more to her words, like she was worried for his health. I saw it, too. He was still so frail.

King Sander placed a hand over hers, closing his eyes. "Take care of it for me. I can't . . ."

"Chanter?" she called over her shoulder.

The elderly servant, his soft white hair bound away from his face, appeared from behind a curtain. He kept his head low and shoulders forward. Feathers, he was good. No one would suspect what he was truly capable of, what he did behind closed doors.

He bowed to Queen Lonacheska. "Yes, My Queen?"

"Take Lady Brendagger to her room," she said. "See that she receives a hot bath and a meal. And have Healer Bandock take a look at her. Her voice doesn't sound right."

"Yes, My Queen."

"And don't let her out of your sight," King Sander growled.

Chanter took my elbow, his grip pinching. "You have my word, dear king."

He was just as angry as King Sander. His rage was a little weaker, but still, it could fuel my power if I . . .

What was wrong with me? This was exactly what Rion had done. This had been how she gathered power. She took it from others so she could spare herself.

Master Chanter dragged me from the Great Hall. As soon as we were alone, walking the corridors, he straightened, his broad shoulders drawing back. "You've made a right mess of things," he said.

"I know," I whispered.

"Then why did you do it?" His grip on my arm tightened. "Do you have any idea what you've put our king through? What he's suffered? He tried to protect you, to keep you here in Meldron despite the risk of Queen Lonacheska discovering who you were. When she did and pushed him away, his heart broke. His health declined. You fled for the Glacial Empire the day he collapsed, the day Toleah declared war." His gray eyes flashed. "He needed you."

If only I could let him know that I had gone to the Glacial Empire on the request of the queen, that I had risked King Sander's wrath to save his unborn child. My feet slowed, but Chanter dragged me forward.

"You should be ashamed of yourself. I've advised King Sander to make a public example of you. Any other subject displaying your defiance would be executed for treason."

I swallowed. "And what is my punishment?"

"It is undecided. Despite what you deserve, King Sander cares for you."

My chest ached. I knew I would hurt King Sander by leaving, I just hadn't realized how much.

"Where is Broderick?" Chanter demanded. "That boy has defied me for the last time. I know he went with you to the

Glacial Empire, despite my wishes. I've half a mind to give him a sound lashing and put him in the stocks for a week."

The image of Broderick lying unconscious on the bed in the upper room of the inn, his face pale and hollow, his arm twisted, and the smell of blood thick and consuming filled my mind. "He . . . he had to stay in Gerom Post."

"What?" Chanter whirled, his eyes flickering between worry and rage. "He said he was returning with you in his last message."

"Did he tell you about the Deathbiters?"

"Yes."

"What about . . . the beast?"

His white brows rose.

I gathered a deep, shaky breath. "There's something you need to know."

## CHAPTER 21

# PRINCE LEANDER

Cold seeped into my back as I sat by the window overlooking the training square, watching the soldiers drill. I ached to be down there with them, but my sword and knives had been confiscated, the door locked, and a soldier stationed outside. I was a prisoner... again.

I ran my fingers through my damp hair, pulling tangles free. When had it reached my shoulders? It was finally long enough to pull into a warrior's tail without annoying strands falling out. I grabbed a leather cord, wrapping it around my hair at the nape of my neck.

The lock clicked.

I looked up as a young soldier entered, her long curls as red as her uniform. She peered around the door, scanning the room as if looking for something. Then she ducked back out.

*Odd.*

I waited for the door to shut.

What was going on?

After a few short breaths, s woman slipped inside, her heavy cream dress moving like a waterfall around her legs. She pushed the door closed, her dark eyes wide and expectant as she looked at me.

I fell to one knee. "Queen Lonacheska."

"Well? Did you find it?"

I swallowed the lump in my throat. I thought facing King Sander would be the worst of my return, but I was wrong. She was the reason I'd defied the king. And I'd failed.

Not just failed. I'd gone down a different path, dabbling in dark magic for my own selfish desire to free Ikane. I hadn't been thinking about the good of Roanfire or the wellbeing of Lonacheska's child. All I'd wanted was Ikane back.

"It wasn't there."

"What?"

"Only half of the letter was there. The important part was missing."

Her hand flew to her abdomen as if she couldn't breathe. "Are you telling me that you don't have a way to save my child?"

I dared to look up. "What happened to Prince Leander? Where do we stand with Toleah?"

"Why are you asking me about Toleah when my child's life is at stake?"

"I think . . . I think Prince Leander knows something."

She moved to the roaring fireplace, orange light flickering against her pale skin and golden hair, illuminating the worry on her brow. She bit her knuckles. "I'm afraid that is out of the question."

The door opened, and the redheaded soldier stuck her freckled face inside. "Someone is coming."

Queen Lonacheska hurried to the door. "We will speak more of this later." She slipped out, and the door locked.

I stood, rubbing my hands against my thighs, listening to the fading footfalls beyond the door. I thought I was to be given to Prince Leander as a token of peace. I expected it. Had things gotten so out of control? Was Roanfire at war? It would explain why King Sander was so livid. We wouldn't survive.

It was all my fault.

The lock clicked again, and this time King Sander entered, followed by Master Chanter.

I returned to my knee, keeping my face lowered.

King Sander stopped before me, his soft leather boots scuffed on the toes. The fire crackled and spit beside us, daring us to break the silence.

"Do you know how low I've had to stoop to spare Roanfire thus far?" His voice was strained like he held back a roar. "I've locked the Tolean Prince in a tower like a common criminal. I've intercepted letters. Lied to Shah Milak about his son's delay. I've offered Prince Leander half the kingdom just to keep the peace. Do you know what he said?"

I shook my head.

"Nothing. He says nothing. He stares at the fire, waiting for the day he is liberated or killed."

My eyes shot up. Killed? Would King Sander go that far?

"Ah, that got your attention," King Sander grumbled. "Do you see the damage you caused by running off? Things wouldn't have gotten so out of hand if you had listened to me."

I swallowed, understanding why Queen Lonacheska had been so distraught. "Let me speak with him."

"You?" King Sander let out a bitter laugh then coughed.

"What harm could it do, My King?" Master Chanter asked.

King Sander turned away, dragging a hand down his haggard face. "She couldn't make things worse."

Chanter turned to me. "I will have the maids dress you suitably."

That meant a gown, jewels, and lace, hair pulled into ringlets, and face painted with sticky colors and rose oil.

"With all due respect, I must decline," I said. "I need to be transparent with him. He needs to trust me. I will not pretend to be something I'm not."

"But you are Lady Brendagger," King Sander said. "You must—"

"That is simply a title I've been given. But at heart, I am a soldier, a warrior, and your humble servant."

King Sander's stormy blue eyes took in the new scars on my face. A question brewed behind them—he clearly wanted to know where the marks had come from but was too angry to ask.

"At least cover those scars," he said.

"She has a point, My King," Chanter replied. "Her scars will add to her character. Let them shine."

King Sander held a kerchief to his lips, coughing again. "Don't think this will spare you punishment. You will pay for what you have done."

"Yes, My King."

Nothing he could do would be worse than what I'd already endured.

Master Chanter delivered a structured sleeveless coat embellished with a simple detail of silver edging. Silver. Not gold. The coat itself was royal blue, not crimson.

I did not ask why they avoided the colors of Roanfire. There was a reason behind everything they did, including the coat's structure.

The high collar and rows of rustic clasps cascading down my bust were not only flattering but ideal for a soldier. Paired with brown trousers, a white cotton shirt, and soft leather boots, I was the best version of myself I could be.

I was not a soldier of Roanfire nor a Lady of Meldron. I was Keatep Brendagger, bastard daughter of the king, a traitor and savior, a rogue warrior.

I scrutinized myself in the mirror, hardly recognizing the woman staring back at me. The scars striping across my skin like rose-gold paint made me look fierce. The scar on my throat, partially hidden by the high collar, blossomed up like a flower.

Master Chanter stepped beside me. "I think you're missing something." He pulled my sword from behind his back. "A warrior needs her weapons."

Holding my sword was like embracing a lost friend. I hastily buckled it around my waist, needing to feel the familiar weight of it against my hip. "Thank you."

"I also brought you this." He handed me a familiar piece of cloth, the kerchief with the geometric designs of Toleah. I felt the object wrapped inside—hard, smooth, and round. I didn't need to open it to know what it was: the rainbow bangle Prince Leander had gifted me the day he asked for my hand in marriage.

"It might help him remember why he came here in the first place," Chanter said.

Or it would enrage him. The engagement itself was what triggered his outburst, the deception of who I truly was. He was under the impression that I was a true hero of Roanfire, the woman who single-handedly destroyed the Leviathan army. Discovering that I'd trained fugitive slaves from Toleah against the treaty between our two kingdoms shattered that vision.

I followed Chanter from the chamber, looking twice at the redheaded soldier who accompanied us. She kept her eyes forward and head high as if she knew nothing of Queen Lonacheska's earlier visit.

"When can I see Ropert again?" I asked Chanter.

"After he's been debriefed. There is a lot to go over, especially after your account of . . . the beast."

"Are you going to send help?"

"Once we have all the facts, we shall see what we can do. Our resources are limited."

We ascended a spiraling staircase, flickering torches burning from iron sconces on the way up. My heart thundered as we emerged on the fourth floor where two guards were posted on the landing, flanking an arched wrought iron door.

I flexed my sweating palms, wiping them on the kerchief in my hand.

The lock clicked.

"Remember, your goal is to simply get him to talk. Do not make any promises or enter into negotiations without King Sander's approval." Chanter gestured to the redheaded soldier. "Corporal Melark will escort you to your room after."

The redheaded soldier saluted. She was so young, so innocent. Had I ever been that way?

Chanter stepped down the spiral staircase. "Oh, and Lady Brendagger." He glanced over his shoulder. "I respect Queen Lonacheska's decisions."

He knew. Feathers, of course, he knew. He probably knew Corporal Melark was working for her as well.

I inhaled, closing my eyes, turning to the door. I couldn't make any more mistakes.

Corporal Melark pushed the wrought iron door open.

Warmth danced up my skin followed by the earthy, sweet smell of cinnamon and clove. A simple bed stood against one wall, a small round table and two chairs in the other.

The prince slumped in the only armchair in the circular room, stretching his bare feet out to the fire, twisting an emerald ring on his finger. He wasn't wearing his blue headscarf. His hair was bound into thick black dreadlocks reaching past his shoulders. Gold bands clamped the strands, looking like stars in the midnight sky. His exotic handsomeness made me sweat.

He didn't tear his eyes from the fire as I entered. His deep-set eyes stared into the flames, anger seething from them.

Thrall roused, provoked by the scent of something that would provide it sustenance. I froze. Even King Sander's anger hadn't been this potent.

*Breathe.* I inhaled, the warm Tolean spices filling my lungs.

The door bolted behind me.

I inhaled again, dispelling the spark in my mind.

"Prince Leander?"

He didn't look at me.

I moved between him and the fire and dropped to one knee.

"You." He stiffened, grasping the arms of the chair with clawed fingers. "How dare Sander send you here! Get out of my sight."

First step accomplished. He was speaking to me.

"We need to talk," I said.

"Talk? I will not speak to a traitor." His accent was thicker than I remembered. He leaned back in his chair, his honey-gold eyes fixating on the fire. I was losing him.

"I can bring you Hala Whitefox."

His eyes moved to me. Feathers, they were stunning. Firelight struck them like sunlight on amber crystals.

"You think that by offering to betray someone you once trusted, I should trust you?"

"I am trying to find a way to stop this war."

A smile pulled on his lips, dark and venomous. "Roanfire will fall."

I stood. "Your life hangs in the balance as well."

"I know that."

Thrall sparked, hot and bright, making me flinch. *Breathe.* I needed to tame his rage. I needed to pacify him somehow, or nothing good would come of this.

"I am done speaking. Leave or stay, it makes no difference." He leaned back in his seat, turning the emerald ring on his finger. His eyes burned like the coals of the fire.

I set my jaw and tightened my fists. He could hold his tongue, but he could not close his ears.

I grabbed one of the small wooden chairs from the table, situated it beside him, and sat.

"Let me see if I understand this correctly. When you came to Roanfire, you were under the impression that you would be asking me, a war hero, to marry you. As a wedding gift, your father would send food to Roanfire, and we would have a new alliance between our kingdoms." I paused, waiting for him to correct me.

He stared at the flames, eyes hard, jaw tight.

"During our negotiations, you discovered that I bear the traitor's brand of Roanfire. That I was once a member of the White Fox Resistance. I admit, we did harbor slaves from Toleah." I touched my shoulder where the brand scarred my skin. "I deserved this."

He shifted in his seat.

"I bear this brand not for my time among the White Fox Resistance, but because I befriended a Leviathan Pirate."

His eyes strayed from the fire but stubbornly locked onto the flames again. He stopped twisting his ring.

It was working. He was listening.

"You see, he wanted to change the way our kingdoms interact. He wanted peace. But so much hatred burns in our history that we are blind to what the future could be."

The logs on the fire collapsed, and the flames died down to a smolder. I slipped from the chair and stoked it back to roaring.

Still crouching by the fire, I turned to him. "I come to you for a selfish reason. I want you to take me back to Toleah with you."

His eyes moved to mine.

"If I must become your slave to do so, so be it."

His dark brows furrowed. "Why?"

I stared at my hands, watching the sprite dust dance and flicker on my palms. "I am looking for the White Wardent."

His eyes turned back to the fire. There was something different in the way they burned, though, a churning.

This was progress. I bit my tongue, waiting for him to speak.

He set his elbow on the armrest, placing his chiseled jaw on his fist. Perhaps it was best for me to leave it here for the night. I didn't want to push too hard.

I stood. "Thank you for listening to me, Your Majesty." I bowed and moved to the door, raising my fist to knock.

"Lady Brendagger?"

I stopped. *Feathers, please, let this be a step in the right direction.* I turned back to him.

He was still watching the fire. "I will listen tomorrow."

I smiled. It was nay impossible to keep it from splitting my face in two. "As you wish."

I knocked, the door opened, and I stepped into the hallway. The soldiers locked the door after me.

"Good news?" Corporal Melark asked.

I let the smile free. "He wants to see me tomorrow."

## CHAPTER 22

# MELDRON

*T*he last Deathbiter fled to the safety of its lair as pale pink light crept over the rooftops. Finally, he was alone. Finally, it was quiet. He shook off the chaos of the night crawling under his skin—the screeching, the biting, the clawing, the noise. It all interfered with the tranquil stars flickering in the sky, unmoving, unwavering, steady and reliable.

Now they, too, were gone.

Windows and doors banged opened to the crisp silence of morning, unpleasant human smells wafting into the street from their night of cowering in overheated buildings. It would be so simple to barrel through an open door or window and tear into every single beating heart inside. But he still couldn't do it. Why? Why was the feeling in his chest so strong?

Voices carried through the streets as people mindlessly greeted one another.

More noise.

He shook his head wildly. Why couldn't he have a moment of peace? He couldn't concentrate on the steady heartbeat of his target inside the building. Master was expecting him to finish the task—and soon.

"Eamon, don't. There must be another way." The voice was warm and motherly, powerful. Her heartbeat struck strong and vibrant, her love for Eamon pulsing behind each throb.

He knew her heartbeat. She rarely left Eamon's side. But something was different. Her heart beat a little faster today, like she was worried about something.

"Everything is in place. We need to stop him now."

Marrok's ears perked at the sound of his voice.

Cautiously, he craned his neck around the corner of the building and saw Erin, a woman with dark curls and a handsome face, clutch Eamon's hand.

"Every day, there are new tracks around the inn. He won't yield until he eliminates me." Eamon's breath puffed in the cold. "I can't keep hiding."

Erin's worried eyes scanned the street, searching corners and crevices.

Marrok shrank back, legs tightening, claws aching to sink into flesh. What was Eamon up to? Why was he out in the open like this? It wasn't like him.

He risked a glance around the building again.

"I wish you would try something else." Erin hugged her shoulders, her face struggling to stay composed. "Set bear traps, dig a pit, anything."

Eamon caressed her elbows. "I am not your late husband, Erin. I am a soldier. Risking my life is part of my job. If that is too much for you to accept, I understand."

Erin threw her arms around Eamon's neck, burying her face into the folds of his cloak. "You're a fool, you know that?" she whispered.

Eamon's arms tightened around her, pulling her against his strong body.

Something pricked Marrok's chest. A part of him longed to have what Eamon did. He slinked back, shaking his head. He wasn't designed for love and compassion. He glared at his clawed hands. He was designed to kill.

"It'll all be over before you know it," Eamon said. "Relax."

*Marrok's mind reeled at the word, a memory slamming into him like a tidal wave, spinning and twisting.*

"Relax." Eamon's hands rested on Ikane's shoulders, painfully massaging his rock-tight muscles. "Let your body move naturally, and your speed will be unmatched."

The boy, barely growing into manhood, shook him off, holding his swords ready. "What is speed against strength? Won't they just smash right through my defenses?"

Eamon stepped around the training post. "Strength is for moving weight. Strength is to protect your joints. Strength is to safeguard an injury." Eamon winked. "Strength is to flex your muscles for an alluring dame."

Ikane pursed his lips, unamused.

"There are two sides to the tension coin, my boy. One is to generate as much full-body tension as possible. The other is to be relaxed." Eamon drew his sword with one fluid movement. He whipped the blade into the mutilated training post, his sword blurring with his speed. "Relaxing will give you two critical advantages." Splinters flew with every ringing blow. "You will be able to strike as fast as a Tolean cobra without losing your endurance." He lashed out at the post six more times then lowered his sword.

Ikane's brows rose. Scales, Eamon wasn't even breathless.

"You must find the balance of relaxed tension."

"The what?"

Eamon chuckled.

Ikane didn't see what was so amusing. How could he be relaxed and tense at the same time? If he didn't know how brilliant Master Eamon was, he would've said he was mad.

"Observe." Eamon took his stance. "If my strike is too loose, I have no power." His sword bounced off the wood, barely leaving a dent. He raised his sword again. This time, his shoulders and back tightened. "Too tight, I will be slow and still have no power."

In the time it took Eamon to hit the post, Ikane could've jabbed at him twice.

"You must learn the exact timing of when to tense, how hard, and when to be relaxed." Eamon stepped back. "You try."

Ikane raised his swords. His shoulders instantly tightened. He stretched his neck, shaking out his muscles.

"Now, don't get too loose, or you'll lose speed. You must find that perfect balance."

Unattainable balance was more like it. Maybe Eamon was going mad.

Marrok shook his head.

What was that? Where did that memory come from? Did he know Eamon? Was he a friend? A mentor?

Impossible. Master said he was a threat. That he needed to be destroyed.

He glanced around the building, his heart lurching into his throat as he scanned the empty street. Where had Eamon gone? He stepped from the narrow space between the buildings, eyes straining as he searched doorways, corners, and crates. Eamon couldn't have gotten far.

Marrok sniffed the air, finding the cold scent of steel and leather of his target. He was close. Just to the other side of the building.

He shrank into the alley, turned, and skirted around the back of the inn. The smell of roast pheasant and spices wafted through the open window, masking the scent of his prey. He slowed as he came to the end of the building, peering down the alleyway littered with crates and barrels. Eamon stood in shadow at the far end, his voice low as he spoke to a soldier.

This was it.

In just three bounds, Eamon's throat would be in his jaw. He could already feel the warm blood on his tongue, smell the iron.

Marrok's body coiled. Three, two, one—

"Ikane, don't." The woman's voice barreled through his skull, sinking into his mind with white energy. The voice was soft and defined, not mingled with a thousand others. That wasn't his goddess. It was the girl.

His clawed feet slipped on loose snow, and his shoulder crashed into a barrel sitting against the wall. It fractured, the crack of breaking wood carrying through the alleyway. Something bit his arm as he tumbled against the wall. He glanced down, finding a piece of splintered wood embedded in his skin.

"Now!"

The cry came from the rooftop.

Marrok's gaze shot upward, finding an archer crouched above him, her arrow aimed at his chest. What sort of weapon was that? It wasn't meant to kill. It was narrow, the tip too fine to detect, but there was a smell wafting from it. A smell he knew from before. But what was it?

Crates burst open, soldiers exploding from their hiding places within the alley. Did they think they could capture him?

Marrok sprang from the wall, launching his frame at the nearest soldier. But his body stopped in midair—something had snapped tight around his ankle, jerking him back. He landed hard on his chest. He whirled.

A thick rope wrapped around his leg, pulled taut by three soldiers. If they thought this would stop him, they were wrong.

"Now. Throw the ropes!" Eamon bellowed. "All of them!"

Marrok pushed himself from the snow as something flew around his neck. It jerked against his windpipe, forcing his body to rock back. Another rope caught his arm, the lasso sliding clear to his shoulder.

"Alina! Now!" Eamon barked.

"I can't get a clear shot!"

It was the archer, her sight fixed on Marrok.

How dare they think they could overpower him, a creature as powerful as the gods! His claws slashed into rope, the thick strands cutting clean from his shoulder. He rolled to his hands and knees, jerking the ropes with him. Soldiers cried out at his strength, stumbling into crates and barrels.

"Alina!" Eamon roared.

"If you want him alive, get me a clear shot!" she cried.

*Soldiers fell on the ropes like hordes of ants, pulling Marrok's body in opposite directions. Marrok's roar was cut short as the rope tightened around his windpipe. His foot jerked from beneath him. Another rope caught his wrist, and a fourth lassoed his other, spreading him wide.*

*He was stronger than this.*

*"Got it!" the archer cried.*

*The whistle was short. Her arrow burrowed into Marrok's shoulder, just below his neck. Fire exploded through his skin, soaring into his head and across his chest. He roared, pulling against rope and man. His heart pounded in his ears, muffling the soldiers' cries.*

*What had they done to him? Poison?*

*The alleyway grew darker, the bright crimson uniforms blurring into shadow. His lungs screamed for air, and his muscles burned with exertion. If these soldiers didn't kill him, the goddess would.*

*He couldn't be caught.*

*Master would not be pleased.*

My eyes opened.

I'd done it.

Somehow, I'd managed to infiltrate the dream. The relief was palpable, my lungs breathing air I thought already there. I rolled onto my back, blinking at the large stones embedded in the ceiling, pushing my hair from my face.

Eamon had caught Ikane. Finally, there was hope.

I sat up, shoving the blankets from my legs. The chill in the room rushed across them, sending gooseflesh up my limbs, but I smiled.

Throwing the window open to the morning light, I sat at the small wooden desk provided, snatched a piece of clean white paper, prepped the inkwell, and wrote.

My dreams had never been wrong, but I needed to confirm that Eamon had, in fact, captured Ikane.

As I blew on the drying ink, a knock sounded at the door.

"Enter."

The lock clicked, and the door opened. Master Chanter stepped inside, dressed in the inconspicuous brown tunic of a servant. He placed a breakfast tray on my table, glancing at my unmade bed and the open window spilling soft light into the chamber.

"You're up early." He rubbed his hands together. "It's freezing in here."

I hadn't noticed. I rolled the letter into a scroll, not bothering to seal it. He would read it before sending it anyway.

I twisted in the chair to face him. "Will you please send this to Eamon?"

He scrutinized the scroll, took it, and tucked it up his sleeve. "I just finished composing my own letter to Broderick. I'll send them together this afternoon."

Rising from my seat, I cornered the washbasin and splashed cold water on my face. "Can I spar with Ropert today?" I couldn't wait to share the news with him. Ikane would find himself again under Eamon's care. I knew he would.

"I can arrange that." Chanter handed me a towel.

"Thank you." I pressed it against my cheeks.

"A man arrived at the castle gates this morning," Chanter said. "He was sent here by Lord Everguard to address the king about the Deathbiters in Kaltum. He says he knows you. Alder Grayhorn?"

I stiffened. "Alder? Here?"

"You don't look pleased."

It was not that I wasn't pleased. This was my second chance. Ikane had pleaded with me to learn from Alder. But did Alder's offer still stand after I shunned him for using the same power I did? "Is he someone we can trust?" Chanter pressed. "Should I be worried?"

"No, no. He's fine. We just didn't part on good terms." I rubbed my face, pinching my lips in my hands. "Where is he staying?"

"I gave him a room in the castle."

"I'd like to speak with him later."

Chanter closed the window. "There is something familiar about him. I feel like I've seen him somewhere before, but I can't place it."

I crouched by the fireplace, tossing kindling inside, and decided to give him a huge hint. "Meldron Library."

He pressed a finger against his lips, eyes distant in thought. They suddenly burst wide. "The White Wardent?"

"Uncanny, isn't it?"

"Indeed," he murmured. "I must do some research on this."

"Let me know what you discover."

"I will."

"You're. Getting. Sloppy," Ropert said between strokes, our swords ringing through the training arena. He dodged my blow, my blade swinging wild as it met no resistance. I hated when he did that.

"Less. Talk." I followed the pull of my weapon, spun, and blocked his next strike. The force jarred through my hands up to my shoulders. I brought my sword up, ripping through the space where Ropert had been.

He was getting faster.

Gripping his sword with both hands, he swung at my head.

I crouched, his weapon flying harmlessly by. He should know better. The move might deliver a powerful strike, but it left him wide open.

Launching myself forward, I dug my shoulder just under his ribcage. A solid *oomph* exploded from his lungs.

"Dagger." He staggered back, clutching his ribs. "Don't do that."

I shrugged. "Then don't give me an opening."

"Oh, you want to play that way?" He raised his sword.

"Lady Brendagger."

I closed my eyes at the voice, my shoulders dropping. This was just getting good. "Yes?"

"I am here to escort you back to your room."

I faced Corporal Melark. "Just a few more minutes?"

She shook her head. "I'm afraid there isn't time."

Ropert slid his weapon into the sheath at his back. "We'll continue this later."

I sighed, sliding my sword home.

Corporal Melark spun on her heel, turning to the castle. A world of trouble waited for me inside. King Sander's wrath. The Tolean Prince. Alder. What I wouldn't give for a day in the sun, my toes sinking into the sand, saltwater lapping against my ankles. Just a day alone . . . or with Ikane under the stars.

Corporal Melark looked over her shoulder. "Lady Brendagger," she demanded.

Ropert smiled at me, jerking his head in Corporal Melark's direction. There was that positivity again, the spark that kept me going.

I followed Corporal Melark into the castle, the thick walls severing the warm morning sunlight. How much time did they think was needed to get me ready to see the prince? I'd bathed the day before. All I needed was a quick rinse in the washbasin, a comb, and a clean tunic.

Corporal Melark stepped off the spiraling staircase a landing too early.

I paused. "My room isn't on this floor."

"I know. Please, follow me."

My hand moved to the hilt of my sword. What was going on?

She led me down the hallway lined with vibrant tapestries depicting exotic scenes and animals. Intricately painted pots, flowering plants, and tasseled runners stretched over long tables carved with budding vines and leaves. Corporal Melark knocked on a door decorated with carved lattice work, flowering vines, and three hummingbirds.

"Enter."

Was that Queen Lonacheska's voice?

The door swung open. Queen Lonacheska rose from one of two cushioned chairs flanking the fireplace. The warmth was too intense after my spar with Ropert, igniting a wave of perspiration on my skin. Perhaps I *would* need another bath.

"Lady Brendagger. Thank you for coming." Queen Lonacheska gestured to the seat across from her. It was draped with soft gray fur like the rooms of the Glacial Empire.

She wanted me to sit? Like an equal? I couldn't do that.

I moved around the chair but sank to one knee. "What can I do for you, My Queen?"

Her lips pursed. "I didn't ask you to bow."

"I am a soldier, Your Highness."

"You think to correct me?" she snapped. "I asked you to sit, and you refuse."

"I didn't think—"

"Did I ask you to think?"

I clamped my mouth shut, rose, and sat on the edge of the chair.

She straightened her seemly neck, perching on her chair like the most delicate bird, folding her hands in her lap. "How are things progressing with the Tolean Prince?"

"I speak with him again this evening."

"So he has opened up to you?"

"He hasn't completely shut me out, if that's the same thing?"

A little smile pulled on her lips. "That is promising. What did King Sander have to say?"

Why was she asking me all these questions? Didn't she speak with her husband? "He's asked me to negotiate a new peace treaty, if possible."

Her brows furrowed. "He hasn't punished you yet?"

"Not yet."

"I am sorry to have put you in this position. Whatever he decides, I will see that it is reduced."

"I appreciate that, Your Majesty, but I will accept the consequences." I glanced at Corporal Melark standing by the door. This young soldier must be in high favor with the queen to be permitted to listen to this conversation.

Lonacheska's lips tightened, her hands absently wandering to her stomach. The movement revealed the slight rounding of her abdomen beneath her honey-colored gown. "I felt her for the first time yesterday."

My stomach couldn't decide whether to flip with joy or churn with fear. It was the first sign of life, the first sign that there would be another princess of Roanfire.

I had to clear her path. She didn't deserve to face what I faced.

I had to find the White Wardent.

## CHAPTER 23

## "HE BOTHERS YOU, TOO"

"I want you to give this to Prince Leander." Master Chanter pressed a scroll into my hand, the red wax seal smooth against my thumb.

"What is this?"

"It is King Sander's wishes."

I blinked at him. "What? I just got him to speak with me. No, not even that. He's just listening. I can't give him this yet. I need time to get him to trust me."

"Time is something Roanfire does not have."

I licked my lips, staring at the wrought iron door waiting for me to enter. Why did he spring this on me now? Was it even fair that he and King Sander had hashed out the terms of a new treaty without consulting Prince Leander?

I rubbed my temples. Who was I to question what the king did? He knew what he was doing, didn't he?

Master Chanter set his hand on my shoulder, squeezing gently. "King Sander has faith in you."

Boulders fell on my back, and my legs suddenly felt like I'd sparred for hours. "So the fate of Roanfire is in my hands?"

He smiled softly, the lines around his eyes creasing deeper. "So it would seem." He nodded to the soldiers flanking the door. The sound of the key turning struck my chest like thundering battle drums. The door creaked open.

Prince Leander stood in the doorway, his appearance drastically different from the day before. His calf-length coat, embroidered with gold and blues, shimmered in the firelight, looking like the autumn woods on a sun-warmed day. The excess fabric of his cobalt-blue turban draped across his shoulders like a waterfall. He gestured to the fireplace.

The chair I'd moved the day before remained where I'd set it. He was looking forward to my visit.

I tucked the scroll behind my back as I stepped over the threshold. The door closed behind me.

"Your Highness." I bowed.

He held out his hand, palm up as if expecting me to place something in it. Did he want to take my hand?

"The letter."

"You heard?"

"I listen."

Gathering a deep breath, I placed the scroll in his outstretched palm. He turned to his seat, breaking the seal.

I sat beside him, rubbing my hands against my thighs. The fire cracked and sputtered, casting long shadows across the rug at our feet. What was King Sander getting me into?

Leander's brows furrowed, his amber eyes narrowing at the black ink. He made a fist, pressing his emerald ring to his lips.

My heart struck fast and hard, threatening to beat right out of my chest. Feathers, this didn't look good. What had King Sander done?

Prince Leander lowered the scroll, his eyes rising to the fire.

"May I see it?" I asked.

He extended it to me without taking his gaze from the flames.

*Shazadeh Leander Polusmed,*
*Prince of Toleah,*

*I, King Sander Noirfonika of Roanfire, cannot apologize enough for the gross misunderstanding between our kingdoms. The last thing I want is war. We have lived in peace for generations, and I pray to the Phoenix that we can make this peace last generations more. I can think of nothing that would atone for what I have done. I am not asking for forgiveness, but I am asking that you not make Roanfire suffer for my mistake.*

*Hiding Lady Brendagger's past was dishonest. Yes, she did things that would make her a traitor in the eyes of my kingdom, but she has proven herself to be loyal and true. She holds great power, as was displayed when she destroyed the Leviathan Army.*

*That is truth.*

*It is my greatest wish for us to mend this rift and return to what we had before. If you desire Lady Brendagger to be your wife, so be it. All I ask is that you honor your original offer and provide Roanfire with enough food to see us through the winter.*

*I eagerly await your reply.*

*With sincere respect,*
*King Sander Noirfonika*

I lowered the scroll, choking on his words. How could he? This was something he should have discussed with me beforehand. This was... feathers, this was my punishment for running off. I'd rather take the lashes.

"You would come to Toleah with me?" Prince Leander asked, his voice soft.

I swallowed, looking back at the letter. My heart struck my ribcage like a battering ram. This was what I'd wanted, wasn't it? This was what I needed to do to spare Queen Lonacheska's child.

"Your king is bold. Why should I still supply Roanfire with food?" He leaned back in his chair, folding his arms across his chest.

"Because it would be the honorable thing to do."

He leaned forward, lacing his fingers together. "I have a counteroffer for King Sander. First, I would like to be released from this tower, moved to a room more accommodating to my station, and have my Ridarri returned to me. I want access to your best scouts and fastest messengers."

"Done."

"Second, you are required to dine with me every evening for the remainder of my stay."

I nodded. "How long will—"

He held up a hand. "Third, I want you to bring the leader of the White Fox Resistance to me."

An energy sparked in my chest, the same elation I'd felt after helping Eamon capture Ikane. This was something I could do, something within my control, something I was good at. "I will."

"This does not mean that I will send food to Roanfire at this time." He took the letter from me, stood, and dropped it into the fire.

My heart plunged into my stomach.

He watched the paper coil and the edges turn black. "But I will have faith in what King Sander said about you." He turned to me, his amber eyes solid and unwavering. "I retract my declaration of war on Roanfire."

The muscles in my shoulders eased like a suit of armor had been lifted from them. I inhaled, breath trembling. "Thank you, Your Majesty." I stood, my legs bursting with energy. "I will see that your requests are honored immediately."

He tipped his head.

My feet flew to the door.

Master Chanter pushed himself from the wall, brows raised in question as I stepped over the threshold. My body trembled as the soldiers locked the door behind me, eyes watching me with the same eagerness as Master Chanter's were.

"He has retracted his declaration of war."

The pent-up tension in the small landing evaporated, audible sighs flowing like wind in summer grass.

Master Chanter closed his eyes. "Thank the Phoenix," he breathed. "How did you do it? Did he read the letter?"

"He did, but he burned it."

Master Chanter chuckled, wrapping his arm around my shoulders, steering me to the stairs. "At least he burned it *after* he read it this time. King Sander will be eager to hear this news, but I'm afraid you cannot see him until this evening. I will see that you join him and the queen for supper."

"I'm afraid I can't. I've agreed to dine with Prince Leander every evening until we leave for Toleah." I bit my lip. "And he refused to send food at this time."

Chanter's smile faded. "I suppose we can arrange a banquet this evening then. What else did you agree to?"

"How do you plan to capture Hala Whitefox?" Ropert asked as he escorted me to the dining room. "That is her name, isn't it?"

The rich blue skirt I wore tangled with my legs, swooshing like the waves on the sea. I tugged on the waist, trying to ease the cinch of the corset. "However I do it, it won't be in this dress."

Ropert chuckled. "Maybe if you wore that for our next sparring session, I'd stand a chance."

"You just need to watch your feet. When you swing wide like that, you square off, giving me an opening."

"I'll remember that."

We turned a corner, the large double doors leading to the dining hall looming at the far end of the hallway. Two soldiers flanked the doors, opening and closing them as servants bustled in and out.

Ropert's pace slowed. "I don't want you to go."

What was he talking about? "It's just supper." Granted, I'd rather spend my time in the mess hall with the soldiers, but dining with the king and queen was a tolerable affair, even if I did have to wear a dress.

He stopped completely, looking at his freshly cleaned boots. "I don't want you to go to Toleah."

Something tightened around my heart, coiling and pulling me into the floor. "I was trying not to think about it."

He gave me a sad smile. "Sorry."

"Lady Brendagger. Captain Saded." The deep voice sank into my chest, burrowing in like an arrow to flesh. My body froze. Alder.

Swallowing, I turned around. His long strides were confident, his head held high, his new tunic and trousers constructed of good quality leather and wool. He looked like a different man without his hood. His silver-black hair flowed like silk down his back, and a leather patch covered his damaged eye. His silver one sparked like moonbeams on water.

Two men accompanied him.

"Alder." I bowed to him, hoping he could feel the apology burning inside my chest. "I meant to visit with you today."

"Think nothing of it." He waved dismissively. "I am here on official business for Lord Everguard. I suppose I must thank you for the opportunity to work with him. Who would have thought a man like me would be given servants?" He glanced at the two men behind him.

One was short and older with hard eyes and a chiseled jaw. The other was young and tall, lean and solid, with a head shaved clean of hair. A thick scar interrupted the dark line of his eyebrow over his left eye. They were the roughest-looking servants I'd ever seen.

"Are you heading to supper?" Alder asked.

Ropert glanced at me, his glass-blue eyes flashing with a warning.

"Are you joining us?" I asked Alder.

He smiled. "It may be second nature to you, but when the king extends an invitation to join him for a banquet, it's not something I would decline." He held out his arm. "May I?"

Why was he being so gracious? Didn't he remember what I'd said? How I drove him away?

I glanced at Ropert as I slipped my arm through Alder's. "How is Lord Everguard?"

"He is well." Alder's hand covered mine, his skin cool and smooth, his long fingers bearing rings I hadn't seen before. "We've conducted a few trials with the Deathbiters and discovered something peculiar." He nodded to the soldiers as we stepped through the door.

"I'm eager to hear," I said.

"In time."

"Ah, Lady Brendagger." King Sander stopped thrumming his fingers on the back of his chair, his face breaking into a forced smile. He rushed to my side, stealing me away from Alder. "What took you so long?" he whispered. "Prince Leander refuses to acknowledge me."

I glanced at Prince Leander. Standing in the far corner, he conversed quietly with his two impressively built Tolean warriors. His midnight coat was embellished with gold trim tonight, and his signature cobalt-blue turban framed his eyes like the sky around two suns. He turned upon hearing my name, his brows creasing as he noted my company.

"Welcome, everyone." Queen Lonacheska moved to her seat, gesturing to the meal spread across the table. "Please, sit."

"Keep him happy," Sander whispered fiercely, steering me toward the Tolean Prince. Then with a louder voice, he added, "Lady Brendagger. Would you please sit with our guest of honor tonight?"

I moved around the table as Prince Leander drew out a chair for me. I sat, tucking the folds of the annoying dress around my legs. Bowls of overcooked soup sat before us, transparent cabbage leaves and carrot swimming in an onion-saturated broth. Two loaves of dark bread sat on the table accompanied by a small bowl of butter. It was an embarrassment that spoke to Roanfire's dire need.

Ropert, the two Ridarri warriors, and Alder's servants took positions along the wall as Prince Leander tucked his chair in beside me. His eyes didn't stray from Alder, who took a seat near Queen Lonacheska. "Do you know that man?" he whispered.

I followed his gaze. "That is Alder Grayhorn, Your Majesty. He works for Lord Everguard of Kaltum."

Leander twisted the emerald ring on his finger, his eyes growing distant and hard.

Had I said something to upset him?

"Welcome, dear honored guests," King Sander said from the head of the table. "We have much to celebrate." He gestured to Prince Leander. "Peace between Roanfire and the Tolean kingdom with the promise of a new alliance." He then turned to Alder. "And a new way to tame the Deathbiters plaguing the northernmost regions of our kingdom. Let us eat in good company and forge new friendships." King Sander sank to his seat, gesturing for us to begin.

I lifted my spoon.

Alder leaned close to Queen Lonacheska and whispered something into her ear. She laughed, the sound bright and true, easing the tension throughout the chamber.

But Prince Leander didn't touch his spoon. He didn't even look at the meal.

"Are you not hungry, Your Majesty?" I asked.

"Have you known him long?"

Was he still talking about Alder? "Alder? No, not really. We met in Glacier Pass on my way back to Meldron."

"Glacier Pass?" Leander sounded alarmed.

"Is something wrong?"

Leander pushed his chair back and stood.

King Sander rose, his eyes filled with unbridled concern. "Is the meal not to your liking, Prince Leander? I'm sorry we cannot offer more. We are—"

"Forgive me." Prince Leander bowed to the king. "I have an urgent matter to take care of." He waved to his Ridarri as he hurried from the room, his embellished coat blooming behind him.

King Sander rounded on me. "What did you say?"

I looked from King Sander to Alder to the door. "I . . . I'm not sure."

"Go after him," Sander barked. "Find out."

I moved quickly, rushing through the doors. Leander was already at the end of the hallway. Feathers, why did I have to wear a dress? I gathered the skirts, sprinting after him, my footfalls echoing through the corridor. "Prince Leander!"

The Ridarri faced me, their bodies creating an impressive human shield. Leander said something to them in his native tongue, and the Ridarri stepped aside.

"It's Alder, isn't it?" I dropped the absurd amount of fabric to the floor. "Something about him bothers you."

His head tipped, his golden-amber eyes scrutinizing me. "He bothers you, too, doesn't he?"

I pressed my lips together. "I . . . I'm torn. There is so much about him I want to trust. So much he can offer. But something doesn't feel right. Do you know something about him?"

"Not yet." Prince Leander twisted his ring again, his eyes fixed on the closed doors at the end of the corridor as if he could see Alder sitting at the table beyond them. "If you'll excuse me, Lady Brendagger, I really must see to this . . . strange matter. I hope you understand."

I bowed, wishing he would share more. He knew something about Alder. He saw the likeness. But why wouldn't he share anything about Yotherna with me? I had to gain Prince Leander's trust, and right now, that meant letting him go. "Will I see you tomorrow for supper?"

"I expect you at my chambers at dusk," he said. "Goodnight, Lady Brendagger." He turned, his strides quick, his Ridarri following.

I sagged against the wall, cool stone pressing against my back as I rubbed my face. I wasn't ready to go back to the dining hall. Everything was too heavy, like I couldn't remove the full suit of armor worn long after battle—rusting, blood-crusted, and bent. When was it safe to take it off?

When was it safe to just be Corporal Brendagger again?

*He flexed his fingers, trying to keep blood flowing through his aching arms. The pathetic soldiers had coiled the ropes around his wrists seven times and reinforced the cords that stretched his arms from post to post by braiding three together. They would be no match for his claws ... if only he could reach them. With his arms stretched wide, he couldn't get enough leverage to break the bonds, let alone move. He'd tried. And now his wrists ached and stung, and his shoulders burned.*

*Thick clusters of snow alighted on his coat, the featherlight touch of a love he'd never know. For once, it was quiet. Even the hushed conversations of the soldiers standing guard became muffled by the falling snow. What were they waiting for? Why didn't they just mount his head to a wall, skin his hide, and lay it in front of a fireplace?*

*It wouldn't be long now before the Deathbiters emerged. Sunlight grew hazy and weak through the thick clouds.*

*He closed his eyes. He'd relish the silence as long as he could.*

*"Ikane?"*

*He stiffened at the voice driving into his mind.*

*"Ikane, can you hear me?"*

*He curled his fists. So much for a moment of peace. Now the girl infested his thoughts. Her presence was like the gentle fall of snow, teasing, melting before he could see the crystal pattern. She was everywhere and nowhere.*

"Get out of my head," he growled.

The soldiers shifted, pointing spears and swords at his exposed chest.

"I know you don't like it when I do this. I am sorry. I just . . . I just want to speak with you. I care for you, Ikane. I want to help you."

"You can help me by getting. Out. Of. My. Head!"

He waited for her stubborn reply, ready to tell her exactly what he would do once Master gave him permission to hunt her down. But she remained silently in his mind like the snow, her presence dominant and true but . . . peaceful? How did she do it? How did she irritate and inspire him at the same time?

"How long has he been quiet?" The unmistakable voice of Eamon came from behind him.

Marrok lifted his head. He twisted, trying to lock eyes with the man brilliant enough to organize his successful capture. He would tear out his heart.

Something in his shoulder popped, and fire soared up his neck, white sparks flashing across his vision. He abandoned the idea of facing his captor.

"He stopped fighting the moment it began snowing," the soldier said. "But sir, I think the poison has worn off. He's getting stronger. We need to reinforce the posts."

Marrok glanced at the heavy wooden beams plunging into the snow on either side of him. They were as thick as a ship's mast and taller than Marrok when he stood at full height. Snow pushed from the base, and a small crater indicated the post had shifted during his struggle. The fear behind the soldier's voice sent a rush of pride through Marrok's body. He could break free, and they knew it.

*Snow crunched as Eamon dared to come face-to-face with Marrok, his hand resting on the hilt of his sword. Eamon was no fool. He knew what Marrok was capable of.*

*Eamon's dark eyes studied him, running up and down the length of his perfect form. "I am so sorry this happened to you, Little Wolf."*

*"Little"? Marrok bristled. He was anything but little. His muscles were twice the size of Eamon's, and he stood two heads taller. He jerked against the ropes, barely moving an inch.*

*"Come on, Ikane. I know you're in there, boy." Eamon's eyes hardened. "You are loved and missed by so many. Keatep, Ropert, Broderick, and your brother, Teilo. Come on, Ikane. Remember."*

*These names meant nothing. They were empty, blank spaces in his mind like sunken ships in the sea.*

*"I will tear out your throat," Marrok growled.*

*Eamon's jaw tightened. He withdrew a sword from his belt. Not the long sword at his hip but a second sword—one made of black steel, the pommel curling into the head of a Leviathan.*

*"This is yours." Eamon held the weapon out to him. "Do you remember? It has a twin. You've always been a dual sword fighter."*

*Marrok blinked. He didn't use a sword. His weapons were his hands and teeth. And he used them now, snapping and snarling at the outstretched weapon.*

*Eamon didn't flinch. He was a formidable opponent, Marrok would give him that. It was a shame he would have to die.*

*"Kea has the other sword," Eamon said.*

*Kea? He meant the girl. The one still hiding in his mind, pretending to be invisible but still invading his privacy. He shook his head, wishing he could shake her free.*

*"I will see your blood flow. I will see hers as well!" He strained against the ropes. The post on his right shifted.*

*Eamon lowered the weapon and stepped back. "Reinforce the posts, and give him another dose of wolfsbane. That should keep him quiet through the night."*

*Soldiers moved to comply. The creak of a bow tugged on his ears, drawing his attention away from Eamon. The archer from the day before sighted down the narrow shaft then released. The arrow sank into his arm, and fire spread through his blood. He roared, pulling against the rope.*

*They couldn't keep him here. They couldn't. He was too strong, too powerful for this.*

*He searched his blurring vision for Eamon. He would kill him. He would do as Master commanded, and then he would go after the girl called Kea.*

*"I'm not giving up on you, Ikane," Eamon said.*

*Weight surged through Marrok's limbs as Eamon turned away. His head sagged against his chest, his knees buckling. Eamon would pay for this. They all would.*

*Darkness fell, and Deathbiter screeches filled the sky.*

A bang hit my window, jarring me from the dream, screeches tearing through the glass. The creature clung to the frame, fangs barred, wings flailing. I flew from the bed, drawing the curtains shut.

Flaming feathers. They were here.

How could we withstand this? The people were already starving, now the Deathbiters. Roanfire could not endure both and survive.

We needed Prince Leander's help now, Hala or not.

## CHAPTER 24

## SHE'S HERE

"Lady Brendagger. Are you awake?"

My fingers paused from tedious task of closing the silver clasps down the front of my structured tunic. The door unlocked and groaned open. Master Chanter stepped inside, his eyes bloodshot and weary, his hair not quite as perfect as I was accustomed to. Something in his face spoke of more than just sleep deprivation.

"What's wrong?"

Chanter eyed my window. Pale sunlight glowed beneath the curtains, a strange silence beyond. No birds sang. The usual ring of swords, grunts of soldiers, and whinny of horses were missing.

"I need your help." Chanter shuffled to my desk, pulled a handful of wrinkled papers from his sleeve, and dropped them. "I received strange messages from a healer here in Meldron a few days ago. I thought nothing of them. But now, I'm not so sure. Especially after Broderick's most recent letter."

"Broderick wrote you? When?"

"His letter arrived yesterday."

"And you didn't tell me?" Feathers, this was wonderful news. Broderick was awake and well enough to compose letters. "How is he?"

"That isn't the point." Chanter jabbed a finger on the papers, his face grave. "Broderick composed this letter a week ago. Look, and tell me what you see."

I slipped into the chair, moving the scribbled pieces of parchment around. The notes on top were from the healer.

*Jette Carter*
*Female. Age, fifteen. Pottergate Street.*
*Cause of death, unknown.*

*Landis Oresman*
*Male. Age, seventeen. Pottergate Street.*
*Cause of death, unknown.*

*Joel Mudotter*
*Male. Age, thirty-two. Peasemarket Hyll.*
*Cause of death, unknown.*

I wasn't sure what Master Chanter was getting at. Unknown deaths were rising in Meldron. Starvation was taking a toll. But I pressed on, setting the notes aside and focusing on the larger leaf of creased paper. Broderick's letters were uneven and dragged across the page as if he had been too weak to hold the quill.

*Master Chanter,*
*I need you to investigate something for me. Healer Malcom and I have been working closely to find a solid, affordable cure for the Deathbiters' bite.*
*However, our research uncovered thirty-eight deaths in previously healthy individuals who have no mark of a Deathbiter. I believe they were mistakenly counted as Deathbiter victims.*

*I've reached out to Shear and Kaltum where the Deathbiters are thickest and found evidence of more strange deaths incorrectly counted as Deathbiter casualties.*

*Please, look into unusual deaths near you. I'm concerned something else is afoot. These individuals did not suffer with fever and hallucinations. They died instantly with an unnerving hollowness in their eyes.*

*I am sorry to put this burden on you. I am still mending from my injuries and cannot travel in my condition, not at the speed needed to outrun the Deathbiters. By the grace of the Phoenix, I should be well enough to travel by month's end.*

*Your faithful apprentice,*
*Broderick Ironshade*

I lowered his letter and looked at Master Chanter. "How can I help?"

Chanter lifted the three notes of scribbled deaths from the desk, flipping them through his scarred hands. "You have seen the way Deathbiters work. You've seen those infected. I have not. I would like you and Ropert to accompany me to view the bodies."

"Let me grab my cloak."

Ropert pulled his cloak tighter as we followed Master Chanter through the streets of Meldron. A fog lingered between the buildings, making it difficult to see the next bend. Frost decorated windowpanes, and our breath plumed like clouds.

"I can't wait for spring," Ropert muttered.

"And when it's spring, you'll wish for summer." Chanter glanced over his shoulder. "And in summer, you'll wish for autumn. You young people, always wishing for something to change. Always wishing for things to move faster. I'll tell you now, enjoy the moments you have. Life will be better for it."

He turned down a side road, the timber-framed buildings shading us from the morning sunlight.

Master Chanter paused by a door and knocked. The door opened, and an elderly woman peered at us down a long nose. "You're late."

"I'm right on time, Madam Winchell." Chanter stepped inside. "Where are the bodies?"

She pressed her wrinkled lips together, stepping back. "This way."

We entered a narrow hallway filled with a strange smell of herbs and rotting wood. The woman immediately herded us into a dark room on the right where the smell hinted at rotten meat and flowers. The bodies were beginning to decompose.

A table stood in the center with a sheet draped over the form of a man. Candles flickered in the corners, casting shadows on two more sheets lying on the floor.

Madam Winchell moved to the head of the table and lifted the corner of the sheet. "They have enough meat on their bones to rule out starvation. There are no signs of poison, assault, or any other underlying condition. They were healthy. But yet, here they lie." She moved the sheet from the man's face. By the growth of his beard, I assumed this to be Joel Mudotter from Chanter's list.

"Were his eyes closed like this when he was found?" Master Chanter asked.

"No," Madam Winchell said. "They were wide open and . . . well, here. Let me show you." She pried the man's eyelid open with a crooked finger.

His iris was white, drained of all color.

I staggered back.

It couldn't be.

Madam Winchell reverently covered the man's face. "I haven't touched those two." She gestured to the two corpses on the floor. "Their deaths are highly unusual. They were healthy and strong, found together on the street. Their parents say they were courting."

Crouching by the sheet, I swallowed hard and lifted the corner. Hollow eyes stared at me as if their souls had been pulled from their bodies.

I dropped the cloth, my heart thundering.

She was here.

"Dagger. What's wrong?"

I couldn't breathe. The walls closed in like a dark cage growing smaller and smaller. Thrall flickered inside me, intrigued by the rush of fear, eager to have a taste. How? How was she here? Why hadn't I sensed her? Were all the other bodies like this, spread halfway across Roanfire? She was gathering power.

But how? She couldn't do it without help.

Had everything been a distraction—the Deathbiters, Ikane—all to keep me from seeing the real threat? Had she been right under my nose the whole time?

"You know what is causing this, don't you?" Master Chanter asked.

Maybe she wasn't here. Maybe she was reaching out across Roanfire, picking at souls too weak to resist her. It wasn't impossible. She'd done it in the past. She had tried devouring me halfway across the entire kingdom.

But that couldn't be right. She always complained of using too much power when she did that. She wasn't in the hands of Master somewhere in Glacier Pass. She was on the move, following my trek back to Meldron.

"Dagger." Ropert took my shoulders, dragging me to my feet. "Let's get you outside."

I allowed him to steer me from the room, through the door, and into the snowy street. My lungs felt trapped, like cords had been wrapped around them, keeping them from expanding. Who would be her next victim? Why was she here? What did she—

The baby.

"We have to get back to the castle, now!"

My legs burned, and my lungs stung from the sprint through the city, up the stairs, and down the corridor. I only hoped I wasn't too late.

Slamming the lever down, I rammed my shoulder against the door, throwing it wide. "My Queen?"

Corporal Melark jumped from her seat by the fire, red curls flying, her sword half-drawn from its sheath.

Queen Lonacheska jumped, jerking the teacup from her lips, the motion sending a splatter onto her lap. "Uh. Lady Brendagger. What's gotten into you?"

I scanned the room for anything out of place, a red glow, a smell, a sound that didn't belong, a presence. No matter how far I stretched my mind, I couldn't find her. Rion was somewhere in the castle. I knew she was.

Lona grabbed a napkin from the table beside her and dabbed her dress as Ropert and Master Chanter staggered in after me.

"My apologies, Your Majesty." Chanter bowed to the queen. Then he grabbed my elbow, and with a painful pinch, steered me to the door. "What do you think you are doing?"

"Wait." Queen Lonacheska rose from her seat, her dark eyes locking on mine.

She saw it. The danger, the fear.

"Please, excuse us," she said, holding her voice remarkably steady. "I would like to speak with Lady Brendagger privately."

Chanter's grip loosened as he turned back to the queen. His brows furrowed. "I am responsible for your safety, My Queen, and the safety of our king. I cannot perform my duties if I do not have every bit of vital information." He shot me a dangerous glare. "I do not like being kept in the dark."

"And you shall have all the information you need once I have spoken with Lady Brendagger. If you please." Lona motioned to the open door.

I hoped Chanter didn't see how badly her hands were shaking.

Chanter's jaw tightened. "As you wish." He bowed then motioned for Corporal Melark and Ropert to follow.

"Master Chanter," I called after him.

He paused.

"Fetch King Sander. He'll want to know."

Master Chanter's brows furrowed once more, but he nodded.

As soon as the door clicked shut, Lona sank back into her seat, her hands trembling as she braced herself against the armrests. Her dark eyes were wide and wild, filled with unbridled worry, pleading for me to explain. "What is it? What happened?"

"It's Rion," I breathed. "She's here. In Meldron. She may even be in the castle."

Lonacheska's hands flew to her rounding abdomen. "How?"

"I don't know." My body ached with energy, ready to act, to fight, to shield. But there was nothing I could do. I paced in front of the fireplace, the warmth penetrating my clothing, sending a shiver up my spine. I dug my palms into my temples, scrunching my eyes. "I . . . I can't sense her."

How could I protect the queen when I didn't know where the threat was coming from? Rion had been gathering power for the past month, possibly longer. All this time, she'd been collecting new energy right behind my back.

But even if I *could* find her, I couldn't face her. My mind was weak, Etheria frail, and Thrall ready to devour any form of rage like a starved viper.

"What can be done?" Lona asked.

I dropped my hands. "You shouldn't be alone. I . . . I can't leave your side." Even that sounded foolish in my head. If I couldn't sense Rion, what good could I do? Rion had been so silent for so long I wasn't sure I'd recognize her if I did feel her.

The door's latch clicked. Lona and I whirled as Master Chanter stepped inside, followed by King Sander. Sander didn't look well. The dark circles under his eyes made him look gaunt and frail, and the worried expression didn't help.

"Lona?"

Lonacheska rose from her seat, rushing into her husband's arms.

"My dear, you are trembling." He gathered her to him, his stormy blue eyes flaring as they found mine, almost as if he wanted to throw me into the dungeons for distressing her.

I bit my lip. Perhaps I had acted too rashly. Rion couldn't do anything with the child until she was born, and even then, she would be too frail to hold all the fire and rage Rion bottled inside.

"The baby is in danger," Lona whispered to King Sander.

"What?" He stepped back, holding her at arm's length, scanning her rounding belly. "How? Are you hurt?"

She shook her head.

Chanter crossed his arms over his chest, silver brows growing darker as he glowered at me. "Out with it, Brendagger."

I'd made a mess of things. But wasn't it better to be overly cautious than not cautious enough?

"Broderick was right," I said. "The killings were not caused by the Deathbiters. They are the work of Rion Noirfonika."

"That fairy tale again?" King Sander groaned. "Kea. Haven't you found peace with that yet? Roanfire is on the brink of starvation, and you are causing a scene about a rumored ancient curse—"

"But it's not." Queen Lonacheska pushed him away. "Don't you see? This is the reason I sent Lady Brendagger to the Glacial Empire."

King Sander's jaw dropped, his eyes flashing. "You . . . you *what*?"

"Yes, I sent her to the Glacial Empire." Lona's voice broke, her eyes shimmering in the firelight. "I did not intend to hurt you, Sander. I know how much you were relying on Lady Brendagger. But there is a curse on our child, one real and strong, and it will claim the life of our daughter if you do not allow Kea to—"

"Our daughter?" King Sander interrupted. The betrayal in his eyes melted away as he took in his bride's figure. "How . . . how can you be sure?"

Tears streaked down the queen's smooth cheeks. "Because of the curse." She hugged her shoulders. "Our child will be the second female heir to the throne of Roanfire in four hundred years." She glanced at me. "If Kea does not destroy it, our child will have no choice but to face a monster that will surely kill her. I can't . . . I can't let that happen."

King Sander looked at me, his stormy blue eyes flooding with shifting emotions. "You truly believe this, don't you? You wouldn't have gone to the Glacial Empire if you didn't."

"No one should have to face what I have," I whispered. "Especially not a child."

King Sander moved slowly, gently pulling Lona against his chest. She clung to him, burying her tear-streaked face into his shoulder.

"What can I do?" he asked.

Something in my chest eased, a crushing sensation I hadn't known was sitting against it. He finally accepted the truth. He finally believed what I had been telling him all along.

"Post half a dozen guards at the door," I said. "Don't trust anyone, and don't let anyone near the queen until we find out who is helping Rion. And I . . . I should stay with her. I'm the only one who can protect her."

Those last words felt like a lie dripping from my lips. But I had no idea what more I could do.

# CHAPTER 25

# TOLEAH'S SECRETS

*I* turned inward, pulling into a place I rarely visited anymore. Where was she? How could she hide so well? There had to be a thread or memory, anything that could lead to her. But my mind was as still as a moonlit pond, lonely and void of Rion's or Ikane's thoughts.

How had this become normal? My mind used to ripple with so many views.

"Lady Brendagger?" Queen Lonacheska's voice radiated through my mind, her touch on my hand drawing me back to my body. How long had I been sitting here? My hips ached, and something in my neck pinched.

Straightening, I blinked at the fire crackling in the hearth. Corporal Melark crouched by the fireplace, stoking the flames.

Lona leaned back in her seat, dropping her hands to the book in her lap. How in the blazes could she relax enough to read anything at a time like this?

"Sir Ropert is here to escort you to supper," she said.

I rubbed my face, glancing at the four-poster bed against the wall where King Sander rested. He still looked pale.

Ropert stood by the door, waiting.

I shook my head. "I can't leave your side." If Prince Leander was any kind of man, he would understand that the queen needed me.

"I will be alright for an hour," Lona said. "You must hold up your end of the agreement with Toleah. We still need their help. Maly will be here. She can be trusted."

I was carrying too much on my shoulders. Yes, I'd agreed to dine with Prince Leander, but I'd also promised to protect my queen and her baby. One hour was more than enough time for someone to slip into Lona's chambers.

Corporal Melark stood. "I will keep her safe," she said.

I scanned the room once more. "No one is to enter. Not even her usual maids."

The young redheaded soldier nodded.

I stood, ran my fingers through my hair, and straightened my tunic. I inhaled through my nose, but it didn't ease the weight crushing my shoulders. I shouldn't be leaving Queen Lonacheska's side. Not even for this.

"Lock the door after me."

Corporal Melark followed me to the exit where Ropert greeted me with a smile, though it didn't quite reach his eyes.

"Ready?" he asked.

"Not really." But I stepped into the corridor where six soldiers stood guard anyway. Ropert closed the door, and the clunk of the key turning echoed behind us.

"I've set up a rotation of every three hours for the exchange of guards," Ropert said as I fell into step beside him. "I'll stand watch this evening."

My chest tightened. Even an army was no match for Rion. I suggested that the door be guarded only to ease Lona's fears. But the soldiers were nothing to her, specks of dust easily blown from her path. The last thing I wanted was for Ropert to stand guard. What if Rion attacked?

An image of Ropert crumpled on the ground flashed through my mind, his vibrant blue eyes turned lifeless and hollow, staring at me.

I slammed my eyes shut, shaking my head. I couldn't think that way.

"Don't let Prince Leander bully you into anything, Dagger. You don't need to agree to all of his demands." Ropert stopped at a door and knocked.

"Even if it means the end of Roanfire?"

"I don't think it'll come to that."

The door creaked open to a pair of large brown eyes. Leander's Ridarri warrior scanned us, her gaze lifting to Ropert's tall frame. She tilted her head at him, her long, midnight hair falling over her tattooed shoulder. "I remember you," she said in a thick accent.

Ropert stiffened and cleared his throat. "And I remember you. You . . . you have to show me how you landed that kick." He rubbed his jaw absently.

Her lips pulled into a smile.

Prince Leander's voice rang out behind her, saying something in his native tongue.

The Ridarri stepped aside, opening the door wider, the smell of warm spices wafting against my face. "Lady Brendagger is here," she said.

"Ah, welcome," Prince Leander said from his place by the fire. He was missing his cobalt-blue headscarf again, and his long black dreadlocks hung down his back.

His second Ridarri—a tall man with broad shoulders—stood at attention nearby.

I stepped into Prince Leander's chambers. I would keep this visit as brief as possible. I'd make up an excuse if I had to.

My feet stopped. Something was different about the room. The cushioned armchairs—typically situated by the fire—had been pushed against the wall, and a short round table took their place. Instead of chairs, thick, colorful pillows lay around it.

Flaming feathers, where had all the food come from?

A vibrant salad of green spinach with bright red radishes and seeds sat beside a bowl of roasted turnips and squash—

vegetables I could only dream of this time of year, not to mention during a famine. A small roast sat beside them. The shape and rich smell suggested it was rabbit.

Prince Leander gestured to a pillow beside him. "Please, sit."

I glanced back at Ropert. I wanted him to stay. There was enough food here for him, and I knew how much he loved filling his belly. I saw the look in his eye.

But he smiled at me. "I'll be back for you in an hour." He gave Leander's Ridarri a quick nod then slipped away.

A strange sense of loneliness came with his absence, but I gathered a deep breath and moved to the suggested seat, sank down, and folded my legs.

Flipping the tail of his long coat behind him, Leander sank to his cushion beside me and nodded to his Ridarri warriors. "Boma. Ciri. Come."

The man and woman moved from their positions and—flaming feathers. What were they doing? Were they actually going to sit at the table with the prince?

They were. Weren't they his slaves?

"We are all equal to Mother Earth," Prince Leander said as he reached for the glistening plate of roasted turnip and squash. "Without her, we would have no food. Without her, we do not live. We are not above nature nor is one man above another."

I didn't understand. With a belief like that, wouldn't the Toleans shun slavery? Owning another human being contradicted everything he had just said.

But I bit my tongue. This was not the time nor the place to confront him. We needed food, and I had to convince him to help us.

Prince Leander handed the dish to me. "Take what you want. There is enough for all."

I hesitated. "Could . . . could Ropert join us next time?"

"Your bodyguard?"

I nodded.

"I don't see why not."

Something about his words eased the tension in my gut. I filled my plate, sampling every dish. I mopped juices with soft rabbit meat, crunched crisp radishes between my teeth, savored the rich flavor of herb and onion. The food tasted of home, of summer in Daram, the smell of rosemary and thyme wafting from Mayama's garden, and the laughter of soldiers dining in the mess hall.

I wiped the grease from my lips with the back of my sleeve. "Where did this food come from?"

Leander's lips twitched with a smile, but he suffocated it. "Do you always eat like that?"

My hands froze, the meal's juices glistening on my fingertips. My stomach clenched. I was dining with the Tolean Prince! Small bites, the napkin, posture, utensils. How could I have forgotten everything Illorce had taught me?

Heat rose to my ears, burning through my face.

Prince Leander chuckled. "I am pleased the meal was to your liking." He laced his fingers, resting his elbows on the table. His eyes were like deep pools of bright honey against his dark skin, flickering with amusement. "Perhaps we should have sent for more food from Toleah. Ciri, when does the first shipment arrive?"

The female Ridarri politely swallowed her mouthful. "Within the week, Shazadeh Leander."

I couldn't chew. What did she just say? "You mean . . . ?"

"Yes." He smiled. "Toleah is sending help."

My hands flew over my mouth. I wanted to run to King Sander, tell him he could stop worrying about the kingdom. We were going to be alright.

"Thank you. Thank you so much, Your Highness. Roanfire will be forever in your debt."

"It is not Roanfire's debt I seek," he said, his eyes watching me intently.

I swallowed hard.

Was it me? After everything, did he still want my hand in marriage?

Leander stood, brushing his gold-embellished dreadlocks behind his shoulder. "You asked me where this food came from." He extended a hand to me. "There is a reason I demanded a room with plenty of south-facing windows."

His grip was firm as he helped me to my feet and steered me to the far end of the room. I hadn't noticed the colorful fabrics hanging from ceiling to floor, cutting the room in half like a strange rainbow wall. At any other time, I would have fought his firm guidance, but somehow, I trusted him.

He dropped my hand and parted a section, holding the curtain for me. "After you."

Ducking, I stepped through.

A gentle humidity touched my skin like a grounding embrace, and a rich smell of earth and decay flooded my senses. Flaming feathers. What had he done to this place?

Greenery sprouted from a garden of pottery, vibrant leaves reaching to warm light spilling from four arched windows. Yellow blossoms opened like stars. Fruit from the very items we'd just eaten clung to plants, thick and ripe. Vines climbed up the walls and sprawled across the floor.

"How . . . how is this possible?"

Leander ducked in after me. "I admit, it is a challenge."

"It's impossible."

He chuckled, a warm and genuine sound. "Not impossible. Come. Let me show you." He wove through the pots, his long coat brushing against the dense foliage. Pulling a small pail from a shelf, he withdrew a stick with frayed cotton knotted at the tip. He offered one to me.

"I don't understand. Why are you showing me this? Just two days ago, we were about to go to war."

"Are you not pleased?"

I folded my arms. "Such generosity doesn't come without a price. I will keep my end of the bargain and bring you Hala Whitefox. But this?" I waved to the garden bursting with enough food to feed the entire castle. "What do you want in return for showing me this?"

"I haven't shown you anything but a garden. I can assure you, I am not giving you any of Toleah's secrets today." He offered me one of his strange cotton-tipped sticks again. "But this garden does need constant tending. Seeing as there are no insects to pollinate, we must do it by hand. Will you help me?"

A spark of guilt stole through me, rousing Thrall just enough to open one eye to the taste. I shouldn't have spoken to him that way. I shouldn't have questioned his generosity. But something about him had been drastically different since the night he met Alder.

Sticking the tip of the swab into an open squash blossom, he made a gentle circular motion, collecting the bright yellow pollen. Deliberately and methodically, he moved the pollen from one flower to another. "The ones with the long stems are male. The ones with the small fruit under the blossom are female," he said. "Be sure to collect from both."

This was more complicated than I thought. I followed his motions, the cotton ball on the end of my stick growing bright with color.

I paused. Did that flower just move?

I stared at the blossom, watching as the yellow petals slowly curled in. The entire plant trembled, and the small green fruit swelled at the base of the flower. I glanced at Prince Leander.

"That," he began, "now *that* is Toleah's secret. The fruit will be ready to consume by tomorrow." He set his pollinator aside, his honey-colored eyes finding mine. The vibrant green plants reflected in them. "And because they grow so quickly, we must harvest twice a day."

The curtain parted, and his Ridarri entered with large wicker baskets on their hips. They began harvesting the unbelievably ripe vegetables, filling the baskets with three varieties of squash, fat radishes, juicy heads of cabbage, pungent onions, and rich orange carrots.

"Tonight, no one in the castle shall go hungry," Leander said as he collected a handful of radishes, brushed the dirt from their red skin, and placed the bundle into Boma's basket.

A strange feeling pushed into my chest, swelling into my eyes, suffocating Thrall. I blinked away the blurriness, unable to hide the smile trembling on my lips. This man was going to save Roanfire. This Tolean Prince, who I judged as selfish and prideful, had a heart rich with giving. Ships were coming, and this garden—however he did it—was a breath of new life in the castle.

"Thank you." My voice broke with emotion. "Thank you so much."

"We will do our best to supply the castle with food until the ships arrive." Leander dusted the dirt from his hands as he approached.

"Why? I mean, I . . . I don't understand why you are doing this for us. For King Sander. He locked you in a tower. You endured things no prince should have to face."

Prince Leander twisted the emerald ring on his finger, his honey-colored eyes scanning the jungle around us. "Perhaps I was tired of the tasteless broths served by your kitchen."

I arched an eyebrow.

His eyes, burning with a startling intensity, locked with mine. "Or it is because I have a feeling that our lives will be more intertwined than I believed."

What . . . what did he mean by that? The gentle swelling in my chest dropped to an uneasy churn in the pit of my stomach. I swallowed hard. Marriage? Is that what he meant? Was I to spend the rest of my life with him in Toleah, away from everything and everyone I loved?

"I . . . I should be getting back."

"Of course." He opened the curtain for me. "I look forward to dining with you again tomorrow."

A part of me did, too.

## CHAPTER 26

# ESCAPE

*M*arrok strained against the ropes. A deep ache settled in his wrists that even his lycanthrope abilities couldn't heal fast enough. The fur beneath the cords lay matted and clotted with blood.

But the post had shifted, the deep shadow between wood and snow indicating a good two-inch gap, even after the soldiers had reinforced it with rock and additional planks.

At this rate, he would break free just as sunlight touched the sky and the Deathbiters fled to their lair.

Perhaps it was his imagination, but there seemed to be fewer every night. He could see the stars breaking through the clouds in small clusters now without black leathery wings blotting his view. What he wouldn't give to see the full scope of the constellations.

There was a time he soared between the stars, wind rushing across his face until his eyes watered, the ship rocking beneath his feet.

He shook his head.

That couldn't be right. He'd never set foot on a ship before, had he? The memory felt like it belonged to someone else.

"No. That is your memory, Ikane. It's true. Every part of it. You love the stars. You were born on the water. You are a Leviathan pirate."

The voice was a whisper, barely cutting through the screaming cries of bats grating through his ears. The girl was in his head again.

"Oh, Ikane, I wish I didn't have to invade your thoughts to speak with you."

"Then don't," he growled.

"Ikane, please."

"What do you want with me?"

"I want you to remember who you are."

What in the shuddering timbers did she mean by that? He was a creature born of magic, bred for destruction, a godlike being. Master told him so.

"Master has told you what he wanted you to hear. Your name is Ikane Ormand. You are the youngest of the seven Leviathan princes. You've risked everything to save your brother, Teilo. You turned against them in the heat of battle to protect me. You have—"

He slammed his eyes shut, teeth grinding together. "Stop. Just stop!"

Her voice fell silent, but he could still feel her inside, leaning against his mind with a tenderness he didn't deserve or want.

"I will tear out your heart, you hear? First, I will destroy Eamon, and then I will come for you. I will hunt you until the last star falls from the sky."

"Ikane, please."

Pain touched her voice, and he smiled. Maybe now she understood the true threat he posed.

"I . . . I love you."

Those three words struck his chest like a wave of ice.

Why would she say something like that? She didn't even know him. He didn't know her.

*But why . . . why did it feel true?*

*A cloud of black invaded his thoughts, suffocating every question in his mind. It roiled with power, expanding like blood gushing from a wound underwater.*

"She is feeding you lies." Master's rumbling voice flooded his thoughts. "She doesn't love you. Do you think she could love a creature who harmed her friend? A creature who hunts her guardian? Break her, shatter her heart, crush it!"

*A faint light pushed back on the shadow.* "No." *Her voice grew in strength.* "Ikane, Eamon is your friend and mentor. He cares for you more than you know. He trained you. Do you remember? Two swords."

"Leave him alone!" *Master roared. A surge of black power slammed into her light, driving her back. The impact rippled across Marrok's mind as if a hammer had been taken to his skull. He ground his teeth together, fists tightening, muscles straining against his bonds.*

*Why did they insist on treating his mind like a battle arena? Didn't they see the pain they were causing him? For one with a body so powerful, he felt like a helpless bystander, a victim powerless to defend himself.*

*The girl's light flickered with her tight words.* "I am sorry this happened to you, Ikane. Your mind should be yours." *Her energy receded.*

*Was she . . . was she leaving him in peace?*

"You think yourself to be so noble," *Master roared, releasing another wave of black power at her retreating light.*

*A whimper tore from Marrok's throat as black danced behind his eyelids.*

"And you!" *Master turned his rage to Marrok.* "I have given you a body that cannot be tamed! Break those bonds! Kill Eamon! Was I a fool to place so much faith in you?"

"No, Master," *Marrok groaned.*

"Then finish the task. I cannot wait any longer!"

*Heat rose in Marrok's chest. He was created to serve Master just like the bats circling overhead. No one could match his* strength. No one could match his speed. Master was right. The girl was lying. No one could love what he was.

Fire spread through his muscles, turning them solid, the cords snapping taut. He would not be beaten by a few ropes or an aging warrior.

Shutting his eyes and digging his feet into the packed snow, he strained, willing all energy into his center. The sound of breaking wood rippled through his arms as they gained more and more freedom.

"That's it," Master crooned.

Marrok eased back, gasping for breath, his arms sagging on the ropes as he waited for the burning to subside. One of the posts leaned against the pile of rocks at the base, deep cracks etching black lines into the wood. One more pull like that, and he would be free.

He jerked his arms tight. The post creaked. With a resounding crack, his arm shot forward, rope and broken beam crashing to the snow at his feet.

His muscles sighed as they dropped to a natural position. He was free.

"Good. Now, finish it." Master's pride and approval radiated through his mind, fueling his next move.

"Dagger." Ropert whispered. "Dagger, wake up." He shook my shoulder.

I blinked at the smoldering embers in the fireplace then at Ropert who knelt beside my armchair, pale moonlight from the window showing his face filled with worry. What was he doing here? He was supposed to be in bed, far away from Lona's chambers. He wasn't even dressed, and his hair hung loose and wild around his shoulders.

Lona was sound asleep in her bed, and Corporal Melark lay curled before the fire.

"What time is it?" I whispered, rubbing sleep from my eyes. My head ached. Master's blows still rippled through my skull. And Ikane . . . Ikane was free.

Feathers, this wasn't good.

"She's in the castle," Ropert whispered.

I dropped my hand, my mind still trying to tear itself from the dream. "Who?"

"Rion."

My stomach flipped, and my mind flew awake. "What?"

"Hush." He held a finger to his lips. "We don't want to alarm the queen. Master Chanter sent me. He wants you to come."

"But the queen..." I swallowed hard, staring at Lonacheska sleeping soundly under her down covers, her golden hair falling across her pillow like sunbeams. King Sander lay beside her, his arm draped gently around her growing stomach.

"There are six soldiers at the door. They won't let anyone in but you or me."

My body shook with adrenaline as I followed Ropert from Queen Lonacheska's chambers. The guards on duty snapped to attention as Ropert claimed a torch from a soldier, the firelight casting long, quivering shadows on the walls around us. Even Ropert was scared.

My legs worked hard to keep up with his long strides. "What happened?"

"I . . . I can't describe it."

We turned down a long corridor filled with rows of windows, blue moonlight falling in perfect arched shapes across the floor. Ropert slowed upon noting a tall figure sitting in one of the windows with a notebook propped open on his leg. Sketches of bats surrounded by scribbled notes filled the page. His long midnight-gray hair cascaded down his back as he watched Deathbiters streak through the sky beyond the windows.

Alder turned as Ropert's torchlight touched his face.

"Put that out," he whispered fiercely.

The fire hissed out as Ropert suffocated it between the wall and his boot. "What are you doing here?"

Alder turned back to the window, the blue light making his good eye shimmer. "I was watching the Deathbiters from my room and noticed something odd. Look there." He pointed his charcoal pencil to a section of castle visible from the window.

Ropert leaned over Alder's shoulder, squinting.

"The Deathbiters have been clustering about that section of the castle for the past hour," Alder said, "but I can't see anything they might be attacking."

Ropert's eyes grew wide. "The servants' quarters," he breathed.

And I thought his face pale before.

I placed a hand on his arm, trying to keep my heart from beating out of my chest. "Ropert?"

Alder closed his book and slipped from the window. "Did something happen?"

Ropert's eyes remained fixed on the Deathbiter swarm outside. "I . . . I think you should both see this."

Alder and I exchanged looks then followed him down the hallway and into a narrow corridor. Ropert's hand trembled as he relit his torch with the flame of another burning in an iron sconce on the wall. Orange light flickered against the narrowing walls, doors growing smaller and tighter as we entered the servants' quarters.

Master Chanter appeared from a shadowy doorway. His eyes, already near panic, furrowed upon seeing Alder with us. "What is he doing here?"

"I think he can help," Ropert said.

Master Chanter turned his attention to me. "It's just like the others . . . but worse." He rested a hand on the lever of the door behind him, paused, then pushed the door open.

Ropert held the torch through the door but didn't enter.

A strange smell of charred flesh filled the chamber, mingled with a flowery perfume. Two bunks sat on opposite corners of the room.

I took a step forward, pausing as I noted the pale skin of a hand lying across my path. A woman—a maidservant I'd seen in Queen Lonacheska's room—lay motionless on the floor, her eyes wide and hollow.

My heart jumped behind my spine, and my legs shook, willing me to turn and bolt. But I couldn't run.

Another body caught my attention, lying across the bottom bunk of the bed at an odd angle. A third lay crumpled at the far wall, and a fourth was only visible by her limp arm hanging over the top bunk.

Four. Four maidservants. Gone.

Everything raced toward me as the room shrunk. Faces gaped at me, eyes frozen wide, empty and hollow. I staggered away, shoulders hitting the wall at my back.

"Close the door." My voice was shamefully weak.

How? How could she have done this right under my nose? I didn't feel a thing.

*Rion, you coward. Show yourself,* I cried in my mind, stretching farther than ever before.

"You say there are more deaths like these?" Alder asked as Chanter pulled the door shut. "All across Roanfire?"

"From Gerom Post to here," Chanter said.

Alder brushed his silken hair back, his face tight. "The Deathbiters are not to blame for this. This is the work of Thrall." He looked at me. "The Deathbiters respond to it. It is how I keep them at bay. Someone must be calling to them." He glanced at Chanter. "Whose attendants were these? Whomever they serve must be in danger."

"They belong to Queen Lonacheska." Master Chanter stared at me. "Go, Kea. We're right behind you."

I turned, my legs driving me through the corridor.

What if we were already too late? What if this had all been a distraction? Rion could have infested the child by now. Four lives at once? She wasn't even trying to hide anymore.

I reached the spiraling staircase, taking the stairs two at a time.

What could I do? I had no lead, no thread, no red spark, no burn to trace. This was maddening. Why couldn't I feel her? Someone had to be protecting her. The same someone who kept Yotherna from me.

It was Master. I knew it was.

I could have confronted him. Just a few moments ago, I'd faced him in the dream. My head still ached from his strikes. But fighting him had hurt Ikane. His mind wasn't the place for a battle. I had to find another way.

My muscles burned as I reached the royal corridor. The four soldiers standing guard jumped from their lazy positions against the wall when I hurried for them.

"Has anyone been here?" I demanded.

"No, my lady."

I hoped the news would ease the pounding in my chest, but it did nothing.

Footfalls echoed down the hallway as Ropert, Master Chanter, and Alder reached me.

"She's safe," I said. "No one has been here."

"Let them rest." Chanter turned to Ropert. "Double the guards, and set hourly rotations."

"Hourly?" Ropert arched an eyebrow.

"This is not a time to gamble with sleep deprivation, boredom, or daydreamers," Chanter said. "Shorter rotations will ensure sharper eyes and minds."

Ropert nodded. "I'll see to it."

"As for you." Chanter turned to me. "You are not to leave Queen Lonacheska's side. Whatever danger she's in, it seems you are the best and last defense she has."

If only he knew how much I disagreed.

"Which means I'll have to make other dinner arrangements with Prince Leander." Master Chanter dragged a hand down his groomed beard. "Let us hope he won't change his mind and threaten war again for altering your agreement." He hurried past the guards and slipped out of view at the end of the hallway.

"Lady Brendagger." Alder's deep voice rumbled through my chest despite his whisper. "You've already been spending every moment here with the queen. It is admirable what you are trying to do. But how long do you think you can manage?"

My brows furrowed. "What do you mean?"

"What I'm trying to say is that I would be happy to assist. I can stay with the queen when you need to attend your nightly dinners with Prince Leander or stretch your legs or spar with Ropert. I am the only other person here who can detect the use of Thrall."

I bit my lip. "You . . . you would do that?"

He smiled.

Feathers, he was gorgeous.

"Of course, I would," he said. "You are my friend, Kea."

The tightness in my chest eased, finally feeling that I no longer had to shoulder this burden alone. "Thank you, Alder. And I'm sure Master Chanter will find your offer most generous."

"I can take watch now if you'd like," he offered.

I shook my head. I couldn't sleep anyway. "I hate to ask since you've already been more than helpful, but you may want to let Master Chanter know of your offer before he upsets Prince Leander."

Alder let out a soft, rumbling chuckle. "As you wish." He tipped his head, his silken hair falling over his shoulders. After nodding to Ropert, he turned and allowed his long legs to carry him into the shadowy end of the corridor.

Ropert stepped beside me, watching Alder go. "I think I misjudged him."

"I think we both did," I agreed.

## CHAPTER 27

# BREAK HER

*M*arrok didn't think it was possible to push his powerful body beyond its godlike ability, but cold splinters shredded his lungs and every muscle in his legs burned and ached. A stitch pierced his side.

It was nothing compared to the waves of pain crashing against his heart, pressing down on him like a relentless waterfall. He collapsed against a thick tree, his claws leaving pale streaks in the bark.

So much red. It flaked from the thick padding on his palms. It clotted the fur on his wrists. It stuck under his long, lethal claws. He tasted it, metallic and sharp, sickening and sweet on his tongue. The smell made his stomach roll.

"You did well, my son. You have finished your task. Now, come to me. I have a new errand for you."

Master's voice speared his mind the same way his teeth had penetrated flesh. Why did it hurt so much? He'd done what Master commanded. He'd followed orders. He did what was expected of him.

Yet the sensation of his fangs breaking into the skin of the man's throat tore into his heart like a thousand daggers. A thousand daggers tipped with venom.

*The kindness had never left the man's eyes, even after he lay in the snow with blood pooling around his body. The man had only ever spoken to him with respect and hope, calling to him like a lost friend.*

*A strange sound escaped his chest.*

*No. It was the call of something deeper. The man had been more than a friend, more than a mentor. He had been a father.*

*The images came clear, the memories strong and vivid. Eamon guiding him through sword drills, late night talks by the firelight, strolls along the beach, fishing, hunting, and scheming against the Leviathan pirates.*

*Bile seared up his throat, his stomach clenching like the sorrow crushing his heart. The trees around him blurred, and water streaked down the fur on his cheeks. The whimper tearing from his throat ripped the last of his strength from his powerful body. He dropped, claws digging into the snow, leaving streaks of blood in their wake.*

*Master told him to strike where it would hurt the girl the most.*

*But Marrok felt like the debilitated one.*

I jerked upright. The muscles in my neck spasmed as I straightened in the armchair, blinking as my mind snapped back to Queen Lonacheska's night-darkened room. Dying embers smoldered in the fireplace, the flickering orange light as real as the pain in Marrok's chest and the coppery-sweet taste of blood lingering on his tongue.

My fingers brushed my lips.

Eamon?

Had he really . . . ? My breath came hard as a deep ache grew around my thundering heart, expanding like a dangerous black mist rolling over the sea, suffocating it. Every heart throb pushed against my ribs as if they had shriveled into a cage too small.

It couldn't be true. Ikane would never do such a thing. He would never . . .

But my dreams had never been wrong.

My hands flew to my chest, digging through my tunic as if I could keep my heart from beating through my skin. A cry tore from my throat. I should have gone back. I should have stayed by Eamon's side.

"Dagger?" Ropert stirred in the chair opposite mine. His brows furrowed as he leaned forward and placed a warm hand on my knee. "Are you alright?"

Oh, Phoenix help me, I couldn't breathe.

Ropert slipped to his knees, taking my hands in his. "What's wrong? What happened?"

My heart was going to burst. I threw my arms around his neck, pulling him close, willing his solid arms to keep my chest from exploding. But even as he encircled me, the pain didn't ease. I pulled on his shirt, fabric straining against my fingers. He needed to crush me. Suffocate me. I didn't want to breathe. I didn't want to feel my heart beat.

"Hey," he said softly. "What's wrong? What happened?"

I couldn't say it. I didn't want to say it. It was a dream. That's all. A dream that showed my worst fears, nothing more. Eamon was fine. Ikane didn't do it. He was with Broderick. They would come back to Meldron soon. I would see all of them again, strong and healthy and smiling before me.

But everything surrounding my heart knew it was a lie.

Ropert's arms loosened.

My fingers dug into his back, pulling him closer. I needed him. He was the only thing keeping my heart from shattering. "Don't let go."

He crushed me, finally squeezing me until my ribs ached. It didn't help. It didn't stop the growing ache in my chest.

"What is going on?" Queen Lonacheska slipped her legs over the bed, dragging a blanket around her shoulders. She approached cautiously, and her hand was soft and gentle against my back.

I couldn't speak. I couldn't think. Ikane's pain was real. He knew what he'd done, and it was crushing him just like it was crushing me.

Thrall woke, a flicker of something hot and famished. For the first time, I wanted it to feast. I wanted it to devour this feeling inside my chest. Swallow it whole. Make it go away.

*It was just a dream. Just a dream . . .*

Lonacheska straightened. "Where is Maly?"

Blinking through the tears and sniffing, I searched the room for the redheaded soldier. She shouldn't have left without telling Ropert or me, but Maly's bedroll lay empty before the fire.

Ropert stood. The emptiness in my chest widened in his absence. I pushed the heel of my palms against my eyes, rocking forward in my chair. Why wouldn't Thrall feast? The pain was deep, strong, and paralyzing. It was what it wanted. Why did it sit like an obstinate cat waiting for its meal?

Ropert cracked the door open, peering into the hallway. "Flaming feathers . . ." He ripped the door wide, and something thumped at his boots. His hair flew as he dropped to his knees. "Maly?" The tone in his voice sent my blood into a panic.

I forced myself to stand, to take a step around the armchair, to blink my eyes clear of tears. Now was not the time to mourn. I needed to stay alert for the queen.

But my feet stopped as Ropert's eyes locked onto mine.

Maly's head of red curls lay at Ropert's knees. Why wasn't she moving?

"Maly?" Queen Lonacheska stepped closer.

Ropert leapt to his feet, whirled, and grabbed the queen's shoulders. "Stay back."

"Maly!" Lona's hands flew over her mouth, strangling her cry.

Rion was here.

At Queen Lonacheska's doorstep.

And I'd felt nothing.

The floor opened beneath my boots like I was falling from the Fold cliffs all over again. My knees cracked against the floor, the impact jarring through my spine. It was too much. I'd relied on Thrall to sense her, but it had done nothing. All it did was push me down and suffocate me in a sea of failure.

And now Eamon . . .

An ugly, shattered cry pushed from my throat as I fell forward on my hands . . . my useless hands. Tears dropped onto my scarred, calloused skin tainted by sprite dust, unable to protect anyone I loved. The daggers going through my chest stabbed again and again.

It was no wonder Queen Damita failed. It was no wonder every queen and princess before her failed, too. This was an impossible task that left nothing but devastated souls in its wake.

The image of Ikane's deformed, hybrid body curled on the snow flooded my mind. His arms clutching his torso, tears streaking down his fur, his powerful growl broken with uncontrolled pain. And the blood on his hands—Eamon's blood.

I couldn't do this anymore.

Ropert's knees hit the ground beside me, his strong arms pulling me to him. He rocked with me, letting my tears stain his shirt and my cries deaden against his chest.

"Send for Alder," Ropert whispered to the queen. "We need him."

## CHAPTER 28

# "I KNOW WHO YOU ARE"

"Dagger?"

My eyes burned. Heavy and swollen lids struggled to open to the candlelight flickering beside my bed.

A calloused hand stroked my hair, and everything flooded back. The blood. The taste of copper. The tears streaking down Marrok's furred cheeks. The tenderness of Ropert's hand was sucked away by the void in my heart.

"Come on, Dagger. I hate seeing you like this." Ropert leaned forward, bracing himself beside my pillow. "Please, tell me what happened last night. I know Maly meant a lot to Queen Lonacheska, and her death is a terrible thing, but you were not mourning her, were you?"

As I squeezed my aching eyes closed, Maly's red curls lying near Ropert's knee flashed behind my lids. Everything was so wrong.

"Kea," Ropert pleaded softly, his fingers brushing a strand of hair from my cheek. Hearing him say my name instead of his pet name for me solidified how much he worried. "Please. What happened?"

My chest clenched, and fresh tears burned my eyes. Oh, when would I stop crying? I might be shedding tears for no reason. Eamon could be alive. My dream could be wrong.

"I need . . ." I swallowed, refusing to give way to the tears. "I need to send a letter."

Ropert ran a thumb across my cheek, stealing the fresh tear that had rebelliously slipped from my lashes. "A letter? To whom?"

"Eamon." His name pierced my tongue, shredding my chest, tearing into my heart.

Ropert's grip on my hand tightened, his pale brows furrowed, and his bright blue eyes pleaded with me to share the weight. "Did something happen?"

Oh, feathers, it was impossible to keep the tears at bay. I leapt up, grabbing Ropert's neck, my body shaking with sobs. "Marrok killed him. He killed him."

"Are you sure?"

I screamed against his shoulder. I wanted to believe it was a lie as much as he did. But I knew in the back of my mind that the truth was there. I was linked to Ikane in a way I wished I wasn't. My dreams were filled with his reality.

Ropert's arms tightened around me like he was trying to become a part of me to share my pain. "I'll find out what happened," he whispered, stroking my hair. There was something in his voice, a rage that simmered just beneath the surface. "Marrok will pay."

How could he think beyond the sorrow?

A knock sounded on the door. "Lady Brendagger? Is Sir Ropert there with you?"

The voice was unfamiliar.

Ropert pulled away and wiped his cheeks with his thumb, sniffing quickly. "Who is it?"

"Alder's man, sir. He asked me to send for you."

The sorrow on Ropert's face shifted to worry. "Alder is with the queen. I should see what this is about."

My arms dropped, the soldier in me pushing past the sorrow. "Go."

Ropert hurried to the door and slipped out. A hushed conversation flowed from the crack.

I lay back down, rolling onto my side, hugging my blankets to my chest, staring at the shuttered window. It was a wall keeping the Deathbiters out and the warmth in. We couldn't see each other, and yet we knew the other was there. Just like the wall hiding Rion from me.

I could blame Marrok. I could blame Master. But all this was Rion's doing. She was tearing me apart without laying a finger on me, without even brushing her feverish power against my mind. Even as a ghost, she was too powerful.

I shut my eyes. I'd lost my home, my friends, my position in the army, my love, and now the man I called my father. What more would she take from me?

"Alright, now. He's gone," the unfamiliar voice whispered.

The door creaked open.

"Hurry," another said. This voice was deeper, more gravely and harsh.

I rolled onto my back, blinking at two figures slipping into my room. One was short and rough-looking; the other was tall, his head was shaved clean, and he had a scar on his left brow. Alder's servants? What were they doing here? Where had Ropert gone?

The younger man lunged across the room. His hands clamped down on my shoulders, pinning me to the bed as the other tore the blanket from my legs.

Adrenaline soared, and my muscles kicked into action. My heel struck the gruff man's shoulder. Grunting, he threw himself across my knees, trapping my legs in his meaty arms.

I clawed at the younger man as his arms slipped under mine, dragging me from the bed, a hand clamping down on my mouth so hard my jaw ached. Flaming feathers. Who were these men? What did they want with me?

"I've got her," he growled to the other in a harsh whisper. "Let's go."

Arching against solid muscle, I tried to find leverage as they carried me to the doorway. The older man peered around the corner into the darkened hallway, barely phased by my struggling. I clawed at the bald man's arms, slamming my knuckles into the nerves on the back of his hands, anything to make him release. Was this man immune to pain?

"Someone's coming," the short man warned.

They shuffled into the shadow of a doorway, their arms tightening around me to the point of bruising bone. My muffled cries turned to frantic gasps through my nose as the bald man's hand pinched my jaw, pulling my head against his chest.

". . . isn't a good time." Ropert's voice carried down the hallway. "She's just received some devastating news."

I screamed his name, but the sound was a muffled squeal in my ears. The bald man's fingers dug into my cheeks as he pulled back.

"It cannot wait." It was Prince Leander's voice. His accent was unmistakable.

My captors pressed into the darkness as Ropert and Leander neared, the light of a torch spreading across the walls.

The older man shot the bald man a look as if to ask what had gone wrong.

I arched, my leg breaking free from the older man's grip. His fist cracked into my side, and white sparks danced across my vision as my ribs gave way to the impact. I desperately tried to inhale through my nose. He trapped my legs again.

Ropert and Leander walked by, the torch in Ropert's hand flickering across our faces. How could they not hear me?

Despite the man's fingers digging into my cheeks, I screamed Ropert's name against his hand.

Ropert paused, holding the torch higher. "Did you hear that?"

My captors grew deathly still.

Prince Leander's golden irises scanned the hallway. "I didn't hear any..." He found our darkened corner, and his eyes narrowed to lethal slits upon seeing my attackers. "Fara karifi," he breathed in his native tongue. "Behind you."

Ropert whirled, the torch hissing by our faces.

The older man dropped my legs. I barely caught myself as he bolted down the corridor, and the young man's grip on me shifted.

"This isn't worth it," he muttered, shunting me in the back.

I stumbled into Ropert's arms.

"Stop them! Guards! Intruders!" Ropert bellowed.

Prince Leander's gold-embellished dreadlocks whipped as he flew down the corridor in pursuit, legs pumping faster than I would have thought possible. With a calculated leap, he planted one foot on the wall, his body arching in an impossible angle around the fleeing abductor. His embellished coat flew around him like rippling water.

A harsh crack rang through the corridor as Prince Leander's strange curled-toe boot slammed against the bald man's head. The man pitched to the side, his body slamming against the stone wall with an ugly crack before he slumped to the ground.

Leander landed like a cat.

Flaming feathers. I knew Toleans could fight. But this was something else. Prince Leander was more dangerous than I imagined.

Whipping around, Leander flew after the older man.

"Are you hurt?" Ropert turned to me, lifting my chin, scrutinizing my cheeks under the light of his torch. His eyes grew hard. "Those are going to bruise. Are you hurt anywhere else?"

I held my side but shook my head. I barely felt the pain through the consuming hollow ache in my chest.

A cry tore through the hallway, drawing my attention back to Leander. He stood with a boot pressed against the old man's back, his arm twisted behind him. If Leander moved even an inch, the man's arm would break.

Four soldiers appeared from around the corner as Ropert marched for him.

"Who are you? What do you want with Lady Brendagger?"

The old man's jaw grew tight.

"Sir Ropert asked you a question," Leander said.

"I don't answer to the likes of you," the old man spat.

Feathers, did he know who he was addressing? I watched Leander's face, waiting for rage to erupt. Even Thrall arched its head, eager to have a taste.

But Prince Leander's face remained as placid as still water as he shifted an inch. Something popped in the man's shoulder.

"Alright. Alright." The man's face burned red as he sucked air through his teeth.

Leander eased the pressure.

"We're bounty hunters, alright?"

I held my bruised ribs, eyes locking with Ropert's as he peered over his shoulder at me. The Leviathan pirates had reached into Meldron castle. Just a few nights ago, these men stood in the same room with King Sander and Queen Lonacheska as they'd dined.

Did Alder know?

"Arrest them," Ropert ordered the soldiers. "Take them to the dungeons."

Prince Leander straightened his coat and brushed his dreadlocks behind his shoulders as the Phoenix soldiers hauled the old man to his feet and dragged the limp body of the younger bounty hunter away. His eyes grew hard and determined as he approached. "I must speak with you."

I was in no shape to greet him. My trousers were wrinkled from sleep, my cotton shirt was bunched around my waist, and I was missing a stocking.

Master Chanter had always made certain I was polished and presentable before meeting with the prince. Now he saw me for who I really was. A nobody, crushed and broken.

Ropert stepped between us. "Can this wait? Kea has been through a lot tonight already."

"I'm afraid it cannot," Leander said. "It concerns this incident and Alder."

For a moment, the pain in my chest subsided as my mind snapped to attention. "Did you learn something about him?"

"May we speak in private? Your chambers, perhaps?"

"Ropert can hear what you have to say."

Leander glanced down the corridor, catching sight of a servant slipping into a room at the far end. "It's not Ropert I'm concerned about."

What information could he have that needed such secrecy? I turned, guiding them to my chambers. I pushed the door open, finding my blanket and pillow on the floor and the bed sitting askew. If the bounty hunters had made it into the castle, no place would be safe.

Prince Leander pushed the door shut, his hand lingering on the lever. "Alder is not who he says he is."

He turned to me, his brows holding a tight crease above his well-formed nose. "I knew I had seen him somewhere before, or someone like him. I know now that his real name is Karreth, and he was imprisoned in Glacier Pass by his elder brother. Only someone with magic identical to his could have set him free."

"I . . . I don't understand."

Prince Leander stepped closer, his golden eyes pulling me into them, searching, daring me to reveal everything. "Tell me true. Are you a princess of Roanfire?"

My chest fluttered in and out of numbness. I glanced at Ropert. He stood stiff, his lips pressed tight.

"I . . . I am not an heir to the throne," I whispered.

"Yes, but royal blood does flow through your veins," Leander pressed.

I bit my lip, giving him one nod.

"Fara karifi," he cursed in his native tongue, turning away. "You are the first female heir born to the throne of Roanfire in four hundred years." He ran both hands over his embellished dreadlocks, locking his fingers at the base of his neck and arching his head to the sky. He whirled back to me. "Do you have the Phoenix Stone?"

I stared at him. "How . . . how do you know about that?"

"I know about the Phoenix Stone and more. Where is it? Do you have it?"

"No." I wished I had a different answer. "It was stolen by the Deathbiters." My hand wandered to the flowering scar on my throat, the skin raised and patchy under my fingers.

Prince Leander's eyes narrowed. "The Deathbiters Alder says he can control?"

Realization cracked into my chest like the force of a hammer on a shield. How could I have been so blind? Broderick had seen it. That was why Master ordered Ikane to attack him. I had been too eager to find relief from this frightening power to believe that Alder didn't have good intentions.

Feathers, everything pointed to Alder from the beginning. My weakness as we escaped the Deathbiters' lair. His tattered and threadbare cloak in the dead of winter. No mount or provisions. The man who used Thrall like a sword.

And the way he collapsed in Shear when I'd unleashed Ropert's trapped fire against Master and Rion.

He *was* Master.

Ropert stepped forward, his eyes wide, a hand on the hilt of his sword. "Alder is with the queen."

Adrenaline drove my body forward. Sprinting past Leander, I ripped the door open and barreled down the hallway. My one stocking slipped on the stone floor as I turned a corner, sending me flying against the wall. I pushed off the stone, sprinting up the stairs.

I should have known this was his plan all along. He wanted to get to Queen Lonacheska and the child. His offer to help was nothing but a lie. He'd planned everything.

But why was he working with the bounty hunters? What did they have to gain? Rion didn't want me alive.

The soldiers blinked at me as I raced for Lonacheska's door.

"Open it," I cried.

The fools didn't move.

I slammed down the lever, throwing all my weight against it. But it didn't budge.

"Your Majesty!" I rattled the lever, banging a fist against the solid wood. "Queen Lonacheska!"

"She didn't want to be disturbed," a soldier said.

This wasn't good. "Where's the key?"

"Alder has it," he said.

"Dagger." Ropert skidded to a halt beside me with Prince Leander close behind.

"It's locked," I panted.

Ropert's face hardened. With a solid kick of his boot, the door's latch splintered and flew wide.

I dove into the chamber—Prince Leander and Ropert following, the soldiers outside watching—and targeted Alder. He stood beside Queen Lonacheska's seat by the roaring fire, hands on the back of her chair, his flawless curtain of silver-black hair falling loosely over his scarred eye.

King Sander rose shakily from the other armchair as if I'd just interrupted a pleasant conversation. "Kea?"

Alder's unbelievable perfection warped into the decrepit old skeleton from my visions—the monster who shielded Rion from me, stole Ikane, and turned him into a bloodthirsty beast.

I let him see the pain, rage, and betrayal in my swollen eyes. "Lona. Get away from him."

Alder arched an eyebrow as Lona rose and slipped into King Sander's arms on the other side of the fireplace. Sander's eyes darted between Alder and me, his brows creased.

"Have you been mourning, darling?" Alder tilted his head at me and furrowed his dark brows as if concerned for my well-being. "I didn't realize you and Corporal Melark were so close."

Heat flared through my chest. How dare he make light of my pain. He knew what he'd done.

I took a step forward, but Prince Leander grabbed my elbow. "Take caution, Lady Brendagger. He is more dangerous than we can understand."

Oh, I understood. I knew exactly what Alder was capable of, and I would not let him intimidate me.

"Where is the Phoenix Stone?"

"The what?" Alder's face shifted to pure confusion.

My teeth snapped together. He was good. But he couldn't fool me anymore. "Stop. Just stop. I know who you are, Karreth."

He blinked at the mention of his true name.

"You stole Ikane from me, changed him into a beast, erased his memories. You made him kill . . ." My voice broke, my throat suddenly too tight to breathe. Tears I thought already shed surfaced.

"Has something happened?" Alder stepped closer.

"Don't pretend to care," I snapped. "Where is the Phoenix Stone?"

He froze, eyes glancing at Ropert and Prince Leander standing behind me. He was trapped, and he knew it.

Alder dropped his head, his long hair falling across his face like curtains. "Just because I can wield Thrall doesn't make me the enemy." He turned to the fire, the flames dancing across his black attire. "I've done nothing but help you. Why would I do that if I was working with Rion?"

That was it. My confirmation.

"I never told you her name, Master." I spat the title he'd given himself. "You destroyed Ikane. You control the Deathbiters."

His head tilted slightly. "I don't just control the Deathbiters, darling." His silver eye met mine. "I created them."

King Sander stepped forward, pushing Queen Lonacheska behind him. "What is the meaning of this?" His eyes were stone, his voice roaring with a warning. "Are you saying you are responsible for the plague across Roanfire?"

"I am." Alder's focus turned to me. "As for your beloved Ikane, he served his purpose." A horrible smile spread on his dreadfully beautiful face. "He relished the taste of Eamon Brendagger's blood."

His words were like a knife to my gut, twisting with heat.

"Eamon?" King Sander breathed, watching me. "Master Eamon is dead?"

"Torn apart by the same creature who maimed her meddling friend, Broderick," Alder said.

Lightning surged through my chest, the black spark of Thrall leaping from its corner, flaring through my blood. I would turn Alder to ash. "How dare you!"

Leander grabbed my shoulders, drawing me back. "Don't let him provoke you."

"Listen to the Tolean, young princess," Alder crooned, taking a step closer to the king and queen. "You wouldn't want to harm your friends now, would you? Although, I am curious to see what that would do to your bodyguard." His silver eye flashed to Ropert.

What did Ropert have to do with any of this?

"There is something about you I don't understand." Alder tilted his head at my broad-shouldered bodyguard. "You are immune to my power."

I glanced at Ropert, who stood as firm as an ancient oak, his hand on his sword, glowering at Alder.

"Do you remember when Deathbiter venom and oils surged through your blood, burning you from the inside out? I tried to heal you. Truly, I did." Alder let out a bitter chuckle. "But my power had no effect. Even in the tavern when you betrayed me to Lord Everguard. You should have felt my wrath, but you didn't even flinch."

Ropert took a step forward, his sword halfway from its sheath. "Care to try again?"

Alder slipped a hand into the collar of his shirt, a red glow bursting between his fingers. My heart stopped. It was the Phoenix Stone. She was here, right in front of me, and I couldn't feel her.

"That's it, boy. Come closer." He uncurled his hand, and the crimson ruby dropped, dangling from a cord in front of Alder's black countenance. The room exploded in red light. The ruby burned with raw energy, ready to consume and destroy.

Why didn't Ropert stop? Didn't he realize what the ruby would do to him?

I had to do something. No sword or man could hope to overpower Alder and Rion—not with the power they held together.

I had to focus. I couldn't rely on the rage, hate, and pain burning in my chest—however strong they might be—to crush them.

Delving beyond the rubble of emotions crowding the surface of my mind, I sank into the pure depths of what my heart was made of. I was born to protect. That's who I was. A soldier. One who would fight for the freedom of others, no matter the cost.

"Guards! Arrest him," King Sander commanded. "Throw him in the dungeons."

"Anyone who touches me will end up just like Corporal Melark," Alder warned, holding the ruby out to the cautiously approaching soldiers with Ropert leading the pack.

"Ropert, stop." I fought against Leander's firm grip on my shoulders. He was getting too close. "You may be immune to his powers, but you're not immune to hers."

Alder smiled as Ropert's feet planted a sword's length away. "Come on, boy. Let's find out what you are truly capable—"

King Sander's arm slid around Alder's throat from behind, jerking the tall, slimy man back. Even in his weakened state, King Sander found the strength to hold on, crushing Alder's windpipe. Alder clawed at the king's arm, the ruby flying dangerously close to his skin.

I wriggled from Prince Leander's grip, rushing forward just as Alder twisted. He thrust the glowing red ruby against King Sander's chest.

The king went rigid, his eyes flying wide.

"Sander!" Lona screamed.

My blood turned to ice as King Sander's stormy blue irises grew dull like the shine of wet ink drying on parchment.

Everything was swallowed in silence as he crumpled to the floor, the golden circlet slipping from his brow, rolling to Queen Lonacheska's feet. I couldn't breathe.

Lona dropped to her knees and pulled King Sander's head into her lap, frantically caressing his face, chest, and arms as she searched for sign of injury. "Sander!" she cried. "Sander, wake up. Please."

Alder staggered back, leaning against the stone hearth, holding his throat and gasping.

My stomach flipped as if I were standing on the bow of a ship tossing in a storm, and my lungs inhaled with frantic, shallow gulps. First Eamon and now . . .

Ropert lunged, his sword racing for Alder's center.

Alder spun away as Ropert's sword hit stone with a clank and sparks. Alder grabbed Lona by the arm. She cried out as he jerked her from the ground, holding her before him like a shield.

Ropert froze, chest puffing as the crimson jewel dangled in front of the queen's rounding belly.

"You know what she can do." Alder's eye grew sharper than my blade fresh from the blacksmith's grindstone.

I couldn't think. King Sander lay on the ground, crumpled and defeated, his hair splayed across stone like grass in water. I hadn't thought the hollowness in my chest could get any deeper, yet it gaped wider, becoming a place I could fall into and never climb from again.

How much more would she take from me? How much more would I lose trying to resist?

"Lady Brendagger," Prince Leander whispered. "This is not the way. You cannot fight them with strength of body. You must find the power in your heart."

What heart? It sat motionless in my chest with a dagger plunged in the center. I'd lost Ikane and Broderick and Eamon—those who meant the most to me—and now King Sander.

Pressure bore down on my ears, a sensation I hadn't felt since . . . my eyes flew wide.

Rion. She was reaching. She was going to take someone.

A soldier groaned. His sword dropped, clattering to the stone floor as he clutched his head. Then another. All four soldiers fell to their knees, faces contorted in pain, blood streaking from their noses.

Ropert staggered back. His sword dropped with a clang at his boots, his fingers flying to his head, digging into his scalp. He stumbled against the edge of the fireplace.

"Ropert!" I caught him before he collapsed to the floor, sinking to my knees with him.

"Dagger . . ." His voice pushed through clenched teeth as he stared up at me, his glass-blue eyes filled with the fiery pain I knew too well. A streak of red slipped from his nose.

"Stop it, Rion!" I screamed at the ruby dangling from Alder's hand. "Stop!"

A groan tore from Prince Leander as he staggered against the far wall, eyes scrunched against her burning torture.

"Please! Stop!"

Ropert's compact, muscular body sagged against me, his head dropping.

"No. Ropert. Wake up. Please, wake up." Trembling under his weight, I guided him to the floor, my hands cradling his head of blond curls. His eyes—his beautiful crystal-blue eyes—stared at the ceiling, empty and cold.

"No." I took his face in my hands. The red stubble on his jaw prickled my fingers, and his face blurred as tears surged into my eyes. "Please, no."

"Rion doesn't need you anymore," Alder said, his voice as cool as a winter wind. "The infant the queen carries is a blank page for my darling Rion to build her future upon."

Lona whimpered as Alder began dragging her to the door. He held the ruby between us like a shield, or a dagger, or a vial of poison.

Somehow, I rose to my feet.

I couldn't live like this.

Alder's brows furrowed as my hand reached for the dangling red jewel, the glittering flecks of sprite dust embedded in my palm flaring with red light.

"Kea, no," Queen Lonacheska whispered.

My fingers clamped around the ruby, suffocating her red glow. The room constricted, warping into glowing fragments of red and black.

## CHAPTER 29

# SHOOTING STARS

*E*ndless clouds of stars burned through a red haze, churning like ink through water, each one a life taken too soon from the world. Each one stolen. Each one murdered by the twisted mind of one too overcome with a selfish desire to live on forever, no matter the cost to others.

Ropert and King Sander were here somewhere among the thousands of souls Rion held captive. The soldiers, Corporal Melark, Queen Lonacheska's servants, and all the poor individuals Alder had helped her consume from Gerom Post to Meldron. How many of them were Leviathan pirates?

"So." Her voice was filled with a thousand others, like the stars whispered the words with her. "You've finally admitted defeat."

I found her in the midst.

Rion, burning brighter than I'd ever seen, her coppery skin rolling with veins of orange and red, her white hair flowing around her like flames in a raging wind, her crimson gown glistening like fresh-drawn blood. A slender, burning vortex stretched from her hand through the heart of the trembling stars to the ruby's domed confinement. Strange green light burned down the fire like a funnel, and flashes of green lightning stretched across the surface of the ruby.

I'd seen her do this before. When she'd tried to take Ikane. This green energy must belong to Prince Leander. It was the only life she hadn't taken yet.

And I wouldn't allow it.

I raced for her, stars rushing by in a blur.

A terrible smile grew on her painted lips as she dropped the swirling vortex like releasing a rope. Leander's green light fled the ruby as she stretched her hand to me. Fire sparked through her fingers, growing larger as I sped toward her.

"Do you honestly believe that you—a weak and feeble-minded mortal—can defeat me?" she roared. Fire shot from her palm, a burning tether slamming into me like a whip. A terrible crack echoed through the ruby, rippling through the stars.

I'd forgotten the true extent of her pain, the way it burned through the soul, wrapping around every broken piece of my heart, burning parts I thought I no longer had.

"You should be groveling at my feet," she snapped, "thanking me for bringing you here to spend eternity with your beloved King Sander and bodyguard. If you had only asked, I could have brought Eamon Brendagger here, too, instead of allowing him to be torn to pieces by that wretched animal. Don't you see the mercy I give? You could have been together."

How dare she say Eamon's name. How dare she think she was doing me a kindness by consuming King Sander and Ropert. It didn't matter what happened to me now. I had nothing left to lose. One of us would meet our end this day.

She took Ikane from me and destroyed him. She killed Eamon, crippled Broderick, and devoured King Sander and Ropert and so many others. She would pay. She would feel what it was like to lose everything.

My mind opened to Thrall like castle gates to the enemy. It crackled through a memory of Mayama wiping her hands on her apron, the smell of garlic and onion thick in the kitchens. A serving boy tripped over a boot—my boot—spilling mugs and dishes under the tables.

It wasn't real, but I let Thrall twist and bend it. Whatever it needed to grow.

Mayama's face burned, her rage as tangible as her meaty fist curling around her wooden—gone.

Thrall didn't care what it ate as long as it was fed. How could Alder live this way, crafting lies to fuel his power? What was real, and what was not?

Even if I had allowed him to tutor me, would he have? Or would he have let Thrall destroy me one piece of my soul at a time?

Thrall sank its teeth into another memory of Eamon standing in a darkened alleyway, raising a bottle to his lips. The liquid dripped down his unkempt beard.

I pushed Thrall another direction. This was not a memory I wanted to change or to forget. I wanted to remember Eamon as he was: a leader, a warrior, a proud father. He didn't drink anymore. The scent had left his clothes and skin. His eyes had never been so alert. But that experience had made him who he was, and I wanted to remember that, too.

But Thrall resisted, swinging back, sickeningly sweet ethers pushing into the lie. Like a half-starved beast, it feasted on the raw pain so fresh it bled.

The throbbing energy raced along her burning thread, holding me captive. Black fire consumed her orange blaze, overpowering her with all the rage and hollow pain in my heart.

It drew into her skin.

Flaming feathers, she inhaled it, like everything I'd allowed Thrall to bend and twist was meant for her. How was it possible for her skin to burn even brighter?

"Is that all?" she laughed. "Don't stop now."

Thrall barreled through another memory like a wolf sinking its teeth into the slender neck of a doe, dragging it down. Ikane stood at the gate of Meldron castle, brandishing a battle-axe, his green eye flaring as he swore to take my head.

*Feathers, make it stop.* Thrall was going too far, reaching memories too deep and precious. This was not my Ikane. He had turned against his own people to save me, his own brothers.

And his weapon wasn't an axe. He fought with twin blades made of black steel. One lay in my room this very moment, awaiting his hand, and the other was with Broderick.

"Breathe." Broderick's voice pushed into my head almost like he'd pressed a bow into my hand.

The memory slipped back into its original form.

Thrall stopped, spitting the memory away like something foul. It whirled on me as if I'd betrayed it.

Rion's eyes narrowed. "Karreth said you were growing stronger. I didn't realize he meant you were becoming adept at resisting the pull of Thrall."

A burning thread shot from her hand into the sea of lights around us, catching a single star. It streaked toward her, burning hot and strong, radiating with a protective energy only a parent could have for a child.

Rion snatched the star in her fist like an insect, her red-painted nails sinking into it like claws into flesh. Its light dulled under her pressure. "Perhaps losing King Sander again will help."

King Sander? The star in her hand was King Sander.

I'd seen her hold a soul like this before. She'd crushed it. She'd consumed it. Just one small squeeze of her hand, and he would be gone forever. "Don't . . . don't hurt him. Send him back. You must send him back. He is the last true heir to the Noirfonika line."

She chuckled, her teeth gleaming in her firelight. "He *was* the last true heir. The new princess is all I need."

Her fist slammed tight.

"No!"

King Sander's light absorbed into her hand, spreading up her arm, feeding her energy with a new wave of brilliance.

"What have you done?" I cried. The ache in my center opened wide like a drawbridge crashing down. Thrall rushed inside, clawing at corners, searching for any fragment of pain it missed.

"Dagger, stop."

*Was that... was that Ropert?*

*Thrall sputtered.*

A star drifted closer, its edge tinged with a red-orange glow. There was something familiar about it, strong and faithful, radiating with an embrace I'd relied on all my life.

"Ropert?"

"I don't understand what's happening, Dagger, but I do know that she'll only use this energy against you."

Rion's eyes narrowed to glowing slits. "How dare you interfere."

"She's trying to make you destroy yourself," Ropert said. "She's baiting you."

"Insolent whelp." A burning thread shot from Rion's hand, racing for the red-edged star beside me.

*So help me, she would not take another life.*

I whirled into the thread's path. The fire hit, burrowing deep. A thousand bolts of lightning raced through every memory and thought, sparking across images and figures, drawing out every moment of agony... draining Thrall. She stole every morsel of power I'd risked gathering to strike her down.

Her brightness doubled, then tripled... while I faded.

"Hold on, Dagger." Ropert's energy engulfed me like an embrace, his warmth and solid arms becoming a barrier against Rion's fire. I could almost feel his muscles crushing me against his chest, smell his scent of leather and whatever food he'd last eaten on his shirt, feel his heartbeat against my ear.

How... how was he doing this? It was a familiar sensation, like when Ikane's silver-blue energy had merged with my white lights of Etheria.

*That's what I needed now. Not Thrall. Etheria. Ropert couldn't shield us forever. Even now, I felt his strength wavering under Rion's onslaught of fire.*

"Dagger." *Ropert's voice was like a warm wind breathing into my soul. And suddenly I held the bow, my muscles straining as I drew back, my lungs expanding with Ropert's vibrant energy. A white star of Etheria flickered between us, and then another, swarming together like insects over a placid lake.*

*Rion's eyes narrowed.* "You're even more of a nuisance than Queen Damita was."

*She reached to the sea of stars, four thin burning threads shooting from her hands into the clouds. The quivering lights scattered like fish in a pond, but her threads snaked after them, hunting, chasing, until they found their prey. The glowing orbs let out painful screams as the threads drew them to her in the form of shooting stars. They flickered out as they sank into her hands.*

*Closing her eyes, Rion lifted her head to the sky, inhaling as a rush of brightness overpowered her.* "You are more like me than you realize, Phoenix daughter." *She waved a hand across the endless sea of trembling stars.* "You judge me for inviting souls to live forever in me when you yourself are draining a life for your own purpose."

*She was right. I was using Ropert. My hold on him eased.*

"Don't listen to her, Dagger." *Ropert claimed my attention as if he had gripped my shoulders and trapped my eyes with his.* "She steals what I give willingly. There is a difference."

*Did he know what he was saying?* "But I'm using you."

"Better you than her." *I could almost see his crooked grin.*

"Listen to him, Keatep." *A new creamy voice brushed against me like a feather. The shape of a tall, slender man with skin as pure as marble solidified beside us.*

"Yotherna," *I breathed.*

"It can't be." *Rion's eyes widened, her fire dissipating. She staggered back, her blood-red gown trailing behind her.*

Yotherna brushed his pale fingers against me as if he were brushing a tear from my cheek. "I tried to reach you sooner, but Thrall was too thick. No matter how hard I tried, I couldn't find you. But once you reached for Etheria, you were like a beacon."

He was here. He was finally taking matters into his own hands. "Will you help me defeat her?"

His beautiful face contorted with sorrow. He looked so much like Alder.

"Alas, I do not have the power to destroy what I created. And I cannot stay long. But I will do what I can to help you buy some time to come to me. Trust Prince Leander."

"Traitor," Rion bellowed. A hundred stars fell from the sky, and the screams of a hundred voices pulled into Rion's burning form. Flames collected in her hands like a catapult's boulder drenched in pitch.

Yotherna whirled, wrapping us in his arms, and a pale sphere of crystalline power engulfed us as Rion's fireball collided with his shield, exploding around us. A grunt escaped his throat as we careened across the weightless expanse of her prison.

"You would help her destroy me?" Rion screamed. "After all we've been through? After what we shared?" A tinge of humanity crept into her voice. It was like seeing him pained her in a way I couldn't understand. How had she any feeling left in her twisted, heartless soul?

Yotherna's breath came hard as he faced her. "You know why I cannot allow it."

Rion scanned the sea of stars, her white eyes traveling longingly to the warped edges of the ruby's border. "You will not trap me in here again." She raised a hand. Thousands of threads burst from her palm, hunting thousands of stars. The clouds erupted with screams as she drew them together, twisting faster and faster into a thick braid of burning light. It slammed into the dome.

"What is she doing?" Ropert whispered.

A strange cry echoed from somewhere beyond the jewel.

*The star-infested line began to pulse fast and light, like the pounding of an infant's heart. With every other distant boom, a light flickered out.*

*She was targeting the baby! She was sending her power into the fetus.*

*How could she even fathom a child so young capable of withstanding such fire? Even Ikane—a formidable Leviathan pirate with muscles of steel—had crumbled under her energy.*

*"Stop her," Yotherna panted, his vision fading as he stretched his slender fingers toward me. "I give you all I can." A surge of white lightning flared through my core, every fleck of Etheria swelling with his light and power. Ropert's orange-red energy flashed with it, enveloping my little white particles of dust in something stronger than I could've ever imagined.*

*But Yotherna was gone. Once again, he left me alone to fight his creation.*

*A scream tore through the ruby, a cry different from the stars. It came from beyond. It was Queen Lonacheska—it had to be. She felt her child's pain.*

*The little heartbeat increased in rhythm, frantic and erratic.*

*What did Rion think she was doing? She'd taken King Sander, and if I couldn't find my way back to my body, then I would be lost, too. All she had left was the unborn princess. If she killed the child now in her desperate attempt to flee the ruby, she would seal her fate by her own greed.*

*Stars howled to her, around her, through her, soaring up the shaft of burning power to the ruby's crystalline dome. The princess's little heartbeat thrummed wildly. Any faster, and it would be a solid hum of death.*

*Perhaps this was for the best. Rion's line would end. Her chance for rebirth would be no more.*

*But would she ever stop feasting?*

*"Don't stop now, Dagger," Ropert said.*

*He was right. This wasn't a solution. It was a bandage for an infected wound. Roanfire would continue to be plagued by her lust for souls.*

*Ropert leaned against me like we so often did when we fought together, back-to-back, shoulder to shoulder, constantly aware of each other's movements. Yotherna's energy surged through us like a sunburst, slamming into the whirling funnel of stars with an earsplitting crack that shook the ruby's surface. Rion spun away in a swirl of blood-red silk, the stars scattering like black birds from a freshly sown wheat field.*

*Ropert's energy replaced the weakness left in the wake of expending so much power.*

*Focus, steady, release.*

*Etheria swarmed around me like snowflakes, building, growing solid with Ropert's red energy. He was growing weaker. I could feel it. And so was I. I had to release it before I used everything Ropert had to give.*

*The lights rushed forward like arrows, spinning around Rion in a vortex of their own. Her bright red lips curled into a smile as the power tightened, her white eyes glowing embers against the suffocating whirlwind. Something in them radiated with triumph.*

*I hesitated. Why was she smiling? What had I overlooked?*

*Etheria slammed shut, encasing her in a solid sphere of white, the red glow of the ruby dulling to a soft rose.*

*Ropert's energy fell away like I'd dropped my sword. A small red-white ember sputtered beside me, as weak and frail as I felt.*

*"Ropert." I reached for him, catching the tender flicker of his remaining energy. I'd used him. I'd used all of him. I'd nearly snuffed him out the same way Rion had done to King Sander. "Oh, Ropert. Please, forgive me."*

*Somehow, I felt as though his warm, calloused hand rested against my cheek. "I'd do it again."*

*"I'll never ask it of you. Never." I clung to him, searching the cloud of souls flickering above us. There had to be a way out, a way to save him. I'd escaped the ruby before. Was it so impossible to think I couldn't bring Ropert with me?*

*But my body had to be in contact with the ruby. Where was it now? Did my hand still clutch it?*

*I paused as a cool blue line like fractured ice lanced across the dome-like surface. Was that a crack? It couldn't be. In all my attempts, I'd never even managed a chip. How had I . . . ?*

*It didn't matter. Ropert's light was fading. I had to save him. I had to.*

*Gathering Ropert to me, I sprang for the escape. A strange weight pushed against me like I was running through a knee-deep bog. Ropert's light, tiny and weak, dragged against me like a waterlogged cloak.*

*But I would not let go. If anyone deserved to live, it was him.*

## CHAPTER 30

# CRACKED SAFE-HAVEN

I inhaled, the coppery scent of blood filling my nose. Cold stone pressed against my bruised cheek. I opened my eyes.

King Sander lay across the room, body slumped onto its side, eyes closed, his peaceful face illuminated by the dying embers in the fire. My chest tightened beyond breath. He was gone. He really was gone. Just like Eamon.

Ropert.

Every muscle ached and trembled as I pulled my hands under me, pushing myself from the floor. Ropert lay unmoving by the fireplace, sword lying in his limp grip, a thin line of blood streaking from his nose down the side of his cheek.

My heart thundered in my chest as I scrambled to his side and cupped his pale cheeks in my hands. So pale. His head lay heavy. "Please, Ropert, please."

I stroked his hair back, and his flaxen curls swept gently around his face. My fingers paused at a section of locks beside his brow. White. His hair had turned white, drained of life and color.

Tears surged through my eyes as I clutched his shirt, burying my forehead against his solid chest. The lump in my throat grew too thick to swallow.

This was my doing. I had used his strength the way Rion had. She was right. I was just like . . .

A puff of air escaped his lips.

I straightened, blinking away the tears, watching every twitch of his face. "Ropert?"

His lips parted with breath.

Relief flooded my core, and my eyes burst with a new rush of tears as I pressed my ear to his chest. His heart drummed. His lungs expanded. Blessed Phoenix, he was alive.

I pressed my lips against Ropert's brow. "I'll never ask this of you again," I whispered.

I'd brought him back. Somehow, I'd rescued him from Rion's prison with the help of Yotherna's power. But even with his help, I wasn't strong enough to destroy Rion. She was still alive. Trapped, but alive. In time, she would break free again. She would rise and destroy with or without Alder's help.

Where was he? Where was the ruby? Lonacheska?

I scanned the silent room. Prince Leander was missing, too. The door stood wide to the evening, four unmoving soldiers sprawled on the floor. Could I have saved them, too? Could I have found them among the clouds of stars so thick and numberless?

It was nothing short of miraculous that I'd brought Ropert back.

Metal ground against stone as I dragged Ropert's sword to me. Planting the tip into the hearth, I pulled myself up and staggered past the empty shells of fallen soldiers.

I leaned against the doorframe, glancing back at Ropert lying at the foot of the mantle. Then at King Sander. If only I'd found him before Rion had.

My chest ached. I wanted to throw myself into a fit of screams, but my body was too spent to shed another tear.

Numbly, I staggered into the hallway. It stood dark in both directions.

Where would Alder go? Where would he take the queen?

My knees shook and wobbled as I chose a direction and hurried down the dark corridor, thankful again to the little firesprite for giving me the gift of sight in darkness. A hazy orange glow illuminated every corner as I stumbled down the spiraling staircase.

I paused as moonlight struck my face through an arched window. Deathbiters darted through the street, clinging to rooftops and chimneys, clawing at boarded-up windows. These were the monsters Alder had created. Monsters he controlled.

"Kea?" Prince Leander's Tolean accent rang through the staircase as he struggled to climb the stairs. He was missing his coat and his sleeveless shirt was shredded. Deep lacerations cut into the smooth dark skin of his face and arms, dark blood dripping from the infected wounds. The acrid stench of Deathbiter overpowered his usual scent of cinnamon.

He didn't look well.

He sagged against the wall, his golden eyes wide and unbelieving. "I thought ... I thought you were dead," he whispered. "I thought you and Ropert and King Sander were all dead."

I swallowed against the pain in my heart. "Where ... where is Alder?"

Leander glanced away, his throat working as he swallowed hard. "I'm so sorry. I tried. I followed him as far as I could, but when he reached the outer doors ... there was nothing I could do. The Deathbiters were too thick."

A fresh wave of trembling surged through my blood. "You mean he took her out there?" I stared out the window at the bats racing from building to building, the silver moonglow touching their wings.

Prince Leander stepped beside me, following my gaze. "He won't harm her, will he?"

Sliding against the wall, I sank to the cold stairs, clutching Ropert's sword. Alder wouldn't hurt her. He needed her healthy and strong for the baby.

I dropped my face into my hand. "How did I not see it? He meant for this to happen. He used me to get to Queen Lonacheska."

Leander trembled as he sank to the step beside me, holding an oozing wound on his bare shoulder. "You cannot blame yourself for this."

I shook my head. "I knew there was something strange about him, but I trusted him anyway. I should have listened to Broderick. He knew. He saw through him." And that was why Master had ordered Marrok to attack.

Leander shivered, his dark skin shimmering with perspiration. "This . . . Broderick sounds like a wise man."

"I wish he were here now. He would know what to do." I dropped my hand. He wouldn't have let it get this far.

"You've done all you can for now," Leander said.

"Alder has the Phoenix Stone and the next heir to the throne of Roanfire." I rubbed my eyes. "We have less than five months before Lona gives birth . . . before the world changes forever."

"You are wrong about one thing." Prince Leander turned his fist up, uncurling his fingers. I blinked, squinting through the firedust in my eyes. A small jewel glowed in his palm, the color of a spring rose. "As long as you have this, we have an advantage."

The Stone. The Phoenix Stone! But how was he holding it? How was Rion not draining his life? "How . . . ?" I blinked at him. "How did you take it without—"

"Without it killing me?" he finished. "When it changed color. I knew you had done something remarkable when the bright red glow shifted. I wish . . . I wish I could have done more, but Alder already stood in the threshold when I seized it." He tipped the faded ruby into my hand.

I stared down at the jewel lying in my winddust-riddled palm. The surface was no longer smooth—a single crack ran down the center. A crack I had somehow dealt to her safe haven.

Something about the fissure brought a fragment of hope to all the darkness crushing my chest. The stone *could* be destroyed.

Clutching the ruby in my fist, I turned to the prince. I had to know. I had to understand. This young Tolean prince knew more than he was letting on.

"What do you know about the White Wardent?" I asked.

The Glacial Rogue

# THE TASTE OF EAMON'S BLOOD

*Marrok's body moved through the slender trunks of night-darkened aspens. He hated how his muscles responded to Master's call. The inbred reaction was like the involuntary shift of the changing seasons.*

*With every step, his mind screamed for him to stop. Why should he listen to the instinctive pull of his body? Why should he carry out any order given by Master? Master felt nothing for the pain he'd caused. Master had ordered him to do the unforgivable, to crush a life too precious to destroy—a life that meant more to Marrok than his own. The taste of Eamon's blood lingered on his tongue like a festering wound.*

*"Marrok."*

*Master's resonating voice floated through the trees, the pull of his tone drawing Marrok forward like a fish caught by a fisherman's lure. His body shook as he resisted the next step. And the next. Why was it so hard to refuse?*

*His hand shot out, claws digging into the bark of a tree, the barren branches above trembling on impact. For a moment, he stopped moving.*

*A hint of ash caught his nose. Heat crashed through his veins. Master was close.*

## The Glacial Rogue

*Claws shredded through the trunk as Marrok's body pushed on. He couldn't stop. His fists clenched, muscles turning to steel. If only he could tear into the monster who made him destroy Eamon, clamp his jaws on Master's throat, feel his warm blood coat his fur . . .*

*Another scent touched the air, sweet and honey-like, entangled with raw fear. Despite the pull of Master's command, Marrok slowed. Master wasn't alone.*

*"Marrok," Master called.*

*Silver-blue moonlight radiated through the trees, touching the snow beneath like a carpet of foam on the sea. Two figures moved toward him, silhouetted by the moon's glow.*

*There was no mistaking Master's lean frame and black cloak. But why was he clutching the arm of a woman, dragging her behind him like prey? This wasn't the girl who infiltrated his dreams. She was older, paler, and her stomach was . . .*

*Marrok's feet finally planted.*

*The woman was with child.*

*What in the name of every beast of the sea was Master doing with a pregnant woman? Her long hair fell over her shoulders in a golden mess. Her cheeks were flushed and tear-stained, and her eyes were red-rimmed and swollen. A bruise swelled at her cheek. By the way her feet trudged through the snow, she'd given up all hope of escape.*

*"There you are." Master's silver eye fell on Marrok. "Come here, and carry this woman. She needs rest."*

*The woman lifted her head, and her dark eyes found Marrok. They shot wide as he stepped through the trees. With a cry, she pulled against Master's crushing grip.*

*"Stop fighting." Master jerked her forward, catching both of her wrists. "Or do you need another warning?"*

*Marrok's eyes narrowed, his feet planting again. He knew Master was referring to the mark on her cheek.*

*Her breathing came in frantic puffs as she watched Marrok, wide eyes scanning his monstrous form, trapped between man and wolf. Something inside Marrok grew hard at the fear rolling from her countenance. She needn't fear him. No matter what Master demanded, Marrok would not harm a hair on her head. Not after what he'd done to Eamon.*

"Come here, Marrok." *Master dropped one of the woman's wrists.*

*Marrok's legs moved forward at the command, but something in him pulled back, fighting against it like an anchor catching rock at the bottom of the sea.*

*Master's silver eye narrowed.* "What are you doing?"

*Marrok sank to his haunches, tail whipping against the snow.*

"Are you still sulking over Eamon Brendagger?"

"Eamon?" *the woman asked, her eyes flashing between Master and Marrok. The worry in her voice had to mean she knew something about Eamon. Perhaps she could help him remember . . .*

"Don't look at me that way. I wasn't the one who ripped out his throat with my teeth," *Master growled.*

*How dare he? Marrok did what he had been commanded to do, and he blindly obeyed.*

*Something inside him flickered awake. A consciousness of who Master had designed him to be. A possession. A puppet. A slave.*

"He was going to kill you. He was feeding you lies, twisting everything I taught you." *Master's eyes narrowed, his scarred one pulling oddly in its socket.* "Come here, Marrok." *He jabbed a finger at the snow by his boots like he was disciplining a hound.*

*Every muscle in Marrok's body ached to heed Master's entrenched command. It pulled at him like the wind filling the sail of a ship. One clawed hand drew forward and sank into the snow.*

*He couldn't resist; it was impossible to try. He was bound to Master in a way he couldn't understand, filled with a strange loyalty that edged on madness.*

*The woman clenched her fingers under Master's grip, watching Marrok with such terror his heart ached. The taste of Eamon's blood filled his mouth.*

*Very well. If Master wanted him to come, he'd come.*

*He let go, his body flying forward, black trees rushing by in a blur.*

*Master's narrowed eyes grew wide when Marrok showed no sign of stopping.* "What—?" *Master threw up his arm, blocking Marrok's jaw from clamping down on his throat.*

*It didn't matter. A bite was a bite, and Marrok's jaw cracked bone. It punctured leather and flesh. Something sweet and metallic exploded across his tongue.*

*Releasing the woman, Master fell back. Marrok landed on all fours atop him, jaw clamped tight to Master's forearm. His claws were next, lethal and sharp. They would shred Master the same way they had—*

*A blinding lightning surged through Marrok's skull. Black rushed across his vision. The noise of the woods grew faint as if he'd sunk into the depths of the sea. His jaw unclamped his quarry.*

"You dare turn against me?" *Master's fist cracked against Marrok's skull.*

*Marrok's body rocked into the snow, ears ringing. Shaking his head, he pushed himself from the earth. He blinked at the blurry shapes around him. The woman cowered beside a cluster of aspens.*

*And Master. The black form rose from the ground, towering over Marrok like a great behemoth, shadow and rage spilling from his body like thick smoke, crackling with black energy.*

"I created you!" *Master's deep voice crashed into Marrok's chest like a tidal wave, pushing him under.* "And this is how you repay me? You are mine, you hear? Mine! You will do as I say."

*The power rolling from Master pummeled Marrok into the snow, driving him to the mud beneath, threatening to entomb him. Every muscle in his body stabbed with the bolts of black lightning flaring through his spine.*

*Marrok trembled as he tried to rise. He would not be subject to this man's commands anymore. He would not—*

Black lightning cracked through his head. Master stepped over him, planting a boot on the side of his skull, and leaned forward, his dark hair falling across his daggerlike eyes. "You are nothing without me," Master said. "I created you, and I can destroy you. The choice is yours."

Master could tear him apart. He could pull the muscle from his bones without raising a finger. A whimper squeaked from Marrok's throat, high-pitched and pitiful.

"Good." Master removed his boot from Marrok's jaw. Cradling his arm, he scanned the trees, his face growing hard when he didn't find the woman. "Now, look what you've done. She got away."

Marrok pushed himself from the snow, eyeing Master's crippled arm as redness leaked from his leather sleeve. Three drops hit the snow.

His tongue ran across his teeth. The flavor of Eamon's blood pushed to the back of his mind.

Master's blood raged across his lips, sweet and sharp. Three drops weren't enough. He wanted more.

"Fetch her back," Master ordered, "and do not harm her. The child she carries is more valuable than all the jewels of Roanfire."

Marrok's body obeyed. It sprinted across the snow, kicking up clumps as he wove through the trees, following her footprints. But his mind roared with vengeance.

*One way or another, he would learn the truth of who he was.*

The Glacial Rogue

# ABOUT THE AUTHOR

When she is not writing or drawing, C.K. Miller can be found working in the garden, practicing martial arts, or studying natural medicine.

www.ckmillerbooks.com

# ACKNOWLEDGEMENTS

This book has taken far longer to write than anticipated. The pandemic of 2020 and 2021 took a great toll on my creativity, as I'm sure it did the creativity of many others. In times of crisis, we turn to survival mode. And when one is being chased by a tiger, the last thing on one's mind is to create.

But finally, here it is. With the help and encouragement of many talented friends and fans.

A special thank you to my dear friend, Brandon Ho, Creative Director of Goldenworks Entertainment, for the many phone calls and messages where we discussed plot and structure. Your insight was invaluable.

Thank you to Philip Smith, author of The Brotherhood (you should check out his book), for being the best angry Scotsman ever to light a fire under my butt. I still replay your brilliant voice message whenever I get the urge to procrastinate.

What is a book without a knowledgeable, legendary novelist like Chris A. Jackson? The award-winning author of many great fantasy novels, and professional sailor who took the time to answer my questions about ships. Thank you so much.

I'd like to thank my forever fan and fellow Leviathan Lover, Amber Kizer, for taking the time to read my first draft and provide me with invaluable feedback.

Thank you, Trina Tolman, my sister and friend, for watching my boys, listening to me vent about bumps in my writing career, and always showing a genuine interest in the progress of my series. And for being an honest beta reader.

A special thank you to Steph Johnsen for her priceless, meticulous feedback on plot, feel, and structure. Her advice made this book, especially the ending, come to life.

I cannot thank my husband enough for taking the kids off my hands, sitting with me to brainstorm and smooth out plot-holes, sending me to the library, taking the family camping and making certain I have my laptop and charger, and for giving me the only space in the house that was his: the office. It is now a place I can flourish with my writing. I would not have come this far without his support, encouragement, and never-ending belief that I could do this.

### *And a shout out to my special Roanfire ARC Team!*

Author Lilia Gestson, Korine Miller, Author Jennifer Ann Schlag, Jennifer Gilmore, Author Ceara Nobles, Laurel Bingham, Ismael Rodriguez, and Karl Sanderson and family.

Made in the USA
Monee, IL
14 November 2023